FORTUNATE SON

Published by Mission Point Press
2554 Chandler Rd.
Traverse City, MI 49696
(231) 421-9513
www.MissionPointPress.com

Cover design by Mark Swan
Book design by Sarah Meiers

ISBN: 978-1-961302-54-9 (hardcover)
978-1-961302-55-6 (softcover)

Library of Congress Control Number: 2024908015

Printed in the United States of America

FORTUNATE SON

BY ANDREW BRIDGEMAN

MISSION POINT PRESS

This book is dedicated to my wife, Kathy.
Thank you for believing in me.

Arnau Farre took a long drag on his cigarette. He blew a trail of smoke through the cracked window of his dented brown Chevette, then flicked the butt off his index finger, watching it bounce and spark against the icy asphalt. He was glad to be alone. Glad to have time to think. But he wasn't happy. Far from it.

For most of the night he'd been thinking about life. And about death. But mostly, he was thinking about loss. He clicked open the glove compartment and reached under the registration papers, insurance documents, and oil-change receipts. He grabbed the Beretta, checked the magazine, then screwed the black suppressor to the barrel.

He idled the Chevette behind a mound of snow, barely visible under the dull orangey lights of the parking lot. The brown car blended seamlessly with the strip mall behind it—two acres of retail hospice wheezing into cracked asphalt. It was seven o'clock. The stores were closed: the VCR repair shop, the place that sold fabric, the family drug store—all on life support, dying a slow death while across the street another brand new Walmart had sprung up over the bones of a local hardware store. Life. Death. And loss.

Arnau considered the Chevette his inheritance after the owner, a disagreeable son of a bitch, had the misfortune of falling through a hole in an icy northern lake—after being shot twice in the chest and once more above the right eye. There were some that claimed possession of the car was 9/10 of the law. Arnau Farre didn't believe in fractions. And he didn't care much about the law.

He had a good view of that Walmart across the street. It would have been better to have waited over there—could have walked over and gotten a coffee at Dunkin'. But it wasn't an option. They had security cameras over there. The dumpy strip mall wouldn't live long enough to get that upgrade.

For the better part of two hours, he'd been watching suburban- ites moping into the Walmart for crappy yellow shovels that were destined to crack down the center or fall off the handle by February. There had been no peaceful transition of seasonal power. It wasn't even Thanksgiving yet. Winter had staged a coup—eleven inches of demoralizing snow, wet and heavy.

For years, Arnau had known this day was coming, but he hadn't prepared himself for just how cold it would feel. He turned slowly in his seat to look into the back. Between two empty child booster seats was an arrangement of red roses in crinkly cellophane, a green rubber band choking the stems.

This was the most important assignment of his life. Ida's too. He knew he shouldn't complicate the handoff by presenting her roses. But he needed her to know how he felt. He'd never been good with words, and love—if that's what this was—well, it was damn complicated. The commercial on TV encouraged him to just "say it with flowers" and that was fine by him. He'd known Ida all his life. She was older and had always looked after him like a mother, or a big sister. But in the past few months, on their long walks together, things had started leaning toward something else. And he needed to know. Because tonight was the last time he'd ever see Ida. Never again. Forever.

He grabbed a pen and stared at the blue florist card. Flowers and a note. That was the plan. And the problem. How do you express what's in your heart on a three-inch notecard? How do you say goodbye? Arnau rubbed his hand across his whiskered face, then through his thick black hair.

He pictured himself handing Ida the roses, then leaning down and kissing her lips, imagining what it might be like to catch her breath in his mouth. Just one kiss. It would need to last a lifetime. He coughed to relieve his anxiety, but what buzzed inside him wasn't a thing to be hacked out. He held the pen over the blue florist card, waiting for inspiration. He stared at the card for ten minutes. What if she didn't feel the same way? What if he was misinterpreting the signs?

Arnau wrote slowly, making sure his words were legible and wondering if, maybe, the flowers were too much.

He slapped the cigarette pack against his thigh and pulled another smoke, hoping the nicotine would clear his head. He pushed the Beretta into the blue pizza warmer on the passenger seat, then looked at his watch. It was getting late. But he was confident the congresswoman and her husband would be leaving the house soon. The spotter phoned when the babysitter arrived. Apparently, the couple wasn't in a hurry to rush out the door. The woman probably couldn't care less about being on time for a Boston Bruins hockey game.

In the end, it would be a very difficult evening for the couple. They would blame themselves—abandoning their two four-year-old boys into the custody of a gray kitten and a high school girl with a blue cast on her arm signed by her friends on the cheerleading squad.

He snuffed out the cigarette before answering the phone. It was time. Years of patience and planning. It would begin with him. Above all the others, it was Arnau Farre who was chosen.

In minutes, the white Lexus was at the intersection, slowing for the stoplight. The husband was in the passenger seat. The congresswoman was driving. Arnau watched her flip the visor down and turn her face into the light of the vanity mirror. Congresswoman Kimberly Hancock was blessed with the holy trinity of political potential: wealth, intelligence, and political courage. If that wasn't enough, she'd inherited a famous name—the beneficiary of generations of American greatness, greed, and leadership. Betting on her political success was easy money. She untwisted a lipstick cartridge, made her mouth an oval, then wiped the corner of her lip with an index finger. The light turned green, and the white Lexus disappeared into the night.

Arnau Farre didn't consider himself a monster for stealing her boys or killing the babysitter. It was a just cause. A down payment on a promise. Tonight, he would drag the first pawn off the board. It would take two more decades for the pieces to move into position.

But that's the way it is with prophecies. They require patience, faith, and sacrifice.

And true believers.

And there were plenty.

Present Day—

Twenty Years Later

1

FBI Special Agent Briar Metcalf's head was pounding with a familiar ache—the kind that usually diminished around noon. Once again, he'd forgotten to add a water wedge between his nightcap(s) of Jameson, straight up. He drove slowly through the gritty Staten Island neighborhood. The slate gray sky seemed to fit the worn, polluted façade—a hard place of dirty brick buildings, grimy steel roll-ups, and chipped stucco. A neighborhood that looked as tired as Briar felt.

He found street parking in front of Sandra Dee's Diner. He popped two chalky aspirin, sipped the last of his coffee, and squeaked the Styrofoam into the cupholder. A blast of city wind snapped through his red bowling shirt. He looked into his locked car; his winter jacket was balled up in the backseat. The effort of unlocking and retrieving it was a little more than he was up for. Besides, the cure for hangovers was forward movement—backward was *no bueno*.

He tucked a thin case file under his arm and with his free hand checked that his wallet and phone were in his khaki pants, that his badge was clipped to his belt, and that his Glock was under his bowling shirt, tight on the hip.

Sandra Dee's was a replica '50s diner. The owners had made a decent attempt on the interior: white tiled walls, red booths, stainless counters, and little tin ashtrays stenciled with "NO SMOKING." The sign on the door advertised a 5% discount for customers in their 50s, but Metcalf wouldn't claim it. He didn't like thinking about his age and certainly didn't want to discuss it with a stranger. But there was no denying he was on the back end of life. His mop of black hair was now white—but still wavy. Still thick. So there.

Briar eyed the hostess. Either management had a poor understanding of the mid-twentieth century or they'd lost control of the dress code. She greeted him in a tie-dye shirt with sparkling green disco shorts. Looking at her confirmed every suspicion he had of the young.

"One?" she asked without looking at him.

"I'm meeting someone."

"You see him?"

"Her. And no."

Briar had planned to read up on his new partner last night. The file containing her bio was on the ottoman. He remembered pouring himself a stiffener to get through it, but he had no recollection of actually reading it. Not that it mattered. Nothing in the file would tell him what he really wanted to know. The only thing he was certain of was that she was a Blue Flame—straight out of the academy; a First Office Agent on her first day in the field. He hoped she wasn't one of those FOAs who thought just because they spent a few weeks at Quantico that they actually knew something. They were a pain in the ass. And could be dangerous to your health.

Briar tried to recall her face. He couldn't. Did he even look at her picture? He cursed his lack of curiosity—another indictment of his advancing age. He positioned himself in the open and scanned the breakfast crowd, searching for the latest item to fall off the FBI conveyor belt.

A hand shot up from a window-side booth in the back. It waved. Twice. Briar nodded, exhaled, and tried to conjure a pleasant persona. It wasn't easy. He'd worked alone for more than a decade—a street agent with seniority. For whatever reason, the SUP had assigned him a rookie, and no matter how much bitching Briar did, the guy wasn't budging. Orders had come from somewhere up the chain.

His black shoes clipped against the harlequin floor. He raised his head to force a grin in her direction. *What's her name? Trisha?*

She was smiling. A minty-white, innocent grin that caught him off-guard. He stared a moment longer than he intended. She was stunning. Maybe more beautiful than his ex-wife had been—before her face had become a scowl, immune to the delicate creams and dainty tubes of crap that crowded out his side of the vanity. But this woman in front of him, his new partner, was dangerously cute. The kind of girl that gets middle-aged men in trouble. And he didn't need trouble.

She had something else that got his attention. A white butterfly bandage stretched across her eyebrow. Briar approached. She launched out of her seat, leaned across the table, and extended her arm. It was a firmer grip than he expected, and he double-clutched to meet the force of it.

He circled his finger at her face. "What happened?"

"Emma Noble. Nice to meet you."

Nope. Not Trisha.

"Briar."

She nodded, as if everything he said was crucial. The rookie was, no doubt, trying to let him know that she was competent and that she shouldn't be underestimated. He looked at her eyebrow. "You get run over by something?"

"It's nothing."

"Looks like something."

"Nope. Not really. So—"

"Is it a secret?" he asked.

"It's just not how I want to start off."

"Why?"

"You're not going to let it go?"

"I'm just curious. What happened?"

She touched her brow. "I took a header in the CVS parking lot. I was running in for Mike and Ike's and…"

"You run for candy?"

Emma sighed. "Yup. This is definitely the kick-ass first impression I was hoping to make."

Briar rubbed the smile off his lips. "Your file said you were uncoordinated."

"It probably does. I'm impressed you read it."

"I'm very thorough."

He swept breadcrumbs off the red vinyl seat before scrunching in. The table hadn't been cleaned. In front of him, yellow globs of yolk had hardened in a spray pattern. Briar reached into his shirt pocket for his glasses and bent his head to the table. The last customer, a lefty by the looks of it, had forked the egg directly into the heart of its sunny side. Briar leaned closer, investigating the yolk—a fleck of fennel. Rye toast, then. But the crumbs he'd brushed away were wheat. Residue from two different customers, then, which meant the staff had ignored the table for most of the morning. Which meant that nobody at this restaurant gave a shit. Which meant Briar Metcalf would be ordering coffee only.

He raised his head to see Emma Noble smiling.

"What?" he asked.

"Just never seen an inquest done on an egg yolk. Suspect fowl play?"

Briar winced. His hangover hated puns. He ran his tongue around the inside of his cheek, unsure whether he liked her yet. "What's your background, Noble? Lawyer, right? That's all the Bureau hires anymore. We used to recruit linebackers."

"Guess you *didn't* read my bio then."

Briar folded his hands on the table and inhaled. "So, not a lawyer."

"I worked at a veterinary clinic while I was in grad school."

"Well, that'll sure come in handy," Briar muttered, unfurling his silverware from a cotton napkin and snowplowing the dried egg yolk off the table with his butter knife.

The server arrived as the yellow crust flaked to the floor. She was too old for her pink poodle mini skirt and looked vaguely familiar. From the blistering, how-dare-you-show-up-here look she was giving him, he got the distinct impression that they might have had some history. Apparently, a forgettable one.

"What'll you have, hon?" she said to Emma Noble.

"Coffee."

"You?" she said without affection.

Briar made the peace sign. "Black."

He waited for her to leave and folded his hands back on the table.

"What's your story, Noble? Why did the SUP order me to partner up with a dog nurse? You have someone pulling strings for you?"

"Pulling strings? I didn't realize you were such a catch."

Okay. He was starting to like her … a little. Briar put the case file on the table. He licked his index finger and flipped through the pages.

"What are we working on?" Emma asked.

"What were you hoping for?"

"Something memorable. After all, it's my first case."

10

"Well, sorry to disappoint. It isn't the crime of the century. We're interested in this guy—"

Emma picked her phone off the table, swept her finger across, tapped twice, and set it down.

He stared at her.

"Sorry. Dropping a pin."

"Pin?"

"My father. I drop a pin—my location—a couple times a day."

"And he lives in New York? Standing by to rescue his daughter?"

"St. Louis."

Briar pinched the bridge of his nose. He didn't thank the aging sock-hopper for the coffee when she slid it across the table at him. Emma looked like she was about to say something—Briar shut it down with a raised index finger. He lifted the heavy ceramic mug to his lips and closed his eyes. His hangover thanked him for demanding silence.

A buzz interrupted the peaceful moment. He opened his eyes to see his phone vibrating on the white table. The caller ID turned his arms to gooseflesh.

"Assistant Director, good morning."

Briar saw Emma's eye widen. The conversation was quick. When it was over, he lowered the phone to his lap and exhaled. He looked up at the ceiling, concentrating on keeping his thoughts in check. It was a reminder he often gave himself at the beginning of things. Focus on what's in front of you. Let it unravel naturally. No mistakes.

"What was that about?"

Briar took a last sip of his coffee and threw a five on the table. "Well, I was wrong, Noble. Apparently, your first case *is* the crime of the century."

2

Rural Vermont had always been a good place to live if a person wanted privacy, and, in the last twenty years, Mrs. Ida Danvers had not been an overly social woman. She was content with the quiet company of her husband. Now retired, they were stoic, independent, and alone—aging in the New England tradition.

Today was an important day. She'd been waiting most of her life for it. Visitors would be coming up the hill. It was important for her to see them as they arrived. From the leaded window over her rust-spotted sink, she could see all the way down her hill. She'd know if a vehicle turned off Route 7 and could follow it all the way up the lengthy drive.

Seeing the visitors arrive was so important for Mrs. Danvers that she had not moved from the window since dawn. She had washed the plates, pots, silverware, cups, glasses, and cookie sheets. She dried every one and then washed them again. Her focus never swayed from the vehicles moving down Route 7.

Her husband, Wendall, did not know about the visitors. He was a man that didn't enjoy surprises.

The Danvers had lived in their worn, yellow colonial for nearly twenty years. Wendall was sixty and his knees couldn't manage much of the labor required to fix the place. Their son wasn't around to help—Ben lived down in Boston with his girlfriend, Kate. The aging couple had ignored the upkeep, allowing the home to weather into desperation. In fairer seasons, it was a decent place. The level ground around the house had surrendered to high grasses interrupted by simple gardens with rolled chicken wire stapled to weathered posts that leaned out of the dirt at odd angles. In summer, ticks infested the hillside weeds that swept down to Route 7. The couple spent most favorable days sitting on their porch, ignoring the highway traffic, and focusing beyond—to a somewhat obstructed view of Harriton Reservoir.

This morning, ten inches of new powder hid the gardens and the grasses and the ticks.

Mrs. Danvers watched her husband. He was on the granite steppers by the split-rail fence in front of the house. He held a red leash attached to their black terrier mix. She watched the fabric of his brown corduroys flap in the wind like luffed sailcloth. Wendall had a knack for underestimating the weather. She watched the dog sniff around a post, then hike his ass—his back legs quaking under the strain of his dump. Wendall smiled toward the window, giving his wife a thumbs-up.

Wendall was a good man—a tender, generous man. He didn't deserve this surprise.

The waiting and the standing were tiring her. She bent her old knees, stretching the joints. Her feet were sore too. She leaned her body against the porcelain sink and ran her index finger into the shoe behind her heel. It did little to comfort her. When her head rose above the sink, she saw the dog snap his attention down the hill. Mrs. Danvers did the same.

The visitors were here. Six black SUVs were turning off Route 7 and streaming up the hill. One after another—a parade of sirens and blue lights. Blinking. Coming fast.

She stepped off the porch and handed her husband a brown jacket. She squeezed his upper arm and leaned her head into his shoulder.

"You seeing this?" he said, pointing at the approaching vehicles.

Wendall took a step forward to meet the visitors coming up the drive.

Ida Danvers didn't give him time to register that the icy feeling at the base of his skull was a gun. Wendall didn't live long enough to hear the shot. His head sprayed across the split-rail fence.

Ida kept a firm grip on the revolver.

The vehicles reached the top of the drive. Ida squeezed her eyes tight and reached into her past for an oath she'd made decades before. *"Mia ĵuro, mia vivo."*

She found her courage in the memory of a man she once knew. A man who had instructions. A trustworthy man who knew what needed to be done. She allowed the thought of him to be the last thing on her mind. Ida sucked the barrel of the gun into her mouth.

The SUVs skidded on the gravel, crunching to a stop as the gunshot echoed down the snowy hill, across Route 7, and into the woods beyond Harriton Reservoir.

3

Ben Danvers buried his icy hand into the pocket of his down jacket, trying to ignore the sting of the wind biting through his fleece Celtics pajama bottoms. He wiggled the leash, hoping it might spur his Australian Shepherd puppy to shit. The dog looked up at him, wagged his nubby tail, then plopped down in the snow. Ben sighed and closed his eyes. Great dog. Bad pooper.

Ben jogged in place. His breath billowed cold smoke. Dawn was beginning to break over the bay beyond Boston's North End. Soon the red brick buildings would yellow in the sun and the nonnas would cinch their quilted housecoats to take their posts by the windows to look down on the young.

A metal gate clanged to his left. In the nascent light of morning, a person would have been forgiven for mistaking the hunching old man dragging two trash bags for an elf or maybe a hobbit. Ben made a small wave at Papa Giordano—a man emblematic of the North End, historic and charming.

He curled his bony finger at the pup. "He makes the shit?"

Ben shook his head, "Nope."

"He likes to make you wait. He a funny dog."

The old man's laugh bubbled up from his belly and rasped through his throat in a guttural spasm of clucks. Meeting there on the sidewalk had become something of a ritual—Ben exchanging the leash for Papa's heavy black trash bags. Ben would toss them in the dumpster, and when he'd completed the small favor, the old man would stand on his tiptoes and give him a peck on the cheek and a slap on the neck.

"Today, you come. Free slice for the *bella donna*. *Doppio* for you."

He laughed again and waggled his arthritic pinky and index fingers in front of Ben. The old man liked to give a wink when he fired off hexes. Some days he wondered if the accumulation of curses might not be a great thing, but he smiled and took his slap.

Ben took care to enter the apartment without making noise. It was cramped—but no worse than most rentals for couples in their mid-twenties. He was at the bottom rung at Cambridge Hill Holdings. Kate was a first-grade teacher at St. Bartholomew's. Financially speaking, they weren't exactly killing it. He turned on the kitchen light. Three cabinet doors were open. A casserole dish and an ice cream bowl hovered perilously over the counter. Kate had a cavalier attitude about fragility; part of Ben's morning routine was battening shit down and rescuing the breakables.

He looked at the clutter on the kitchen table: Elmer's glue, tongue depressors, cotton balls, construction paper. The trash can was filled with art failure. Kate had no talent for crafts, but she was good with kids and they loved her.

He bent over the kitchen sink, hand-washing the dishes. The TV news kept him company. The volume was off. These days, it was the only acceptable way to watch. Like most cities in America, Boston was fraying at the seams. He glanced over at the replay of last night's eruption: flames and batons, bullhorns and horses. The protest had come within walking distance of their apartment. Across the nation, a rising tide of hate, fear, and conspiracy theories had overwhelmed the levees of common sense—a river of anger was winding across the country, heading straight for Washington, DC.

Ben looked away. He ran a sponge across the countertop and put away the glasses.

In five days, Peter McGill & Kimberly Hancock would be sworn in. A neophyte politician with his running mate, the Senator from Massachusetts—dubbed by her opponents as the "Prickly Princess." There were some who thought the new administration had a fair chance of unifying the country. It was the minority opinion.

Ben poured coffee into Kate's mug and creaked open the bedroom door. The light cast an expanding brightness across the lump on the bed. Buried beneath the white comforter—snuggled deep in the tangle of sheets—was his girlfriend. Only a single toe periscoped from below. He considered putting the coffee on the nightstand and tunneling in to warm himself around her body. He thought twice. His cold skin against hers would not end well. Besides, the dog had already claimed her, dancing over the bedding. He pinched the exposed toe. A groan muffled up from below. Ben turned on the bedside light. The puppy's oversized paws burrowed into the sheets. A frizz of hair sprouted from the depths—the rising of Kate Malone.

"Morning," he said.

She pulled herself up on an elbow and squinted at him with one eye. She held her hand out for the coffee. "What time is it?"

"Six forty-five."

"Benjamin, what the fuck? I was perfectly clear."

"Oh, shit."

"I told you I was off today. Dick move."

He kissed her forehead. Kate sighed and sat cross-legged on the bed in a purple LSU nightshirt. The dog snuggled next to her. She rubbed behind his soft ears while Ben waited for the hot caffeine to melt the frost.

"My boyfriend out there?" she asked.

"He's too old for you."

"But he's *so* cute. You want to know what the old women say?"

"I'm sure I don't."

Kate pressed her palms together and widened them. "Like a donkey."

Ben scrunched up his face as she laughed into her coffee.

"You hear back from Rocky on your idea?"

Ben nodded. "She emailed. Said it was brilliant."

"Really?"

"She's going to present it this morning."

"And take all the credit. Ben, you need to assert yourself. You're the smartest one in the room."

He shrugged and walked out of the bedroom. He'd never spoken up in an acquisition-strategy meeting before. In fact, he'd managed not to speak up at any of the meetings in his brief career with Cambridge Hill Holdings. He decided he wasn't the kind of person who had things to say at work. There was wisdom in keeping a low profile. Management played Whack-A-Mole with young heads that popped out of their holes. Of course, Rocky was the exception to that rule. Everything came easy for her. Management loved her.

Ben stripped down in the bathroom and turned on the shower. He didn't care if Rocky took his idea and ran with it. She was a friend. And he owed her. Without her introduction, Kate and he would never have met.

He turned and stuck his head out the bathroom door. "What'd you say?"

"I said—Rocky told me she thinks your talent is being wasted in Risk Management."

"Yup. Okay."

Before he could close the bathroom door, Kate caught it with her hand. She was wearing his bathrobe. It hung loosely off her thin frame, barely concealing her nakedness. She smiled and lifted her chin. "You must look inside yourself, Simba. You are more than what you've become."

"Such wisdom, Mustafa," Ben said, reaching for the velour sash and pulling it slowly until the robe opened completely.

"*Mu-sta-fa?*" she said, feigning annoyance. "Simba's father is *Mufasa*. How can I be with a man that doesn't—?"

"I don't care what his name is," Ben whispered, planting kisses behind her ear and down her neck.

4

"Crime of the century?" asked Special Agent Emma Noble. Briar edged out of the booth. "Not here."

Emma stood. She was taller than he expected—uncomfortably tall, at least six feet. He wasn't quite five-nine in dress shoes. The aging FBI agent pulled his shoulders back and lifted his chin, waving her forward.

Briar hastily picked fast-food wrappers out of the passenger seat of his vehicle and threw them in back before unlocking the door for his new partner. The gray Chevy Suburban was his assigned Bureau car, or bucar as it was called—the FBI was creative like that. He thought to apologize for the garbage in the back, but there was no reason to bring attention to it.

"So, what's going on?" Emma asked.

She was impatient. But he wasn't ready yet. He wanted another moment for the adrenaline to course through him. He'd missed this feeling. The rush. He looked out the side window, pretending to be interested in a man sweeping glass and debris off the sidewalk in front of his boarded storefront. It was happening. Finally. He'd been waiting a long time.

"Briar?"

He put his elbow over the wheel and faced her. Noble was a coiled spring, hungry to pounce on actionable information. That worried him a little. He needed to keep the leash tight. He placed his keys in the front cupholder.

"Yes?"

19

"Well? Are you gonna tell me?"

"Yeah. The call was from Billy Monroe, assistant director of CID. That means Criminal Investigative Division—in case you haven't gotten a handle on our acronyms yet."

"Super helpful. Thanks. What'd he say?"

"This case is classified. Closed loop. Just for you, me, and the A.D. You'll understand why. We'll get support, but no one knows what we're working on. Not yet, anyway."

Briar took his time putting his seat belt on.

"Jesus, Briar. And…?"

"An old kidnapping case—twin boys taken outside of Boston twenty years ago. They were never found—I never found them."

"You kidding me?"

"Do I hear bells ringing?"

"The Hancock kidnapping? Really?"

Briar nodded and pressed the ignition button.

"That was your case? Holy shit. So, what's going on? What happened?"

"Put your seat belt on."

He lit up his cherries and berries and lurched the SUV into the street.

"We might have found one of them—and, maybe, the kidnappers. We'll know later."

"Jesus. Wait…. Now? We're finding them *now*?"

Briar told her about the two teams of agents: one descending on a small home in Vermont, the other picking up the person who'd gotten flagged in the system.

"What do you mean, flagged?"

"There was a DNA test. One of those online kits. The genetic code triggered the flag. They sent it to Monroe—his eyes only."

"This is nuts."

"We're going up to Boston—Chelsea Headquarters. They're bringing everyone to us. We'll conduct the interviews. See what we've got."

They cruised over the Verrazano Bridge into Brooklyn. Briar needed to stop by the "O" for the files on the Hancock case before heading to Boston. He thought back to the night the children were taken. It was still vivid. Hard to believe it'd been twenty years already.

The car was quiet. Noble was keeping her thoughts to herself—and Briar was fine with that. Glimpses of the Manhattan skyline rushed between bridge structures and tall borough buildings. She was staring out the window with the silent fascination of a child riding shotgun. She caught his eye and straightened up in her seat.

"I wrote a paper on the FBI response to 9/11."

"A page-turner, I'm sure."

"You were working back then. What do you remember?"

Most every American of a certain age had an acute memory of the morning. Where they were. What they were doing. Briar had been driving out of a church parking lot when he heard the news. He'd been in a morning meeting when the attack occurred. It was the kind of meeting where a stranger says, "Hi, I'm Briar," and the room responds, "Hi, Briar" and waits for the stranger's personal darkness to be revealed. Except, that morning, they hadn't said "Hi, Briar." In this group he went by "Steve."

Steve was probably an alcoholic. Briar Metcalf was a squared-away FBI agent. At the encouragement of their ever-optimistic counselor, his wife had thrown a tiny life preserver at their marriage. *"Get sober and we'll see."*

After the meeting on that September morning, Briar got pulled away by a morose alcoholic in the parking lot. The guy liked the sound of his own voice, and Briar had become captive to his rant. When he finally extricated himself, he learned about the attack. The Bureau had been trying to reach him all morning. Every agent in the country was scrambling to respond while Briar Metcalf was sitting in a circle of metal chairs under fluorescent lights in a church basement in Boston, mired in the muddy lives of strangers. That was his memory of 9/11.

"It's not really something I enjoy talking about."

He looked out of the corner of his eye. She had shifted away from him, craning her head to see the commotion on the street: two policemen dragging a black man toward a squad car—an angry crowd shouting and filming the incident on their phones.

Upon arrival, Emma and Briar matched strides, walking down the hall of the New York Office. The "O"—26 Federal Plaza. Briar had been coming into the "O" for years but didn't really know anyone—not beyond sports chitchat. The only effort he made was to learn which agents were rabid Jets fans, just so he could give them shit. That was about it. His lack of familiarity didn't bother him. He enjoyed being alone.

An agent in a blue suit burst through a door, hip-checking Briar against the wall. It wasn't much of a collision, but enough to send his reading glasses skidding down the polished floor. Briar winced when he bent for them. At least Noble didn't ask if he was okay. The kid in the blue suit didn't apologize, just ran down the hallway like a dickhead—another adolescent in a suit. They were all urgent. Overflowing with purpose. Fit and young. The bright shiny apples of the FBI.

Emma Noble pointed to the women's restroom. Briar continued toward his cubicle. Like most of the other offices on the floor, his was cramped and windowless. He stopped in front of his desk. A drip of condensation fell onto his forehead from an overhead pipe. He threw his jacket over the black cabinet. Paint was chipping around a fist-sized dent in the side. Briar rooted his index finger into the paper clip cubby of his metal desk, searching for the key. The bottom drawer of the cabinet rattled out, revealing two thick, green file folders. The accumulation of hours and days and years of failure, hanging in the black coffin at the back of his cubicle. Fifteen years buried.

He laid the files down and glanced at the picture at the back of his desk. It was a photograph of his family staring at him from a wooden frame. It was taken on the sidewalk outside a theatre on Broadway. His ex was burying her face into his shoulder, laughing into his armpit. His son was holding a stuffed lion, showing off his missing teeth in a ridiculously wide smile. Briar stood rigid, smirking at the camera. He'd kept the photo on the desk through the divorce, her remarriage, and the boy's name change. It was the only documented happy moment from a loveless marriage. Briar sometimes regretted not making a better effort to smile for it.

"Nice family," Noble said.

He scooped up the green file folders. "Let's go."

5

The thermostat was set too high in the large conference room on the tenth floor of Cambridge Hill Holdings. A drop of perspiration released down Ben Danvers's neck and trickled into the small of his back. His good suit was creating a mercurial atmosphere against his body—too hot to sustain life. He prayed the Senior VP would remove his suit coat. The rest of the room would stay business until the leader went casual. Apparently, the exec ran cold.

Ben sat in a small chair against a wall the color of rotting salmon. Above his head was a large painting in a heavy gold frame—a wooden ship struggling against a mighty storm, its bow drowning under a breaking wave. The art in every room and hallway at Cambridge Hill shared the same theme: imminent death. Ben thought it a not-so-subliminal message regarding the tenuous grip one should feel about their employment. Rocky believed it had something to do with overcoming challenges.

The high-back leather chairs at the conference table were reserved for the alpha dogs. Ben liked sitting in the outer ring. It gave him an excellent view of Boston's Back Bay: the swooping seagulls, the heavy-beamed wharfs, anchored fishing boats rocking with the tide. Rocky sat next to the VP.

He scanned the sleepy faces in the conference room. Nothing decelerates the cerebral cortex like heat and a poorly delivered PowerPoint. The presenter had flown in from somewhere in the heartland, hoping for approval to buy a competitor. He was a minor cog in Cambridge's vast network. The guy's neck was pink and splotchy. His words came out jumpy. For a while, Ben felt bad for the guy, but the longer he spoke, the less sympathy he had for him.

"Mackin Industries is an advantageous purchase that will excite our current platform and offer tremendous synergistic…"

The guy had been speaking too long and had gone through too many decks not to have made his case. Now he was repeating himself. Ben thought it might take a tranquilizer dart to get the guy to wrap up.

He crept his phone to his lap. His fingers were long and bony around the knuckle. A junior-high music teacher had once told him his hands were perfect for piano and offered to give him private lessons. Ida had shot that idea down, telling Ben the man was likely a pervert. She had a talent for keeping strangers off the stoop—and everyone was a stranger. Ben dismissed the recollection. He was good at keeping that spigot tight. There was no purpose in dwelling on the loneliness of a cloistered childhood. But still, there were drops that leaked out every so often, catching him off guard.

Ida had been like the weather; there were sunny days and there were horrible storms. But mostly it was cold, and as a boy, he'd learned how to sniff out low-pressure systems and read the winds. There were lots of kids like him—forced to adjust to living in shitty climates. Sometimes he had to remind himself that those days were over—he'd made it out and taken that long-awaited left at the bottom of the drive. Into freedom.

He scrolled through the news. It was political garbage. Outgoing president making excuses. Incoming guy making promises. Political pundits spewing their bile and hate in ten-second sound bites. Ben turned his phone off. At least the election was over. In five days, the new administration would begin.

"All right, Wally. I think we've got the picture," said the VP.

Ben looked at the presenter, imagining a yellow-feathered dart sticking out of his neck.

"What's your take, Rocky? Should we rubber-stamp this thing? See if Wally's group can make a home run out of them?"

Make a home run out of them? Ben tilted his head and smiled at Rocky. Her eyes flashed back with a twinkle. Then he watched her face harden. *Game time.* She leaned forward, pressing her palms on the table.

"How you manage it, Wally? You tuck 'em?"

"Sorry?" he responded.

"I don't see a bulge so—I'm just wondering where the hell you put them?"

Ben winced when the guy looked down at his own pants.

"What?"

"I've got your numbers from last year—hot off the press. Christ, Wally, it's a massacre. A slaughter. The pages are dripping red. But here you are, standing in front of us, telling us you want to buy a company. So, it's a simple question: Where are you hiding those magnificent balls?"

"I just—"

"Wally, nobody wants to hear about your testicles."

His face was drowning in maroon. "But we need Mackin, because if we don't—"

Rocky interrupted. "You'll have to fire some good people in Ohio. I know."

"Indiana. We're from Indiana."

Ben smiled.

She lifted her chin. "Anyway, nobody at Cambridge Hill will let you heap more debt on yourself. Unless, of course, *you're* smart enough to come up with a less expensive alternative."

Ben felt sorry for the poor bastard. Rocky didn't play touch. Work was tackle football. Old-school, without helmets. Only her close friends knew that behind the gristle was a big-hearted woman. But at work? Rocky was all bulldog. She took what she wanted, and, in a moment, the room would understand why she'd just eviscerated the guy from Indiana. It was her windup. She was about to slay the room with the idea he'd come up with. Rocky lived for moments like these.

Instead, Ben watched her push her seat away from the table and cross her legs. She looked him in the eye, cocked her head, and winked. That was when the first flash of panic drummed in his chest.

Keep going, Rock.

Don't do this.

She was staring at him, nodding slightly.

Ben shook his head. He had no intention of speaking up.

"Does anyone disagree?" asked the VP.

Don't do it, Rocky.

"Ben, you have some thoughts on this?" she asked.

25

"Ben? Where is Ben?" asked the VP, craning his neck. "Ah, there you are. Wanna weigh in on this one?"

It was an ambush. Rocky and Kate had conspired against him. The packed employees shifted in their seats, searching to find him in the large conference room's outer ring. Ben felt his face flushing.

"Um. I agree. You can't afford it," he said a little faster than he intended.

He peeked at Rocky.

"Any interesting ideas on how it *could* work, Ben?" she probed, doubling down.

His mouth went dry. "Um."

"Sorry, Ben, could you please speak up?" asked the VP, leaning to see him more clearly.

Breathe. Fake it till you make it. Act like you've been here before. Project confidence. Raise your chin. Speak from the heart. He knew all the words from *The Secret to Igniting Your Inner Power,* the book Kate had given him for Christmas.

"So, Mackin is—I mean, you know—it's highly leveraged. No one is going to lend them more money."

He was acutely aware of the silence in the negative space of his words. His brain was drifting away—his thought balloon fleeing the scene. Everyone was staring at him. Ben looked down and spoke into the carpet. "Their major supplier is a tiny electronics mom-and-pop in the middle of farm country."

Ben dry-swallowed, then coughed into his fist.

The VP interrupted. "I'm sorry Ben, but we can't hear you."

"Well, um." He cleared his throat. "They supply a certain critical component that is made custom for Mackin. They'll go bankrupt without that supplier."

He looked up. No one was tracking anything he was saying. They were bored with him. It was exactly the nightmare he knew it would be.

"What are you saying, Ben?" Rocky asked loudly.

He looked over. She was smiling. Enjoying the shit out of the moment. To her, work was nothing but a bullshit game. Maybe that was the secret. *Go with it.*

"You're buying the wrong company," Ben blurted with an authority that caught him, and the rest of the room, by surprise. The match struck. He felt the blue-yellow flame shooting from his fingertips, exactly like the book said it would. "If you buy the mom-and-pop, you can starve Mackin and buy them later for pennies on the dollar."

The VP scribbled something on a paper, then looked at the Indiana guy. "Wally, you know this company?"

"Yes, sir."

"Is what Ben says true?"

"It seems like a good idea."

"That's because it is. Nice work, Ben."

The alpha dogs gently slapped the wooden conference table in recognition. Ben's heart was double-timing. Rocky was grinning. He mouthed a silent "thank you" to her.

He was enjoying the moment too much to register that the door to the conference room had opened. Rebecca from reception entered first. Behind her were four men and a woman, wearing blue windbreakers.

"He's right there," she said, pointing a finger in the vicinity of the drowning ship.

Ben was in the after-chills of his first workgasm. His mind registered nothing of the FBI agents storming the room. It wasn't until one grabbed ahold of his elbow that Ben's eyes went wide.

"Benjamin Danvers? FBI. You're coming with us."

"What's going—?" It was Rocky. She was standing up.

"Now, sir."

There were hands on him. Multiple sets of hands. On his shoulders and on the back of his neck, hustling him out of the room and down the hall past coworkers poking their heads out of offices, watching him being pulled across the tan commercial-grade carpeting. The elevator doors by the reception desk were closing but the agent with the brown ponytail caught it and ordered everyone out. Ben knew those people, and they knew him. They were staring. He couldn't think what to say. He looked over his shoulder at them as the doors closed.

"What's happening?" he asked at last.

Silence.

"I don't understand. What's happening?"

Still no response. The only thing he could think to do was ask to see their search warrant.

"What?" replied the tallest FBI agent, genuinely perplexed by the question.

The woman shook her head at her colleague. It seemed she might be in charge.

The elevator dropped. So did Ben's stomach. It turned watery, and he felt pressure pushing against his colon. The agents whisked him through the marbled expanse of Cambridge Hill's entryway—past the security guards Ben greeted every morning, but who now ignored him and stood at their posts like FBI wannabes. He felt like a criminal, and as he passed the people in the entryway, he knew he looked like one, too. The agents pushed him into the revolving door. A black SUV with a rolling blue light waited on the other side.

"Mr. Danvers, we're escorting you to FBI Regional Headquarters. We'll be there in fifteen."

"Please. I don't understand."

"That's all we can say."

"I'm sorry but—"

"Fifteen minutes," the female agent said as the driver flicked on his sirens and merged into the street.

6

Emma Noble braced herself against the stench drifting out of the backseat of Briar's gray Suburban. Whatever was back there, it had defrosted in the past hour. She clenched her eyes. It wasn't just one thing. It was a cocktail of sewage. She could almost taste it: notes of rancid garbage with a hint of athlete's foot. She was sure the flavor profile would get more complex before they reached Chelsea HQ.

Briar had spent the first few blocks of the trip swearing at everything in Midtown that was on or near the road: cabs, buses, streetlights, pedestrians—anything that threatened to impede his progress. He was overly dramatic about it, but she had to give him credit. He was an enlightened curser.

He sizzled into a proper rage when traffic clogged on FDR Drive. Hundreds of protesters had marched onto the highway. Briar triggered his siren and flipped on his blue lights. The vehicles in front worked to get out of his way, inching over where they could. It took a while for a seam to open in the traffic. To Emma's right, a few idiots had exited their vehicles, adding their rage to the powder keg. She watched a guy charge into the demonstration with a two-handed grip on a 3-iron that he'd pulled from the trunk of his Mercedes. Emma asked if they should stop and get the situation under control. Briar told her that the "cum bubble" deserved everything he was about to get. Getting to Chelsea as fast as possible was the mission.

He swung his left arm out the window, shouting for the mass to move. It took a few minutes for the protesters to holster their "fuck you" fingers and let them through. Emma, being a midwestern girl, waved them a thank you—which did nothing to lighten Briar's mood. When they broke free, he burned a hole through the open left lane.

Emma had questions. She wanted to learn more about the Hancock kidnapping—and about Briar himself. But the veins in his neck were engorged and she thought a cleansing silence might be the best medicine to keep him from stroking out. For twenty minutes, she said nothing.

She looked over at him. The quiet had gone on long enough.

"You know, your car kinda smells like a fishing derby."

Briar narrowed his eyes and Emma decided more silence might be in order.

She counted the mile markers—a new one coming into view every forty seconds. They passed an amateur highway memorial, three tilted crosses and an American flag shivering in the wind.

"You think the chatter's legit?" Emma asked.

"What chatter?"

"The terror threat."

"I don't do gossip."

"So, no fear of domestic terror, then?"

He shrugged. "Who the fuck knows? But if you look around at this country and you don't think we're heading for an ass-puckering nightmare, you're not paying attention. It's going to be civil war. You agree?"

"It's my first day. They told me I'm not allowed to have opinions for a couple more."

"But you *don't* agree, do you?"

The violence and hatred were undeniable. It was in front of her every day. On the street. On the news. Almost everyone she knew had bounced out of the middle and planted their flag on the far side of a political fringe. But Emma was an optimist. It might take a while, but she believed America was too good for what it had become. It would get better. Eventually.

"I might have more faith in people than you do."

Briar shrugged. "Believe what you want. But it's coming."

She let the conversation burn itself out. He was an intense guy, and his face was showing some tough miles; blue spider veins unspooled across his cheeks, and the skin around his jaw sagged south. For decades he'd probably been witness to the worst things humans could do to each other. Briar Metcalf was a thorny dude, but he was the real deal. She'd read his bio three times. SUP said he had the best instincts of anyone he'd ever worked with. She intended to learn as much as she could. As much as he was willing to offer.

"The Hancock files are in the gray bag in the backseat. Get yourself up to speed," he told her.

"Do I need a tetanus shot to reach back there?"

"Don't push it, Noble. I'm not sure if I like you yet."

"What? Everybody loves me."

• • •

Ben Danvers was an aquarium attraction—an awkward fish swimming alone behind the giant window of the FBI's conference room. Agents walked by and stared, then moved on. He had stopped trying to flag them down. No one was saying anything. He had developed a routine. Stations of anxiety: staring at the black and white photographs of former FBI leaders on the paneled wall, studying the complicated phone console on the table, standing by the window to view the traffic going up and down Route 1.

The northbound vehicles were slowing for construction work. An orange-vested crew was filling in potholes, the hot tar steaming off the frozen road. Ben breathed in and exhaled slowly. His initial panic had relaxed into a rolling tension. He was thinking about Kate. Rocky would have called her immediately. He knew she was worrying. The FBI had taken his phone and his wallet. "Protocol," they'd said. He tried to prop himself up with the hope he'd be able to call her soon. They'd laugh about the mix-up. She'd make a joke about dating a dangerous man. He wasn't convincing himself, though. In fact, he was nervous as hell.

He hadn't been involved in last night's violent protest. And he'd be the last person the FBI would come to if Cambridge Hill were up to something sketchy. He could only admit to a couple of crimes: twice he'd driven after a party when he shouldn't have; he'd smoked pot a few times before it was legal; he'd pirated NFL games over the internet. But that wasn't why he was here. Also, he wasn't in handcuffs. They weren't treating him like a criminal.

The agents hadn't fingerprinted him, but they *had* steamrolled him

31

into agreeing to swab his cheek and take a blood sample. *DNA test?* His chest thumped a little faster. Maybe they'd found the answer to the most important question in Ben's life.

Where's my real father?

When he was eight years old, Ida had abruptly told him that Wendall was his stepfather. No warming words. Just said it and walked away. Ben had burning questions about who his dad was. She refused: *"I don't have to tell you anything."* He asked every day until she got sick of the inquiries and started walloping him in the ear. That put a stop to the questions.

Ben had always wondered where his father was, inventing tales of him, fantasizing that the man lived in an exotic place having adventures, biding his time until Ben was old enough to be rescued. One day, he'd skip up the porch stairs, hug Ben tight, and tell Ida, "The boy is coming with me," and they'd leave Vermont in a station wagon. Or maybe on a horse.

Ben had spent his childhood in a stale bedroom, waiting by the window—watching the traffic rolling up and down Route 7.

The guy never bothered to show.

Maybe the FBI knew why.

7

The security gate raised in front of Briar's gray Suburban. He looked up at the FBI's regional headquarters. It was a new building—an eight-story, windowed box in the middle of a field. Boston had been his first office when he'd graduated from the academy, but the building he'd worked in was four miles down the road and a hell of a lot shabbier than this.

At the ribbon-cutting a few years ago, A.D. Billy Monroe stood next to the director of the FBI. He even had some things to say for the cameras. Briar had soured on Monroe a long time ago. They had started out together. Monroe had been a comically poor investigator, and he knew it too. Back in the day, he would beg Briar to help him with his cases. The smartest thing he ever did was to jump into management the first chance he got. Turned out Billy Monroe was a political savant. A professional kiss-ass who had a talent for sniffing out the right rectum.

Briar hadn't been surprised to get the call from Monroe this morning. The A.D. always called him when the stakes were high. Besides, the Hancock kidnapping was Briar's old case, and his one and only glaring failure.

"Pretty wicked first day, huh?" Emma said as they entered the building.

"We'll see."

A woman was waiting when the elevator doors opened. She was short, but ramrod straight and serious. Behind her, FBI suits rushed between cubicles, conference rooms, and offices.

"Agent Metcalf? Theresa Michaels. Special Agent in Charge. We spoke on the phone."

The SAC's grip was almost as strong as Noble's. She was young to be in charge, but then again, everyone looked young to Briar.

"The A.D. requested that we extend every courtesy and resource to you."

Briar thanked her.

"We have Mr. Danvers in Conference Room A. He's been here a few hours."

"And the Vermont people?"

The SAC jerked her chin toward the end of the hall. "My office, please."

Briar and Emma followed her into the bright, windowed corner office. It resembled all the SAC offices he'd ever known. They decorated from the same recipe: three parts patriotism, two parts family, one part humble brag. In Theresa Michael's case, the last ingredient was a photograph of her laughing with the red-headed director of the FBI, minutes after she'd completed some kind of mud race. It was a dirt-glopped, post-race photo intended to remind visitors she was just another fun-loving athlete who also happened to be friendly with the director.

"There was an incident in Vermont. I wanted to tell you in person."

She handed Briar her phone. He was looking at a photograph of a woman in a blue wool sweater, face down in blood-soaked snow. The next photograph was more graphic. He felt his face flushing. He looked up at the SAC.

"Self-inflicted. As my guys were coming up the drive. She did her husband first."

Briar looked down at it again and exhaled.

"You okay?" asked Emma.

"Yeah, of course." He showed her the screen.

Her eyes widened, but she kept it together pretty well. So far, Briar thought, she was handling herself just fine.

"What would you like them to do?" asked the SAC.

Briar was looking at the photograph again. "I'm sorry? What?"

"My team's still at the scene."

"Sure." He inhaled and handed her back the phone. "Need pictures

34

and prints. When they're done, have local PD secure the house. You said the kid's here?"

The SAC nodded.

"How is he?"

"Holding it together. He's nervous."

"What about the kit?"

"Done."

Briar shot her a look. "Done-done?"

"Waiting on the results. Should be soon. You want to meet him?"

He shook his head. "Not yet."

"Roger. You can wait in my office. And I'm sorry about Vermont— nothing we could do."

They didn't have to wait long. A knock came and a thin blue folder was handed through the door. It had one piece of paper inside. Briar retrieved his glasses and skimmed down the page, stopping at the word he'd been looking for.

MATCH

He reminded himself not to rush. No shortcuts. Every move mattered now. He tucked the thick green file folders under his arm and handed Noble the blue folder. She read it as they walked toward Room A.

8

The conference room door popped. Ben's chest jumped. He stood. A young agent, roughly his age, came in first. She gave him a hollow smile and looked back at her partner, a white-haired older guy in a bowling shirt. He held file folders under his arm and a gray bag over his shoulder. Ben felt his mouth go dry. The hairs on the back of his neck were coming to attention.

The agent with the files nodded. No smile. Ben held his stare. There was nothing calming in those icy blue eyes. It felt as if they were carving into him, opening a window into his every weakness and secret.

"Please, sit," the agent said, pointing to a chair at the table.

His voice was gruff. Ben expected nothing less.

"Mr. Danvers, my name is Special Agent Metcalf. This is Special Agent Noble. I understand you've been made to wait. I apologize for the inconvenience."

It was as if Ben had dropped the reins of his mind. It was galloping too fast to calibrate what was happening. "I'm sorry. I didn't get—?"

This time, it was the woman who spoke, repeating their names. It came more gently from her mouth. Agent Metcalf seated himself directly across from Ben.

"You have questions. We'll get to them. This is an ongoing investigation; we need some information. Maybe you can help us. If you feel you can't proceed without your attorney present, we understand. It's certainly your right. Frankly," he said with a wink and an unconvincing grin, "I'd like to just dive in, but it's your call. Any reason you need an attorney here this morning, Mr. Danvers?"

Ben looked at the woman. She nodded. And smiled. It looked sincere.

He'd seen enough TV crime shows with Kate to know that, when presented with the option of a lawyer, you 100% said "yes." Shit always went sideways for the accused when they did otherwise. The thing was, he didn't know any criminal-defense attorneys. And he'd already spent hours waiting. Ben looked again at Agent Noble. She had kind eyes.

"Any reason you need an attorney this morning, Mr. Danvers?" Metcalf asked again. This time there was no grin.

Ben shook his head.

There was a camera in the corner of the room attached to a beefy tripod. Metcalf dragged it across the carpet. He fiddled with the switches and the toggles and the zoom. He looked frustrated. After a couple of minutes, his face reddened. The guy was getting pissed. Ben didn't want the guy to be pissed.

Agent Noble pushed her seat back and stood. "Can I—?"

"I got it."

"Power button on the bottom?" she asked quietly.

Metcalf grumbled and the red light came on.

She smiled and whispered to Ben, "I have advanced degrees in audio-visual."

Her delivery was half-hearted, but it was friendly enough.

"Agent Noble will take notes. I'll record our conversation. Let's get to it."

Metcalf pulled reading glasses from his shirt pocket and placed them on the green files. He peered into his gray bag. Every movement he made was slow. He took his time retrieving a ballpoint pen, then dug deeper into his bag, coming up with a small black notepad, which he placed on the table next to the thick green file folders. He lifted the glasses and perched them at the tip of his nose.

Ben's knees were not bouncing under the table—they were spasming.

The agent tilted his head toward the camera. "For the record, this is Special Agent Briar Metcalf with Special Agent Emma Noble interviewing Mr. Benjamin Danvers, who is meeting with us freely and of his own accord. Is that right, Mr. Danvers?"

Ben leaned forward. "It is."

Metcalf stared over his glasses. His eyes were arrows. "Full name and date of birth."

"Benjamin A. Danvers. July 10, 1995."

"What's the A stand for?"

"Arnau."

The agent wet his finger and flipped a couple of pages into the front of his green folder. His mouth moved, but he wasn't saying anything. He scribbled into his small notebook.

"Parents?"

"Ida Danvers. My stepfather is Wendall Danvers."

"Biological father?"

"Did you find him?"

"Find him?" The agent cocked his head and looked at Ben over his glasses. "When did he go missing?"

"He's always been missing. I've never met him."

Metcalf gave an exasperated sigh. "No … this has nothing to do with him."

Ben's heart double-timed.

The agent hesitated, leaning forward as he spoke.

"You have brothers? Sisters?"

"No."

"No?"

Ben shook his head. He paid attention to the quizzical look the agent shared with his partner. Agent Metcalf continued questioning him about relatives: aunts, uncles, grandparents, cousins. He wanted every branch of Ben's family tree, but there weren't any. The only family he had were Ida and Wendall.

"Where did you grow up?"

"Through high school, Rutland County in Vermont. I went to college in New Hampshire for business. I live in Boston now."

With every answer, he looked at the agent, trying to gauge his reaction. The guy wasn't giving anything away. He turned to the woman. No smile. Metcalf cleared his throat. Ben watched his posture change. The easy questions were over. Something was coming.

"Last time you saw your parents?"

"I think July 4th. Wait—no, it was um, Thanksgiving. Sorry."

The agent put his notebook down and swiveled in his chair, his fingers tapping against each other in a pyramid. The guy wasn't saying anything. Just staring at him over his reading glasses.

Ben thought it might be time to assert himself, "I'd like to know—"

Agent Metcalf cut him off. "Why don't you tell me about your parents' criminal activity. All of it. Start with your knowledge of anti-American activity and links to terrorist groups here and abroad."

What the hell?

Agent Metcalf folded his arms across his chest.

What the hell? Ben turned to Agent Noble. Gone was the softness in her face.

"What are you—? My stepfather is a retiree. He worked road crew for the city and my mom is … she's just a mom. They're not…. This isn't right. I can't believe you—"

"Mr. Danvers, your cooperation here is essential. I'll ask again. Are you aware of your parents' criminal activity?"

"No. I, uh … I don't know what's happening here."

The agent put his elbow on the table. He sunk his chin into his palm and turned his gaze out the window and kept it there for a minute. He grumbled something inaudible and looked at Ben.

"I'm going to get us coffee. How do you take it?"

Ben didn't respond.

"Agent Noble, join me?"

• • •

Briar extended his arms and let the counter in the FBI's mini kitchen take his weight. He blew a clearing gust from his mouth and turned on the faucet. "What'd you see?" he asked, massaging wet fingers into his eyes.

"You mean, do I think he was lying?"

Briar nodded.

"Nervous. But no. I don't think he's got any idea what's going on. Do you?"

"Nope." Briar sent a thousand-mile stare toward the sugar container.

"What now?"

"We tell him."

It would be hard for the kid to hear what happened in Vermont. And that was only the first course. It was his job to rip the band-aid off. It wasn't summer camp, for fuck's sake. The kid would deal with it, or he wouldn't. Briar chucked the paper towel into the plastic trash container.

"Okay. Here we go."

9

Ben paced the conference room. His parents were retirees living in the Vermont woods. Criminals? Anti-American activity? Terrorists? Complete bullshit.

Agent Metcalf held the door for his partner who entered balancing three Styrofoam cups. She put them where he'd been sitting. Ben didn't walk back to the table.

"I've got—black, cream, and cream and sugar," she said. "I didn't have a hand for the black and suga—"

Ben stared at her. He had no use for the damn coffee. "I don't know what's going on here, but—now? I want an attorney."

Metcalf nodded and sat down. "Don't blame you. Sure. We can stop."

"That's what I want," Ben said, gripping the back of a chair.

Agent Metcalf made a show of sliding the thickest of the green folders toward Ben. He placed his glasses back on his nose and pointed to the file. "Some interesting things in here. Stuff about you," he said, running his index finger inside the folder, teasing it open. "Why don't you sit back down, Mr. Danvers. Let me tell you a story."

"I'm not answering any more questions."

"Noted. If, when I'm done, you want an attorney, we'll make that call."

The agent tapped the bulky folder twice with his index finger as if he was preparing a sleight-of-hand trick.

Ben waited while Metcalf took off his glasses.

41

"It was late November. Twenty years ago. I got the call about 2 AM. They said it was a kidnapping. I was kind of 'the guy' in the northeast for those cases." Metcalf got out of his chair. He turned off the camera and dragged it back into the corner.

"I come up on this nice house in the suburbs. Police, ambulance, fire are on the scene—their lights flashing up into the trees. The place is a mansion. Sits in the woods. No homes nearby. Even at night and with snow on the ground I can tell that the lawn, the hedges—everything's manicured."

Metcalf folded his arms and leaned against the wall.

"The cops outside gave me a quick debrief and then I come in through the front door. First thing I see are red streaks in the carpet, so I follow the drag marks. I find the babysitter face down behind the couch. She's cold. Stiffness already starting to get into her. I roll her on her side. The carpet is blood-wet. Two gunshots in her chest. One in the head. Right here," he said pointing above his right eye. "Apparently, she was a real good kid. Just fifteen."

Ben looked over at Agent Noble. She was leaning forward like it was one of her favorite stories.

"I had to concentrate on blocking out the crying coming from the kitchen. That's where the parents were waiting to speak to me. There was no sign of forced entry. Maybe the babysitter knew her killer. Maybe she opened the door to a stranger. It was too early to guess. I'm walking through the house, making notes. When I think I've got the lay of the land, I go into the kitchen."

Metcalf sat again, in a new chair—uncomfortably close to Ben— and leaned in.

"I've seen gruesome things. You know what stays with you? Not the blood. Not the gore. It's the sounds of people in anguish. That's what gives you the nightmares. The thing that leaves the echo—the residue. I go in and the husband's as quiet as a cat, rubbing her shoulders. But that woman's cries? Haunting."

Agent Metcalf paused, leaning back in his chair to give Ben some breathing room. "You want me to keep going?"

"What does this have to do with my parents—or me?"

"We're getting there."

Metcalf stood and walked to the window. He looked down at the highway for a moment before speaking.

"This couple had been out with friends all night. They come home and the wife is the first one in the house. She sees the blood. Finds the babysitter. She screams up the stairs to look for her twin boys—identical twin boys. She's checking the rooms. She's looking in closets. Under beds. She's opening the vanity doors in the bathroom, praying the children hid themselves but knowing they were too young to be afraid of a stranger."

Metcalf looked at the coffee cups in front of Ben. "I'll take the black if you aren't going to."

He took a few sips, then ran his index finger over the edge of the Styrofoam. There was something about the agent's confidence that gave Ben an uneasy feeling.

"Mr. Danvers, back then I was something of an optimist. I thought we had a decent chance of finding the kids alive. Yes, there was a dead body, but the scene didn't have the hallmark creepiness that pedophiles leave behind. The parents were wealthy. All signs pointed to this being transactional—someone looking for a big payday. We set up our recording devices. Install our cameras. We're waiting for the ransom call. We wait three days. Five days. Two weeks. Nothing. No call. Weeks turned into months. Months into years. The kids vanished. Gone."

The agent returned to his seat. He rotated his coffee cup on the table like a dial.

Ben inhaled. "What does this have to do with me?"

"I'm going to tell you. You see, the Bureau has these big old computers. Terrific, powerful things and they're always scanning for stuff—like genetic code databases. Someone gets a DNA test, and the sequence is checked against cold cases—people we're looking for. Last night we get a ping from an ancestry site. The code matches the DNA of one of the twins kidnapped twenty years ago. The young man lives in Boston."

Ben's chest began to feel heavy.

"We do a quick internet search and we've got everything on this young man. And the couple that raised him in Vermont."

Ben's mouth dropped. "Are you—?"

"Understandably, this is an interesting development. We've got questions, right? Is it really the kid? Who are these people in Vermont? Are they the kidnappers? Whole bunch of question marks."

Ben could feel his world fissuring. Agent Metcalf slid a thin blue file folder in front of him.

"So, we send simultaneous teams: one to pick up Wendall and Ida Danvers in Vermont. The other gathers up their son at his workplace. We give the kid a DNA swab and a blood test."

The agent opened the blue folder and pointed at the paper. MATCH.

Ben tried to swallow, but it was as if he had forgotten how to inhale properly. "I want to speak to them. Please."

Agent Metcalf hesitated and looked at his partner. Agent Noble was looking down at the floor.

"Mr. Danvers, this part's going to be tough to hear."

Ben focused on the polished conference table, listening while Metcalf told him how Ida had shot Wendall and then herself. He watched his own tremoring index finger trace a knot in the wood. "I don't believe you," he murmured.

"I'd prefer not to show you the pictures, son."

The gearbox in Ben's mind slipped as the fragments of what he'd heard assembled.

Kidnapped.
Identical twins.
Killed Wendall
Shot herself.
Kidnapped.

Ben slumped in his seat.

"You okay?" asked Agent Noble.

He couldn't speak. He was only half aware of the knock on the conference door or Agent Metcalf answering it and leaving the room.

"Mr. Danvers? The FBI has a special division for victims. It's called VSD. We'll get you all the assistance you need," said Agent Noble. Her softness had returned.

He heard a familiar voice shouting as the conference room door opened, "We're going to sue *all* your asses."

Rocky. She was charging through the door, pulling on the sleeve of a nervous guy in a blue suit. It was Wilbur Gimple, the corporate trust attorney from the seventh floor. Kate entered a couple steps behind them, wide-eyed and worried.

"We demand our client be represented by counsel. This is an outrage," Rocky yelled, not sure to which agent she needed to direct her threats.

Gimple was visibly relieved to learn that his extremely limited talents would be unnecessary. Ben asked for privacy. Rocky and the FBI agents gave the couple the room. He told Kate what he knew, and she listened, shaking her head in disbelief and covering her mouth with her palm. When he finished, she grabbed his hand and held it tight.

"I'm so sorry. What can I do? What do you need, babe?"

"Get me out of here."

Agent Metcalf cracked the door open and stuck his head through. Kate spoke first. "We'd like to leave now."

"We're not done yet. Mr. Danvers, there's more you need to know."

10

Arnau Farre's brown winter jacket was in a heap, lying stiff in the snow. Two dozen smashed cigarette butts littered the clearing at the edge of the woods. The only sound coming out of that remote northern place was the staccato *crack* of axe blade slashing into oak. It echoed out of the clearing, through the tree line, and across the frozen lake.

Every three swings, Arnau would spit into his thick hands, rub them dry on his faded jeans, and straighten his orange knit hat. Then he'd twist the heels of his black muck boots into the snow and attack the wood once more. His thin black shirt was matted in sweat. He ignored the bite of the freezing wetness against his skin. He could push down pain when his mind was on other things. This afternoon, his thoughts were on Ida. He sent another angry swing into the log—the axe smashed through, sending the split parts flying and lodging the blade deep into the stump.

He threw quartered logs at the day's pile of firewood. He loaded the toboggan with as much as it could hold. He tucked the wedges, the sledge, and his axe in as well. The sun was getting low. He needed to get moving. There were still things that had to be done.

Arnau's head clocked in the direction of the sound. For the past hour, he'd thought something was out there—circling him, sizing him up. Now he was sure of it. He could hear the panting. He knew it was a pack of coyotes before they showed themselves. Arnau made quick calculations: the serrated knife on his belt was too short to be effective,

46

and the axe would be good for only one swing before it stuck into bone and meat. He grabbed the sledgehammer and a log.

Eight hungry, rib-thin coyotes growled into the clearing, snarling and snapping.

Arnau watched how they moved together, trying to determine which was the leader. The alpha would start the attack; the others would hang back until they could exploit an injury. It wasn't long before the alpha showed himself. It stepped forward, hackles raised—a yellow patch between its eyes.

Arnau threw the chunk of firewood, striking him in the yellow of its head. It yelped and retreated. But only for a few feet. It turned and snarled with a spine-chilling ferocity that left no doubt about its intention to kill.

It leaped.

Arnau twisted his heels into the snow and swung the sledge across his body, as if the alpha were a meaty curveball floating into the strike zone. *Crack.* The coyote dropped at Arnau's feet. The rest of the pack barked and howled but had the good sense to stay back. The animal was broken and lying in the snow, blinking its eyes passively. It flared its nostrils, the shallowest fog of breath escaping its dying chest. Arnau dragged the limp coyote by its forepaws to the stump. He took a moment to center the head. He swung the sledge high, bringing the iron crashing down to finish it off. Arnau spit into his hands and rubbed them on his jeans. He straightened his orange hat. He lifted the heavy sledge once again, smashing it into the dead alpha's snout, the crack of the collision exploding fang shrapnel into the snow. The next blow caved in the side of the coyote's head. Arnau swung again. And again. Swinging. And swinging. Pulverizing the coyote until its skull was flat and unrecognizable. Until the animal and the stump had become one.

Arnau pulled his serrated knife from his belt and sawed through the dead animal's belly, extracting the organs. He threw them into the woods for the scattered pack to eat—if they ever came back.

He scooped crusty snow into his hands and rubbed them until the icy grains turned his fingers and knuckles clean and pink. He strapped his black muck boots into snowshoes and tightened the toboggan rope across his chest. He grunted the load forward, trudging through the deep snow—out of the forest and across the wide frozen lake. Wispy funnels of powder blew across the flat white, squinting his eyes and stinging his weathered face. In the distance, gray woodsmoke drifted from a cabin's stone chimney.

Arnau unstrapped his snowshoes and leaned them against the cedar shingles by the side of the house. He stacked the logs on the porch. His thighs sank into snowdrifts as he walked the perimeter of the cabin. When he was satisfied that it was secure, he removed his muck boots and entered the honey-dark interior. The cabin was built by homesteaders a century ago. Now, it was a humble retreat for a man with an obscenity of money. But the Father was no hypocrite. The Father was pure. And for his children—Thy Will Be Done.

Arnau warmed his hands in front of the crackling fieldstone fireplace. He stared at the picture on the mantel. It was a yellowing photograph of children. A hundred or more in rows. In the center stood Ida, holding Arnau's hand. Her green dress. Her long hair.

He remembered everything about that afternoon. The sun in his eyes. The cameraman aiming from a rickety stepladder, trying to make them say, "cheese." The Father, his arms folded, scanning hawkishly for misbehavior. Arnau remembered because that was the day when his life changed. The day Ida took his small hand and walked him into the forest, dried his tears, and sunk her knees into the moss and pine needles and gave him his first-ever hug. The day his crying stopped. And the loneliness ended. In those sun-dappled woods, she gently held his face and asked him to make a vow—an innocent, childlike promise—to love her and obey her. Forever. And in return, he would never be lonely again. Arnau had kept his promise. And, until today, she had too.

He heard the creak of stairs and turned. The Father was descending—his large hands gripping the wooden railing where a silver garland still wove through the balusters. He wore a red flannel shirt tucked into denim jeans. His hair was white, but he didn't carry himself like a man nearing eighty. Those who understood him were careful in his presence. The Father was smart, dangerous, and unpredictable—like a half-domesticated animal, capable of extreme tenderness and ferocious cruelty. Still strong. Still imposing. And his followers still believed in him. Everything that was about to happen—everything they were about to do—was for their love of the Father. And their fear of him.

The man walked into the kitchen and came out a few minutes

later with a peanut butter sandwich on white bread—crust removed. He handed it to Arnau.

"You should have taken the snowmobile."

Arnau didn't respond.

The Father looked at the picture, then gave Arnau's neck a gentle pat.

"It's done," he said. "She made her sacrifice."

Arnau stared into the flames. He already knew she was gone. A hollowness had passed through him when he was in the woods, and he'd sensed it was Ida. He shifted his weight to put some distance between himself and the Father.

"Stop feeling sorry for yourself. You knew this day was coming. You are not a child, Arnau. Everyone is relying on you. Do you understand? Look at me. Look at me when I'm talking to you. You understand?"

Arnau stared at the old man, letting his eyes answer for him. The Father smiled and kissed his forehead.

"Of course you do."

11

Ringo's, across the highway from Chelsea FBI headquarters, was in the last throes of its lunch buffet. Kate had pleaded on Ben's behalf: if they had more to say, let it not be in an FBI conference room. But the restaurant was no less depressing. The curtains were drawn. It was dark and nearly empty. The salad bar was picked over and wilted—brown lettuce drowning in melting ice water. The pizza was well beyond the resuscitation of warming lights. Ben skipped the food and filled a fountain drink. Kate put her palm in the middle of his back. Ballast.

He took a deep breath and prepared himself.

The four huddled in a spacious booth at the back of the restaurant. The agents sat against the wall, looking at the entrance. The green file folders waited in front of Metcalf, about to spring open again like an information jack-in-the-box.

"Okay," said Ben, "I want to get this over with."

Agent Metcalf folded his hands on the table. "It's still an active investigation. We need to locate your brother. I need at least 48 hours."

"You've been looking for twenty years. What makes you think you'll have success in two days?" asked Kate.

Metcalf nodded at his partner, giving Agent Noble permission to answer.

"The boys are identical. We can use facial recognition software," she said.

Metcalf added, "Secret Service also needs to finish a background check on you. They've asked for a little time."

"Secret Service?" asked Kate.

Metcalf deadpanned the punchline. "Your birth mother is Kimberly Hancock."

A shot of electricity cracked through the booth—the moment before thunderclap.

"BEN!" Kate covered her mouth, then whispered, "Oh, my god—you're one of the twins!" She grabbed for his hand, "My god."

Ben stared at Metcalf, stunned.

Vice President-Elect Kimberly Hancock?

He knew her story. The entire world knew her story. Kimberly Hancock was a descendant of American royalty. Wealthy beyond measure. Her toddlers, twin boys, were taken from her. Within five years, her husband, a medical researcher—*my real father*—was dead from cancer. Politically, no one could land a punch. She was untouchable. The country had mourned for her and cheered her rise from tragedy. Her voice had become thunder. The Prickly Princess.

"Christ, the whole world was looking for you and your brother."

Ben blinked to slow the world down. It wasn't working. He stared down at the varnished table, knowing they were all watching his reaction. Kate was stroking the back of his neck. It didn't make sense. What would Ida and Wendall have to do with Kimberly Hancock? And why?

He looked up at the veteran agent across from him. "You believe my mom and stepfather kidnapped me from *her* and killed a babysitter in the process?"

Metcalf shook his head. "I always assumed it was a single person. You don't think Ida and Wendall were capable of it, right?"

"No. They are—*were* nonviolent."

The agent shrugged. "I saw the pictures. It got pretty violent today."

More silence. Kate's consoling fingers rubbed his upper back. A memory came to him. He must have been seven or eight. A sleepover with neighborhood friends. Wendall had pitched a tent for them in the backyard. He stared at the wall, trying to remember the rhyme—the one he and his buddies recited in their sleeping bags. The one they used to scare themselves.

Wee Willie and Little Fred
Just a-sleepin' in their bed
The children bled

The Creeper fled
Everyone knows Willie and Fred
Are FUCKING Dead!

"Babe? You okay?"

Ben looked at Agent Noble. He wanted to hear it from her.

He whispered, "Am I Willie or Fred?"

She looked over at her partner. "I'm sorry, we don't know your name."

Ben felt himself untether. He was not who he thought he was. He was no one. A tear dripped down his cheek. Kate pulled him in. Held him with strong arms. She kissed his ear, his cheek, and his temple. "Hey," she said, waiting for his eyes to connect with hers, "you're *Ben*." She pushed a hard kiss against his wet eyelid and held it.

He looked at the FBI agents across the table. They were staring at him dispassionately—evaluating him. Their eyes were asking questions. Is he authentic? Do we believe him? Can he be trusted with the vice president?

Ben wiped his face. "You're wondering about me. Trying to figure out how fucked up I am."

"None of *my* business," said Metcalf.

"You're wondering if I'm some kind of threat."

"If you are, the Secret Service will handle it."

"Do you think I am?"

"Babe, it's okay. No one thinks that."

"Do you, Agent Metcalf? You think I am?"

Ben watched Agent Noble glance over at her partner, as if maybe she wanted to know the same thing.

"Professional opinion? No. But listen—what do I know? I'm in charge of Lost and Found. You're found. I move on."

"Then, please find my brother."

Agent Noble nodded. "We'll do our best."

Ben took his hands off the table and leaned his back against the booth, a signal he was done with the FBI agents if they were done with him. Metcalf closed the green folder and grabbed his jacket. He stood and looked down at Ben.

"If it's me, I keep this quiet for as long as I can. Try to enjoy the last of your privacy. Your life? It's about to get complicated."

12

Emma Noble watched her partner in motion, taking laps around the temporary office they were given at Chelsea HQ, his cell-phone planted in his right ear. He had Associate Director Monroe on the line, giving him updates on what they'd learned in the past seven hours. Emma was tasked with communicating with F.A.C.E. Services, searching for Benjamin Danvers's identical twin. Briar worked NGI-IPS for priors on Ida and Wendall Danvers. There were loud voices in the hallway. Metcalf scowled and planted a finger into his free ear while he listened to Monroe in the other.

"Yeah, that's how it looks. Doesn't seem like Wendall Danvers had anything to do with this. He didn't meet the woman until after the kidnapping. No priors. Grew up in the town they lived in. No sketchy affiliations. At this point, we're thinking he was just a victim."

In the past few hours, Briar's bristly personality had improved. He was more patient and helpful than Emma expected he'd be. As an investigator, he was in his element—in control and in charge. As a human, he had some things to work on.

"No, sir. That's a different story. Ida Danvers is a ghost. We found nothing on her. I mean *nothing*: no driver's license, Social Security number was bogus. It's like she never existed before coming to Vermont. Yup. Understand." Briar raised his eyebrows, "Yeah. We got it back. My partner, Emma Noble, did the work on that. I'm going to pass the phone."

53

Emma inhaled, taking a calming breath before speaking to Monroe, a man destined to become the next director of the FBI.

"Assistant Director, Agent Noble here…. Yes, we located the twin. No, sir. It's *not* good news. His name was James Reid. He's deceased … a boat explosion on a lake in Missouri when he was a teenager. Four died in the accident: Steven and Beverly Reid, the Hancock boy, and one of his buddies…. Yes, we're sure. Agent Metcalf spoke to the investigating trooper from Missouri. All the victims were identified at the scene and confirmed with dental records…. The trooper didn't see foul play, sir. It was just an accident. Old boat, old fuel lines…. Yes, sir, I expect it does require a second look. Of course. He's right here. Thank you, sir."

Emma handed the phone back to Briar. She dried her palms on her pants legs and listened while he told the A.D. what they'd learned about Steven and Beverly Reid. It was a now-familiar story. Steven Reid married a single mom. They raised the boy together. And Beverly Reid, like Ida Danvers, was a ghost.

"Okay, Billy. See you soon." Briar dropped his phone into the front pocket of his bowling shirt.

Emma waited for him to speak.

"Monroe wants us to give a formal debrief in Washington—day after tomorrow. They're notifying Vice President-Elect Hancock. For now, we're done."

"Done?"

"We'll drive back to the city in the morning. As of right now, we're just spectators."

"What about Benjamin Danvers? Who's going to tell him about his brother?"

Briar shrugged and pulled his phone out of his front pocket.

Emma stood quickly. "No. I want to tell him."

Briar passed the phone to her.

She pushed his hand down. "In person. He deserves that."

• • •

Arnau Farre took the stairs, his palm gliding over the oak rail. He entered the small room and sat on his childhood bed. He needed to get some sleep before he left. But first, he wanted to read them one more time. He pulled open the drawer on his nightstand and pulled out the bundle of mail. The stamped envelopes were addressed by hand and secured by rubber bands.

He had not seen Ida in twenty years. He'd not spoken or written in that time. It was, of course, not permitted—she had a son and a family. Receiving a letter from another man would have made her difficult life even more troublesome. And dangerous. But Ida, if she was careful, could write to him. And she did. The letters were clever. She'd always been the smart one. The first few pages were written from her. The following pages—from her imagination of how he might respond. Ida's words were so much better than his would have been. Over the years, she'd invented arguments that played out over several mailings, then reconciled in subtle and wonderful ways. By using letters, she had tended to their friendship. And then, somehow, she'd let them blossom into love—all without a word from Arnau himself. Those letters. That love. They remained the most real thing in Arnau Farre's life.

The envelope on top was blue. The last she ever sent. He brought it to his nose searching for a hint of her scent. He ran his hands over the places where her hands had been. This letter was different from the others. There were no pretend words from Arnau. The letter contained a command—not a wish. Something that would make Ida's sacrifice more bearable. She trusted that Arnau would fulfill it—no matter what.

And he would. *No matter what.*

He removed the small picture from the envelope and tucked it into his wallet. He put the billfold on his dresser and before turning out the light, brought the letter once more to his face. And pressed his mouth into the stain of her lipstick.

• • •

Emma Noble struggled to parallel park. She finally got the bucar tucked into a line of frozen vehicles mated against the curb across from Giuseppa's Pizza in the North End of Boston. She sat in the dark, taking small bites of a Wendy's cheeseburger as she watched Benjamin Danvers and his girlfriend through the restaurant's picture window. Emma wasn't meeting him at his apartment for another forty-five minutes. She considered her early arrival as *stakeout lite,* which made it sound more professional than what it really was—voyeurism.

It had been a high-voltage day. Emma felt like squeezing a bit more juice out of it. She was fascinated. Seeing them together—knowing what they were talking about. Knowing they were trying to make sense of it all. She sipped Coca-Cola from a white, waxy cup. She replayed the day. Re-examined the events and her impressions. She had been paying careful attention to Benjamin Danvers throughout the interrogation. Briar had asked the right questions, and Emma had zeroed in on Benjamin's reactions.

On the trip north, she'd thought about what he'd be like. Would he have a personality defect? Or something worse? Emma had studied him, but she didn't see anything unusual. He was a normal guy with painfully authentic reactions to impossible news. She agreed with Briar—he was simply a victim. But, unlike her partner, it gutted her to see Benjamin Danvers's life explode in front of her.

She wiped a napkin across her lips and dropped the half-eaten burger in the bag. Benjamin and Kate were huddled together, their heads touching. They looked good together. They fit. You could tell when you saw it, and whenever she saw "it," she couldn't help but feel a twinge of jealousy. It had been a while since she'd shared a pizza with a guy with potential to be more than a friend. Forever ago. She'd settled into being a professional third-wheeler—a date appendage for her friends.

All things in their time. That was her dad's advice. *Keep yourself out there—it'll happen.* It was sweet. And not super helpful, but it was all she'd get. Her mother had been the one with the right words and the soothing tone and the gentle embraces.

She touched the base of her throat. The tingle had been there since morning. Sometimes Emma believed she had a sixth sense. Or maybe a kind of psychic awareness. She was no spoon-bender, a miserable rock-paper-scissors player, and she'd never guessed correctly in the "I'm thinking of a number between one and whatever" game. But she could see the sorrow and anger and fear behind a stranger's eyes when others couldn't. Maybe it wasn't a sixth sense—maybe it was only empathy.

She watched Kate kiss Benjamin's cheek. Emma exhaled forcefully enough to fog the windshield. It was good to see that Ben had someone in his corner. Someone there for him on his very worst day. That was a good thing. The most important thing.

An old man in a white apron approached the table, wiping his palms across his chest. He had a broad smile and spoke with his hands. They were grinning up at him. The man kissed Kate's forehead and leaned over to ruffle the top of Benjamin's head. Emma relaxed her shoulders. Benjamin had roots. He had people. He'd make it through this.

She watched the couple walk arm in arm across the street toward their apartment. Emma was supposed to arrive in five minutes. They would be waiting for her. The moment wasn't lost on her. Her first solo flight as an FBI agent. She turned up the volume, leaned into the headrest, and allowed the harmonies of ABBA to drift into her like a comforting breeze. *You got this, Emma.*

13

Kate Malone invited Emma to sit in the best of the furniture in the small apartment, a tan lounge chair. Emma owned something similar; she'd found it on the street a few days ago, then dragged it four blocks and up five flights. Benjamin and Kate's apartment was budget-chic. A smattering of new and old. She recognized the effort to make do with what's cheap and available—adding a unique flair here and there. The lounger was probably their big purchase. The coffee table had seen better days. They'd planted it in front of a couch that was wrapped in a blue cloth cover. Emma guessed that under the fabric was an upholstery horror show.

Their Australian Shepherd puppy was over his initial excitement of having a guest in the house. He sprawled in the middle of the room, scraping his teeth across a plasticky brown bone clutched between his overgrown paws. Benjamin sat with his girlfriend, sharing the same couch—her hand resting on his mid-thigh, her fingers flexed into him.

The couple was about the same age as Emma. They all spoke the same shorthand. They could have grown up together—been high school friends. But tonight, there was an ocean of difference between them. One a giver, the other, a receiver of important news. For the first time, Emma felt the profound power of owning information.

Briar had had second thoughts about her doing this alone. She'd stuck to her guns. Benjamin Danvers deserved to hear the news from someone with more warmth than Briar could muster. He'd finally consented. *"No spitballing. Don't pretend to know things you don't."*

The couple was leaning forward, waiting for her to begin.

"We got news on your brother. I'm sorry...."

She told him about the FBI facial-recognition program and the boat explosion. Emma watched Kate's head turn back and forth, taking in the information, then looking over to make sure her boyfriend was okay.

Emma had worried about how he'd take the news. He handled it fine. At least the bad news had come quickly enough for him not to have gotten his hopes up. She rose from the lounge chair. It had not been an easy first day, but it was a good one. She'd done her job. And for the first time, Emma Noble felt like a *real* FBI agent.

"What happens now?" Benjamin asked.

"I'm told someone will be in touch."

Briar would have been happy with that answer. Vague.

"How'd you guys meet?" Emma asked, grabbing her jacket.

Kate answered. "We were introduced by a friend of mine who works with Ben at Cambridge Hill. It'll be two years in April. Love at first sight."

"I'm glad you have each other," Emma said, wondering to herself when she'd find her someone. "I'll leave you guys. Benjamin, remember what I told you about our victim services. They might help. Okay?"

"They're going to want me to contact Hancock, right?" he asked before Emma could get to the door. "Do I have to? Can it wait?"

Emma saw Kate stiffen.

"What?" his girlfriend said.

"Kate, it's not crazy for me to think about this first," he said defensively.

"There's *nothing* to think about. Twenty years, Ben. *Twenty years.* How could you make that poor woman wait one more second?"

His eyes pleaded with Emma, like she had some power to resolve this. His world was crashing around him. But it wasn't her business. "I'll see myself out. You've got my card."

Emma walked to the car. She'd call her father. Tell him it had been an interesting day. He wouldn't press her on the details. He knew better. She'd tell him about her coming trip to meet the bigwigs in DC the day after tomorrow. Her father would want her to visit Uncle Gunny. And then, she knew, he'd spend the rest of the call complaining: a neighbor who played music too loud; a rotten meal that they'd charged him too much for; that there was too much snow in St. Louis—or not enough. She'd laugh and tell him to suck it up.

Tomorrow she'd be back in New York City. The job would slow down. She was okay with that.

• • •

Neither of them spoke. Even the puppy sat up and watched, understanding something important was about to happen. Kate sat at the kitchen table, her knees tucked under her chin.

The call had come an hour ago. He hadn't recognized the acronym they'd used to identify themselves, but the person made sure Ben wrote down Kimberly Hancock's personal cellphone number. They made him repeat it, twice. He'd written the digits neatly on a slip of paper. Ben had his phone in his hand, in calling position. He laid it on the counter. "I don't want to do this. I don't want to become someone else."

"Meeting your real mother doesn't change who you are."

"It'll change everything. You know it will."

"It doesn't change *us*. I won't let it. Now, stop being a puss."

Ben turned. She was grinning. Kate looked at the phone on the counter and raised her eyebrows. "Benjamin, call your mother."

He felt his chest constricting, but he dialed anyway.

A woman answered, her voice tight and unsteady.

Kate's hand moved to her mouth.

"Hello? My name is Ben. I think … I may be your son."

DAY 2

14

Ben couldn't sleep. He was wide awake. Other than a trace of street-light filtering through the blinds, his room was black. That thin illumination created stripes across the ceiling that angled at the corner and sliced down the wall. His eyes followed the geometry of light, but his mind stayed in the dark places. They had been appearing to him all night—the images and sounds of his childhood. Once true memories, now something else. False. Scattered scraps—soap bubbles floating outside the window of a bullet train. Ida on her knees in the garden with her blue gloves, black with dirt, the metal clang of Wendall's wrench falling under the hood, a tucked-in kiss, the click of the bedside lamp, the "goodnight," the closing door, and the extinguishing light from the hallway. The blackness of his bedroom.

Ben had lost feeling on his left side. Kate pressed into him, her arm draped over his stomach, her leg hooked into his. The puppy had spread his weight across Ben's knees, pinning him down. It was a gentle suffocation. He let them bind him—a suture for his wounds.

Ben believed that he was half of something. It seemed right that there'd been another—a puzzle piece that would've snapped into the curves of his hollow caves and made him whole. He assumed he was the weaker, quieter half. His twin probably carried the noise, the laughter, and the strength. He should have had a brother and a friend. He tried to imagine what they might have done together. What would it have been like never to be lonely? Ida had taken that away from him. She'd stolen his childhood. Taken everything.

Ben looked down at Kate's head nestled into his chest. He found her hand and slid his fingers through hers. "I love you," he whispered. She mumbled a "you too," and Ben released her hand and blinked up at the ceiling. Waiting for dawn.

· · ·

Arnau Farre didn't need an alarm to wake him at 2 AM. His eyes were open and acclimated to the darkness. He sat upright and rolled stiffly out of bed. The bags were packed: a green duffel, a large suitcase on sturdy wheels, and a steel camber-top toolbox. The duffel contained clothes, toiletries, a handgun, and a custom-fitted bullpup sniper rifle—the other cases were not for him.

The Father's door, at the end of the hall, was ajar. Arnau heard the steady rumble of deep sleep. Only the back of the Father's white head was visible, the rest of him tucked under a heavy comforter. Arnau closed the door.

It was snowing—a light dusting. Arnau stepped into his muck boots and walked to the shed. He pulled the chain. The yellow bulb lit the interior's old, dark wood. Four fishing rods leaned against the back wall by a shelf with hand tools and a chainsaw. Two metal gas canisters and a gray plastic jug of two-stroke were on the ground behind a three-year-old snow machine.

He secured the bags and hopped on the cold seat of the snowmobile. The headlights illuminated a hemlock by the side of the cabin. It was catching the falling snow in its green branches. He paused and admired it—the tree Arnau had climbed as a child, where he'd hung his first deer. The tree he might never see again.

He gunned the snowmobile across the lake. The frigid wind revived his leathery face. He felt free. A memory rushed to him of a summer day when he was young. The day he had pedaled a bicycle down an asphalt road that was so new and black that it felt like his tires were racing on glass as he followed a girl in a green dress, her long hair flying behind her—the pink tassels from her handlebars snapping in the wind.

The day he'd first killed a man.

15

Summer 1978

The housing developers put the roads in first to prove to prospective buyers that they were committed to making a neighborhood out of the dusty, treeless expanse. Red survey ribbons fluttered in the breeze and concrete foundations lined the new road like open tombs. The couple living on Nathan Hale Drive had bought the model home. It was the only complete, move-in-ready house available in the Colonials subdivision outside of Boston. The couple's excitement had waned some since late spring. They had not expected the incessant rolling and beeping of heavy machinery—had not expected the crusting film of blown dirt that caked to the windows and the white, vinyl siding.

It was a quiet morning. On Sundays, the diesel CAT across the street slept. Mr. Atamian's wife was gone, visiting her parents. The man opened the window. He heard kids laughing. He flicked the red button on his Mr. Coffee, and it began gurgling through its cycle.

He sipped at his steaming mug, tightened his bathrobe, and opened the front door. His yard was dead. The landscapers had scattered clumps of straw across the seeded brown dirt. The grass hadn't taken root. Every soaking rain threatened to carry the seeds into the curbside sewer. He turned on the spigot and watched the green hose jerk and uncoil. The sprinkler popped and ejaculated weak, limp strips of nourishment across the arid ground. He picked up the paper from the stoop.

"Hi mister!" a girl said as she whizzed by on a blue bicycle.

A boy behind her lifted his butt from his yellow banana seat, pedaling hard to catch up. Mr. Atamian sipped his coffee and waved. He returned to the kitchen and sat at the table to scan the headlines. Seconds later, he lowered his head into the sports page. The Red Sox were on a tear. No way the Yankees would catch them—not with Yaz, Fisk, Rice, Lynn, Evans, Tiant, and Eckersley. Up eight in June already. Barring a disaster, they had a real chance to win it all. Beantown would go nuts.

He was settling into the crossword when the doorbell rang. He tightened his bathrobe and opened the front door to see the bicycle kids on his stoop.

"My little brother has to go terribly bad. Can he use your bathroom?" said the girl.

The dimple-cheeked brother looked to be no more than eleven years old. He was red faced and bouncing. Mr. Atamian opened the door wide.

"Down the hall. First door on the right."

The kid ran into the house. The girl in the green dress stood in the foyer. She had a pink book bag over her shoulder. In the city, kids her age were smoking pot and wearing bell bottoms.

"You rich?" she asked.

He laughed, "Not hardly. Where'd you kids come from?"

"Another street. Way over there," she said, pointing to nowhere in particular. "My name is Ida." She walked into the kitchen. "Are you doing crosswords?"

He nodded.

"Can I help?"

"It's very difficult."

"Ask me one."

He exhaled and looked down at the puzzle. "Greek personification of darkness. Six letters. Ends in 'S.'"

Ida scrunched her face and looked up at the ceiling. "Erebus?"

He studied the puzzle, bouncing the eraser of his number 2 pencil across the boxes to confirm the fit. "How old are you?" he asked.

"How old do you think I am?"

"Fourteen?"

"That's probably a good guess."

"You're very smart, Ida."

"The Father only takes the smart ones. Ask me another."

"I don't understand."

"I said, ask me another one."

The boy in the bathroom didn't rush. He laid the glass vial and the long needle on the silver shelf under the mirror. The boy suctioned the poison from the vial into the needle, the way they'd taught him. He slipped off his sneakers and tiptoed toward the kitchen.

"Is it … assent?" Ida said.

Mr. Atamian chuckled and filled in the boxes. The boy moved silently toward the back of the man. He made eye contact with Ida. She pointed to the puzzle and Mr. Atamian's head dropped, exposing his neck. Arnau Farre buried the needle deep. Barry Atamian slapped at his neck to cover the sting.

"Ow! Shit."

Mr. Atamian lost control of his arm. It dropped to his side. His head drooped. Then it rolled awkwardly over his shoulder. His eyes remained open. Aware. Ida leaned over the table and studied his face.

"This is Arnau. The Father says he's one of the most important children at our school. You know all about our school, don't you?"

The man's eyes dilated with recognition. Ida reached into her book bag and laid the contents on the table: sketchbook, folded plastic sheeting, carving knife. Drool slipped from the corner of his mouth.

"Don't talk." Ida handed Arnau the sketchbook and the man's number 2 pencil. "Arnau's an excellent artist. Seriously, he's really good."

She reached for the folded plastic sheeting and rose from the table, spreading it on the new hardwood floor like she was doing up a guest bed. She smoothed the wrinkles with her hands. Then Ida cinched Mr. Atamian's open robe, pulled a pen out of his ceramic mug, took a sip of his coffee, and began finishing his crossword puzzle.

Mr. Atamian's eyes drifted while Arnau drew.

Ida looked at her watch and put down the pen. "Want to show him your drawing?"

The boy turned it around.

"Ha! Look how good that is." She put the sketchbook in her bag. She leaned into the man's face so his eyes could follow her. "Mr.

Atamian, the Father sends his condolences on your death. He said you shouldn't have taken Paula away from us."

Arnau gripped the top of the man's chair. He pushed his weight into it, rocking the seat until the adult man in the robe poured out onto the plastic. He landed on his stomach. Ida lifted the hem of her dress and curtsied down to his ear.

"The Quicker Cleaner-Uppers are coming. You won't be here when your wife gets back. It was nice meeting you, Mister."

Arnau put his knee into the man's spine and grabbed a clump of his curly black hair. He jerked the head back and slid the carving knife across Barry Atamian's throat. Minutes later, the girl and the boy were racing their bicycles down the new road, and for a short time Arnau took the lead, the wind blowing into his happy face.

16

Arnau accelerated the snowmobile across the frozen lake and down the narrow trail that intersected with a private country lane. Every two weeks he made the trip for groceries at the four-pump gas station a mile away. In forty years, he'd seen attendants come and go, but they were all the same—bored. Bored with asking people which pump they were on, bored with giving out-of-towners directions, bored with handing out restroom keys. The workers at that gas station recognized Arnau Farre, and they liked him because he had nothing to say and didn't need directions or a key to the shitter.

He turned off the engine 50 yards from the end of the trail. He flicked a bright LED flashlight on, then off, twice. High beams from a vehicle responded. Arnau unpacked his bags and trudged the rest of the path. There was a woman in the driver's side of the F-150. It had probably been idling a while. He knew it would be gassed up and ready for the trip. She opened the door and slid out, bundled up in layers of coat and scarves. The woman was in her mid-fifties. She was thick and carried herself with a punch-first personality. She handed Arnau a cinnamon roll.

"You ready?" she asked.

"Make sure he takes the statin. He forgets. I left the bottle by the sink."

She nodded and held his forearm, "Good luck."

"Tell me about the truck."

"Belongs to a third-shift guy at the mill. He won't know it's missing until he gets off. I'd guess, it'll be reported between 7 and 8 AM."

He nodded. That was fine. He was going to ditch the car in the city before anyone missed it. Arnau opened the door of the truck and put his bags into the back. He climbed in and put his Beretta in the console. He planned on driving the speed limit, not attracting attention, but you can never be sure. It would be a tough morning for the cop that tried to pull him over.

Arnau watched the woman walk down the path toward the snowmobile that would take her to the Father. She stopped and walked back to the truck. She stepped up on the footrail and put her arm through the open window and got a hold of his shoulder and held it tight.

"You come back, Arnau Farre. You hear me?"

He patted her hand, gave it a quick squeeze, then pushed it away.

• • •

The stolen truck rolled through the empty midtown streets without hitting a red light. The only vehicles on the road were a bakery van, a sanitation truck, and a few cabs—the city was still sleeping. Arnau made a right turn into an alley and parked behind a green dumpster by a wall scribbled with red and white graffiti. He turned off his headlights and waited.

For ten minutes he scanned the alley until he saw movement in the rearview mirror. It was the shadow of a man coming toward him. Without taking his eyes off the target, Arnau reached for the Beretta. The man stopped a few car lengths from the truck and leaned against the wall to light a cigarette. Arnau recognized the face glowing in the match flame. He lowered the gun and counted—the orange ember brightened every fifteen seconds.

The man in the shadows smoked three cigarettes before the last guy arrived. Arnau saw his silhouette coming down the alley. The Greek was wearing soft pants with a silver stripe running down the leg. He walked like an athlete, heel to balls of the feet, each step controlled and strong. His broad chest filled out the zippered tracksuit. The brim of his baseball hat was low enough that it was impossible to see his face. But Arnau knew it was the Greek.

The smoker threw down his cigarette and stepped to the passenger side door. The Greek walked in front of the hood toward the driver's side open window. He lifted his hat so Arnau could see his goddamned nose. It ran east and west on his face. Years ago, he had needed to learn a lesson. Arnau was an excellent teacher. He'd redecorated the Greek's face until an understanding had been reached. And not forgotten.

"Burner number?" asked Arnau. The Greek gave it to him, and he put the digits into his phone. "Bag's in the back."

The Greek took the roller bag and raised the handle.

"Text me when you're clear."

The Greek nodded. He gave a small wave to the man at the passenger side of the car, then turned up the alley, dragging the heavy roller bag behind him.

Arnau put the Beretta back in the console and waited for his passenger to hop in.

"Hey, Arnau."

He addressed the man by his alias. "Morning, George."

George had a round face with a stubby nose and wide, bulbous eyes that didn't seem secure in their sockets—like they could fly across the room with a healthy sneeze.

"Where am I going?" asked Arnau.

"Parking garage on 27th," George said, tightening his seat belt. "Third floor. Purple Camry."

Arnau put the truck in gear, wondering why the idiot would have chosen a purple car.

"Ida?" George asked.

Arnau nodded.

George shook his head and sighed. That was all that needed to be said. They ditched the truck in the parking garage and took the purple Camry on a circuitous trip to rural Pennsylvania.

17

Three suitcases guarded the apartment door. Another lay unzipped on the bed next to Ben. It was his suitcase, and he'd "fill it." That's what he'd told Kate fifteen minutes ago when she was being super helpful. Now he wished he'd let her do it. It was a difficult wardrobe decision. What are you supposed to wear to a meeting with the soon-to-be vice president of the United States? He looked online. Unless it was a formal affair—suit and tie. But it was a double occasion. Ben was returning from a kidnapping. What do you wear for that?

Ben pulled a pair of khakis over his briefs, buttoned up his button-down, and had just put his arms through a blue blazer when Kate walked into the room. She looked him up and down.

"I just called St. Bart's. Told them I'd be out for the rest of the week. Rocky's handling everything for you at Cambridge Hill. You hanging in there?"

Ben wasn't hanging in there, but it was good that Kate was taking charge. Last night, she'd spent an hour working out the arrangements with the "person" from Kimberly Hancock's office. She'd written the details on a piece of yellow construction paper and run through the itinerary while Ben was drying from his shower. The information came too quickly, and he decided he didn't really need to understand it as long as she did. Kate was good at handling stuff like this.

A representative from Camp Waggy Paws had picked up the puppy at 7 AM. Ben and the dog shared a look on the way out the door; he was blinking pathetically from his cage, not ready to be whisked away. Ben

71

wasn't ready either. He threw sneakers, underwear, some comfortable shirts, and a pair of jeans into the suitcase. Kate was pacing the living room floor. Ben waited for her to pass, then placed his luggage with the others.

He spent his final five minutes at the kitchen table, looking out the window at the people on the street walking into their ordinary day. Ben loved ordinary days. Today would not be one of those. He felt fingers kneading his shoulders, digging into the back of his neck.

"You're tight," she said.

"Shocking."

Kate laughed and kissed the back of his head. "It's going to be fine, babe."

The knock came right on time. Ben opened the door to see a giant in a blue suit. Kate tried to hand her suitcase to the massive man. He ignored it.

"The car's at the curb. I'm Greer. You're going to walk directly behind me—your palm on my back. If your hand leaves my suit, my gun comes out. Understand?"

Ben nodded.

"What should I do?" she asked.

"Whatever you'd like, ma'am. I'm not here for you."

Kate shot Ben a look, then chuckled—mumbling that she'd just take care of herself then.

Ben sat in the backseat of the black Town Car staring at the back of Greer's head in the passenger seat, his noggin wedged into the roof. It was the biggest melon he'd ever seen. The trip didn't take long. In minutes, the car turned into the drive of a private airfield in the suburbs. A worker in heavy boots and a blue parka opened the metal gate and waved the car toward the tarmac.

Ben saw the plane descend, gliding into a landing. Not until it turned did he make out that it was a Gulfstream. A very shiny Gulfstream. On the tail was the letter "H" in stylized cursive. Kimberly Hancock was inside. He wondered what he should call her. Not mother. Madam Vice President-Elect felt too formal and clunky. Senator seemed a bit past tense, with the inauguration just days away. Kimberly was way too familiar. He gave up.

Ben's hair blew stiffly in the chill wind waiting by the side of the car with Kate next to him, her arm folded formally into his elbow—something he couldn't remember her ever doing. She was nervous too.

The Gulfstream's hatch lowered. A thin-looking man in a tight suit prepared the stairs. He stood up and turned, talking to someone inside the plane.

Ben inhaled. She was coming.

And then he saw that, no. She wasn't coming.

The guy bounding down the stairs had gray, CEO hair that didn't lift in the breeze. He wore an expensive suit and a fine, bright smile, and extended his arm before he was in range of Ben's hand.

"Benjamin! My god. What a thing. I'm David Plimpton," he said, pumping with a sure grip. He smiled. "And you must be Kate. We're glad you're here."

Kate looked at Ben and inhaled deeply.

David Plimpton put his arm behind Ben's back and turned him toward the Gulfstream. "Your mother wanted to be here. I advised against it. The press follow her everywhere. She'll be waiting for you at the airport—in a private area so you can meet her without paparazzi jamming cameras in your eye."

Ben thanked him for that.

Plimpton stopped and braced Ben's shoulder.

"I can't imagine what you've been through in the past 24 hours. We're all getting our head around it. But she's overjoyed—it's everything she's ever wished for. But the timing of this is terrible. We're under a lot of stress with the transition. Don't judge her too quickly. She's wonderful."

Ben stepped into the cabin of the G550 Gulfstream. It smelled new car fresh. The interior was over the top: high-polished burl wood accents, baskets of fruit, vases of colorful flowers, soft leather seats with the letter "H" embroidered on the pillows. The vice-presidential seal hung on the wall, wrapped in thin, clear plastic that would be ripped off a few days from now. A photographer at the back of the plane was steadying his camera against a leather seat, a sturdy woman in pearls and a black wool dress by his side.

"Benjamin," said David Plimpton, "this is Riley McGraw. She's in charge of public perception. You're going to need her for a while. Riley's as good as they come."

"Everyone is overjoyed to welcome you home," said the woman in the black wool dress.

David Plimpton waved the couple into seats across from him. For the first time in his life, Ben was facing the wrong direction on an airplane. It felt odd. Everything felt odd.

Plimpton leaned forward and clapped his hands. "Kate, I'm going to need a favor. We're thinking of putting you in a private car when we land. You'll get reconnected with Ben soon. The vice president-elect is eager to meet you, but let's just give her a few moments alone with Benjamin. Without other distractions. How's that sound?"

"I'd like her with me," said Ben.

Kate shook her head. "No. He's right."

David Plimpton gave them a winning smile and got up.

"Riley, they're all yours," he said, reaching into his pinstripe for his phone.

The woman lowered herself into the seat. She inhaled through her nose, then sculptured her face into a wintry smile that lasted uncomfortably long. Ben stared back, not understanding what he was expected to say. Riley McGraw tilted her head at Kate and gave her the same mannequin smile. In Ben's experience, people that made smiley faces like that almost never had anything amusing to say.

"Benjamin, have you done any public speaking? Spent any time in front of the cameras?"

He shook his head.

"What does a risk manager for Cambridge Hill Holdings do?"

"I, um, look at potential things that might, uh—"

She raised her eyebrows. "Okay, so you're *not* a great communicator."

"He's just nervous," Kate said, "but he's one of the smartest—"

"And what do *you* do?" Riley McGraw clipped.

"I teach first grade."

"I see," she said, giving Kate an impatient smile. She asked Ben to turn to the right and to the left. "You have a pleasant appearance. Good eyes. Sad. People like faces like yours."

Ben looked over her shoulder at David Plimpton. He was on the phone, speaking fluent Mandarin.

Riley McGraw waited for his eyes to return to hers before she continued. "The press has the story. Which means there's going to be a crowd to manage at the airport." She caught the attention of the flight attendant and mimed that she needed three waters. "The press always gets what they want. If you have a secret, they'll find it. You're hoping I can keep them out of your life, aren't you?" She stared at him. "I don't ask rhetorical questions. You hope I can keep them out of your life, don't you?"

Ben nodded, "Yes."

"I can't. I'm not that good. No one is. And just so you know, if they can't find it, they'll insinuate it or, if it's a slow news day, just make it up. Does that give you anxiety?"

"Yes."

"Congratulations—you're human. And it means you will never break the most important commandment. Thou shalt never speak to the press without me or my team present. Should I repeat it?"

"No. Don't talk to reporters," he said.

The woman dug through her handbag for her phone and pressed the red record button. "Now, I need everything about you. And, so we're clear, I work for your mother. My job is to make sure your mud doesn't land on her shoes. Got it? Great."

Kate held Ben's hand. For the next hour, he answered the woman's questions. Riley McGraw nodded and, by the end, seemed visibly relieved to learn Ben was less damaging than she had feared.

He felt the vibration of the Gulfstream's wheels lowering under his feet. He looked out the window to see enormous mansions abutting blue water, expansive golf courses winding through expensive property; as the plane lowered, he saw baseball diamonds and suburban neighborhoods. The scenery changed as the plane descended toward DC: potholed, looping highways, blocks of boxy stores, rows of houses without yards, graffiti-scrawled tenement buildings. Ben lowered the shade and leaned into the soft leather seat, dreading what was coming next.

• • •

The Greek swept his palm across the six-hundred-thread percale sheets. He fluffed the pillows behind his head, then propped his elbows so he could see the fancy room in its entirety. One of the naked people must have set the wake-up alarm. And he was glad they had because the Emerald Point Hotel had a kick-ass service—no alarm buzzing out of a clock radio or the rude awakening of a phone call from the front desk. In the penthouse suite of the Emerald Point Hotel in Midtown, it was an orchestration of bird songs soaring over the calm gurgle of a stream—all in surround sound. The room brightened with soft, verdant lights that emanated from hidden sconces.

His knapsack was at the end of the king-sized bed. The roller bag was by the bathroom door. The naked couple was on the couch where he'd dragged them. Everything was still where he left it. He yawned and leaned his back against the headboard. He listened to the birds coming through the speaker and wondered what species they were—but the thought didn't keep his attention. The Greek put his hand below the silk sheets and played with himself, masturbating to the nudes he'd arranged so carefully and in such a naughty way.

When he had satisfied himself, he flushed the toilet and walked across the room and opened the blinds. The city was awakening—bustling a hundred floors below him. He looked at the skyscraper across from him. So close. So convenient. So impossible to miss.

18

The Gulfstream taxied. It seemed an eternity to get to its designated hangar at the far end of Reagan National. Ben lifted the shade. Their small plane was rolling past men and women in lime vests and ear protection that had stopped their work, pointing at Kimberly Hancock's Gulfstream. A few of them waved.

What Ben could not know was that millions were watching the progress of the small plane: from their phones, their televisions, in bedrooms, on buses, at the gym, in break rooms like Cambridge Hill Holdings, and in family rooms like the one in a remote northern cabin on the shores of a frozen lake.

"You got this, babe," Kate said, hugging him hard.

As they parted on the tarmac, Ben wished he would have put up a better fight to keep her close. He needed her. The car drove away. Her hand waved out of the backseat window.

A blustery wind lifted the corner of the narrow, black entry carpet. Ben could feel David Plimpton and Riley McGraw behind him, waiting for him to move. The photographer from the plane was prowling on his right, snapping at him. Dave Plimpton put his arm on Ben's shoulder.

"It's going to be fine."

Ben walked the black carpet. Someone opened the door for him. He took the narrow steps, hesitating at the landing where the polished hallway widened and turned to the right.

Treason. That was it. He hadn't been able to put a name to what he'd been feeling, but there it was. Despite what he'd learned about the kidnapping and the murder of Wendall, he couldn't help feeling that being introduced to Kimberly Hancock was a traitorous act. What would Ida think about this meeting? *After all I did for you?*

Ben shivered.

"It's going to be fine," Plimpton said again.

It was a gentle push. But a push just the same. Ben walked down the hall to the lounge area. It was a large room with tall windows, green plants, and minimalist brown furniture. The photographer was getting closer. Ben heard a gasp—in unison—from more than thirty people standing in front of the windows. They were all looking at him. Some through their phones. Some were crying. But for Ben, they were little more than a cluster of well-dressed strangers … and that's when he saw her.

The woman from the television.

Except not really. There was little resemblance to the maverick from the political commercials. This was no Prickly Princess. She was leaning into the woman next to her, gripping her arm to keep herself upright. Kimberly Hancock's face was blotched red, her eyes were wide.

The camera kept firing at him. Closer. Closer. He wanted the guy to go away. He wanted everyone to go away. This was not where he wanted to be.

Kimberly Hancock made two hesitant steps, then charged, galloping to him. An animal sound came up from the back of her throat as she flew into him and crashed against his chest. Her manic arms and hands and fingers groped across the skin of his middle back, squeezing and holding tight. She buried her head under his chin and wilted. He held her while she sobbed. It was gallons of suffering and despair and worry and anger and false hope gushing into a thimble of moment.

Kimberly Hancock unwound herself from her son and looked up into his eyes. Her hands reached for his face. They held him while she took in every eyelash, and pore, and dimple. She put a hand on his head and stroked his hair—and another sobbing tide rose out of her. Ben had never seen so much joy in a person.

She was trying to carry words to him. "I'm so sorry. I'm so—"

They were impossible words to lift.

"I'm okay. I'm okay," he heard himself saying.

• • •

Emma Noble got into the passenger seat of the gray Suburban. She turned her head into the backseat. It was clean. A pine-scented air freshener hung from the rearview mirror. She smiled to herself and clicked her seat belt.

"Morning!" she said.

"Shh."

"Jesus, you look like shit."

"Mmhmm."

"Big celebration last night?"

Briar rubbed his fingers into the white stubble of his chin, then across his cheek and under his eye. "What?"

"Never mind. You want me to drive?"

"No," he coughed. "How'd the kid take it?"

"He dealt with it. I guess he can take a punch, right?"

Silence.

"You see the news?"

Briar shook his head and backed out of the Hampton Inn parking spot.

"It was on every channel. They're saying it was extraordinary work by the FBI."

"Do you have to yell?"

She whispered, "The news people think you're very special."

As Briar drove for New York City, Emma Noble watched the coverage from her phone. She'd seen the shaky camera shot from a helicopter hovering over a two-story, yellow colonial in Vermont with the crawl at the bottom of the screen that read: "*Kidnapped Hancock Twin Found.*" She'd seen the college and high school pictures of Benjamin Danvers. Most of the reporting was accurate. They were piecing together the story of the boat explosion at the Lake of the Ozarks. Now, she was watching the live coverage at Reagan National of Kimberly Hancock and her son pushing their way through a swarm of photographers and journalists.

"Was he abused?"

"What was the motive behind the kidnapping?"

"Have your feelings about the FBI changed now that they found your son?"

"Benjamin, are you happy to be home?"

"Willie or Fred?"

Emma watched as mother and son were hustled into a waiting black SUV. The camera froze on a blurry picture of Benjamin in the backseat. He looked miserable. Emma exhaled and turned off her phone.

19

"Now I know how the beetles feel," Kimberly Hancock said, smoothing out her blue blazer.

"What?" asked Ben.

"The Beatles. Now I know how they must have felt."

"Oh, right."

The black SUV pulled away from the crowd of reporters—two police motorcycles in front, another SUV tailgating behind. Kimberly Hancock was next to Ben in the back of the spacious vehicle. She reached over and touched him—lightly on the big knuckles of his slender hand. It was awkward and intimate. She pulled it back.

"You met David, right?" she said.

Ben nodded.

"We all work for David."

Plimpton turned. "Lies. Your mother's the captain. She steers the ship—I just manage the sails."

Kimberly Hancock smiled and put her hand on the shoulder of the seat in front of her. David Plimpton gave it a squeeze. He smiled at Ben.

"We're heading back to the house. Tonight, we'll have a private celebration at Drew McDuffee's downtown—you like steak, right?"

"What about Kate?" Ben asked.

"Of course. All set."

"How long have you two been together?" she asked.

"Two years."

"It will be nice to meet her."

Ben nodded. Outside the window people gathered on the sidewalk, watching the small parade go by. They waved and smiled. He rubbed his palms against his thighs. The conversation had stalled. Ben knew the incoming vice president, his mother, was waiting for him to say something. He agreed. He should say something. But he had no idea what.

"I have bottled water up here," said David Plimpton. "Can I interest anyone?"

"Sure," said Kimberly. "Benjamin? Water?"

Ben nodded.

He took a sip and looked at the people waving. There were hundreds lined up along the street. Kimberly Hancock leaned across Ben and waved back. A young woman on the sidewalk jumped up and down and fell laughing into a friend next to her. Ben chuckled. His mother did too.

She slid closer. "Wave. You'll make their day."

Ben did. His mother pressed next to him, and their faces filled the window. The smell of her hairspray. Her perfume. Her hand lotion. He didn't recognize her scent. And yet, to the people looking at the two faces in the window, there was no doubt they were mother and son. They shared the same blue eyes and high cheekbones. The same thin lips.

The black SUV sped onto the expressway, the sidewalk people disappeared, and Kimberly Hancock slid back to her side.

• • •

Briar barked into the windshield. "Go! Douchebag!"

City driving had revived him.

"Missouri plate. You see what I'm talking about? Noble? You listening?"

"Yup."

"Move! Why? Why are you Midwesterners afraid of making a fucking left?"

"Not polite to clog the—?"

"Polite? Bullshit. They're all pussies. Move, dickhead!"

A man in a black overcoat ran into the intersection, nearly getting creamed by a bus. A woman followed. Emma squinted down the street. It was an eruption. Everyone running. Away from something.

"Briar?"

"Shit," he said.

A hunk of twisted metal blasted into the pavement ahead of them. Flaming debris rained down, shattering car windows. Emma bent low to look up through the windshield. Black and gray smoke billowed from the top of a skyscraper.

"Oh no," she said.

Briar's impatience had stuck him to the bumper of the Missouri vehicle. The bread truck behind him was glued to his exhaust pipe. He accelerated, pushing Missouri far enough for him to turn. But there was nowhere to go. He swore, turned the wheel, and drove up on the sidewalk and, for half a block, managed to avoid hitting the scramble of men and women running out of buildings.

He parked. Emma followed him out of the car with no clear idea of what to do. He threw a ballistic vest at her from the trunk. The sirens were deafening—long fire engine blasts, police squelches. Emma stood by the trunk of the gray Suburban, waiting for Briar to lead. He grabbed binoculars. Smoke was pouring from the top of the building. He lowered his arms and looked around.

"What should I—"

He ignored her and yelled at a cop standing in the road. "Hey!" he said, waving his arm in a circle. "These people are too close. Push 'em back!"

Men and woman were pouring out of the entrance of the smoking skyscraper.

"Should we go in?" yelled Emma.

The first responders were arriving. Briar shook his head at Emma and pointed to them. He shouted over the noise. "They do *their* job. We do *our* job."

He crossed the street, ignoring the debris raining down in front of the building. He was bent at the waist, strolling around the outside of the building like he was searching for seashells. Emma mouthed a haphazard prayer and ran to him. Briar kneeled over a piece of twisted steel. He put his hand over it, checking that it was cool enough to handle. He nodded at Emma. They lifted it together and brought it behind a fire truck.

"What are we looking for?" Emma yelled.

Briar put his glasses on. He didn't have to look very long.

"See this?" he shouted.

Emma crouched with him. The steel was peppered with pockmarks. "High velocity explosive."

Emma nodded. She'd hoped it was a gas explosion, something accidental, but this was intentional. People were dead. Dying, because of someone's outsized hate.

Briar looked up at the stand of skyscrapers around him. He pointed to one on his left. "We need to get up there," he said, jogging over to the building.

They came out on the top floor. It was empty—everyone had already evacuated. Emma stayed on Briar's heels, running to the east side.

"Find out what building that is," Briar said, pointing at the smoking skyscraper.

It was impossible to see anything through the thick, gray smoke billowing next door; grains of concrete clinked against the glass, and funnels of paper scraps skipped across the window.

Emma found it quickly. "Mansion Media Building."

A helpful wind released the thick cloud, giving them their first view of the devastation. Emma could see through the top of the building: the raging fire, the crushed metal, the slabs of tipped concrete. Briar dialed a number that leapfrogged four levels of command. He held it to his ear and handed Emma the binoculars.

"Look for anything out of place," he told her. "Yeah. Billy, it's Briar. I'm in Manhattan—we got a problem."

Emma scanned the blocks and buildings around her, dividing her line of sight into a search grid. She didn't see anything out of place until she focused on the awning of the Emerald Point Hotel and worked her way up the side of the building.

"Briar?"

"Hold on."

Emma handed him the binoculars. "Emerald Point Hotel. Top floor. Corner window."

It took him a moment to find it.

"Yeah," he said into the phone. "We got a hole in a window in the top floor of the Emerald Point Hotel. A perfect damn circle."

20

The sirens at street level were deafening. Emma Noble bent her head, pressing her index fingers into her ears as she followed Briar out the revolving door. Police had barricaded every cross street for over a mile, opening an emergency artery through Midtown. Firefighters and emergency workers rushed through the right-side doors of the Mansion Media Building—a line of clean, baggy uniforms and clunky helmets. Their brothers exited out the left, exhausted and soot-faced, squinting at the light, hurrying victims into an ambulance or a triage tent a few blocks away. A powdered victim, a woman maybe—it was hard for Emma to tell—embraced a firefighter outside the door. She watched the guy catch his breath, then get back in line on the right. Once more into the breach.

The posh lobby of the Emerald Point Hotel showed no signs of damage. The brass railings were in high shine as were the marble floors. Not a bulb in any of the crystal chandeliers had broken. It was eerily quiet—all the guests and staff had evacuated. Emma and Briar turned toward the ding of the elevator. A tall guy in silver-tipped cowboy boots stepped out, a hotel security badge clipped to his brown suit.

"That was fast," he said.

"What was fast?" asked Briar.

"Just called you."

The guy wasn't in a panic. He was amped, but in control. Disciplined. Emma recognized the way he handled himself. She knew people like that. Uncle Gunny. Her father. She guessed this guy in the silver-tipped cowboy boots had seen things. And when he handed Briar the master key and said it "wasn't good" up in suite 1008, Emma believed him.

"Security tapes are on the fourth floor. I'll be waiting for you."

Briar pressed the elevator button, then dug into his pocket. "You want gum?"

Emma shook her head. "I'm okay."

The room was freezing, but that wasn't the first thing she noticed. The only sensory perception she could focus on was the color red. Red pools in the carpet. Red smears on the wall. Red splatters against the window. Red streaks across the upholstery. Red, still dripping off the sofa.

Two blood-smeared naked bodies on the couch.

Emma's stomach clenched, turned over, and flew up her throat. She pushed past Briar and hurled herself into the hallway, blowing her bitter guts into the carpet. Kneeling and bent over, she waited for the nausea to pass. Her eyes were watering, her chest heaving. She rubbed her face and leaned against the wall, trying to distance herself from what she'd just seen. In training, they'd told her about this moment. Not everybody could do the job. There were only two choices: ignore the crime-scene horror and do your job or turn in your badge and gun. She wasn't quitting. Emma inhaled deeply and stepped back into the suite.

"You want that gum now?" asked Briar.

"Yeah," she whispered.

Emma stood by the hole in the window so the blowing wind could clear her head like a cold electrocution. The bodies were gruesome. Emma guessed the murderer had taken his time with the killing and with the pornographic display. She stared at the man on the couch. He looked familiar. Emma took a step forward and crouched in front of the body. She turned her attention to the woman, gazing into her wide eyes. *No way.*

"Is that…?" she asked.

"I think so."

She wondered how the press would report it. The married prince of right-wing media found dead with his lover—the progressive news network's most beloved pundit—in the honeymoon suite of the Emerald Point Hotel.

"You understand that?" Briar asked, pointing to the wall.

Libereco pensi mem was written in blood on the wall.

"Latin maybe?"

There was no doubt what was scribbled like an afterthought over the sofa.

Your Opinions Are Boring As Fuck.

Briar stooped to look out the hole in the window. "The circle was cut low," he said, walking backward in the room, looking at the carpet and the window from different angles. "The terrorist fired from a kneeling position."

"What was it?" asked Emma.

"Shoulder mounted. Maybe thermobaric."

"Bunker buster? How the hell?"

Briar shrugged. They both turned at the quiet knock at the door. A bald guy in glasses was in front. The rest of the forensic team was milling around in the hallway.

"You guys done?" he asked.

"Yeah," said Briar.

"That ours or theirs?" he said, pointing into the hallway.

"What?" asked Briar.

"The chowder in the hallway."

Briar pointed at Emma.

• • •

"Everybody calls me Vegas," said the guy in the cowboy boots, waiting for them in the fourth-floor security office.

"I'm Metcalf. This is Noble. What's the story with the deceased couple?"

"Worst kept secret in the hotel. Mansion Media pays for that room and those two come in a couple times a week under aliases. You recognized them?"

Emma nodded.

"I know, right? Let me show you a couple of things."

A giant screen took up most of the wall of the security room. It was divided into a hundred small squares displaying the public areas of the hotel from a few different angles. Vegas pointed at the screen.

"We've got shots of the stairwells and elevators. Lobby and the entrance doors here. Front desk. Kitchen. Café. All entry points and exits."

"And?" asked Briar.

"I've got timestamps of the couple entering the suite. He comes in last night at 10:12. She arrives 10:35. No one else takes the elevator to that floor until 12:10 AM. Then this guy pops in."

Vegas tapped his keyboard, and video from the elevator played on the giant screen. It was a man in a tracksuit, a baseball hat scrunched low on his head, a knapsack over his shoulder. The picture was excellent, but they couldn't ID the face.

"Nothing happens on that floor until 4:45 AM. Track Suit gets back on the elevator. Takes it down. Now—look. Here's the lobby camera. He leaves. Goes right out the door."

"So, not our guy?" asked Emma.

"Wait. See? Nine minutes later, he comes back in through the lobby. This time he's got a roller bag. Takes the elevator back up."

"You're sure he isn't a guest?" she asked.

"No. I've accounted for the other nine suites. He doesn't belong to any of them."

"Show me how he leaves," said Briar.

"Here's the playback from the time of the explosion and the sounding of our hotel alarm a minute later."

The screen showed eight people gathering by the elevator on the hundredth floor, coming in groups of twos. Their body language showed the expected anxiety of the moment. None of them carried bags. Only coats. The elevator doors opened. The group stepped in. A woman held the door for someone.

"There! Freeze it," said Briar.

Track Suit was the last guy in, coming from off camera with the knapsack and a roller bag. His head was still down.

"I can follow him out," said Vegas.

Emma watched the screen. The terrorist stepped out of the elevator and into the lobby. Up to that point he'd done well keeping his head down, but he couldn't help himself. He walked to the large windows and looked up at the Mansion Media Building to see his handiwork. The camera froze on a perfect picture of the man's face and his easily identifiable nose.

"Got ya, dumbass," said Briar.

21

The awkward atmosphere inside the black, armored SUV evaporated when David Plimpton handed his phone to Kimberly Hancock, showing her the text he'd just received.

"When did this happen?" she asked.

"Just now. Mansion Media Building."

"Oh god, David—we have friends there."

Ten minutes later, she'd finished her first phone call. On the second call she was impatient for more information, peppering the person with a salvo of rapid-fire questions. Her third conversation was deferential. Ben guessed she was speaking to the president-elect.

"Don't apologize. It can't be helped," she said, hanging up.

David Plimpton turned, waiting for an update.

"He wants everyone." She looked at Ben and sighed. "I'm sorry. There's been a terrorist attack. I need to drop you at the house. I don't know how long.... I'm so sorry."

"I understand," said Ben.

The vehicle slowed to enter the gated community where brick and stone mansions towered over the streets below—sprawling lawn after sprawling lawn. Secret service agents huddled together in the cold at the end of Kimberly Hancock's driveway. They snapped to attention at the approach of the black SUV. An iron gate swung inward and the car proceeded up the narrow, crushed-oyster drive where mature dogwoods lined the road and acres of brown lawn meandered toward a grand old home with cedar shingles that had weathered into a gray patina. Massive brick chimneys jutted from multiple roof lines and an immaculate red barn to the right of the home stood proud and straight. At the top of the drive, Ben could see the blue-green water of the snaking Potomac River in the distance. He stood by the trunk watching the driver take his bags out. Kimberly Hancock gripped his elbow.

"I'm sorry. I'll see you soon, okay?" she said, giving him an uncomfortably long hug.

The massive wooden doors opened. Kate was standing at the entrance. She looked nervous. Fidgety.

Kimberly Hancock made her hands a prayer. "I'm so sorry, Kate. There's been an emergency. You and Benjamin make yourself at home. I'll be back as soon as I possibly can."

They waved together from the stoop as the armored SUV retreated down the drive. When it was out of sight, Kate pulled Ben through the front doors. "Dude. This house…. Have you ever seen anything like this?"

Ben followed her, taking it all in: the wide-plank antique oak floors, the intricate mahogany millwork, the floor-to-ceiling stone fireplace, the expansive kitchen, the river views at the back of the house. Kimberly Hancock's home was decorated with intent to be two things at once: imposing and casually comfortable. Ben was struck by what it lacked. There was no musty onion fust coming from the pantry; no need to move a chair to squeeze past the table to get to the window; no sweaters balled up on couches to serve as second pillows. It was a magnificent, sterile museum. He tilted his head toward the ceiling, listening to the thwack-thwack of the news choppers circling above the house.

"This is nuts," he said.

"Which part?"

He raised his eyebrows at her, then shook his head.

"You doing okay?"

"Better now."

"Was it weird?"

"Oh, yeah."

"What's she like?"

"Fine. Nice I guess."

The family room was twice as big as their Boston apartment. Kate turned on the TV. The terror attack in New York was on every station. There had been casualties, but less than expected. The building was structurally intact—no danger of collapsing. The attack had turned the reunification of Kimberly Hancock and her long-lost son into a below-the-fold headline. Kate turned down the volume and put her chin on the blade of Ben's shoulder. She stroked his chest while they sat for a while in silence.

"You know…." she said.

"Hmm?"

"If you grew up in a place like this … you'd probably be," she hesitated for effect, "such a dick."

Ben chuckled and held her hand.

She whispered in his ear. "I saw you on the news. You looked good. Almost handsome."

"Almost? Come on now." Ben leaned in, bringing his lips to hers.

The moment was punctured by the slam of the front door.

Riley McGraw waddled into the room with a young woman behind her, probably an assistant—the girl's arms weighed down with a stack of folders and binders. "Good. You're both here."

Ben took a deep breath, preparing himself for a fresh round of misery.

"We're off to a good start. America isn't asking about your politics."

Ben shrugged. "Why does that matt—?"

"It means half the country doesn't hate you … yet."

"What happens now?" asked Kate.

"We need to introduce you."

Ben gave her a sour look. "What does that mean?"

"Just a couple of TV interviews. One on your own and one with your mother. We've got to do them right away."

"Why?" asked Kate.

"The focus needs to be on the president and his first 100 days. So, we'll get it out of the way before the inauguration."

Ben was shaking his head. "No way. I'm not going on TV."

"Of course you are. You're holding the golden ticket. Welcome to Wonka," said the woman.

"He's not a polished speaker," Kate explained.

"We've established that," she said without looking over. "But it isn't necessary. I want authentic, not polished." She motioned her assistant to put the papers and binders on the coffee table. "So, tomorrow, you'll go on Mattson & McCall's Morning Show."

Ben shook his head. "No way. Uh-uh."

"Yes. You will. It's the only way to regain your privacy. In a week, you'll be old news. We've already worked out the rules—they'll ask you the questions in that red folder."

Kate looked through the papers on the coffee table. "What's the rest of this?" she asked.

"Talking points. Your mother's political positions. Things that might be helpful—if you're asked."

"But, you said they'll only ask me the questions in the—"

"When the cameras roll, reporters can't help themselves. They go off reservation. But don't worry, Mattson knows I'll cut his dick off if he tries something dumb."

"I can't do this."

Kate leaned into him. "You can. I'll be right beside you."

"Actually, no, you won't be. The two of us are going to have breakfast tomorrow while Ben's at the studio. We need to have a little chat about expectations and boundaries." Riley McGraw looked Kate up and down, then frowned. "And maybe we'll carve out a little time for some clothes shopping."

Ben rose from the couch and walked into the kitchen, hoping to get some distance. Some breathing room. But McGraw and her assistant followed.

"A car will be here for you at 5 AM. You go live at 6:45. It's a thirty-minute exclusive. You're back here by 8:30. Easy peasy, lemon squeezy."

Kate looked into the red binder. "Where did you grow up?" she asked Ben.

"What?"

"I'm reading the questions they'll ask. *Do you remember anything from your childhood before the kidnapping? Has it sunk in yet that you're the son of the incoming vice president?*' Babe, these are softball questions. I don't think there's anything here you have to worry about."

"There's plenty to worry about."

92

22

Emma Noble leaned down to put a few more playing cards under the leg of her rickety kitchen table. Taped-up moving boxes were stacked in the hallway of her tiny apartment, waiting to be unpacked another day. She adjusted her laptop and rubbed her fingers into her tired eyes. The "O" had been a disturbed hive of energy all afternoon: agents yelling over their cubicles, running down hallways, shouting into their phones. Emma had spent it hunched over a desk, filling out paperwork on what they'd seen in the suite at the Emerald Point Hotel. She'd found the meaning of the words written in blood on the wall of the hotel room. *Libereco pensi mem.*

It was Esperanto. The translation: "Freedom to Think for Yourself."

There was no country of Esperanto. It was a language invented in the 1880s by a Polish eye doctor who believed there should be a universal, borderless language that could unite the world. It had periods of popularity in the 20th century, but never caught on the way he'd hoped.

Emma's involvement with the attack in New York ended when she handed in the report. It was DOMTERR's concern now. The next item on the agenda was tomorrow afternoon's meeting in DC with Monroe for a debrief on the Hancock case. Briar told her he'd do the talking. That left her with a lot on her mind and nothing to do. Her partner wouldn't be joining her on the early-morning flight. Apparently, he didn't fly—or ride commercial buses or take trains. He said they were "petri-dish deathtraps." Uncle Gunny was picking Emma up at the airport and taking her to breakfast ahead of the big meeting.

She wasn't satisfied. There were too many unanswered questions. She poured a glass of wine and continued her research, trying to find more on the phrase *Libereco pensi mem*. There was only one reference. It was from an obscure essay written by an anonymous author in the mid-twentieth century. The phrase was the first of the *Tri kolonoj de la libereco* (Three Pillars of Freedom*)*. The second, *Libereco de mono*, was freedom from money. The third, *Libereco de registaro*: freedom from government. She tried to tie the ideology to anti-fascist or white nationalism. It didn't fit. She was looking at something new.

Emma copied her research and attached it to an email to the DOMTERR team leader. Her energy was used up. She took to the couch with her wineglass in hand, flipping through TV channels, hoping a show would distract her from what she'd seen in the Emerald Point Hotel. She sipped red wine and closed her eyes. It wasn't working. Nothing could stop her mind's eye from entering Suite 1008. Nothing could stop her from seeing the blood. So much blood.

• • •

There had been no celebratory steak dinner. Kimberly Hancock still wasn't back from her meeting with the president-elect. Ben and Kate shared take-out food in the great room. They ate while she tossed practice questions at him from the red binder. It had gone on for hours. He wasn't enjoying the help.

Remember to speak up, Ben.

I think you should try to look at the host. Not at the camera. Right?

Try to smile more.

It was past ten o'clock when Ben halted the study session. He wandered the massive home alone: checked out the wine cellar in the basement, peeked into the theater room, glanced at Kimberly Hancock's office.

He walked the far section of the house. It was older than the rest of the mansion. The hallway was narrower. At the end were two carved wooden doors. Ben turned the brass doorknob. The room was dark. He reached his hand around the inside wall, feeling for a light switch. He flicked it on, but the room remained in darkness. Judging by the box of matches and the wax candle in the brass holder, the lights hadn't been on in this room for a while. He struck a match and lit the wick. The room was chilly, and the floorboards creaked under his feet.

His eyes took some time adjusting to the dim light. Ben raised the candle over his head, illuminating the dark shadows. It was a library. An old library. It had high ceilings with heavy beams of dark wood—a masculine room with mahogany walls. White dust covers draped over the chairs and couches. Ben walked in farther. The library contained hundreds of leathered volumes, ribbed in ancient ochre and weathered sienna, drooping on the shelves, weary with age. And there were portraits—oil paintings of men frowning from across the room.

"The wiring needs to be replaced."

He turned to see Kimberly Hancock under the transom. She had changed out of her smart outfit with the American flag lapel pin. Her hair was down. She wore blue sweatpants and a green T-shirt under an untied, pink terrycloth robe. She held a binder in front of her like it was something that might go off.

"Let's put a fire in," she said.

The dry wood in the hearth crackled to life. The library glowed with an orange, warming light. Each took a side of the sofa's dust cover and lifted. They folded their corners and walked forward, meeting each other like steps in an old folk dance. She pressed her hand over Ben's and smiled before taking the folded cover and placing it in the hutch. They sat together in front of the fire, neither saying anything for a long while. Ben stared at the painting above the mantel—the portrait of a famous man in a powdered wig.

"You know who that is?" she asked.

"Yes."

"As a young girl, I was in awe of this room. Then, when I understood the expectations, it made me anxious." She looked around at the men on the walls. "It still does." She picked the thick binder from the floor and put it on her lap. "They compiled a dossier on you. Everything they could find: your school grades, papers you wrote in college, interviews with people that know you—I'm not completely sure of everything that's in here."

"They didn't waste any time."

She nodded and snapped open the silver rings and pulled the paper away. The sofa creaked as Kimberly Hancock leaned forward and threw the pages into the fire. "That isn't how I want to get to know you." She grabbed an iron poker and pushed the papers into the center of the flames, where they burned brightly, then became black and crisp—fragile, gray ash that flittered up the chimney and into the heavens. She stared into the fire.

Ben could see she was struggling with the moment. Kimberly Hancock was more vulnerable than he'd expected her to be. He'd seen the debate—he'd watched her slay all the men in the room except one. She was a warrior. But this person standing by the fire? This Kimberly Hancock was not who he expected.

"I kept your clothes. For seventeen years, I kept them. In a cardboard box. I would take them out on your birthdays—and always on Christmas. And sometimes when I just needed to see them. I'd lay them out on the bed—they were so small. I'd sit there with them. Lift them up and inhale them. I imagined myself buttoning and zipping you and your brother into them. Imagined you playing in the backyard in them. The way you used to."

Ben watched her wipe her nose and gather herself.

"Then, I made a decision to stop torturing myself. It was a rainy day. I drove into the city and put the box by a bin outside a Goodwill. I sat in my car across the street until a man came out and lifted the box on his shoulder and took it inside. That was the last day I cried for you and your brother. Until yesterday."

She looked at him. Ben recognized her brokenness. He lowered his head and stared into the glow of the embers.

"I was grateful when I heard you never knew you were kidnapped. You didn't have to suffer the way we did. But today—seeing you? I can't imagine what you're going through." She touched his hand. "I'm sorry."

Ben nodded. Her hand clasped his. They were warm, and her fingers slid around his like they belonged there.

"You remind me of your father. You look like him. He was gentle, and kind. Like you. Roger was my compass—the man always pointed toward true north. I wish you could have met him, and he could have seen you all grown up like this." She stared up at the ceiling and exhaled. "I have a strong urge to shackle you to my wrist and never let you out of my sight." She gave an unconvincing chuckle, "I don't suppose you'd be up for that, would you?"

Ben smiled and she patted his hand.

"I don't know what I expect to happen now. You have your own life, but … I'll take as much of you as you'll give me. I promise, I'll be okay with whatever that looks like. But Ben, you have to know—I've been waiting and hoping. For so long." Her eyes pooled and her voice caught in her throat. "I'm desperate. To be your—" She shook her head and smiled, then ran a thumb under both eyes. "You know?"

Ben nodded and waited for Kimberly Hancock to gather herself.

"You're going on Mattson & McCall tomorrow?"

He started feeling the drumbeat of anxiety pattering through his chest.

"I can see it in your face. This is overwhelming, isn't it? We've thrown you right into the boil."

Ben forced a tight smile.

"Riley McGraw says the interview has to be done. If not, I'd put you out of your misery and cancel it straight away. I'm sorry. I understand all of this must be so uncomfortable for you—and probably very scary?"

Ben hardened his face so she wouldn't see the fear in it. "It's just you know—"

"I do know. It *is* scary. You need space." She looked into the fire for a moment, then shot him a confident look. "You'll take my car tomorrow. You'll go to the interview alone, without Riley's assistants breathing down your neck." Kimberly Hancock reached into the pocket of her robe and pulled the ignition key from the fob. She hesitated a moment, then put it in Ben's palm. "It's in the garage. You'll do just fine."

97

DAY 3

23

Ben parked the Land Rover under a blue sign that read—*Reserved for Guests of Studio C.* He glanced at the red binder on the passenger seat. His breath caught in his throat—anxiety was serving oxygen on tiny plates from a slow kitchen.

Earlier, he and Kate had shared a coffee in the den. She said it was going to be "fine." And reminded him to "just have fun." At the moment, Ben couldn't think of a less fun thing to do. But he understood that this was the toll he had to pay to get his privacy back. And he didn't want to disappoint Kate. Which is why he got out of the car and stood in the parking lot of the national news studio before dawn, by the hood of his birth mother's Land Rover, holding a red binder and waiting to see if the bright LED headlights would turn off on their own.

Ben walked slowly through the dark toward the illuminated interior of Studio C. An overcaffeinated person at the front desk made him sign a paper and asked him to wait "just a skosh" for the Assistant Something or Other to take him in. Ben paged through the red binder. His eyes scanned the questions, but his once-reliable brain had chosen this morning to go on strike. He felt his stomach lurch.

"Benjamin Hancock! Welcome."

"It's Danvers," he said, swallowing hard.

The assistant's face twisted. She scribbled on her clipboard, then turned her back and whispered frantically into her headset. In a flash, she returned her attention to him, bathing Ben in faux joy. "All set—catastrophe averted."

She grabbed his elbow and guided him into a spacious room. There was a snacks table in the back: a silver coffee carafe, boxes of donuts, a large brown plastic jug of something. At the far end of the room, sitting on a bright stage, were Mattson & McCall, speaking casually to people in headsets.

"We're in commercial," she said. "I'm bringing you to Tony. After he makes you even more beautiful, we'll get levels, do a light adjustment, and then get out of your way so you can speak directly to the world. This must be exciting for you."

"Just the questions in this, right?" he said, pointing at the red binder.

"May I?" She reached for it and flipped through. "I don't think we have this."

"But Riley McG—"

"Oh, Tony. This is Benjamin Danvers. Can you be a dear and take him back with you?"

For twenty minutes, Ben was brushed and dabbed and powdered. And dabbed a few more times after that. Tony put his chin on Ben's shoulder and looked into the bulbed mirror at their reflections.

"I can, literally, see your heart pumping through your shirt."

Ben swallowed and tried to make a smile.

"We haven't lost anyone here. Not yet. Just have fun." Tony tilted his head and winced. "But, honey, you've got to stop sweating or you're gonna get me fired."

Ben waited by the snack table. The brown plastic jug had a peeling label that read "juices." His stomach was in no condition to drink juices. The set fell silent. Cameras were rolling. Ben watched Mattson & McCall on the monitors, shooting the breeze. Smiling. Teasing the interview with Kimberly Hancock's kidnapped son.

"Stay tuned for our exclusive interview."

They went to break. The room became two minutes of madness. The host made a beeline for Ben. "Hey, man, Dick Mattson. Terrific you could join us today. Gonna be great. I hear you're really nervous. They told me to make you comfortable. You gonna make it?"

Ben shrugged.

"Terrific. Me too. See you in a few." He winked and bolted somewhere.

"Mr. Danvers? We're ready for you," said a woman. She pointed at a chair that had been added to the set.

He squinted at the impossibly bright light and shifted in the seat; on the monitor to his left, he saw himself shift in his seat. He looked away and wiped sweat from the back of his neck. His mouth had gone dry. The table next to him lay bare.

"Ready, Bill? Please say something Mr. Danvers."

"Could I have some water? Please."

"Bill, how was that? Good?" she said, giving a thumbs up. "Thanks, Mr. Danvers. Stay right here. We're running the network's original footage from the kidnapping. Live in five minutes and thirty seconds."

Ben felt queasy. "I need a bathroom please."

The assistant pretended she didn't hear him.

"Restroom. Please."

"Is it an emergency?"

"Yeah, pretty sure it is."

She smiled, but her eyes looked angry. "Melissa! Show Mr. Danvers to the restroom. Quickly. Please!"

For two minutes, Ben did some unproductive dry heaving in the handicap stall. He sat on the porcelain, his head in his hands—praying for a small earthquake or lightning strike, anything to keep him from walking out in front of all those people. The bathroom door opened far enough for a woman's face to call out.

"Mr. Danvers. We need you. Please. It's time."

He heard the door slam shut.

Ben stood in front of the sink and tucked at his shirt. He looked at his perspiring face, thick with make-up. *What am I doing?* It felt like he was in the helpless grip of a riptide—an unforgiving current carrying him out to sea. Ben looked at his sweaty reflection. Saw his tremoring hands. This wasn't for him. He couldn't be here. He had to escape.

Leave. Now.

He opened the bathroom door, shook off the grabbing arm of the clipboard-headset-lady, walked past the donut-coffee-juices table, jogged through the reception area, and ran through the dark morning toward the silver Land Rover.

Ben laid his head against the steering wheel. Kate was going to be disappointed, maybe angry. Riley McGraw was definitely going to be pissed. Kimberly Hancock? Who knew what she'd think. There would be hell to pay, but he'd deal with that later. He turned off his phone and started the engine. Where was he going? What was out there for him? The image of the yellow colonial in Vermont came to him like an answer. He needed to go back—to swim upstream. Back to where things started. He had a full tank, more than enough to get him to Vermont. Maybe Ida had left a message waiting for him in the house—some clue that would help him understand. Ben dropped the Land Rover into gear and in minutes was on the expressway, heading north.

Running away from home. And running back to it.

24

Arnau Farre didn't care that the rented house smelled like cat piss. He ignored the yellow circles in the carpet and the splinters in the dark paneling installed during the Nixon administration. He didn't spend any time admiring the framed print of the giant ark bathed in heavenly light and the forever queue of docile animals waiting for salvation. The two-bedroom ranch in Pennsylvania farm country served one purpose. It was on a dead-end street in the middle of nowhere.

The house didn't disturb Arnau Farre. But he *was* disturbed— because he worked with morons. The Greek had been careless. His nose had become a breaking news story.

Arnau alternated between sipping coffee from a pink flamingo mug and reassembling his rifle. Finally, he leaned back into the high-sheen, overstuffed, blue couch and shook his head. It was impossible to ignore the snoring coming out of the back bedroom. It hadn't relented. All night, George Engel wheezed and snarled like an animal caught in a sack.

Arnau was plenty disturbed with George too. He'd had the responsibility of getting a clean, untraceable car for their trip south. A simple task for a simple man. Arnau didn't listen to the excuse. Because he didn't care. George Engel had rented the purple Camry from the largest national agency at the largest airport in New Jersey.

He opened the finger-smudged sliding glass door at the back of the house and stepped onto the square deck. The rust-red paint was bubbled and blistered. Beyond the stiff brown grass was a white garage that backed up to frozen fields. There were no homes nearby, only acres of farmland as far as he could see. He inhaled deeply through his cigarette and thought about the work to come. Two jobs. One today. One tomorrow.

The inauguration was three days away.

The Prophecy—everything the Father had envisioned. All that his brothers and sisters had worked for. The victory that Ida had sacrificed her life for. When his work was completed, the FBI wouldn't bother looking for him. He just needed to keep his two morons from doing anything stupid for a little while longer.

The sound of a car engine coming down the dead-end road startled him. He flicked the cigarette over the deck railing and darted inside. A dented jeep turned into the driveway. Arnau worked quickly, sliding the short rifle under the couch, then fastening his serrated knife to his belt. He draped his T-shirt over it and double-checked the back windows, making sure no one was moving behind the house.

The driver was alone. Arnau opened the front door and leaned against the jamb, casually sipping from his flamingo coffee mug, waiting for the driver to exit. A middle-aged woman waved to him from the driveway. She was in her fifties or sixties. Her hair was gray and unkempt.

"Morning," said Arnau, moving his coffee mug to his non-dominant hand.

"Hello, Mr. Engel? I hope it's not too early."

Arnau shrugged. He could be Mr. George Engel for a few minutes if he had too.

"I'm Karen."

"Okay."

"Your host? Maybe, you didn't read my profile. Oh, I got something from Turkey Hill for you." She held up a bag of powdered donuts like it was some kind of prize.

"It's not a great time."

"How was your stay?" she said, walking toward the front door.

"Fine."

"Great. Let me put these on the counter for you."

Karen barged in. She rotated around the room long enough for Arnau to understand she was doing a silent inventory of her belongings. Making sure all her shitty stuff was still there.

"What can I do for you?"

"Just checking in. I hope you'll give Casa Karen an excellent review."

A toilet flushed in the back bathroom. She looked at her renter.

"My brother," Arnau said, sipping bitter coffee.

She folded her arms, and he registered the immediate change in mood.

"Your reservation said one guest. It doesn't change the price much—but next time, pay a little more attention to that."

"Sure. Well, nice meeting you."

She looked toward the back bedroom.

"First time to Mountville, Mr. Engel?"

Arnau nodded.

"I was curious because you have New Jersey plates, but you're from Chicago."

"Rental."

"I see. Rented it in New Jersey then?"

Arnau nodded and glanced out the window at the white garage. "You and your husband do this on the side?" he asked, trying to sound kind.

Karen took a step toward the coffee table and looked at the plastic bag filled with gun cleaning paraphernalia. "What's that?"

"I asked if you had a husband."

"No, I um—don't."

"Good for you. An independent woman," Arnau said. He walked over to the sliding glass door. "And that's your garage, right?" He pointed. "I heard some noise coming from it."

"Doubt it. It's locked."

"Maybe an animal got in. Probably lots of them around here. I hate to think of you getting surprised by something rabid."

"I'm sure it's fine."

"Nonsense. Let me help you. I'd feel horrible if something happened to you."

"It's unnecessary."

He opened the sliding door. "What's the harm?" Arnau sent her his best smile, and she followed him into the backyard.

"I don't hear anything."

"Pretty sure something's in there. You unlock it, then I'll open it—just in case something with big teeth jumps out."

The double doors squeaked open, just wide enough for a feral cat to strut into the sunlight. Karen dropped her shoulders and laughed.

"There's your dangerous animal, Mr. Engel!"

He closed the distance and looked down on her. "No, Karen. That's not the dangerous animal."

• • •

Arnau Farre looked down the barrel of his silenced rifle at the hole he'd made in the side of the white garage two hundred yards away. The sights were still off. He dialed two down and one over. He twisted his heels in the dirt. It was a challenging shot. The gagged, gray-haired woman kept moving her head. Arnau lifted the scope and focused his aim above her crazy-looking eyes. And fired.

Bullseye.

George clapped from the deck.

They lifted her limp body into the trunk of the purple Camry, pulled the car into the garage, and locked it. Arnau smoked four cigarettes while George scrubbed the red from the white siding. A half hour later, they drove her dented white Jeep Cherokee toward Washington, DC.

With enough plastic explosives in the trunk to level two city blocks.

25

Emma Noble said goodbye to the nun seated next to her. She yanked her carry-on out of the overhead compartment and bent to peer out the oval window. It was the first time she'd been in DC since her father's retirement. A business traveler across the aisle was staring at her bag. She knew why. It looked sketchy. The zipper had gotten stuck this morning. She'd rushed the repair by mummifying the suitcase in duct tape. She didn't care what anyone thought. Emma was just happy to stretch her long legs out of their cramped confinement.

Uncle Gunny was waiting by security in an expensive black suit and gray tie, his shoes in a high polish. He was a short man with a broad chest and muscular arms. The only sign that he was in his late fifties was the crow's feet around his eyes. He didn't have to worry about laugh lines. But Uncle Gunny's most memorable and endearing feature was his ears. They looked like they belonged on another person. A far larger person. She'd once called him Sergeant Potato Head. Once.

"Hey Squirt."

She hugged him. Then stepped back.

"Look at you! Uncle Fancy-pants."

"Nah. Just another workin' stiff."

"That's not what I hear."

"Your dad's full of shit. Let's get out of here." Gunny saw her suitcase and halted. "What the hell is it that?"

"Luggage. I gave it some flair this morning. You like it?"

The last time Emma was in a limousine it was her junior year in high school, drinking shots of Jolly Rancher with her classmates in a brand-new black dress. It was prom. The night she had to abandon a sweet guy so she could keep Holly Thorpe's hair from falling into the toilet. This second limo experience with Uncle Gunny was nice, but not quite the same.

The maître d' welcomed the former marine by name and brought them to a private table by the window. According to her dad, Uncle Gunny was the smartest jarhead he'd ever met. After he retired from Langley, he started a security business, leveraging his spotless military record and enviable connections. Uncle Gunny was now a very rich man. He and Sam Noble were best friends. Sam and Emma were the only family he had.

"Well?" he said.

"Well, what?"

"Let me see it."

He held out his palm. Emma felt her face blushing. She unclipped her FBI badge and put it in his hand. He studied it, then handed it back to her.

"And?" he said.

"It's been interesting."

"That's what I hear."

"What do you mean, 'that's what you hear?'"

"It's what I hear. What? Why the face?"

"What does my dad know?"

"I didn't say your dad knows anything."

Emma sighed and looked up at the Chihuly chandelier. The two of them were so goddamn frustrating. They always did this. It was code to let her know they had their eyes on her while not admitting to prying into her life.

"Whatever. Yes. It's been interesting."

Uncle Gunny looked around the restaurant and leaned in. "What do you make of Kimberly Hancock's son? What's his name? Benjamin? Bit odd to have his coming-out party only a few days from the inauguration, don't you think?"

"Why would I have an opinion on that?"

"Yeah, right. So, what's your opinion?"

"Not that I know anything, but I bet he was just as shocked as everyone else."

"Well, something's off. Your dad says so too and his instincts—well, you know. The attack in New York wasn't a one-off. Something's happening. We're looking into it. But keep your eyes open and your head down. Okay, Squirt?"

Uncle Gunny shifted the conversation to things more pleasant. When his plate was clean, he wiped a heavy napkin across his lips, then belched into his fist. Emma pushed her seat back, but he grabbed for her wrist.

"What's the word?"

Uncle Gunny wanted to know if she remembered the signal that would bring two men with very dangerous skills racing through hell if she needed them.

"Blossom."

It had never changed. It had been her word since she was six. From her favorite *Powerpuff Girls* cartoon character. A word she'd never uttered.

Not even in spring.

26

"Everybody in town's behind you. Anything you need—just say the word."

Ben thanked the cop at the end of the driveway. He said they'd been busy keeping gawkers off the property. Ben turned the silver Land Rover off Route 7 and headed up the long driveway. The yellow two-story colonial came into view, standing in front of him like a back-lot façade—a movie prop from a fake childhood. The frozen wind ripped across the hill. Ben closed the car door and made the familiar walk to the house. He was grateful for the three inches of new snow. He didn't need to see the red mess Ida had made by the split-rail fence.

He was careful walking up the rotting porch steps. A green metal chair by the front door stopped him in his tracks. It was Ida's. He could picture her there. Staring down the hill. Silent. Lost in her own world. Her ghost was probably there now, rocking in the metal chair with a cigarette in her hand, asking him, *"Were you surprised with my little secret, Benny boy?"*

Ben ducked under the yellow tape and stepped into the house. Out of habit, he removed his shoes in the entryway. He inhaled the familiar odor—the scent of rosemary, cumin, smoke, and mildew bleeding from the walls. He hoped to find something in the house that would make sense of what she'd done. Something that only he would understand. Maybe.

The small entry table held a pair of bifocals, a few ballpoint pens, and a pinecone. Everything in the family room was how he remembered it. Wendall's brown chair sat in front of the television. Ida's was next to it. The room was an organized mess: VHS movies stacked in corners, hunting magazines piled beneath windows, ceramic cardinals clumped in curio cabinets. He had to remind himself that they were dead. It seemed any second that Wendall might come down the stairs and ask what the score of the Celtics game was—and they'd watch it together until he drifted off to sleep in his brown recliner while Ida did her crosswords at the kitchen table.

He walked into the kitchen. Appliances crowded out the counter space—toaster, bread box, coffee maker, and flour and sugar containers. It was clean. Ida always kept a clean kitchen. But there was nothing unusual. There was nothing in the dining room. Literally. It was never used. He looked up at the carpeted stairs. If Ida left a message, it would be up there. Normally, he took the stairs two at a time. Not today. He took them slow. The walls were lined with pictures. He studied each one. He was the star of the stairwell. Framed school pictures. Team sports pictures. Ben with a trout. A merit-badge ceremony. The last photograph at the top of the stairs was his graduation from business school—a picture of the three of them.

There were no baby pictures.

He opened the door to the spare bedroom. A cheap blue comforter was spread over the bed. There was no pillow. A monstrous black vacuum tilted in the corner against the floral wallpaper. He couldn't remember anyone that had ever spent the night in this room. No guests or relatives or friends from out of town.

Ben stepped into his old room with its ribbons and plaques, trophies and awards. He had done nothing exceptional to earn them—it was the shit they gave to everybody, but he hadn't cared. It was cool to get a trophy. Over his bed were certificates push-pinned into the drywall: math Olympics, distinguished honor roll, Vermont Mountain Survival, Pro-Marksman. He opened the bureau drawers. Empty. The closet was piled with old sweaters, sneakers, a couple of junior high track ribbons. He retraced his steps—lifting the corner of his Celtics comforter, looking under the bed. It was exactly as he'd left it.

Ben opened the metal drawers of the cabinet in the small office across the hall. He flipped through five generations of appliance manuals. He rifled through another drawer packed with pink receipts in manila envelopes, at least a decade old. The large bottom drawer held junk: tape, batteries, screwdrivers, scissors. He made a cursory check of the hall closet. Nothing.

It was becoming clear—Ida had nothing to say to him.

He walked down the hall to the master bedroom. The queen-sized bed was made up, an Amish quilt folded at the foot. A small TV with rabbit ears sat on an unstable metal stand. A chipped laminate dresser hunkered against the wall. Over the bed, Wendall had nailed a macrame owl with googly eyes. Across a sea of rust-colored carpet, a pencil drawing hung on the wall. It was of Ida. She was in her twenties. It wasn't like the portraits in Kimberly Hancock's library. A master did not create this. It was amateurish. But Ben had spent countless hours staring at it. Not because it was a drawing of Ida. But because of who she'd said the artist was.

"Your real father drew that."

Ben simmered at the drawing. *Real* father? The only real father he had was Kimberly Hancock's husband, Roger—now deceased. The DNA test proved it. So, everything Ida had told him—it was all bullshit. The asshole who drew this garbage picture wasn't his father. Why did she do that to him? He was just a little kid.

Lying motherfucker.

He punched the picture—smashing the thin glass and exploding the wooden frame off the wall. It landed broken on the carpet. There was nothing in Vermont for him. Coming here had been a mistake. The house was toxic. He needed to get out. And he was about to. That's when he saw it—the corner of a blue card.

Ida had hidden it in the picture's frame. Something she'd intended no one to ever see. Ben was reaching for it when he heard a voice yell from below the stairs.

"Hello? Boy? You heya?"

There was only one person who still called him "boy." Ben walked out of the master bedroom and looked down the carpeted stairs. Ray Buckmeier stood on the entry mat with his wool hat under his armpit, his greased brown coveralls tucked into black rubber boots. Ray was Wendall's best friend. The next-door neighbor everyone in town called Truckmeier on account of the rusting vehicles half buried in his front yard.

"Hey, Mr. Buckmeier."

The man shook Ben's hand without looking him in the eye. He

spoke toward the wall with a nasal wheeze. "Gawdawful, Boy. Just gawdawful."

"Yeah."

"You holdin' up?"

"Doing my best."

Truckmeier nodded. Ben invited him into the family room.

"Which one is Wendy's?"

Ben pointed to Wendall's brown recliner. Truckmeier stared at its emptiness for a while before wiping the seat of his coveralls and low- ering himself into the sofa next to it. Wendall and his friend had spent decades at the property line, rolling their own cigarettes and talking about nothing—and everything. They were full-blooded Vermonters, and they could say most of what needed to be said with an "ayuh."

Ben Danvers waited, because in this part of the world, men with something to say didn't leap into it the way they did down in Boston; they didn't raise their voice with blubbery nonsense or fill a conversa- tional pause with jabber. The men and woman in northern New England took their time warming up to what needed to be said. They thought about their words—even if they weren't always big words—with patience and in a careful, neighborly way, and when they'd gotten out what needed letting out, it was time to move along.

"Coffee?" asked Ben.

"If it's no trouble."

He prepared it while Truckmeier flipped through Wendall's old *Field & Stream* magazines.

Ben had an odd realization. This was the first time he'd ever seen Truckmeier in the house. He was Wendall's oldest friend and had never been allowed in. Ida refused visitors.

Truckmeier thanked Ben for the coffee and sipped as he looked around the room. "This from the can?"

"Folgers."

The old-timer nodded. It was a throat-clearing question. As was the query about who would plow the drive now. Ben waited, because there was a reason Truckmeier had walked through the deep snow to be here. It took a few more minutes for him to end his preamble. He looked over at the recliner.

"So, Ida done it?"

Ben nodded.

"Bitch." He was silent for a moment and added, "Wendy deserved better."

"Yup."

Truckmeier nodded and wiggled his toes in his stocking feet. "You go down to DC? You meet the princess yet?"

"Yup."

"Politics aren't my porridge, but I'm glad for her." Truckmeier looked up at the ceiling and shook his head. "You know, this is the strangest goddamned thing that's ever happened in Rutland County—I can tell you that."

For the first time since he'd walked through the door, the man looked him in the eyes. Whatever needed to be said, it was rounding the turn and heading for home.

"Tilda never trusted her. Not after."

"After?"

"I feel damn bad about this, boy. I shoulda said something to Wendy. Was going to but—couldn't bring myself to it."

"What?"

"Ida entertained a man from out of town every summer when you and Wendy were gone camping. I asked him once if Ida had any brothers. I was careful about it—didn't let on about the visitor. Wendy said she didn't have family. I dropped it and didn't think no more on it. The next year, Tilda sees he's there again. Stayed all day."

Ben squinted, trying to work through who'd be at the house. He couldn't come up with anyone. Ida didn't allow visitors.

"So, the next summer, when you both went north, I set up the game camera in the tree line. Pointed her right at the porch steps. Same guy came back. Got a picture of him."

Ben leaned forward. "And?"

"That photo sat on the counter most of the summer. Waitin' for me to make up my mind to show Wendy. Couldn't bring myself to it. Thought it weren't none of my business to be meddlin' with his marriage and that, maybe it weren't nothin' he needed to be concerned with." He sighed and spoke more softly. "And then she went and killed him. If I'd said somethin'...." Truckmeier looked down at the carpet and pinched his nose. "Ayuh."

"Not your fault."

"Maybe. Maybe not."

Ben got up and walked into the kitchen. He fiddled with the cof-
feepot and ran the water in the sink until Truckmeier had enough time
to find his sea legs.

"You still have that picture?" Ben asked.

"Oh, doubt it. Maybe in the cellar but there's little chance findin'
her down there without an excavatah."

Ben pulled a sticky paper off the pad next to the yellow wall phone.
He wrote his phone number in small block letters.

"I'd really appreciate if you could…."

"I'll look for the picture. I promise it, boy."

"Thanks, Mr. Buckmeier. Text it. You know how to do that?"

He held up his old phone. "The flipper hasn't let me down yet."

With that, Ben realized the odds of getting a text from Truckmeier
were very long indeed.

"Refill?" Ben asked, knowing the answer.

"Nope. Came by to say my sympathies. They're from the both of
us. Tilda told me to give you a hug—but if it's all the same…."

Truckmeier held the handshake and looked Ben in the eye. "Boy,
you oughta know something, and I don't know who else would tell
ya but me. To Wendy, you *were* his son. As real as if you were blood.
And I know that for a fact."

The old-timer was polite enough to turn toward the door and pull on
his black boots while Ben unbuckled his lip. The old man waved over
his shoulder and said his goodbye and trudged back across the granite
steppers toward the snowy tree line where two old friends would never
again roll their own cigarettes and talk about nothing in particular.

27

Emma Noble boarded the RS-DP Bus on Pennsylvania Avenue and smiled her way down the aisle. She caught herself on the gray bar as the bus lurched toward North Rosslyn. It was a short trip—just across the river. Her afternoon had opened up. The meeting with the associate director had been pushed back—maybe later tonight, possibly tomorrow. She scooched into a row and put her hand on the back of the seat. Her finger sank into gum. She pulled away, but it was fresh enough to cling and stretch. It became a six-finger extraction. Emma held her sticky hands out in front of her until a woman across the aisle came to the rescue with a clump of antiseptic wipes.

She'd spent the morning wandering the J. Edgar Hoover Building. There were all sorts of things to see. But not much to do. She was waiting to hear from Briar, but he hadn't answered her text yet, so she'd eaten lunch alone in the cafeteria. She was an enthusiastic over-listener. That's how she learned about the GSA storage facility in North Rosslyn. If the women behind her were to be trusted, the building was more than a motor pool. It was a repository of used furniture that was free to employees with a government ID. Apparently, it was mostly desks and office chairs, but one lady said she got a great lamp and had her eye on a couch. Emma had experienced all the museums and attractions in the nation's capital. Shopping at the *"We Don't Take Money"* store seemed like a fine way to kill some time. And she was not deterred by the fact that she'd flown in from New York City and had no means to bring anything larger than a pencil holder back with her. No, Emma was a woman in her twenties. It was free shit. There was always a way.

. . .

Ben poured Truckmeier's coffee down the sink. Through the kitchen window he saw six cars parked off the highway, taking pictures up the hill at the two-story yellow colonial. He scrubbed out the coffee mugs and dried them with the raggedy blue towel hanging off the oven handle. He walked up the stairs. Daggers of glass lay in the rust-red carpet. The corner of the blue card peeked from under the frame's black mounting board. He reached and pulled it free.

It was a florist's card, thin and yellowed at the corners. He flipped it over. *Rosen's Flowers, Rome, NY* was scrolled at the top in thin cursive. Whoever sent the flowers had written the message in ink with a neat, careful hand.

> *Dear Ida,*
> *I will miss you at Summerton*
> *Your Friend,*
> *A*

It was an oddly impersonal note—the kind of thing a graduating eighth-grader writes to an underclassman in the back of a yearbook before summer break. But this was anything but impersonal to Ida. She had kept it. *No, hidden it.* It had meaning to her. Ben looked at the drawing of Ida on the carpet. She had lied to him and said that "A" was her real father. There was no reason to do that. Unless it mattered to *her*—deeply.

He returned downstairs with the card that might hold the key to unlocking Ida's past. He turned on his phone. It was almost out of juice. He hadn't thought to bring a charger.

Ben opened his messages and cringed. There were two screenfuls of text notifications. Kate was worried about him. There were also messages from an unknown number that he guessed was Riley McGraw. He was in deep shit for running out of the interview. He knew what he *should* do. Call. Right away. Apologize. It was the only mature decision. Face the music. Ben put the phone on the table and stepped

118

away from it. He couldn't do it. He knew it was childish. And, yes, he understood the longer it took to call, the worse it was going to be. It had been eight hours since he ran away—and that was a long time for Kate to worry. Soon. He'd call soon.

He opened his search browser and typed *Rosen's Florist in Rome, NY*. There were no shops with that name in upstate New York. He typed *Summerton*. Ben's thumbs raced through the results. Summerton Hardware, Summerton Stop & Go, Sandy's Summerton Oysters—all in New Jersey. Ben tried the entire phrase I WILL MISS YOU AT SUMMERTON, and pages of obituaries for people with the last name Summerton filled his screen.

Summerton Rome New York

Ben had to work his way through pop-up ads for New York Mortuary Services, Tipton Headstones, and Mr. Stiffies All-Natural Salve. Scrolling beyond the nonsense was something that caught his attention. It was a land acquisition notice from 2015 in Westonberry, New York, for a property abutting the former Summerton Academy. He typed *Summerton Academy Westonberry New York*. There was nothing. Dead end.

He got up and looked out the kitchen window. A news van had joined the cluster of cars parked off the highway at the bottom of the drive. They were taking pictures and it gave him an idea. He clicked on image search and studied every *Summerton Academy Westonberry New York* picture on the first page of results. Most photos showed teenagers smiling in front of brick buildings. The last photograph was a small green building with a wraparound porch. He spread his fingers across the screen. A sign hung over the door: Established 1971, *El Mallumo—Lumo*.

Ben's heart raced. He didn't need to look up the translation. It was Esperanto. "Out of Darkness—Light."

Esperanto had been Ben and Ida's language. When he was eleven, she'd told him about Esperanto. A month later, he surprised her with a handmade Mother's Day card that he'd translated out of a library book. There were very few things that made Ida smile. The card was one of them—and that was all the encouragement Ben needed. In the coming years, he found more Esperanto resources, and studied

119

in his spare time. It had connected him to Ida like nothing else. They would speak Esperanto across the dinner table just to annoy Wendall; sometimes she'd belly-laugh. There was no doubt—Ida had attended this school. With "A."

Ben looked at the link under the picture. It was attributed to Albanyinquirer.com. Ben clicked through. The page linked to the newspaper's home page. He tried their online search tool, but it was a dead end. The *Albany Inquirer* was an hour and a half from the house. It was 3 PM. If he left now, he could be there before they closed.

The phone went to black. The battery died in Ben's hand.

He drove the Land Rover down the hill. The gawkers stood by their cars at the end of the driveway, filming him on their phones. The camera from the news van followed his progress. Ben slowed and faced the cameras. He waved and gave a thumbs-up, then peeled away. In minutes, Kate would learn that he was in Vermont and doing fine; now, worry wouldn't get in the way of her disappointment and anger. He turned south on Route 7 and sped toward Albany repeating the phrase *El Mallumo—Lumo*.

Out of darkness—light.

28

As far as tourist attractions went, the Marriner S. Eccles Federal Reserve Building in Washington, DC, wasn't much of a money-maker. The last time the public took notice of the white, neoclassical building was in 1937 when Franklin Roosevelt dedicated it. But, if the Apostle Paul was correct and money was the root of all evil, then the Eccles Building was Satan's favorite flower. Behind the heavy iron doors, bespectacled economists pored over data and figures and tables and forecasts. Those quiet folk in worsted wool controlled the money supply for the United States. Their technical decisions on rates and bond purchases quaked Wall Street, sent aftershocks through world currencies, and made it possible for a young couple in Toledo, Ohio, to afford a home loan. Or not.

They were the Federal Open Market Committee, and they were in session. The Board of Governors and the twelve presidents of the Federal Reserve took positions around an oval table under an ornate chandelier. They argued about FDIC premium costs and overnight RRPs in civil tones—barely above a whisper. Behind them, in comfortable upholstered chairs, their staff made notes and tapped through complicated spreadsheet calculations, while in the marble hallways, walking two by two, armed agents from Federal Protective Services kept them safe.

Some of the staff were not pounding through complicated math problems. They were watching the stock market on their phones. Trading had halted yesterday after the New York attack. This morning

121

the markets had opened lower, tripping a 15-minute circuit breaker. The last few hours had seen another 5% drop.

The economists around the table didn't concern themselves with one day's movement in the market. The country and the world relied on them to be a steady hand—the unrattled, unshakeable adults above breaking-news and sniping politics. They were the last reliable American institution free from partisanship. And most agreed that, as long as the current chairperson was at the helm, the rich on both sides of the aisle were going to be just fine.

There was one staff member, a woman in the corner of the room with large, black-framed glasses, who was not punching numbers into spreadsheets or looking at the stock market. No one paid much attention to her. In a room full of introverts, she was invisible. Under her professional dark jacket, her heart was racing. Today was her last day. Then again, it was everyone in the room's last day.

The chairperson led them to the next agenda item. Small talk brushed around the woman in the black glasses. She paid no notice. Her chest thumped in time with the ticks of the second hand. She looked down at her phone. If the clock at the back of the room was correct, she'd be getting a text right now. The long wait was over. It would say one of two words: "yes" (it was a go) or "no" (postponed).

Her phone buzzed.

She glanced to both sides, making sure no one could see. She opened the message. It was a cartoon of a black ball. With a sparking fuse. The moron had sent her a bomb emoji.

The woman put her purse over her shoulder and slid her laptop under the chair. She made no excuse for leaving, and no one noticed her. She walked toward the door, fighting an urge to glance back for one last look at her colleagues.

At 3:35, the ranking FPS agent in the Eccles Building marched into the FOMC meeting flanked by two muscular agents who moved to the back corners of the room—feet shoulder width apart, heads on a swivel.

"Ladies and gentlemen, we are under Bomb Threat Protocol. Please rise. Bring your credentials. Leave your personal items. Follow the agents down stairwell #3. If anyone needs help, raise your hand."

All eyes looked to the chairperson. He pushed himself from the table and ran his hand through his wavy, gray hair. He gave them the "it-is-what-it-is" shrug.

"This real?" he whispered to the agent in charge.

"Phone-in threat. We'll clear the building. Try to get you back in a couple hours."

Armed agents guided the officials to the basement and through a rarely used hallway that led to a tight passageway under the street. Guards unlocked a steel door and the members and their staff entered a dimly lit concrete garage waiting for a Homeland Security bus to take them to a secondary location.

• • •

Emma Noble walked off the city bus toward the GSA storage facility in North Rosslyn, Virginia. The place was massive, and, maybe, filled with lots of free goodies. Her phone dinged with a text.

-*Where are you?*

It was Briar. She told him.

-*Meeting w/ AD rescheduled. Forty-five minutes.*

Damn. The next bus wasn't coming for another hour. After a few ripe expletives, Briar agreed to drive four miles out of his way to pick her up—after he finished eating his ham sandwich.

Emma hung up and watched a white Homeland Security bus speed out of the concrete building, its lights flashing, noting that the vehicle was in a hell of a rush.

She stood by a green commercial van, checking her social-media accounts, chuckling at clever memes sent by friends. Hearing footsteps, she looked up again and smiled at a bug-eyed man in a mechanic's uniform strolling out of the building.

• • •

The economists didn't have to wait long for their rescue. The white Homeland bus met them in the basement. They boarded quickly. It glided up the cement ramp toward daylight. Security sunk three bollards into the ground at the exit and waved them through. The bus turned right

123

on C Street between two police escorts on the way to an undisclosed location. It motored toward the E Street Expressway Tunnel. The men and women in charge of overseeing America's money supply sat quietly, drumming their fingers against their thighs and staring out the window.

The woman in the large, black-framed glasses closed the last stall of the women's room on the second floor of the Eccles Building and walked to the row of sinks. She balanced her handbag on the edge of the counter. She unwrapped the silver foil from a stick of gum. Her hands were shaking. She turned on the faucet and dabbed her neck and face, refusing to look at her reflection in the mirror. She ripped a paper towel from the dispenser, dried herself, and opened the door into the marble hallway and acted just as surprised to see the bomb squad as they were to see her.

29

Amy Munson needed a victory. And she was driving fast to see that she got it. The BMW was a wedding present from her new husband. She didn't need it. What she *really* needed was the acceptance of his daughter. The angry eight-year-old was stubbornly set against her and "hated her so much." Amy had made every known insta-mom mistake, and had, maybe, invented some new ones. Every error sounded the elimination buzzer: "You're not my real Mom."

Amy Munson needed a victory. And if not for the dipshit in Tallahassee, she would have had it. She'd made a good plan. Her stepdaughter was acting in a school play. The drama club was giving the kids a celebratory party afterwards. Amy had jumped on the opportunity to volunteer. She dismissed any offer of help from the other moms. The party would rock and her new eight-year-old daughter would see how cool she could be.

She turned on to 19th Street. The party tub of lemon gelato was dripping condensation in the backseat. Bubbles of yellow were forming under the lid.

Things had not gone to plan. A work emergency. The asshole in Tallahassee had offended the company's most important client. It had taken most of the day to untwist the damage. Amy had already missed the play. But she could recover, as long as she could get to the school in time to put up the silver decorations, the balloons, and the comedy/tragedy masks before the bell rang.

She raced down 19th Street toward the E Street intersection. The light ahead was green. One hundred yards away. She slammed the pedal down and made a foxhole prayer to whatever gods were in charge of streetlights that they stay green for another six seconds. She needed this goddamn victory.

The light held. She was going to make it. As she turned the wheel, she caught the police lights blowing through the red. She slammed the brakes. Her tires squealed. The BMW fishtailed. Solid German engineering kept her from crashing into the cruiser. She waited for the small parade—a white Homeland Security bus and another police car tailgating behind.

She didn't need this shit.

She followed the procession. The little caravan of lights was in no rush. Amy looked at her speedometer. They were rolling ten miles under the speed limit. She lifted her eyes into the rearview mirror. A stream of yellow was running down the side of the gelato tub. *Please don't take the turn for E Street Expressway.*

The three-vehicle impediment did exactly what Amy had begged it not to do. They turned toward the E Street Expressway tunnel. She looked at the digital clock on the dash and slammed her palm against the wheel.

• • •

Arnau Farre wore a gray windbreaker, blue jeans, and a black cap. He sat on a bench on the grassy berm of a small park that faced the on-ramp of the E Street Expressway. He dipped his hand into a brown bag, throwing breadcrumbs sidearm into a flock of pigeons. The birds had multiplied in the past hour, strutting around the bench. The park wasn't a particularly bucolic setting to relax and enjoy nature. Arnau looked over his left shoulder. The lights of a police car crested the hill. A large white bus emerged behind it. He did not reach into the bag for more seed. Instead, as the bus motored into the expressway tunnel, his hand moved inside the pocket of his gray windbreaker.

• • •

Amy Munson had to pass. It was a dumb move, but she needed a victory. Hell with it. If it came, she could live with the ticket. The BMW darted across the double yellow and she hit the gas and passed the first police car. She pulled alongside the bus. The windows were tinted black. She felt a fleeting curiosity about who might be on board, but she shifted. The BMW roared over the speed limit, passing the cops and tearing through the short tunnel.

She would later tell investigators that the only thing she remembered hearing was a CRACK, like lightning when it rips through the sky—dangerously close. And then her windows exploded. The BMW seized when the tires shredded—sending the vehicle tumbling side over end, until the new car skidded to its death four hundred yards past the tunnel.

· · ·

The pigeons exploded into the sky. An inferno of shrapnel burst through the entrance of the E Street Expressway Tunnel, incinerating vehicles in its path. There had once been a fine city road with planters in the median that crossed above the tunnel. It was gone. Now, black smoke and flame poured from the hole like the entrance to hell. Arnau Farre walked slowly from the scene, melting into a sea of bystanders rushing to witness the horror.

· · ·

The BMW landed right side up. Amy Munson had a gash over her eye. She was alive. The inside of the car was covered in glass and lemon gelato. She sat on the brown, cold, grassy berm—dazed. After paramedics had checked her out, a reporter stuck a microphone in her face. She spoke into the camera, and in answering the man's questions, she mentioned her stepdaughter's name three times. The interview played on the national cable news network all evening. She watched it from the couch in her living room, her eight-year-old daughter curled into her bruised ribs.

Amy Munson had her goddamned victory.

127

30

Emergency vehicles soared past the gray Suburban. A fire engine. And another. Then police. Lots of cops.

Emma looked over at Briar. "What the hell?"

He nodded, checked the side mirror, and followed the sirens. They turned a corner and saw thick black smoke rising in distance. There was really only one excuse for missing a meeting with the associate director. This was it.

The twilight sky flickered with bright flashes of red and blue. Onlookers packed behind barricades in the road and on the sidewalks, trying to get a look at what had happened. Emma and Briar had to push their way through the crowd. When they did, they came face to face with the charred husks of smoldering commuter cars. Black, acrid smoke rolled out of the entrance of the E Street Tunnel. Emma's eyes watered. She pulled the collar of her blue windbreaker over her nose to fight the nauseating stench—burned-rubber, with a hint of short ribs.

The scene swarmed with fire trucks spraying water into the smoking debris. First responders in yellow coveralls looked into burned vehicles for signs of life. Unlike the Mansion Media Building, this wasn't a rescue operation. This was an investigation. Emma knew there wouldn't be many survivors. Certainly, none in the tunnel. ATF agents, explosive specialists, forensic chemists, bomb technicians, and engineers were joining the frenzy. To the untrained eye it might have seemed a chaotic response. It wasn't. It was an investigative ant hill, each expert crawling the scene with a specific, urgent duty.

Briar left Emma's side and wandered into the fray seeking information. When he came back, there was a twinkle in his eye. Emma was learning to recognize the look—in emergencies, the older agent came alive. He told her the smoldering black spot in the tunnel had been a white Homeland Security bus loaded with VIPs. That's all he knew. It was another attack. And somebody'd had the balls to do it within five blocks of the White House.

Every bomb had a unique signature. The most sophisticated labs in the country were within walking distance of the attack, but it would still take a day or more to decipher the handwriting. That didn't mean Emma couldn't make an educated guess. Detonation velocity was measured in feet per second. A gas explosion in a home was low-velocity—the debris stayed on the lawn. This was no gas explosion. Judging by the ATF agents collecting evidence in the distance, this had been high-velocity. Probably some kind of plastic explosive. Twelve ounces of Semtex had blown up a plane over Lockerbie, Scotland. Based on the destruction she was looking at, the attackers had used at least that much on the bus.

Mobile generators hummed to life, flooding the scene with construction lights. Briar walked into a small park and stood on a paint-chipped bench to survey the scene. Emma followed. Information was coming in random, unverifiable bursts. She saw a man with an I'm-in-charge face flanked by four agents in ATF ballistic vests. He'd know.

"Excuse me, sir. Do we have intel on the bus victims?"

The guy didn't acknowledge her, but one of his agents peeled off. He answered her question like he was giving a football score. Emma wasn't entirely sure what the Federal Reserve did. But she knew they were the people behind the curtain. They had something to do with money. *Money.*

Libereco Pensi Mem (Freedom to think for yourself) had been written in blood on the wall of the suite at the Emerald Point Hotel. The Mansion Media Building represented an attack on the first pillar of the *Tri Kolonoj de Libereco*. The second pillar was freedom from money. There was no bigger money target than the Federal Reserve.

But there was something different about this attack. It was less lethal in terms of body count, but far scarier. It was clear that the terrorists were capable of more than brute force. The Mansion Media Building was a fixed, known structure. It required no special intelligence to attack it. Whoever was responsible for this bombing had access to classified information. They knew bomb-threat protocols and probably much more.

"I've been thinking," she said, looking up at Briar standing on the bench. "Maybe three ways somebody does this: One, a suicide bomber—either on the bus or driving up next to it. Two, it was planted in the tunnel and set remotely."

"Three?"

"It was already on the bus."

Briar nodded and waited for her to continue.

"If it's the first or second, there's nothing much we can do here—"

"Noble, are you anywhere close to the punchline?"

"Before you picked me up, I saw a Homeland bus racing out of the GSA lot. I'll bet money it's the one that exploded in the tunnel. I think we should get back over to North Rosslyn and check it out."

Briar weighed the idea, then reached into his windbreaker and pulled out his car keys. When the vehicle pulled into the GSA facility, Emma knew something had happened there; three police cars and an EMS ambulance were parked outside the building. Four cops were huddled together talking by a side door. There was no urgency to their movement. Whatever had happened, this was clean up. Emma was first out of the car. The cops turned and looked her up and down, then nodded at Briar like he was a lucky guy.

"Your friends are in there," said a cop, thumbing toward the door.

"I don't have friends," Briar said.

The guy made a sour face and told him more explicitly that two FBI agents were inside.

Emma asked, "What's going on?"

"A security guard was murdered inside. He was dead when we got here. Bled out. Nothing we could do for him."

Emma looked above the door at the tinted dome camera pointing at the parking lot. It would have an unobstructed view of who came and went. The cop seemed to read her mind.

"Agents are checking the video."

The door opened a crack. An officer hustled over to pull it wide for the EMS team. The gurney bounced and clanged over the threshold. FBI agents followed the stretcher out the door. They nodded to Briar, then looked at Emma. Up and down. It wasn't subtle. She watched them share a look—like high school boys ogling in a hallway. Choice words were forming in her head, but theirs came quicker. They yelled and reached for their guns—

"Hands!"

Emma stared back. *What?* She looked at Briar, who was equally confused.

"Hands! Now! Fingers laced behind your head."

"What the—"

She raised her arms. One of them stepped to her side and ripped the Glock from her hip.

Briar said, "You're making a mistake."

"Don't think so," muttered the agent with Emma's gun.

"Pretty sure you are," she told him.

"Hands behind your back."

Briar stepped forward.

An agent with a tight grip on his service weapon blocked his path. "Stay back."

Briar put his palms in the air and let them go about their business. Emma's wrist was pulled off her head and shoved behind her back, a metal cuff snapped over it. He repeated the movement with her other hand.

"Seriously, what the hell are you doing?" asked Emma.

"Taking you in."

"For?"

Emma thought maybe she didn't hear him correctly. He repeated it for her again while pushing her head into the backseat of the police car.

Murder?

She pressed the side of her face into the cage divider to see what was happening outside. Briar was talking with the agents. Emma leaned back and rolled her shoulders, hoping to relieve the pain in her wrists and hands. She tilted her head back. The only thing she could see through the back window was the dome camera above the door.

She had just been there, waiting for Briar to pick her up. Her face would have been on the tape. They'd see that all she was doing was just standing there, waiting. It didn't make sense. She had just been standing by the green commercial van with the mechanic. And then, suddenly, it did make sense. Her head dipped into her chest.

She was in deep shit.

31

The Land Rover rolled into the parking lot, its headlights illuminating a painted sign poking from the snow. *Albany Inquirer; Truth, Commitment, Virtue*. It was a low-slung brick building with a flat roof. In the 1950s, the *Inquirer* was the paper that landed on every doorstep. These days, it was Albany's fourth favorite newspaper. Ben Danvers parked against a snowbank in front of a hedge that hadn't been trimmed in years. The cement path from the parking lot was cracked and out of level, but the lights were still on, and that was all he cared about. He entered and a bell jangled above the door. The interior reminded Ben of his vet's office—piddle-proof linoleum floor with yellow plastic chairs.

"Yeah?" said the receptionist, looking over her sandwich.

"I was hoping—"

"If you want to put in a classified, we do that online now."

"No. I'm not here for that."

"Who do you need?"

"I have a question."

She took a bite off the corner of her sandwich. "What kind?"

"I guess it's complicated," he said.

She took another bite and nodded. "Yeah, well, that's too bad. Everyone here's an idiot. Except Barney. He's just a prick."

The receptionist looked down at the novel on her lap. Ben waited by the desk. After a minute, she raised her eyebrows like it surprised her that he was still there. "You can wait over there. He's in a meeting. Not promising he'll see you, though."

Ben sat on a plastic chair and wondered what he needed to ask. *I'd like to speak to the person in charge of putting your paper's name under images on the internet, please?* He picked up today's issue of the *Inquirer*. It was thin.

There was a noise at the door. An orange-jacketed girl was having a tough time pulling the door handle while balancing a tray of drinks in one hand and two fast food take-aways in the other. A white Starbucks bag was clenched in her teeth, bouncing off her chin. Ben opened the door and she rushed to the front desk to put down her baggage. She handed the receptionist a cola.

"You're late. Barney came out twice looking for his food."

The girl unzipped her orange jacket. She turned and thanked Ben for his help. Her full cheeks were rosy with the cold. She leaned over the reception counter.

"I'm done being the Door Dash bitch; they can kiss my—"

She turned around slowly. And stared.

"Are you the Hancock kid?" She walked closer to him. "You are. Aren't you? Benjamin Hancock, right? What the hell are *you* doing *here?*"

It struck him that rushing to a newspaper looking for help had been a terrifically bad idea.

The receptionist took another bite. "He has a question, but they're in a meeting."

"You've been waiting? We made *you* wait?"

Ben got up. "I should go."

She rushed him. "No! I'm Tasha. Please follow me."

"You know Barney's waiting for his food...."

Tasha tilted her head up at the ceiling and swore under her breath. She looked at the bags and drinks on the counter. "I need you to stay right here," she said, pumping her palms. "Bethany don't let him leave. Don't leave. Please. Don't leave. One minute."

Tasha took to the hallway with her bags, spilling cola over the linoleum as she ran. She was back in less than a minute. She inhaled deeply, then swept the hair from her cheek with her index finger. "Please follow me to my office, Mr. Hancock."

"It's Danvers."

Her office was the size of a walk-in closet. The tiny desk was covered with papers. A photograph of a cat stared from a silver frame

133

by her computer screen. There was only one chair. And they were both staring at it.

"Let me get another. Have a seat. I keep Pop Tarts in the top drawer if you're…. Why am I offering you Pop Tarts? Sorry. Okay, so—I'll be right back. I'm going to close the door. Stay right here. Sit, please."

Ben thought of Riley McGraw's commandment: Never talk to the press. *Never.* Not much gray in that. But the *Albany Inquirer* could hardly be considered "the press." And Tasha was anything but intimidating. Ben looked at the wall. Her diploma was thumb-tacked to it—so fresh it hadn't even made it into a frame. He could handle this. Ben heard a clack-clack sound in the hallway.

"Tasha!" boomed a far-off voice, "that's my chair. Bring it back."

"Get your own goddamned chair. I'm in a meeting."

She struggled to get the big roller through the door. The wide arm-rests were the problem. She tilted the chair, trying to gently negotiate it through the door. When that didn't work, she put her weight behind it and forced it in. She flicked the hair from her face and lowered herself gently into the seat, their knees almost touching.

"So, how can I help you?"

"I'm trying to find information on a school in upstate New York called Summerton Academy. It's not there anymore."

Tasha listened as Ben explained what he'd found. She brought the image up on her computer, studying the link to the *Inquirer*. Ben was pleased with himself. It was just enough to get a search started, but not enough to reveal much else.

"Why is this important to you?"

"It's a little personal."

"How so?"

"Just something—"

"Does this involve your kidnapping?"

Ben shifted in his seat.

"It does, doesn't it?"

"You know what? This is a bad idea. I should head out."

"No! Don't go. You need answers. I'll do anything. I can help. Seriously, I'm the person. I'm *your* person. All I do is research. I spend all day in the records room. I'm the research queen."

"I don't know…."

"It'll be great. I promise."

Ben wavered. "None of this can be public."

Tasha took her time answering. Finally, she leaned forward. "Okay. But under one condition. You have to make a promise."

"What?"

"You have to promise to give Tasha Maidlow your first exclusive interview."

"Who's that?"

"Me."

"Well, that's really not my call."

"Wasn't it *you* that made the call to bail on Mattson & McCall this morning?"

Ben had no answer for that.

"I'll drop everything to help you. If you promise me the exclusive."

"Nothing gets out?"

"Nothing without your authorization. I promise—if you do."

Ben nodded. "If you can help me, I'll do it."

Tasha's eyes widened. She looked as if she was going to burst before gathering herself. "I'll get to work on it right away. Where are you staying?"

"I guess I'll find a hotel."

She shook her head. "No. You can't do that. They'll be all over you. That would be bad. Um, you can—" she hesitated, "use my apartment. It's just down the street."

"No. I can't."

"I live with my brother. Seriously, it's not a big deal. You should stay out of sight for a little while."

"Your brother isn't going—"

"My brother won't even know you're there. I doubt he even knows where *he* is most of the time."

Tasha scribbled her address on a piece of paper. She grabbed keys out of her purse. "Here's the one to my apartment. I have a cat. Do you mind feeding him? I don't trust Craig to do it. There's a can in the fridge, it's the one … it's the one with the cat on it. Shit, you know how to feed a cat. Here's my number. I'll be here all night if I have to. You can take my bedroom or sleep on the couch. Whatever you want."

"You sure? I don't—"

"Oh. I am *so* sure."

"Okay."

"Okay? You'll go?"

"Okay."

"Really? You're not going to ghost me?

"What's the cat's name?"

"Mr. Spock. Seriously? You'll go?"

Tasha was awkward, but sincere. He believed she'd keep her word. And keeping out of the public eye for a while seemed like a good idea. "How many scoops for Mr. Spock?"

She gave him the Vulcan salute.

"Two scoops it is."

32

Emma Noble sat handcuffed in the back of a police car for a half hour before a DC Bureau Supervisor showed up. The SUP entered the building with Briar and the other agents. Fifteen minutes later, he came out. The guy glanced into the police car and shook his head at Emma. She was escorted into the Hoover Building for an emergency meeting with a woman from the Office of Professional Responsibility. The woman had a lot of questions and every one of them led to the same conclusion—Emma Noble was guilty of being a dumbass.

For almost an hour now she'd been sitting alone in front of a glass conference table just down the hall from the associate director's office. Briar was in with the A.D.

Emma rubbed her wrists. They were sore. But it was the ache in her stomach that bothered her. She hadn't felt this anxious since waiting in the hospital for word on her mother's condition. The door opened. Briar sat down across from her. He said nothing. Instead, he stared while making steeples and churches out of his fingers. Tapping away. Staring at her. He cleared his throat, and whatever he was warbling up to, Emma was sure she didn't want to hear it.

"Windshield wiper. Very clever," he said.

"Don't."

"I didn't know you were such a good samaritan."

"Briar, really. Just don't."

"Apparently, they're having some trouble scrubbing your image out of the background of their Most Wanted picture."

Emma inhaled. She wasn't going to give him the satisfaction of crying.

"Personally, I think they should send out the one of you shaking his hand."

"Briar—"

Emma looked up to see A.D. William Monroe enter the room. He was tall and, at this late hour, his suit was still crisp—his tie knotted tight over his Adam's apple. This was the most senior FBI leader she'd probably ever meet. This wasn't how she wanted to be introduced. Not like this.

"We're waiting for one more," he said.

The A.D. was massaging the fingers of his left hand when the door opened for the last guest. Emma squeezed her eyes shut. *Oh god, no.*

His hair was redder than in the pictures. The ones that hung on every wall at Quantico. William Monroe's boss was a little a shorter than people might expect, but more imposing. The director of the Federal Bureau of Investigation, Fred O'Toole, didn't sit before speaking.

"I read your statement to OPR. I've seen the video. Not your finest hour, Special Agent Noble—not that you've had many hours with us. Tell me in your own words, please."

Emma felt dizzy. But she inhaled and tried to speak with authority.

"I was waiting outside the GSA facility in North Rosslyn for Briar Metcalf to pick me up for our appointment with the associate director."

"And why were you at the facility?"

"I understood there to be free furniture, sir."

Director O'Toole squinted at her. He raised his eyebrows and motioned for her to keep going.

"A gentleman came out of the secure facility—"

"And who did you assume this was, Agent Noble?"

"He was dressed as a mechanic. I was standing next to his green work van."

"And?"

"He'd locked his keys inside."

The director of the FBI put his index finger in the air and Emma halted.

"So, when you meet him, he's just planted a bomb on a Homeland Security bus and killed a guard inside the GSA facility. He's making his getaway and he's locked his keys in the van? Then, this idiot—who must have the worst luck of any criminal in recent history—finds a Special Agent with the Federal Bureau of Investigation standing beside his truck. And what is it that you do, Agent Noble?"

"I helped him unlock the vehicle, sir."

"By stripping the rubber off the windshield wiper and using the rod to gain access to the lock. Then, you shook hands with the suspect and waved goodbye as he made his escape?"

"Yes, sir. That's what happened." Emma kept her chin up, but she was crumbling on the inside.

Director O'Toole palmed the back of his neck. He walked behind his chair and leaned his arms into it. "You know what I'm doing after this meeting, Agent Noble?"

"No, sir."

"I need to update the president of the United States. Then, I need to call the president-elect. I'm not looking forward to telling them how one of my agents assisted in the escape of the nation's most-wanted terrorist. Or do you think I should skip that part?"

Emma stared back, hoping the question was rhetorical.

The director's face turned from pink to red. "We're up to our eyeballs in terrorists. I got agents working their asses off, and, single-handedly, you make us look like the gosh-darn Keystone Kops. And the Bureau has to take the heat for it."

William Monroe shifted uncomfortably in his seat. This was it. Emma was going to be fired from the FBI in her first week. Every agent started their career on probation—it wouldn't take much paperwork to get rid of her. She imagined telling her father. And Uncle Gunny. They'd be kind and consoling. But under their hugs and "don't worry about its" would be disappointment and pity. She would be a failure. Fired in shame by the director of the FBI.

Emma's face was burning red, but she looked the director in the eyes. She would face the firing squad without a blindfold.

He puffed his cheeks and stared at the carpet for a while before speaking. "If not for two considerations, your FBI adventure would be over. First, Agent Metcalf has made persuasive arguments about your conduct in your first few days of service. He says that you show the qualities and competence found in the best of us and that you deserve a second chance. That about right, Agent Metcalf?"

Briar nodded at the director.

139

"The second consideration is personal. I won't go into the details, but I owe your father a debt. You can tell him this clears it." The director put his hand around the doorknob and looked at Emma. "Don't make me regret this."

Emma thanked Briar for what he said, then picked herself out of the chair and followed him to the elevator. Her hands were shaking. She shoved them in her pockets so he couldn't see. *Make the FBI proud. Make my father proud.* Those were the promises she made to herself on the day she graduated from the Academy. It took less than a week for her to fail. She put her back against the elevator as the doors closed. She shut her eyes and waited for the descent.

The elevator didn't drop. She opened her eyes to see Briar standing in front of her, his arms folded across his chest.

"Who's your father?"

"Not now."

"I want to know. Who is he?"

"Just press the button."

"He a spook?"

"He drives a pickup"

"And?"

"And he brews his own beer. And he hates the designated-hitter rule."

"I can find out."

"Fine. Whatever. Just press the button."

Emma bit into her lower lip. Her anger and self-hatred were turning into something else. Jet fuel. She balled her fists. She would find the bug-eyed asshole with the green van. No matter what.

33

"Eat shit, camper!"

Tasha's brother, Craig, threw his game controller at a couch cushion, then stomped down the hall.

Ben shifted his weight carefully. It was happening again. He closed his eyes. Never once had he thought about the guts of a beanbag. He'd learned from the rip in the red cover that beanbags were not self-explanatory. They were filled with white grains of something that he assumed was probably toxic to cats, and no matter how careful he was, they poured out of the rip every time he moved—then he would pick through the fibers of the shag carpet to find them and push them back into the hole. It was a Sisyphean effort, but there were only two choices—the beanbag or sharing the couch with half-naked Craig.

The blaring blasts of video warfare had subsided. It was a potty-break cease-fire. Ben got up and an army of white pellets spilled into the high pile carpet. He needed to call Kate. His phone was charging on the kitchen counter. Now. No excuses.

Craig walked back into the room, digging a finger into his navel. A Rorschach of drips darkened the crotch of his gray briefs. He inhaled a lung-full of bong smoke, then turned to Ben like a puffer fish. He declined the offer. And within seconds, the truce had ended. Gunfire once again ripped through the apartment and explosions detonated in surround-sound. It would be a tough place to make an apologetic phone call. Ben decided to send a text. A brief, vague text.

-I'm okay. Call tomorrow. Don't worry. Sorry.

It was more like a twentieth-century Western Union telegram. He was a dick for not walking outside and calling her. Kate deserved better. But he didn't want to face her disappointment and anger for running out of the studio and leaving her to fend off Riley McGraw and her staff alone. He pressed send. And turned off his phone. It was the day's last act of cowardice in a day already chock-full of them.

• • •

Arnau Farre relaxed in a wicker chair on a porch in Virginia. The outside lights were off. He sat in the dark listening to the snap of an American flag blowing stiffly in the night wind. He lit a cigarette. It was warmer here than what he was accustomed to. It felt like a mini vacation to sit outside in January and blow smoke at the moon. And, if not for the sounds of the television coming from inside, Arnau Farre might have been completely at peace. George was still wired from this afternoon's success and Arnau didn't have the patience to sit with him any longer.

He crossed his legs at the ankle and took a pull on the cigarette. The tough stuff was behind him. Others were handling what came next. There was only one thing left for him to do. It was not such a big thing to accomplish, but for Arnau, it was the most important work of his life—the fulfillment of Ida's last wish.

A secret. And a promise.

He reached for his wallet and pulled out the picture Ida had sent him a month ago. It was too dark to see. He walked to the window and held it in the television's light. You could tell just by looking at the young man he had been raised by a fine mother. The boy had a confident smile. He was looking forward to meeting him. Again.

The Father would be very angry. All his life, Arnau had obeyed his every command. But this was different. Benjamin Danvers was Ida's boy, and she'd commanded Arnau not to kill him. So it was just tough-tittie that the Father wanted him dead tomorrow. As of now, Arnau Farre was in the protection business.

He returned to the wicker chair. Where would they go? Maybe somewhere even warmer than Virginia. They'd have to stay hidden for a time—but not forever. He blew smoke at the flag, then flicked his ash over the porch rail. Wouldn't it be something if he and the boy could become friends? It wasn't such a crazy idea. They both loved Ida. They had that in common. Yes, he could see them becoming friends. But it might take some time. Benjamin would have to be convinced.

Beyond the fields, a great distance away, Arnau could see the soft white glow of a convenience store. Across the street was a train station. They sold duct tape in that store. He hoped they had zip ties, but he could manage without those. He could go right now and get the chore done. But the job wasn't urgent enough to interrupt his mini porch vacation.

It was a clear night. He looked up at the galaxy of stars. Ida and he had tried to count them one summer's night. They lay next to each other in dry grass by the edge of the lake while shores of peepers echoed around them. That was the night Ida had told him those weren't really stars at all. They were pinholes in a black curtain. When you died and got to the next place, you could put your eye up to the fabric and peer through—at the living. In her last letter, Ida had promised she would look for him every night.

Arnau walked off the porch and stood on the lawn. He tilted his head back and spread his arms wide. With a cigarette in his lip, he sent a wave up to her. She was smiling back.

He knew it.

DAY 4

34

It was midnight, but Emma Noble wasn't clock-watching. She sat in a cubicle in the J. Edgar Hoover Building, her hands flashing across the keyboard. She was alone. The overhead lights were off. Her face glowed in the blue light of her computer screen. A wax candle on the desk flickered in a silver tin. The thought of retreating to her hotel room never crossed her mind. Nor did sleep. She was focused on one thing—finding the location of the terrorist, George Engel.

The FBI was no longer looking for the green commercial van. They'd already found it—engulfed in flames under an overpass in Baltimore. That was six hours ago. George Engel had a good head start. The only lead Emma had was the security card he'd used to access the building. It was better than nothing. She drew a line down the center of a yellow legal pad and labeled each side—Body/Mind. She started on the left. There was no need to write down the description of his face—it was burned into her. They were similar in height—he might have had an inch on her. She wrote *6'1"* on the pad. He had a round face, but he wasn't overweight. *Solid- 215?* She rolled her memory back and forth. He wasn't an athlete. He was *slow*. And *beefy*.

She tapped her pen on the right side of the column. Emma had watched him walk out of the building. He'd just wired a bomb to a bus and killed a guard on federal property. But George Engel hadn't been in a panic. He didn't race out to make his escape. He strolled. Not a care in the world. And when he saw that he'd left his keys in the car, he didn't seem surprised—like that kind of shit was always happening

146

to him. Which was a good thing. Maybe George Engel was prone to making mistakes. Sloppy was good.

She flipped back a few pages and reread her notes. The most important piece of evidence she had was the fact that George Engel didn't break into the secure facility in North Rosslyn. He had used an active and authentic GSA card. It was no forgery. The PIN number connected to his identity.

That kind of ID required a lengthy application and intrusive background checks. It took months for a card to be issued. But not for George Engel. Someone had approved his security clearance on the same day he applied. It had taken Emma three days to get a library card. No one got vetted for security access that quickly. Which meant that George Engel had a high-level accomplice in government. Maybe more than one.

Emma pulled up his application on the screen. She made a note of the date. It was a couple months ago—second week of November. She chewed on her pen. George Engel's face was taking up most of her computer screen: stubby nose, big eyeballs. There was nothing particularly evil-looking about him. He was smiling. He had the kind of face you find behind a grill—rolling hot dogs, telling stories, and drinking Stag beer.

She typed her password into the Bureau's query system. Follow the money. It was a cliché because it was true. She defined the search by time and location—the Northeast region to include any purchases made in the past 48 hours. It was narrow, but she might get lucky. She leaned her head toward the glow of the wax candle burning in the silver tin. Hygge Wax. It smelled like home. She inhaled, and in the two minutes it took the computer to populate, it transported her back to her mother's kitchen.

The computer flashed the results. A George Engel from Paterson, NJ, bought a Whirlpool dishwasher from Best Buy yesterday. Another George Engel ate dinner at a Ruth's Chris in King of Prussia, PA, this evening. No hotels. No rental cars.

She instructed the computer to widen the search to purchases in the United States in the past six weeks from anyone with the name George Engel, Geo Engel, or G. Engel. She pressed "enter" and waited for the network to scour millions upon millions of consumer purchases that occurred in the height of the holiday season. A white progress bar appeared on the screen. It looked like it might take a while.

George Engel's application said he was from Chicago. She doubted that was true. There probably wasn't one factual thing in the entire application. She typed *George Engel Chicago* into the browser on her phone, not expecting to find anything useful. She opened the first result from Wikipedia. George Engel was a toy store owner in Chicago. He was born in 1836 and executed in 1887—by hanging. She expanded the page. He had led the Haymarket Riot. Eleven people died, including seven police officers. Before they dropped the scaffold, his last words were "Hurrah for Anarchy!"

She scribbled *"anarchists"* on the yellow pad and underlined it three times.

The progress bar on her computer moved to the fifty-yard line. When it finally reached the end-zone, it showed 1,732 results. She blew a gust of air and got to work sorting the information. Over the next hour, she weeded through purchases by people named Engel. There were four promising leads—all travel related and from the past week: Marriott Hotel in Richmond, Airbnb in Pennsylvania, airplane ticket from Phoenix to DC, rental car from JFK Airport.

The hotel in Richmond responded quickly with an imprint of the guest's license. It wasn't her bug-eyed George. The Airbnb wouldn't have information for her until morning. The airplane ticket's dates didn't match the attack. That left the rental car company. She looked at her watch. There were no All-Stars taking the field for rental car companies at this hour—and not so many during the day either. It took too long to get the night manager in New Jersey on the phone, but the guy tried to be helpful and promised to send the driver's license. She kept him on the line until it popped into her email.

There he was. George Engel. With a valid Illinois driver's license.

"I got it. *Please* tell me you have GPS locator on this vehicle?"

"Oh yeah. Sure do."

"Terrific. Tell me where the car is."

"I have no idea."

Emma dipped her head toward the candle, hoping it would offer her the calm she required.

"Let's start over. The vehicle has GPS locator?"

"Yes."

"Who can tell me where it is?"

"Do you want me to transfer you to corporate?"

It was an excruciating maze of transfers and holds to get the right person on the phone. And, after confirming that, yes, she was a real FBI agent, they gave Emma the current location of George Engel's rented purple Toyota Camry. It was on private property in Mountville, Pennsylvania. Emma researched the ownership and found that it had an Airbnb registry. No coincidences. Bingo.

Emma called the owner. She wasn't answering. The woman's social media account was very active—until today. For the first time in months, she hadn't posted. Emma had a bad feeling about that.

The cafeteria was empty. Emma refilled her venti cup of dark roast from the carafe. It was lukewarm. She didn't need the caffeine. Her heart was pumping just fine. The State Police in Pennsylvania were putting a team together, heading to Mountville. They'd call her when they had something. She was pouring her third cup of java when the phone buzzed.

Pennsylvania was calling.

35

"Just a sec." Arnau Farre turned on the bedside light and rubbed his eyes. "Okay. What's happening?" By the end of the next sentence, he was fully awake. "Say again. What do you mean 'the kid's missing'?"

Arnau hung up the phone, stopping himself from throwing it against the wall. He took his anger out on the lamp instead. How could Benjamin Danvers be missing? It was impossible. His face was all over the news. How could they have lost him? He sat at the end of the bed, staring at the broken shards on the floor. The entire organization would be searching for the kid. Their only priority now was to find him. And when they did, they'd be very efficient about killing Benjamin Danvers. None of his brothers or sisters would hesitate to put a bullet in the kid's skull. They would have eyes everywhere: on the Vermont house, on the Boston apartment, on the girlfriend in DC.

Arnau had lost control of the situation.

The only thing that mattered was protecting Ida's boy. For the first time, he doubted himself. He rubbed his palms over his whiskered face. He had never been prone to panic. There was no reason to start now. He just had to think it through. But the kid could be anywhere. Which meant Arnau needed to be on the move. If he guessed wrong, Benjamin was dead.

He strapped the green duffel across his back and left the bedroom. He ignored the sound of George's strangled snoring coming from down the hall. Arnau opened the front door, stepped off the farmer's porch, and walked down the long gravel driveway toward the convenience store by the train station. That's where he was going. He'd figure out the rest later. He headed toward town, not realizing that he had left something behind. Something he shouldn't have forgotten.

• • •

Emma listened to the Pennsylvania trooper explain where they'd found the purple Camry. And who was in the trunk.

"Anything else?"

"No, ma'am."

Emma looked up at the ceiling. "It would be strange to take the woman from her own house, kill her, then dump her in the garage of an Airbnb, right?"

"We've never had a shortage of 'strange' in Mountville, ma'am."

"Right. But still. *Her* car wasn't in the driveway or down the street?"

"No, ma'am."

"Thanks for your help. I'm sorry to have ruined your night."

Emma went to work finding records on the recently deceased Karen Pilkington. She drove a white Jeep Cherokee. The car was seven years old and paid off. Emma wrote the VIN on her yellow pad. Driving records showed she was in an accident a month ago. Side-swiped. The left back quarter panel was dented. Now it was a white Jeep Cherokee with damage—that was good, but George Engel could have driven through five states by now.

It would have been a nice thing if Ms. Pilkington had GPS on her car, too. Emma chewed on her pen for a while. She remembered a friend complaining that her insurance company was tracking her with some contraption they plugged into the vehicle. She said it wasn't worth the discount to be monitored by Big Brother. Well, it was worth a try. She tested the insurance company's 24-hour hotline.

"Yes. I understand you can't share her private information. And I understand you would be more comfortable speaking to your manager first. I'm telling you this is a national security issue. Can you at least tell me—are you giving her the Big Brother discount?"

"The what?"

"The doo-hickey that you guys use to monitor their driving."

"Yes," the customer-service woman said.

"Yes, you can? Or yes, she's getting a discount?"

"Yes. To the discount part."

"And is it through a phone app or is it hard-wired?"

"We don't have the phone app."

Emma smiled. "You're going to need to wake your boss now."

The insurance manager she spoke to was groggy and unhappy and very concerned about client privacy. The only thing he could divulge without a warrant was the time the engine started and when it was shut off—and the miles driven. He didn't think that would be of much use. He was wrong; Emma quietly pumped her arms in the air. With that information she could calculate a radius. But, depending on how far George had driven, that radius could be unmanageable.

Emma tapped the pen against her teeth, trying to figure out how she could narrow the search. An idea presented itself, and Emma leaned over her computer and prayed that the woman had a toll pass in her car. *Who* doesn't *have a toll pass? Please have a toll pass.*

Yes. Thank God.

A half hour later, Emma had a record of the tollbooth locations that the Jeep Cherokee had passed since leaving Mountville. George Engel was not five states away. He'd only driven forty-two miles. He passed a toll in northern Virginia at 8:30 PM and turned the car off at 8:35 PM. On country roads, he probably wouldn't have gotten over three miles from the toll. She drew a circle on the map and tried to remember her high school math. Pi squared something. She cheated and looked it up online and narrowed the search area to 28 square miles. She hopped out of her chair and did an awkward dance. The dab at the end was unnecessary, and she promised herself, once again, never to do that.

Emma grabbed her jacket. Then she sat down again. *Shit.*

"Squirt? What the hell?" said the voice through her phone.

"Rise and shine," Emma said cheerily.

"3 AM?"

"You're my favorite uncle. You know that, right?"

"What?"

"I said you're—"

"No. What do you need?"

"Wheels. Kind of urgent. And a big flashlight if you've got one."

"What're you up to?"

"Nothing."

"You're a lousy liar. You need backup?"

"It's no big thing. Just a little drive in the country—checking something."

"Why do I think this is a bad idea?"

"Because you assume women are fragile little teacups that—"

Gunny interrupted her with a loud sigh. "Car's on its way. Going back to bed. 'Night."

A sleep-deprived driver employed by a grumpy former Marine threw Emma the keys to a black Audi. She pushed the seat back and looked at the road ahead. Her training told her she should call this in. But what if she was wrong? She never wanted to feel the way she did in that conference room in front of those men. Ever. This was only a hunch, and she wouldn't gamble her career on it. She'd just drive around a bit.

No harm in that.

36

Emma exited the highway in Ewell, Virginia. She paid the toll and drove directly into the parking lot of a glowing convenience store. She came out of the restroom significantly slower than she'd gone in. "Morning," she said, putting a stick of gum on the counter. The guy took her money without looking up from his phone.

She stood by the car. Ewell's three thousand citizens were still asleep. The tollbooth at the end of the road was lit up. Eight hours ago, George Engel had driven through it. Five minutes after crossing the toll, he'd shut off his car. He could have driven for five minutes or idled for five.

She walked to the curb and looked down the main road. There wasn't much going on in downtown Ewell. Past the red blinking light lay rural countryside. She would search in town first, then head into the country. Her confidence that George Engel was nearby sagged when she saw the dumpy train station across the street. If there was a dented white Jeep in the parking lot, it meant the terrorist was long gone.

Emma entered the lot, driving slow, pointing her flashlight at the vehicles, looking at the make and model of every car in the lot. It was fortunate she wasn't looking under the cars. If she'd seen the man with the green duffel hiding behind the Ford Explorer, he'd have killed her in an instant.

George Engel's car wasn't there. She kept searching. First, behind an auto supply store, shining her light into the dark corners. Emma did the same at the shuttered greasy-spoon diner farther up the road.

After turning into the parking lot of a small hardware store, police lights flashed in her rear-view. Emma shut off the ignition, turned on the interior lights, and placed her hands on the wheel—her FBI badge in plain sight.

"Morning, Officer."

The deputy took the badge and identification and studied it a while. He was an older guy and she guessed the night shift might be his part-time gig.

"What's the FBI doing in Ewell?"

"Tracking terrorists."

"Uh-huh. Sure."

The cop flashed his light into Emma's eyes. "You seem a little unusual to be an FBI agent."

"I think I'm more awkward than unusual."

"I mean you're a woman."

"Yup."

"When'd that start?"

"For me, pretty much right away. But if you mean the FBI—about a hundred years ago."

He turned his light off and said something under his breath.

"We good?" Emma asked.

He nodded and walked back to his cruiser and drove off.

Thirty-five minutes later she had worked her way through the downtown area—roughly three quarters of a mile. If George Engel was in Ewell, he was in the countryside. She took the main road east. The homes were small, but they had acreage—far apart and well off the road. Every three or four hundred yards Emma would stop at the end of a driveway and shine the powerful beam across the property, looking for a dented, white Jeep Cherokee.

She reached the outer boundary of her search area. Dawn was still a couple hours away, but lights were popping on in houses. Cars were on the road. Ewell was waking up. She drove a little farther. If she found nothing in the next half mile, she'd turn around and park by the tollbooth. When it got light, she'd call Briar and tell him what she'd found. If the cavalry needed to be called, she wanted to use *his* trumpet.

Emma slowed the Audi in front of an unpaved gravel driveway. She set her foot on the brake and shined her light across the lawn, past the flagpole, illuminating the farmer's porch. She swung the beam

155

over to the carport at the end of the drive. There were no vehicles. No lights on in the house. Nothing to see. Emma turned off the flashlight. But she kept her foot on the brake. Instinct told her something was there. Something her eyes had seen but hadn't communicated to her brain. She put the Audi in park and pointed the flashlight. Again, the powerful bulb lit the yard, driveway, and the house. Emma took her time searching for what nagged her. There … in the landscaping by the side of the house. The bushes were broken. Like they'd been run over by a car.

Emma looked through her yellow pad and ripped out the page she was looking for. She shut the door quietly, leaned her back against the Audi, and inhaled deeply.

Let's see what's in the backyard.

37

Emma zipped up her FBI windbreaker to ward off the chill breeze. It was pitch black—the clouds had snuffed out the full moon. The only sound was the jangle of an American flag slapping against the pole. She took two crunching footfalls in the gravel drive, then moved to the lawn, using careful, creeping steps to approach the house. Listening. Watching. Her heart banging in her ears. She stopped by the farmer's porch and looked in the window. No lights. No signs of life. Nothing moved but the flag on the front lawn.

She reached the carport. In three steps, she'd be past the house. Emma tilted her head and listened. She waited.

It was nothing.

Her mind was playing tricks. She was freaking herself out—it was something she'd always had a talent for, especially in the dark. She inhaled through her nose and blew out a long, steady exhale, then stepped over the landscaping.

The backyard was big and sloping. She squinted. It was too dark to see. She bent at the knees and scanned the property. There was something interrupting the horizon line. A shape. She thought it might be big enough to be a car—or a shed. Maybe a swing-set. Emma stayed in a crouch, unsure if she should move forward or back.

She thought about her options: go back to the car and call for help, which would come in the form of a part-time county cop with an AARP card, or wait for federal agents to arrive. It might take an hour or more. And what if, in the light of day, it *was* a swing-set? No way she was going to put herself through that bullshit. What she needed was more information. And a little courage. She stood. And stepped quietly into the backyard.

Holding her breath. Walking silently.

Emma moved, closer and closer to the shape. Her eyes were adjusting. The small hairs on her arms raised when she saw that, yes, it *was* a light-colored vehicle parked near the back door. Emma studied the house. Still no lights. Nothing moving. She let the glow of her phone show her the grill. JEEP. She looked once more at the house. Her chest was a drum circle.

She had to be sure. One minute to check the VIN. She would confirm it and call it in. The number would be under the windshield on the driver's side. She turned her back to the house and pulled the yellow paper out of her pocket. She repeated the rhyme in her head like a calming mantra: *Confirm the VIN, call it in. Confirm the VIN, call it in.*

She spread the paper out on the hood with her left hand. She leaned into the windshield, holding her phone to see the first eight digits. 1C4RJEBG. She looked at the paper. They were the same. So far. There were more numbers to check. Fifteen more seconds. She dipped her head in front of the windshield. 9DC—

Emma never heard him coming. A fist yanked a clump of her hair backward, then slammed her head forward. Her ears exploded with the *crack* of shattered cartilage. Her face became a faucet. Her mouth was flooding in blood. A rough, callused hand was driving her face into the glass. Her eyes seared with pain. His weight pushed into her, pinning her to the vehicle. She twisted and pushed against the Jeep to try to clear herself. He was too heavy. She kicked back. He leaned his beefy thighs into her. She tried to free her legs. He was too strong. He mashed his whiskered cheek against the side of her face—his stale breath hot in her ear.

He tugged at the bottom of her windbreaker, searching for her gun. Emma screamed and flailed her right arm. His forearm was grinding her face into the blood-smeared windshield.

A hand moved under her windbreaker. An inch from her weapon.

She swung her arm backwards, beating his hand away with her fist. She was choking on blood. No way to land a real punch.

His hand was on her weapon.

Emma forced her smaller hand over his. She pressed down, fighting to keep the gun holstered. He was too fucking strong.

The gun was coming out.

Emma punched at his hand.

She screamed and pushed at his wrist.

The gun was coming out.

Emma grabbed for his thumb and twisted as hard as she could. He grunted. His weight shifted. She kept forcing the thumb in the direction that thumbs don't bend. His weight shifted again, and Emma's face broke free from the windshield.

He sent a glancing blow against her ribs. She turned into him, tearing at his face with her free hand. He punched her again. She stepped in closer and dug her fingernails into his face. He punched, but she was too close for the swing to pack any power.

Emma planted her thumb into the corner of his eye.

And pressed. And pressed harder.

Until she felt it release under her thumb.

He screamed.

Emma took a step back, drew her weapon, and, with a two-handed grip on her Glock, fired three times into George Engel's chest.

His body didn't wilt or crumple. It thumped heavy into the lawn, like a flour sack thrown from a truck. She stood over him, pointing her gun at his chest. He didn't move. Emma didn't holster her weapon for a long while. She laid her trembling hand under George Engel's chin. No pulse.

She leaned over his body and took a deep breath. She stood upright and brought a tentative finger to her face. Her nose was gushing. She spat blood and lifted her face into the wind, gulping at the fresh air. Her nose was wrecked. She wouldn't be breathing through it anytime soon. Pain was radiating through her face—pulsating across her eyes, across her cheeks, and down her nose. It was swelling. It hurt to blink. But she was alive.

Emma paced until she'd caught her breath, then sat down on the grass next to the corpse of George Engel. The wind blew across the brittle blades and dried Emma's face into a crust of cracked maroon. Finally, the clouds released the moon and the stars. From the lawn of that north Virginia property, next to a dented white Jeep Cherokee, George Engel and Emma Noble stared up at the night sky.

After a minute, she punched the dead arm next to her. "Fuck you, George."

She lay there a while longer, staring up at the stars and the moon. The realization came to her slowly. She smiled. She was okay. Really. And then Emma Noble chuckled because it hurt too much to laugh.

She was okay.

38

Tasha returned to her apartment at 6 AM and threw her jacket over the arm of the couch. She looked at Ben. "Did you have coffee?"

"No. How'd it go?"

"I've got hazelnut or some kind of coconut blend. What's your poison?"

"Doesn't matter. Find anything?"

"Let's do the hazelnut."

"Tasha?"

"I found the beginnings of something. Was my brother a dick?"

"No. What do you mean 'the beginnings of something?'"

"That's good—I was a little worried. Breadcrumbs."

"Breadcrumbs?"

She walked into the galley kitchen and turned on the faucet, pouring water in the carafe. She sniffed the open bag of hazelnut, then scooped the grounds into the filter basket.

"Tasha? Breadcrumbs?"

She rubbed Mr. Spock behind his ears. "We had a reporter. Back in the '70s. He was working on a story about Summerton Academy. They killed it."

Ben slumped.

"But the reason they didn't run it was odd. Lawyers from Summerton were threatening a child-endangerment lawsuit."

"Why would a newspaper be threatened with child endangerment?"

"I don't know."

"So, that's it? We're done?"

She made a face at him and pointed a finger in her chest. "Dude, I'm a professional journalist—ain't no quit in me."

. . .

Every town has a building like the Haystack—an old brick two-story at the far end of Main Street that reincarnates every decade as barbershop, reform church, dance studio, insurance agency, or driving school. Tasha parked her brown Solara by the curb.

"Thanks for doing this," Ben said.

"Just remember your promise."

She dug her keys out of her down jacket and blew on her hands. "No one comes in here except me and the maintenance guy."

"What is this?" he asked.

"It's where they dump everybody's crap."

She unbolted the glass door and pushed. The bottom scraped against the dingy floor. The Haystack was cold and smelled like mildew and plaster dust. Tasha pulled a chain on the low ceiling and the room turned a sickly blood red.

"Bulb from the old darkroom. Nothing wasted at the *Inquirer*."

Ben squinted. The space was a blur of unhelpful light and shadow. Shit was piled everywhere.

"And nothing thrown away," he observed.

"I made a path."

Ben tripped on a ten-speed bicycle. His arm knocked over a bundle of newspapers balancing on the edge of a wooden credenza. He caught himself on a metal table that leaned against a mountain of stacked office chairs and spent toner cartridges.

"It's back this way," she said.

"What is?"

"Fritz LeChien."

"We're meeting someone?"

"No, he was the reporter. We're looking for his shit."

Ben followed Tasha into the back half of the building. She flipped on the light. The room flickered into white fluorescence, revealing clutter everywhere. Someone had tipped over black filing cabinets and had stacked rib-exposed and water-damaged cardboard boxes on them.

White banker boxes covered the floor and were stacked high along the wall. Some were sealed with brown packing tape; others had no lids. Ben guessed there were two or three hundred of them.

"Ralph, the maintenance guy, told me that back in the day, any reporter worth his salt died at his desk. They'd wheel out two gurneys—one went to the morgue, the other brought his shit to the Haystack. I've found crap in here from the early '50s."

"We're looking for this reporter's box?"

"Yep. Fritz LeChien. You start over there. We'll work our way down."

Ben stood on his tiptoes and pulled a box off the top. He ripped off the tape and opened the lid. Under twelve issues of old *Playboys* was a brown mug, a box of paper clips, and a pack of Winstons. He put the box on the floor and grabbed the next.

Thirteen boxes later, no sign of Fritz LeChien.

"You sure his stuff is in here?" he asked.

"Nope. Welcome to Investigative Reporting 101."

Ben continued opening boxes, flipping through files, closing lids, and stacking them away, working his way down the wall. He rolled his neck and curled his shoulders forward. Tasha was watching him.

"What?" he asked.

"I'm just—I can't imagine. You find out the woman who you thought was your mother, actually kidnapped you, and your real mom is a trillionaire and the next vice president. Seems like a lot."

"Yeah."

"What was she like? As a mother?"

"I don't have anything to compare it to."

"I mean, was it normal? Like unconditional love and all that?"

"If unconditional love is normal—then no. It wasn't normal."

"If you could choose, would you rather be kidnapped and never know it or deal with the truth of it all and be rich?"

Ben didn't turn around. He was hoping she would stop asking questions.

"I think I'd like to be rich," she said. "That's what I'd pick."

Ben ripped the tape off the box in front of him. File folders were stacked on their backs. He pulled them out to see the tabs. Underneath the folders was a black Day Planner from 1978 with *LeChien* taped to the front. He sat on a black filing cabinet, the banker's box in his lap.

"You find something?" Tasha asked.

Ben flipped through a few of LeChien's files. They were stuffed with pay stubs and pension data. The thinnest of the green folders had an opaque yellow tab. *Westonberry*. There were only two things inside the folder: a handwritten note and black-and-white picture. The note was written on *Albany Inquirer* stationery dated August 5th.

Fritz-

You're a dick taking this up to Peck after I told you to shit-can it. I'll shove this story up your fat ass. The school's lawyers are going to peel your face off and Jonesy's not lifting a finger to help you this time. Every goddamned Summerton file on my desk—TODAY! No copies. You're done with this shit. I'm serious.

Ben studied the black-and-white photograph. It was a teenage girl. She had black hair and thin lips. Her eyes looked empty. It was a haunting photograph. The date written on the back in ballpoint pen was July 1978.

"You think she's from Summerton?" Tasha asked.

Ben shrugged. "There's nothing else in the file."

Tasha flipped through the Day Planner. She soft-tossed it to Ben. "Check out the last entry."

Ben found the scribbled words from August 12, 1978: *Father/ Volkov? Barry Atamian missing. Wife?*

Ben flipped through the planner. Fritz had crossed out the 25th and written *W'berry* across it.

"It looks like he wasn't giving up on the story," Ben said, flipping farther into the planner. "But there's nothing else in here. For the entire year. You think they fired him?"

Tasha didn't answer. She was looking at her phone.

"Get this. Werner 'Fritz' LeChien, respected reporter for the *Albany Inquirer*, died Wednesday, August 25th, in a one-car accident in upstate New York." She raised her eyebrows.

"What?" Ben asked.

"He drives upstate, working on a story that no one wants him to look into, and he dies in a car crash?"

"People die in car crashes all the time."

Tasha walked closer. "Your mother? This Ida person. You think she went to Summerton. Don't you?"

He nodded.

"Look at my arms. You see this shit? My hairs are standing on end. No, I'm serious—look at them. See?"

"Yup. They are."

"They *killed* Fritz LeChien."

Ben picked up the black-and-white photograph of the pale girl with the sad eyes. The girl knew about Summerton, but she wasn't telling anyone. The reporter had found something. But, whatever it was, it had died with him. Ben stood up. Maybe the reporter was killed. Maybe he wasn't. There were no answers here. It was foolish to keep going. He needed to drive back to DC and see Kate.

"Thanks, Tasha. I think we're done."

Ben hadn't seen it hidden under the cardboard flap inside the box. Tasha tilted her head. She reached in and held it up for Ben to see—a clear, cracked plastic case. A Memorex cassette tape.

"No. We're not done yet."

39

Emma Noble dabbed the blood off her mouth and chin with a warm washcloth. She was in the upstairs bathroom of the farmhouse in Virginia, her blouse a blood-soaked disaster. She inspected herself in the mirror—her nose was a pink balloon. Toilet paper was stuffed up her nostrils; yes, she was battered, but still standing.

She looked down the hallway at the bedrooms that faced one another. George Engel's mechanic uniform was balled on the floor of the first, a steel camber-top toolbox standing next to it. No way in hell she was getting anywhere near that. She'd leave it as a present for the bomb squad. When she peeked into the second bedroom, a chill shot through her heart. The comforter had been pulled back—someone had been sleeping in this room too. Shards of broken ceramic from a shattered lamp littered the carpet.

Two people had been in the house. *Jesus, Emma*! She'd lain on the lawn congratulating herself *before* clearing the house. If George Engel's friend had still been there—no doubt about it, she'd be dead. That was a big, hairy mistake that she vowed never to repeat—or tell anyone.

Emma knelt on the carpet, looking at the broken lamp. Why would someone smash it against the wall? An argument with George maybe? She stood up and looked around the room. Something was on the bedside table—the white glossy back of a photograph. She held it by the edge and flipped it over. He was a little younger, had a bowl haircut, and the beginnings of a bad moustache, but Emma recognized him. This was Benjamin Danvers's senior high school picture.

Why would a terrorist have this?

Her internal logic was sending her in only two directions. Either Kimberly Hancock's son was a target. Or Benjamin had some role to play in the attacks. All she knew for certain was that, as of now, the kid was directly linked to terrorists. And that was very bad news because, in two days, he would be standing by his mother at the inauguration—only feet from the next president of the United States.

Emma slid the photograph into a sandwich bag she'd found in the kitchen, then tucked it into the pocket of her windbreaker to show Briar. Maybe he could make sense of it.

The police sirens were getting closer. Emma walked out the front door onto the wraparound porch, sat in the black wicker chair, and waited for the federal cavalry to descend upon Ewell.

• • •

Tasha hovered the Memorex tape over the cassette deck in the dash of her Solara. "Do you know how this goes?"

"I'm not sure. You think maybe in this way—or like this?"

"Maybe that way?"

Tasha inserted the cassette into the mouth of the player. There was a popping sound, a crunch, and then a crackle. The car speakers made a hollow, open mic sound that lasted long enough for Ben to think the tape might be blank. A gravelly cigarette voice burst through the speakers of the Solara.

"No, this'll be easy. Start with your name."

"Beverly."

"Last name?"

"It's just Beverly."

"You don't know it?"

"I don't have one—I don't think."

"How old are you, Beverly?"

"How old do you think I am?"

"Jeez, I have no idea. Fifteen? What grade are you in?"

"Form 9."

"At Summerton Academy? You're nodding your head 'yes.' How long have you been at that school?"

"Forever. I've always been there."

"And your parents? Where are they?"

"There is only the Father. And the teachers."

"So, you're an orphan?"

"We are the Father's children."

"Why did you run?"

"I was scared of the Punishings."

"You're safe now. You don't have to be scared anymore."

There was a long silence.

"Beverly, what are the Punishings?"

"It's for when you break the first rule."

"First rule?"

"Loyalty. Loyalty to the Father and to the Community of the Fatherhood. We are the bearers of the new order. We pledge our lives and our fealty to the Father and to the Son. Breaking the first rule is a great sin."

"What made you break the rule, Beverly?"

"I didn't! It was the boy! The Greek pulled me into the woods and touched me. I said I would tell on him. So he made up lies about me. And they believed him!"

"I'm sorry that happened. Don't cry. I didn't mean to make you cry—you're doing great. How about we take a little break?"

The open mic sound filled the car. Tasha and Ben exchanged a look and waited. Fritz LeChien's chuckle boomed out of the speakers.

"Of course. You can have as many Cokes as you'd like. Tell me more about the Punishings. What happens?"

"No one knows. The kids are never seen after that. It's bad. Everybody knows it."

There was a brief silence, and then, the sound of a chair scuffing against a floor.

"Beverly, I'm worried about your friends at Summerton. You'd like them to be safe, wouldn't you?"

"They are safe. The Father loves us all very much. We swim and climb trees. Everyone likes it there."

"I'm not sure about that. Do they even teach you anything at this school?"

"Yes. About the Prophecy."

"Prophecy? What's that?"

"That, one day soon, the Son will come. He will bring righteousness and the tyranny of the evil will crumble at his feet. The Prophecy says we must prepare ourselves to assist him when he does."

"How are childr—young people, supposed to do that?"

"The Son will come when we are in our places."

"What places?"

"We will be everywhere."

"I don't understand."

"We will be *everywhere*. All of us. Waiting for the Son."

"Who is the Son?"

ZZZZZTWWPPPPP. The cassette screeched, and the brown tape vomited out of the dash. Tasha fumbled with the "STOP" button.

"Summerton's a cult," she said, looking to Ben.

He nodded and rubbed his hand over his mouth. Beverly and Ida were probably the same age—probably grew up together. The Solara's windows fogged as they silently digested the information on the old tape.

"Summerton lawyered-up when they found out the *Inquirer* had the kid."

Ben nodded, thinking about what had become of the children. *Where were they now?* He pointed at the Day Planner. "It mentions the Father on one of those pages, right?"

Tasha read, *"Father/ Volkov? Barry Atamian missing. Wife?"*

Ben looked at the page. "Should we—"

"Look up Barry Atamian? Already on it."

Tasha found the information quickly. The disappearance was mentioned in the Boston papers in the summer of 1978. Police had questioned his wife, Paula Atamian. There was no body—which meant there was no murder. Barry Atamian had simply disappeared.

"Paula Atamian lives in Medford, Massachusetts. She's a retired schoolteacher," Tasha said, shifting in her seat.

She stared at Ben.

"What?" he asked.

"I'm wondering."

"Wondering what?"

"You were kidnapped by a woman that went to Summerton Academy. Your birth mother is the vice president. Those children were taught to wait for the arrival of the Son."

"Yeah."

"Sooo ... maybe?

169

"What?" Ben gave her a harsh look as he realized what she was suggesting. "That's crazy. The tape is from the '70s. Long before Kimberly Hancock was married—decades before I was born."

"It's a prophecy. Someone knew you were coming. And they planned for it, or they designed it. Either way, you were expected." Tasha nodded her head. "Benjamin Danvers, *you* are the Son."

40

Emma sat on the top step of the farmer's porch, tilting her head at the sky. An EMT's rubber gloves probed gently around her face. Emma had not invited the agent from DOMTERR to join her for the examination, but there he was, keeping up a monologue about life in the domestic-terror racket. He seemed a little too excited that the country was ripping at the seams. In the end, she wasn't sure if he was trying to convince her to leave CID or go for dinner and drinks.

The EMT shined a light in her eyes. "Do you remember what you were doing right before you were hurt?"

"Checking a VIN—1C4RJEBG9DC."

The EMT lady turned off her light and smirked. Apparently, the concussion protocol questions were over.

"I don't think you've got facial fractures, but you should get an X-ray."

The DOMTERR agent leaned in and winked at her. "I'll check in with you when I'm in the Big Apple next month. We'll talk some more—see if you want to move forward."

Emma gave him a half-hearted nod as the woman stretched white tape across her nose. She was pretty sure she didn't want to work or date anyone who called New York City the "Big Apple."

"Can I borrow her?" said a guy in a brown suit standing on the lawn in front of the house.

"In a minute," said the EMT.

Emma didn't know who the brown suit was, but she'd already

171

talked to a few suits. Each wanted an oral report on what went down. A written report was expected by the end of the day. The internal investigation into the shooting had probably already begun. Tomorrow, she was ordered to attend an early morning meeting with her SAC in New York City for an after-action Hot Wash. He and his team would dissect every decision she'd made in the past twelve hours. Being a hero turned out to be a dis-incentivizing administrative hassle—no wonder there weren't more people doing it.

Emma looked across the street. Uncle Gunny was getting out of a vehicle. Big ears in a sharp suit. Of course, he'd already know what had happened. He and her father knew everything. Emma thanked the EMT and jogged over. Gunny wasn't smiling. His phone was at his ear when Emma got to him.

"Yeah. I got eyes on her.... Like shit. Smug too.... No, she's okay.... You too."

Uncle Gunny put the phone away. Emma shrugged, wondering why he'd hung up without letting her talk to her father.

"Now's not the time," he told her, reading her mind.

"Huh?"

"Let's just say he's got some adrenaline to work off."

"K."

He spoke more softly to her. "You're okay?"

Emma beamed back at him.

He returned the smallest of smiles. "Get back to work."

She gave him a hug, then pressed the keys to the black Audi into his hand.

The conversation with the guy in the brown suit lasted twenty minutes and might have gone on longer if not for a gray Suburban rolling over the curb and parking on the lawn. It was as good an excuse as any to extricate herself. She walked over to Briar, standing by his vehicle. Along with having her nose professionally taped, she had white cotton-rolls filling her nostrils.

"Hey, Bwiya." She pointed at her nose. "Bwoken."

He shook his head slowly. "Shopping for Mike and Ike's again? Or something more dangerous—like Nutterbutters?"

She gave him the finger. "Vewy funny."

"You shouldn't have been out here by yourself."

Emma nodded. She took the cotton out of her nostrils and put them in the pocket of her windbreaker.

"What happened," he asked.

"Get me outta here. I'll tell you on the way back."

• • •

Tasha's Solara was still at the curb in front of the Haystack. The defroster hadn't been able to keep up with her tsunami of theories. Ben had offered little in the past fifteen minutes except nods and shrugs.

"What are you going to do now?" she asked.

"I'm not sure. Maybe see if I can talk to Barry Atamian's wife. She lives a few miles from my apartment."

Tasha said little on the drive back to Ben's car. She gave him an awkward hug by the Land Rover. "Be careful. Okay?"

"None of this gets out, right?"

"As long as you keep your virginity pledge—no whoring with other reporters behind my back."

"Deal." Ben smiled. "See you soon."

• • •

Arnau Farre took the aisle seat. His green duffel took the window. The train slowed into Union Station in DC. National Guard soldiers walked along the platform. Police in lime vests held leashes on sniffing dogs. He heaved his bag across his back and walked off the train, mixing in with the crowd and keeping his eyes low. The Great Hall was teeming with people. State police and DC cops patrolled, no doubt carrying pictures of the Greek.

His duffel was army green. His salt and pepper haircut, high and tight. The most dangerous man in Union Station looked like he played for the home team—or once did. He wasn't going to chance anything by staying out in the open. He scanned the crowd, then slid into a bakery and ordered a black coffee. He sat facing the bathrooms at the back of the cafe. He needed a cigarette. His indecision was causing him anxiety—Benjamin Danvers had last been seen in Vermont. Arnau could get a train to Rutland or Clarendon Station, then make his way to Ida's old house. That's where he wanted to be. To see how she lived.

To see the kitchen table where she wrote her letters. But, of all the places her son would be, Vermont was a long shot.

The kid might have returned to DC. If he had, he was dead or on his way to being dead. Arnau couldn't protect him there. The organization had too many resources in the nation's capital. Smart money was on the kid showing up in Boston. The Greek was watching Benjamin's apartment. The train to South Street Station didn't leave for another hour. It was a seven and half-hour trip. Arnau wouldn't get in until after 9 PM. The timing sucked, but it was the best of the three miserable options. He picked up his phone and texted the Greek.

-Any sign?
-*No.*
-I'm coming. Do nothing until I get there.
-*It's MY job.*
-Wait for me.

No Answer.

Arnau strangled the phone. He drained his coffee. At the newsstand he bought two packs of cigarettes and a warm diet 7-Up. He had an hour more to chain smoke and let his anger steep.

41

Emma looked out the windshield as the wipers slapped the snow flurries away. "Storms coming. Looks like Boston's going to get creamed."

Briar didn't comment on the weather. He hadn't said much since Emma had told him about finding Benjamin's picture in the house. He wasn't an agent who liked to spitball ideas with his partner. There was no give and take. When Briar Metcalf was working out a problem, he got quiet. And Benjamin Danvers was his oldest problem. He blew a long exhale.

"What are you thinking, Briar?"

"He's a target, or he's involved. He's got to come willingly."

"So ... we ask nicely?"

"Exactly. You've got his number. Call him."

• • •

Ben hunched over the wheel, tracking the taillights of an eighteen-wheeler. The freezing rain began pelting the Land Rover outside of Albany. It had softened into snow—thick gray flakes falling from a thick gray sky. And it was accumulating faster than the plows could keep up with. The white lines had vanished a while back. He hoped the trucker knew where the road turned. Ben had lost track of the number of vehicles that had slid into the median or slipped off the shoulder.

Wendall had taught him how to drive in these conditions. His voice entered his head now: "*Keep right. Keep slow.*"

It should have been a two-and-a-half-hour drive from Albany to Medford, Massachusetts. Not in a snowstorm. He guessed that if the plows didn't pick up the pace, it would take five.

Shit. He still hadn't called Kate. He was an asshole for not reaching out. He glanced at his phone. Kimberly Hancock had called three times. Kate had called eleven. *Eleven?* She was worried. And when she found out he was okay, she'd be furious. Time to take his medicine. Ben dialed, feeling a groaning discomfort in his stomach.

It gave him a childish sense of relief when Kate's voicemail came through the Land Rover's sound system. Two minutes later his phone rang. It was her.

"Hey, I'm fine," he said quickly. "How are—?"

"You're okay?"

"Yup."

"Christ, Benjamin!"

Silence.

"Where the hell are you?"

"Driving to Boston. How're you doin'?"

"Doin'? You wanna know how I'm doin'? Doin' terrific, Benjamin. I'm in DC with a bunch of strangers asking me where my boyfriend is. I don't know what to tell them. That's how I'm doin'. How're *you* doin'?"

Ben winced. Kate could be difficult when she was angry, and he deserved everything he was getting. After five minutes, she let him get a word in.

"Wait. You're telling me you tracked Ida to a defunct school in upstate New York because you found a florist card in the back of a picture frame in her bedroom?"

"Yup."

"And that makes you think she went to this academy, which—if what you're saying is true—is a cult?"

"Yup."

"A cult, training children to fulfill a prophecy? And now you're on your way to bother an old lady in Medford?"

"Yup."

Silence.

176

"Kate?"

"You're not acting like yourself, Ben. I'm worried about you. You shouldn't be alone. How about—"

"I'm fine. Seriously, Kate. I'm just trying to get answers. It's important to me. I need to understand."

He waited through the silence.

"Benjamin, you're kind of scaring the shit out of me."

"Sorry."

"Please get down here. I need you."

"I'm coming. I promise. I'll drive down tonight—wake you with a coffee and a kiss. Okay?"

"I love you," she said quietly.

"You too."

• • •

Emma looked at Briar. "Voicemail again."

"Text him. Leave a message. Make sure he calls us."

Benjamin, this is Special Agent Emma Noble. Call us as soon as you get this message. Any hour. Any time.

The snow was steady. The flakes flashing in the headlights danced in front of her eyes. Briar was submerged in thought. Emma watched the wipers. Her eyes were heavy, sagging from the strain of a sleepless night and an adrenaline-fueled morning. She wedged her head between the seat and the window. She closed her eyes. The thwap-thwap of the windshield wipers waved her out to sleep.

• • •

Ben squinted at the road. It had gotten dark and snow was flying into his headlights on the horizontal. For hours, it felt like he couldn't blink without going off the road. He exhaled his thanks when the vehicle's navigation system told him he was a mile from the Medford exit.

He turned off the engine. The air in the Land Rover stopped circulating and he got a proper whiff of himself. Ben was still dressed in yesterday's TV clothes. He'd slept in his good shirt and his blue suitcoat had been balled up in the backseat for days. Mrs. Atamian's first impression would be a guy entering her room like he was coming off a three-day bender.

He'd been rehearsing what he would say when he met her. He would apologize for not calling first. That's about as far as he'd gotten. He wasn't good at this sort of thing. The salespeople at Cambridge Hill gave presentations about how to speak to clients. They said, "the key is to get them to like you. Then they'll write a check. And keep on writing them." According to the sales manager, customers came in four sizes: extroverts who wanted to laugh and joke around before they'd buy; number-crunchers who loved a good, complicated spreadsheet; and beautiful souls who just needed to confirm you were a good human before they wrote a check. The fourth type was a little trickier; those people just wanted you to get to the goddamned point, then get the hell out. The sales team at Cambridge Hill Holdings were experts at teasing information out of every personality type. They were chameleons.

Ben wasn't like that. He wasn't comfortable around strangers. And, as he exited the vehicle, he wasn't feeling great about invading the privacy of an old woman to ask her about the disappearance of her husband all those years ago.

The lobby of the retirement community had a country club vibe: wide stone fireplace, a green tartan carpet, a high-shine mahogany piano, a coffee station. There was a small bar in the corner with a sign over it: Happy Days. There were no residents sipping cocktails and laughing—no one at Elm River Assisted Care seemed to be enjoying Happy Days.

"Can I help?" said a woman not old enough to live there.

"I'm here to see Paula Atamian?"

She spoke into a cord hanging from her neck. The woman had one earphone in, the other dangled over her shoulder.

"Reggie? There's a gentleman in reception that would like to see Mrs. A. Hold on." She looked at him. "What's your name, sir?"

"Ben Danvers."

"Mr. Ben Danvers? Okay, Reggie." She smiled, "He'll be down soon and will show you up."

Five minutes later, a husky guy, equal parts muscle and fat, came down the stairs. He was tall and had a gun and heart neck tattoo. He gave Ben a long look.

"Is Mrs. A expecting you?"

"No. Kind of a surprise I guess," Ben admitted.

Reggie stared back for an uncomfortably long time before nodding. They rode the elevator up to the fourth floor. The big man was crowding him. Ben's last elevator ride had been three days ago with an FBI entourage pulling him out of Cambridge Hill Holdings. He was starting to hate elevators.

The doors opened into a wide, handicapped-accessible hallway. Tan carpet. Tan walls. Tan doors with tan entry mats. Only a wilting pink birthday balloon expiring on the carpet and a green "Get Well" card taped to a door brought any color to the hallway. Ben walked while Reggie breathed down his neck.

Outside each door was a small glass case. Most contained photographs of the resident's grandchildren. Room 405's case had only one small frame—a picture of newlyweds taken in front of a rustic, covered bridge. The couple was leaning against a copper, four-door Granada with streamers attached to the bumper. The woman was young and beautiful.

"I can hear you out there," said a voice from inside.

Reggie knocked anyway.

It was a small apartment. PBS news was on the TV. The walls were covered with construction-paper Santas. Paula Atamian sat in a pillowy green recliner by the back wall. She was bone thin. Sickly thin. A crocheted afghan was draped over her lap. Her exposed hand held a Robert Olmstead novel. The other was keeping warm under the blanket.

"He said he came here to surprise you, Mrs. A."

"I don't like surprises," she said blankly, squinting at Ben. "And I don't know you." She cocked her head. "Wait. Maybe I do. You're the one that was on the news."

Ben nodded, looking around at the construction-paper artwork, thinking about Kate.

"My kids," she said, following his eyes. "Thirty years a third-grade teacher. I put them up every year." Her eyes narrowed. "But you're not here to talk about *those* children, are you?"

She stiffened and raised her chin. Reggie took a step toward Ben.

Mrs. Atamian pulled the blanket away.

She had a gun pointed at Ben's chest.

42

Ben cocked his head, his brain a little slow in registering what his eyes were seeing. The infirm old woman in front of him, surrounded by construction paper Santas, was aiming a gun at him. The weapon was too heavy for her to lift. She rested the weight of it against her thigh. But her thin, arthritic fingers had a solid grip on the weapon. Her index finger was in the trigger well. And the barrel was pointing directly at Ben's chest.

What the fuck? His eyes widened and he retreated into Reggie's chest. The big man pushed Ben's arms to the side. He was rough with the pat-down. Reggie pulled the Day Planner out of Ben's suit pocket, thumbed through it, then handed it over to Mrs. Atamian. The old woman stared at the cover of the planner for a few seconds, then lifted her eyes.

"Did Alex send you?"

"Who? No. I uh."

"Why are you here?"

"It was a mistake. I'll go."

"Sit." She waved her free hand toward the couch. "If Alex didn't send you—then how would *you* have found us?"

Ben pointed to the Day Planner. "It's a reporter's calendar from 1978. He was investigating Summerton. I think he wanted to speak to the wife of Barry Atamian—the man who disappeared."

"Barry didn't disappear."

Ben looked at the gun. There was no reason for an old woman to be holding a gun on him and yet, there it was—still pointing at him. He turned his head. Reggie was blocking the door. He looked every bit as intimidating as the gun.

"My mother kidnapped me when I was four. I think she attended Summerton Academy. I've been trying to figure it all out. Someone released my DNA to the FBI so I could be found; maybe it was her, I don't know. There's some kind of prophecy—it might involve me. I don't know *anything*. I came here looking for answers."

Mrs. Atamian looked over at Reggie. She leaned her weight into the armrest and shifted her position. The movement pained her. She laid the pistol on her lap.

"You'd like some tea, wouldn't you, Mr. Danvers?"

Ben agreed. And he was going to keep on agreeing with whatever the woman said as long as she had a gun on her lap.

"So, instead of reuniting with your birth mother, you're chasing ghosts?"

"I, uh—"

"I don't really care. You know Alex is making his move?"

"You mean Alexander Volkov, the Father?"

"He's nobody's father."

"What did he do to the children at Summerton?"

She corrected him, "It's what I did to the children. Right, Reggie?"

The big man shook his head. "You're a saint, Mrs. A. You did your best."

"I don't understand," Ben said.

Paula Atamian pointed Ben to the couch, then pulled the afghan up over her shoulders. She took her time with the story—about her drug use in the late 1960s and her sexual affairs with Barry Atamian and Alex Volkov. She told Ben about the Vietnam War and how they marched and protested against it. How they became more violent after the Kent State shooting.

"A few of us made plans to break into government buildings and set fires. Alex wouldn't let us. He said our dicks weren't big enough to fuck the system. The only way to kill the machine was from the inside."

"From the inside?"

"He said the only way to bring down the system was to grow a virus. A human virus." She rolled her thin neck, closing her eyes and wincing. "With his money and intelligence, Alex could have done anything. Been anything. His parents emigrated from Russia. He was a first-generation American and hated the place—but he never left. He bought hundreds of acres in upstate New York for his friends to join him. He called it his Idea Farm. We all dropped out of school and joined him—hung out, gardened, built lodges and cabins, did lots of drugs. We'd sit around campfires at night, our minds well medicated, and he'd ask us to imagine a world where no one had to waste their lives crawling for a dollar. A world not ruled by out-of-touch old men. A world without bullshit from teachers and ministers and parents. Everyone would be happy. Stone-age happy. And, at Summerton, we were."

Reggie handed Ben a white mug with flowers painted on it. Mrs. Atamian accepted her tea. She took a sip and placed it on a coaster. She grabbed the pistol by the grip and placed it near her tea.

"One day he tells us he's starting an orphanage. We helped him. Alex was meticulous. He personally chose each child. Every one of them for a purpose. Alex went on a search to find the most brilliant children stuck in the system. He'd be gone for months, recruiting all over the world. And son? He wasn't just looking for smart kids. He needed deviant children, too. And believe me, he found them."

"No one noticed what he was doing?"

"He filed the paperwork. It was legitimate. The orphanages back then didn't ask many questions. They were happy to get rid of the expense. Alex was good with the children. They loved him. And then, he taught them about the Prophecy."

"He brainwashed the kids?" Ben asked.

"We were all believers. Fierce believers. It was our religion. We believed everything Alex told us. He was our church—brilliant and charismatic. We were his army of disenchanted students and disgruntled Vietnam vets. We loved him. It was sick—but it was wonderful too."

"But you left."

"Barry stole me away. Grabbed me, threw me in his car, and drove me back to my parents. I wanted to kill him. It took a long time to get healthy. But what he did saved my life. We got married in the spring. He was murdered that summer." Mrs. Atamian took a sip from her mug. "I tried to make up for what I did. I found Reggie. Thank God I convinced him to leave."

Ben stared.

"You're wondering why I didn't go to the police, aren't you? I should have. It's because I'm a coward. I knew if I said something, he wouldn't hesitate to kill me and everyone else I loved. Alex Volkov is an animal. So, I stayed quiet."

Ben watched her wince as she straightened up in her chair.

"Now, the question, Mr. Danvers, is what are *you* going to do?"

"Do? I don't understand. What do you mean?"

She took another sip of tea and rubbed her thumb along the edge of the mug. She stared at him.

Ben tilted his head, thinking about Tasha's theory. "Does this have something to do with me?"

"You mean, do I think you're the Son?"

Ben leaned forward and nodded.

"Do you think you are?"

"I don't know."

She smirked. "Don't you think you'd know it if you were?"

Then, the old woman shifted in her seat, in obvious pain. She looked up at Reggie and nodded.

"Time to go," said the big man.

Ben didn't need help to get off the couch, but Reggie insisted.

"Mr. Danvers?"

Ben turned.

"I assume that, by now, the virus is in the machine. In some very dangerous places. I'd stay clear of DC if I were you."

"The inauguration?"

She shrugged. Then placed her mug on the table and closed her eyes.

43

Ben turned out of the Elm River parking lot too fast. The Land Rover fishtailed, almost side-swiping a pole before he corrected the slide. The roads were shitty and getting worse. Visibility was near zero. He was ten miles from his apartment, and in this storm, it would be an adventure to just get home. There was no way he could drive to DC tonight. Ben turned off the radio and concentrated on the last two things Mrs. Atamian said to him.

The first had given him clarity—and a sense of relief. She said, if he was the Son, he'd know it. Of course. Which meant the prophecy had nothing to do with him. Alex Volkov didn't need him. Summerton didn't need him. It was likely that whatever they hoped to achieve twenty years ago when they'd kidnapped twin boys hadn't panned out.

The streetlight turned yellow. Ben braked. The Land Rover skidded into the intersection, sliding to a stop under the red light. That was enough for him. He pulled into a McDonald's parking lot. The plows needed time to catch up. Ben tilted the seat back and stared up at the snow falling onto the moon roof. He thought about the *other* last thing Mrs. Atamian had said.

Stay clear of DC.

The presidential inauguration was in 39 hours. If Alexander Volkov had designs on crippling the country, that would be the place to do it. Ben understood risk. He knew how to assess threats. He'd studied Enterprise Risk Management in business school. No matter if you were protecting a company from a hostile takeover or defending a country from terror, it was all the same—had been for centuries. It was castle defense: shore up weakness, build a moat, construct high curtain walls, display superior firepower, deploy spies in the village.

This week, the biggest and most important castle in the world was the inauguration in Washington, DC. The entire political structure of the United States would be in attendance. The Joint Chiefs would be there. The Supreme Court.

But it was impossible to imagine someone laying siege to the inauguration. There were no better defense strategists than the men and woman of Homeland Security and the Secret Service. And, after the attack on the Fed this week, they'd be on high alert. DC *should* be the safest place in the world.

But no castle was impregnable. History showed that if an attacker was patient, they could accomplish almost anything. And Alex Volkov was patient. If Mrs. Atamian was right, he'd been waiting decades for an opportune time to strike. A time like now. The greatest superpower in the world was weak. It was in a state of madness. The streets and airwaves and social media overflowed with anger. America trusted their conspiracy theories more than each other. The nation was in a cold civil war. The high castle walls were cracking.

Mrs. Atamian said the virus was in the machine. *Stay clear of DC.*

He needed to call Kate. Convince her to get out. He grabbed for his phone and saw the text—

Call us as soon as you get this message. Any hour. Any time.

Emma woke to a phone buzzing in her lap. She brought her head up and pain seared through her face.

"Briar, it's him."

"Put him on speaker."

"Benjamin? This is Agents Noble and Metcalf."

"I got your message. I have things you need to hear."

"This is Metcalf. You're in DC?"

"No. Boston. I have a tape. Ida was in an orphanage at a place called Summerton. There's a prophecy and—"

"Slow down. We need to meet in person. How're the roads in Boston right now?"

"Impossible."

"Then, tomorrow morning."

"No. I need to get Kate out of DC."

"We're coming north and you're going south. There's a diner in southern Connecticut off the highway. We can meet there. I'll have Agent Noble text you the address. Bring this tape and whatever else you have. 8 AM. Okay?"

"Okay."

"This is Agent Noble."

"Yeah."

"Where are you staying tonight?"

"My apartment."

"Lock the door."

The call ended and Emma turned to Briar. "What the hell is going on?"

"I don't know. I'll tell you what I find out."

"What do you mean what *you'll* find out?"

"Don't you have a Hot Wash in the city with the SAC first thing in the morning?"

"Shit."

• • •

Ben drove slowly through the North End. The cars along the curb had turned into white snow hedges. He needed food, a shower, and sleep. Ben paid the attendant 30 dollars at the open lot next to his apartment building. He walked gingerly in his brown dress shoes across the icy street toward Giuseppa's for a slice. He slipped in the wet snow, catching himself on the corner of a white van idling in front of the restaurant. He looked through the windshield at the driver and waved an apology.

The guy with the crooked nose smiled and waved at him from behind the wheel.

Ben shook off the snow and stomped his feet on the mat. The restaurant was warm. The smell of garlic seeped from the walls. It was good to be off the road and in a familiar place. He fell into a snug in the back corner. He needed to talk to Kate.

He dialed.

Voicemail.

• • •

All the airports north of Philadelphia were closed on account of the snowstorm. Buses weren't running. The only public transportation moving through the blizzard was the heavy, northbound Acela train. Not only was it powering through, it was still on time. If the schedule held, Arnau Farre would arrive at South Street Station in minutes. There wouldn't be any cabs outside the station to drive him the one mile to Benjamin's apartment. He'd have to hoof it. According to the chatter, no one had seen the kid yet. It meant he was still alive. It meant there was still a chance that Arnau could save him. He texted the Greek.

Be there soon.
Too late. He's here.
Do nothing. Wait for me.

There was no reply. If the Greek got to Benjamin, the kid had no chance. Arnau balled his fists and texted again.

Wait for me or you're dead.

No reply.

44

The staff at Giuseppa's Pizzeria fawned over Ben; they shook his hand, they hugged him, they told him they'd seen him on the news; wasn't it incredible that their favorite customer was the son of the vice president? Ben tried to be patient, but he was eager to get across the street to his apartment. Papa G shooed his employees away and sat down.

"Where's *mi bella donna*?"

"I left her in DC."

"You leave her? Why you leave her?"

"I made a mistake."

He shrugged, "Men. Always we make the mistake, yes? You fix it. *Nessun problema*."

Ben nodded.

Papa pointed out the window. "All day the news is on my side-walk. They point the cameras at everyone. Everyone but *me*. I ask the reporters—but they no put me on the TV. I wave. I bring the pizza. *Mi ignorano*," he said, bulging out his lower lip and brushing his hand at the air.

Ben smiled.

Papa G reached across the table and held Ben by the wrist. "But it's no good for you, Benjamin. I have the face for the TV. Not you. I worry for you. You okay?"

"I'm fine, Papa. Thanks."

"Okay," he said, slapping Ben on the neck, then leaning across the table to kiss him on the forehead.

Ben crossed the street to his apartment. The snow had lightened. It would take most of the night for the plows and salt trucks to catch up. But this was New England. The roads were always magically clear by morning. He looked into the white van as he passed. The driver was gone.

Ben walked up the stairs and down the carpeted hallway to his second-floor apartment. He traced his index finger along the solid white walls. A long, hot shower would be nice. He unlocked the door—it swung open quietly. He slammed it shut, then dropped supine on the couch. He thought about Summerton. About Ida. And the virus in the machine. And about Alexander Volkov—the Father. He thought about the inauguration. About Kimberly Hancock. And the FBI. But most of all, he was thinking about Kate.

• • •

Regina Puleo leaned on her cane. She frowned when she heard the slam from the apartment down the hall. Why that boy had to swing that door closed with such force was a mystery. Well, her now-famous neighbor was home. People would want to know that—not that she'd be saying anything. All that gossip about the young man was disgraceful. It was all anyone seemed to want to talk about. She tied a floral apron over her yellow quilted housecoat. Her white slippers were stained with dried, red gravy.

Every other Tuesday, Mrs. Puleo would dress for the market. She was a light eater, and she cooked only for herself. Tonight was an exception. The gravy was simmering for Larry. Her son. He was coming from Phoenix on an airplane tomorrow. For her birthday. She lifted the lid and scowled into the pot. Four complete stirs with a wooden spoon—counterclockwise. She covered the lid, washed the spoon in the sink, and took off the apron.

"Okay. Momma's here," she whispered to the spider plant by the window. She poured water from a small, green plastic jug.

Mrs. Puleo always looked out the window when she fed her baby. Tonight, she couldn't see without cupping her hands to the glass. It was a good storm. Not like '78, but a good dusting for sure. Larry's plane didn't arrive until the afternoon—he'd arrive fine.

189

Giuseppa's was closing later than usual. The streetlight was out again at the corner. She noticed only one person on the street—a man running with a large green bag on his back. And again, she noticed that Mrs. Bartemolo's Pontiac was still taking the handicap spot—eight months after her hip surgery. Disgraceful.

• • •

Arnau Farre's lungs were on fire. The snow was deep. He'd been running through it for a mile already, the heavy duffel bouncing off his back. The Greek's white van was by the curb. He looked in—no one there. He scanned the buildings, trying to read the numbers. Ida's boy lived across the street from the restaurant. He found the old brick building; Benjamin Danvers's apartment was on the second floor. There were only two windows with light glowing behind the shade. He didn't bother with the front door. Arnau rebalanced the duffel across his back and stepped into the narrow alley. The outside light had been broken at the back of the building. The door had been pried open. The Greek was already here.

Arnau's chest tightened with anxiety. He ran in, taking the steps to the second-floor stairwell two at a time. *Please be alive.* He rounded the corner. There, at the end of the hallway, was the Greek: his knees sunk into the welcome mat, his head leaning into the doorknob, hands at work picking the lock.

The Greek pivoted, flashing his gun. Arnau pumped his open hand. The Greek smirked and returned his weapon to the pouch on his waist.

Arnau listened through the door. A radio was playing inside the apartment. Judging from the echo, it was coming from the bathroom. He patted the Greek's shoulder and stepped behind him. He took the duffel off his back and leaned it against the wall.

Arnau Farre was an experienced, emotionally detached killer. But the man kneeling in front of him was his brother. He disliked him. But he was family. They had lived and worked together since they were children. Killing a brother was beyond the pale—a traitorous act. There would be no going back. Ever.

But his loyalty was with Ida. It had always been with Ida. He'd made a solemn vow. *No matter what.* Arnau Farre's only mission was to keep Benjamin Danvers alive and hidden—until it was safe.

He reached under the hem of his jacket and unsheathed his long, serrated blade. The Greek's head was in front of him. One thrust and a twist of his long knife would sever the brain stem. The Greek wouldn't feel a thing. A clean, painless death.

Arnau brought up the knife and stepped into the thrust, driving the blade forward. Whether it had been the long run from South Street Station, or the cigarettes, or the effects of age—Arnau was too slow. The Greek saw the flash of silver in the doorknob's reflection. He jerked his head to the right. The blade sliced through his ear. The Greek was quick and athletic. An experienced fighter. He swung his legs out and curled backward. In the same lightning motion, he had his weapon out of his pouch.

Before he could swing the barrel, Arnau kicked him squarely in the face. The gun spilled out of his grip and onto the carpet. Arnau stabbed down—another glancing slice that ripped into the Greek's upper thigh. His eyes were wild with pain.

Arnau kicked the gun down the hallway.

The Greek got his feet under him and charged, smashing Arnau against the wall. He had a solid grip on Arnau's wrist, trying to keep the knife from turning into him. And he was strong. Maybe stronger than Arnau. His wrist was wilting under the Greek's power. Arnau grimaced, then slammed his forehead into the Greek's face. He head-butted him a second time, hearing the reverberating crunch of the Greek's orbital bones breaking across his face.

"Stop this instant!"

Arnau snapped his head toward the voice. The demand was coming from an old woman in a housecoat leaning on a cane in an open doorway. He ignored her and smashed his head one more time into the Greek's face. Arnau twisted his elbow, breaking the Greek's grip on his knife hand.

He was quicker this time—punching the blade. One-two. Into the Greek's stomach.

Arnau marched him backward, pushing him inside Mrs. Puleo's apartment. The Greek staggered, his bloody hands laced over his gut wound. Arnau swept his legs under the wounded man's ankles, dropping him hard on his back. He threw himself over the body, finishing the Greek with a deep, killing slash through the throat.

45

Arnau Farre took a cleansing breath, then wiped the blade clean across the dead man's shirt. He looked around the room. The frightened old woman in the housecoat was backed against the wall. She wasn't screaming or making a fuss. There was no one else in the small apartment. Arnau pulled off his jacket and threw it under the window.

He stepped to the woman and spoke into her ear. "Will you keep quiet and do as I say?"

She nodded.

"I have my things in the hallway. Come out with me. If someone sees us, you introduce me as your son. Understand?"

"Larry," she said.

"What?"

"That's my son's name, Larry."

"If you scream, I'll kill you."

"I understand."

"Okay, you first."

She shuffled out the door, leaning heavily on her cane. Arnau stopped by Ben's door. He pressed his finger to his lips and listened. The radio was still on inside. Everything was okay. Back on schedule.

He picked the Greek's gun off the hallway carpet and tucked it into the back of his pants. He slung the strap of the green duffel across his chest. They went back to her apartment. Arnau locked the door behind him. He stood the duffel under the window by his crumpled jacket and looked down at the body. The Greek's eyes were wide open in a death stare. The color had drained from his face. His once ruddy complexion had turned pale and yellowish.

The old lady's eyes were wide, too. She had backed herself against the stove. She was staring at the dead man and at the blood pooling on her hardwood floors, the red stain seeping into the white fringe of her rug. Arnau thought the woman was handling the intrusion better than most would. He'd kill her quick. She wouldn't feel anything when it was time.

He took the Greek's fanny pack off him. He unzipped it and found what he needed—the keys to the white van. Inside were four condoms and a pack of Kools that Arnau threw toward his jacket. He pulled out the Greek's phone and held it over the dead man's face until the device unlocked and brightened to life. He took a moment to gather his thoughts, then tapped out a quick message to the Father from the corpse on the floor.

Ne zorgu pri la bubaĉo infano. Ĉio estas klara. La knabo estas mortinta. (Don't worry about the problem child. All is clear. The boy is dead.)

Now, they'd stop looking for Benjamin. The Father's plan was back on schedule. All Arnau had to do was keep the kid hidden for a few days. He took the SIM card out of the Greek's phone and snapped it in half. Soon, he'd do the same to his own. Because, in a matter of minutes, he and Ida's boy would start their adventure.

His lungs were still catching up. Arnau found Tic Tacs in the dead man's pouch. He sat on a black wooden chair by the kitchen table, his chest rising and sinking. He flipped the cap and poured white pellets into his mouth. He chewed calmly. No need to rush. The kid wasn't going anywhere tonight.

"Smells good," Arnau said.

The woman in the quilted housecoat nodded.

"What is it?"

"Red gravy. For my son. It's my birthday tomorrow."

She didn't add that she wanted to be alive to see him when he showed up. It was written all over her face. Her hands were shaking.

"What's your name?"

"Regina Puleo."

"You're Italian?"

"Sicilian. Will you hurt me?"

"Of course not. We're friends now, Regina."

It didn't look like she believed him.

"Why did you kill that man?"

"It's a long story."

"Could you, at least, turn him over?"

"Of course."

Arnau pushed the Greek over on his stomach. He sat back down at the kitchen table. His breath was returning. Not much longer.

"Your son's lucky to have a mother that cooks."

The woman hesitated. She tried to make a smile, but she was too nervous to be convincing. "Come, I'll give you a taste."

Regina Puleo turned her back and dipped the long wooden spoon into the pot. Arnau stepped over the Greek's body and came up behind her. She was leaning on her cane.

Such a frail little bird.

Mrs. Puleo turned. She held the piping hot spoon to his face. He took it with two hands and blew into the tomato and garlic sauce. His lips touched the spoon. The smell of the sauce filled his nostrils.

The woman dropped her cane.

A wilting pain tore through Arnau Farre's torso. Regina Puleo fell backward against the stove, watching him. In that instant, he wasn't sure what happened. His adrenaline was spiking. He looked over the old lady's shoulder. The knife block on the counter had an empty slot.

Arnau looked down, stunned. It was as if he was seeing someone else's problem. Not his own. The old woman *couldn't* have just plunged an eight-inch chef's blade into *him*.

A second wave of pain doubled him over. Arnau's mouth opened in a silent scream. The bitch put the entire blade into him. Up to the hilt. He winced into a standing position and stepped forward. Adrenaline flooded through him. He was going to kill the bitch.

Regina Puleo tilted her jaw. "Sicilian," she said, flipping the back of her hand from under her chin.

He snapped her neck like it was a dry twig. But the small effort to kill the old woman sent a crippling pain through him. He couldn't stand straight. Arnau leaned his head into the wall, trying to rock the burning pain away. It was excruciating to pull the shirt off his back with one hand and get it over his head. His breath was coming in gasps. He looked down. Blood was streaming out of the wound. He knew it would gush when he pulled the knife. If his organs were perforated, death would come in minutes. Even if it was a lucky wound, he could still bleed to death.

Arnau flipped the gas burner to high and laid the second biggest knife over the flame. Every movement created a storm of whipping pain. His left arm was numbing. He stumbled into the bathroom and opened the closet, searching for anything useful. There was a box of adult diaper pads. He pulled out a handful and put them under his armpit. The reflection in the mirror was not what he was accustomed to seeing. He was pale and his face was shiny—he was going into shock. He leaned his forehead against the glass and tried to calm his breathing. He opened the medicine cabinet. It was a pharmacy of opaque orange bottles, all with impossible names. He inspected each, bringing them up to his face, then throwing them on the floor. Plastic bottles were strewn in the white sink and around the toilet when he finally found a label that said *for pain.* It was filled with white tablets. Just twisting the cap was an excruciation. He shook the bottle into his mouth and crunched down on four of five bitter tablets.

The blade was still sticking out of him. He walked gingerly into the kitchen. The steel of the knife on the stove had turned orange. He closed his eyes and tried to keep himself from passing out. He needed duct tape—it was in the green duffel. He reached down for it. The pain sunk him to his knees. It took a long time to get himself on his feet and over to the stove. He rehearsed the steps in his head. 1) Pull the knife. 2) Cauterize the wound. 3) Cover it with the old lady's pads. 4) Duct tape.

Arnau huffed the air in and out of his lungs. It would require strength and concentration. But he was Arnau Farre. He could do anything he put his mind to. He flinched as his hands wrapped around the protruding blade. He pulled it out evenly. Slowly. It was agony until the knife clanged to the floor. He could feel the rush of wet falling off his torso. Arnau didn't look. He wrapped a floral kitchen towel around his hand and grabbed the handle of the red-hot knife. He exhaled and laid the blade across the wound, hearing the PSSSHT of hot steel melting into his skin. He whiffed his burned flesh. The third and fourth steps would have to wait.

Arnau Farre's eyes rolled back in his head and the lights went out.

DAY 5

46

Arnau felt Ida's soft fingers lightly touch his cheek, tracing his lips, then down his chin, into the scruff of his neck. Her face was in a golden glow, smiling over him in her green dress. The flecks of her long hair held the light of the morning sun. She kissed his ear and whispered. Arnau's lazy eyes blinked open. His head was in a thick fog, but he knew where he was. The old woman's bed. He lowered his chin and looked down toward his toes. The movement sent ripples of washing pain from the wound up into his arms and down his legs—but it was a distant pain. He was aware of it, but it didn't consume him. The duct tape was still wrapped tight against his skin. The gray adhesive had become muddy brown, but the bleeding had slowed—maybe even stopped, he wasn't sure. He didn't care about much of anything. He just wanted Ida to come back to him.

She'd visited twice in the night, told him to bind the wound and take more medicine. Arnau squinted at the orange plastic bottle on the nightstand. He tried to remember what Ida had just whispered. He stared at the ceiling, floating deeper into his pharmaceutical fog. His thoughts slipped and he watched fragments of ideas float by him, the flotsam and jetsam of an overly medicated mind—contrails of a thousand tiny wings looping through his mental mist.

Somewhere a door slammed. Arnau squeezed a slow blink. He had a moment of semi-clarity. The boy was leaving. He should get up. The pain of rising was not distant. It snapped through him. Every step. Every small exertion sent shock waves through him. Arnau stood by the window in his underwear.

Benjamin Danvers was crossing the snowy street. Arnau's eyes drooped. The fog in the back of his head was humming a distant tune. He watched the boy walk to the parking lot with a knapsack across his back. It was like a movie—the kid was an actor in a silent film. It fascinated Arnau, watching Benjamin scrape his windshield, turning the frost and ice into mowing lanes.

He heard Ida whisper. *Get the boy.*

Arnau nodded and realized that he, too, was in the film; tying his boots, wincing the heavy green duffel across his back. He saw himself walking on the hallway's carpet; then he was on the stairs. He watched himself smile at an old man with black trash bags. Then he was behind the wheel of a white van ... a fascinating film.

• • •

Ben spent the nearly three-hour drive from Boston to "America's Diner" in southern Connecticut thinking about Kate. She still wasn't picking up. Not late last night. Not this morning. He needed to get to DC. But first, he had to meet the FBI. He'd be quick about telling them what he knew. Right now, getting to Kate was the most important thing.

The blizzard that pummeled Boston had barely grazed southern Connecticut. He pulled into the parking lot of "America's Diner" a few minutes before 8 AM. It was a dumpy little restaurant next to an abandoned gas station at the end of a road. The asphalt was broken and wrinkled with frost heaves. Dirty water pooled in potholes the size of dish platters. There weren't many cars in the lot, just a handful of dented Pontiacs, sun-blistered Civics, and bald-tired Oldsmobiles. Kimberly Hancock's silver Land Rover was out of place here. He locked the vehicle and looked across the street. A scraggle of wild bushes grew by the roadside in front of a metal fence where trash hung in the brambles like urban fruit. Beyond was the Housatonic River. A stretch of dark woods loomed behind the restaurant. He grabbed the restaurant's cold aluminum rail and hopped up the steps and through the entrance.

The diner's carpet was a dull green, probably original to the building; booths were upholstered with slashes of mauve and gray. The only art hanging off the walls were the framed silhouettes of dancing Hopi stick figures playing the flute. The three old-timers at the counter didn't look up when Ben entered. The place didn't look promising, but maybe the food was good. The sign scotch-taped to the unmanned register said "seat yourself."

Ben took a booth by the window so he could look out on the blue-gray drift of the Housatonic—a dirty waterway infected with PCBs, a forever gift from the GE plant upriver in Massachusetts.

• • •

The white van ran rough. Every bump, bounce, and jostle sliced through Arnau Farre. Mrs. Puleo's pain medication was wearing off. He refused to take more. Not for a while at least. He needed to think clearly. In his current state, there was no way he could muscle Benjamin into the van. It wasn't how he wanted to do it, but he'd have to stick a gun in the kid's face. If luck was on his side, the kid would stop and get off the highway soon.

Arnau got his wish when the Land Rover put its blinker on in southern Connecticut, taking an out-of-the-way exit. He followed, keeping his distance, watching the kid pull into a diner in the middle of nowhere. Another stab of pain shot through his side. Arnau gently put his hand over the wound. It was wet and sticky. He needed a new dressing. He pulled into an abandoned gas station across the street. Once he'd gotten himself cleaned up, he would drive over and park next to the Land Rover. No problem. He'd grab the kid when he left the diner.

Arnau lifted his shirt and looked down at his chest. He didn't like what he saw.

47

Ben couldn't help from fidgeting in his seat when he saw Agent Metcalf park next to the Land Rover. The FBI agent slammed his door, took a moment to smooth his mop of gray hair, then looked into the window of Ben's vehicle. The agent sulked into the diner, demanding coffee from the server as he passed her in the aisle. He hung his black overcoat on the hook, then slouched into the booth without a "good morning." He scanned the diner, following the lack of progress on his coffee order.

"Is Agent Noble coming?" Ben asked.

"She had a meeting in the city. It's just me and you," he said gruffly.

Ben tried not to look disappointed. He liked the other one better. Metcalf was kind of a dick.

"That's your Land Rover, right?"

"It's the soon-to-be vice president's."

"That what you call her?"

"I don't know what to call her."

Metcalf smirked. He lifted his bundle of silverware, tearing off the white napkin, laying the fork to the left and the knife and spoon to the right. He took his time finger-straightening each utensil before leaning back into the booth and tilting his head to the side. "All right. Let's get to it. What'd you find?"

"I was in Ver—"

The phone in Ben's jacket pocket chirped, and his heart jumped.

Was it Kate? He pulled it out. *Shit.* A text from a Vermont number. Not Kate.

"Please. Don't mind me," said the FBI agent.

Ben caught the sarcasm, but he opened it anyway. It was from Wendall's old friend, Truckmeier.

Tilda found the picture of Ida's boyfriend. But the flipper is being troublesome.

Ben put the phone in his jacket and looked up at the server sliding a coffee toward him. She dropped two menus on the table. Metcalf didn't thank her.

"So, what's going on?"

"I found out some things."

"Okay. All ears."

"I went back to Vermont. I found out Ida was an orphan, raised by a frightening guy named Alexander Volkov. There might have been a hundred kids with her in upstate New York."

"She had a tough childhood. So did a lot of people."

"You don't understand. It wasn't an orphanage. It was a cult. Volkov brainwashed the kids into believing in a prophecy—that a Son was coming and they needed to help him when he did."

"To do what?"

"To bring down the United States government."

Briar raised his eyebrows.

Ben nodded. "I know it sounds crazy, but he was raising those children to be an army of insiders—hidden in the government. They're in their fifties now. They've had decades to move into powerful positions."

Briar Metcalf folded his hands together. He tilted his head and exhaled. "That's kind of a lot. Don't you think?"

"You don't believe me, but I can prove it." Ben reached into his pocket and handed over the Memorex cassette. "I also found a woman that taught at Summerton. Her name is Paula Atamian. She lives in Medford, Massachusetts. She thinks Alexander Volkov is planning something at the inauguration tomorrow."

"Planning what?"

Ben shook his head. "I don't know."

The FBI agent sipped his coffee and calmly looked out the window like none of it concerned him. It meant he wasn't believing any of it. And why would he?

Metcalf studied the cassette in his hand, rubbing his thumb over it. "Where did this come from?"

"A teenage runaway. A reporter from the *Albany Inquirer* taped an interview with her in the '70s and—"

"In the '70s?" Metcalf said, raising his eyebrows again.

Ben powered on. "Yes, I found his notes. We think Alexander Volkov's group killed the reporter."

"We?"

"Yeah, Tasha—um, I can't remember her last name. She's a reporter too. With the *Albany Inquirer*."

Agent Metcalf squinted. "Who else?"

"What do you mean?"

"Obviously, I'm going to have to get their statements."

"Right. Well, there's Reggie. He was actually one of the children. He works at the retirement community where Mrs. Atamian lives."

Metcalf wasn't writing any of it. He was just staring Ben down. The guy was an asshole.

Ben grabbed for his coat. He needed to get out of America's Diner and get to Kate. "That's it. Now, you know everything. I'm going to skip breakfast. Long drive ahead."

Agent Metcalf put his index finger in the air and reached into the pocket of his overcoat. "I have a question or two," he said, sliding the teenage photograph of Ben across the table. "We found this on the terrorist who blew up the bus in DC."

"That's my school picture. Why would he have it?" asked Ben.

"You tell me."

"Did you get the guy? What'd he say?"

"Agent Noble killed him. Self-defense. He didn't tell us anything."

Ben stared at the picture.

Metcalf leaned in. "So, Mr. Danvers, let me ask again. Why would a terrorist have this? What's your role in all this?"

"You're kidding, right? How would I know?"

"I'm interested in your theory."

Ben shifted in his seat. "Well, I guess I thought it had something to do with me."

"You thought that *you* might be the Son?"

"Yeah."

"But now you don't?"

"No."

Briar Metcalf sipped his coffee and studied Ben. "Then, why do *you* think they kidnapped you?"

"I thought it was a mistake."

"You thought they accidentally kidnapped you? Like whoops?"

"No. Maybe their plans changed, or something happened and they didn't need me. But now—I don't understand why they'd have my picture."

Ben's phone dinged. He turned it over quickly. Not Kate. It was Truckmeier again.

"Sorry."

"Be my guest."

Ben opened the message. Truckmeier had apparently figured out how to send a picture on his flip phone. It was a grainy photograph of a man on the porch of the yellow colonial—Ida's supposed boyfriend. Ben bent closer, expanding the picture. The guy's face was in shadow. He was wearing a collared short-sleeve shirt. That's all he could see. *Thanks anyway, Truckmeier*. Ben put the phone on the table.

"Everything okay?"

"It's nothing. I have a neighbor up in Vermont that thought Ida might be cheating on Wendall. Some mysterious person showed up every summer when we went on camping trips. He set up a game camera. It doesn't matter—infidelity was the least of her crimes."

"And?" he asked.

"Shitty picture. Can't tell anything."

Agent Metcalf sipped his coffee and stared at Ben. The phone sounded again. Ben didn't jump for it.

Metcalf exhaled loudly. "Why don't you just go ahead and get that."

Ben shrugged and opened the new text. It was another picture of the visitor, this time, walking off the porch—his face in bright sunlight. Ben knew who it was. Recognized him immediately. A chill shivered up his spine. He stared at the picture. He didn't need to make it bigger—he knew the man. He was sitting across from him.

It was a photograph of Special Agent Briar Metcalf.

48

*F*uck. Ben held his breath. He kept his eyes fixed on the phone. Agent Metcalf had been the lead FBI investigator on his unsolved kidnapping case. There was no reasonable explanation for visiting Ida in Vermont. His heart raced. Agent Metcalf was a part of it. He used his position to make sure the investigation never got traction. He was one of the Summerton children. A terrorist.

Every nerve in Ben's body fired with panic. He laid the phone down on the table and reached for his coffee, willing his hands not to shake. He exhaled slowly, knowing Metcalf was watching him. Ben didn't look up. He tried to act calmly, but his eyes were darting around the diner—at the old men at the counter, then at the server talking to the kitchen staff. He swung his head out the window to look at the diseased river. His body was in flight mode. His every movement betrayed him. He was as calm as a tweaking meth addict.

"Something interesting?" Metcalf deadpanned.

Ben shook his head and looked into his coffee.

"No? Nothing?"

Ben inhaled. "Well. That's all I know. I'm going to get on the road. Good luck with everything."

He'd meant to say it with conviction—a firm statement followed by a confident walk to the door. But he was no poker player. Ben's voice cracked in the beginning and trailed off at the end.

Metcalf rocked his head. "I don't think we're done yet." He pointed at Ben's phone. "Show me."

"What?"

"Let me see."

Ben exhaled and looked around, hoping for rescue. "It's nothing. Sometimes Kate sends me personal photos that aren't for—"

"Give me your fucking phone."

Ben slid it across the table, and Metcalf pushed it back.

"Unlock it."

Metcalf put on his glasses and looked down his nose at the picture of his younger self. He stared at Ben, running his tongue under his bottom lip.

Ben blurted, "I don't—"

"Shh," he said, dropping Ben's phone into the pocket of his black overcoat. "Congratulations, you're a much bigger pain in the ass than Ida led us to believe. You were supposed to be the easiest part of this thing. Then you go missing."

"I can just—"

"You were supposed to be dead already. Not sure how you managed that trick, but it doesn't matter."

"I'm—"

"Shut up. Here's what's going to happen—when I tell you, you're going to stand in the aisle and put your coat on. You're going to lead the way out the door. And then we'll go for a little walk. Screw up these simple instructions and I'll handcuff you here, put you in my car, and dump you upriver where nobody will ever find you. Understand?"

Ben nodded.

"Okay. Now. Move slowly."

"Can I use the bathroom?"

"No, fucknut, you cannot use the toilet. Get up."

Ben did as he was told.

The server yelled from across the diner, "Where you going?"

Metcalf pulled back the flap of his overcoat, displaying his badge. "Duty calls. Sorry, hon."

"Thank you for your service."

He gave Ben a friendly pat on his shoulder, then pushed him toward the door.

Ben tried to convince himself that it would be okay—maybe the guy just wanted to talk. But in his heart, he knew better. He could run. And Metcalf would shoot him. He could fight. And Metcalf would shoot him. It seemed like every option ended with catching a bullet. The only thing to do was follow directions. There was a still a chance he'd let Ben go. He swung open the door. The cold slapped him across the face. *He's definitely going to kill me.*

"Walk behind the building."

Ben glanced back at Metcalf's gun. "You and Ida were lovers? That's why you were at the house?"

"She was a frosty bitch—no one ever got her to room temperature. Keep walking."

They took a narrow, snow-covered footbridge over an icy gulch. The path weaved left into a section of trees. Metcalf marched him deep into the woods. It was quiet back there. Ben looked over his shoulder. The diner was out of sight.

"Keep going," said Briar.

Fifty yards later they came out of the woods and into a clearing where acres of half-birthed headstones jutted out of the snow. The cemetery sloped up a long hill. Only the top of a steeple crested in the distance. Ben saw it for what it was: a solitary place where no one would come to help him.

"Is Kate okay? Please—"

"You should have stayed in DC. Believe me, this is not my goddamned job. And now I have to kill this reporter and the Atamian woman. Oh, and Reggie—the douchebag. You've created a lot of work for me."

Metcalf pulled a pistol from his ankle holster and returned the service weapon to his hip.

"No. Please. I'll—"

"Stop whimpering. It was bad luck—like being born with a genetic disorder. Something you inherited. It was always going to end this way. You served your purpose. The Prophecy will be fulfilled—a small sacrifice on your part for the promise of a better world." He waved the gun, motioning Ben to the grave marker in front of him. Metcalf rested his hand on the white headstone and curled his body to see the details. "Gerome Wallace, died in 1872. Get on your knees and face Mr. Wallace—and say hello from me when you see him."

"Please."

"Get on your goddamn knees."

Ben sunk his corduroys into the frozen ground. He felt the release of warm piss soaking his inner thigh. He squeezed his eyes shut and lowered his head. His chest was heaving. His eyes pooled with tears. It wasn't fair. He should have had more time. With Kate. With kids of his own.

The blast from the trigger-pull echoed through the graveyard and up the cemetery hill.

49

Arnau Farre cupped his hand over his eyes and concentrated on not passing out from the pain. He crawled from the back of the white van into the driver's seat. His Beretta was in the passenger seat. The Land Rover was still where Benjamin Danvers had parked it, but now, next to it, was a gray SUV. In a parking lot, mostly empty, he wondered why the vehicle was parked so close to Ben's. Was Ida's boy meeting someone at the diner? Arnau drove the white van through the lot, behind the vehicles, to get a closer look. The gray SUV had government plates. Arnau gritted his teeth. He had a pretty good idea who the vehicle belonged to.

He parked at the far end of the lot—the best vantage point to see the entrance, the vehicles, and the back of the building. He woofed his breathing to keep the pain from debilitating him. If it *was* Briar Metcalf's gray SUV, the boy wouldn't live to see lunch.

He fought through the pain, keeping his eyes on the door until Benjamin came down the steps. He was holding the railing—looking nervous. Behind him, in a black overcoat, was Briar Metcalf sliding his hand under his coat, unholstering his Glock. Arnau grabbed for his Beretta. It was reflex. Under normal circumstances, he would have taken Briar down in the parking lot. But not today. Not in his condition. A gunfight with Metcalf would end badly for him. He put the Beretta back on the seat.

Arnau watched them walk into the woods. He inhaled as deeply as the pain would allow and unzipped the green duffel bag. He pulled out clothes and toiletries, scattering his shit on the floor of the van until he could unearth his short sniper rifle. Arnau opened the door and stumbled into the woods. There was no path here. He moved as quickly as he could through the snow. Arnau pulled himself through thicket and thorns, trying to keep parallel to where the two had gone in. He was concentrating on getting to Benjamin Danvers, and, for the moment, it was helping him keep the pain at bay. At least it was, until he slapped the magazine into the rifle. The effort brought him to his knees. Arnau leaned into a tree and pushed his shoulder into the trunk to right himself. He took three steps and slipped. He fell headfirst down the frozen hill, landing hard on his duct-taped stomach—the crash ending when his neck and head plunged into an icy stream. Arnau choked and coughed, spittle draining out of his mouth. He struggled to his feet. Blood was pouring from his gut wound. He muffled a cry with the back of his hand and fought to pull himself up the other side of the gulch and through tree branches and more thicket.

He lost his bearings in the middle of the woods. He listened. Nothing. He brought the scope of the rifle to his eye and panned. No sign of them. He lowered it back down and stumbled farther into the woods—repeating his promise to Ida as he went.

No matter what.

No matter what.

He fell against an old rock wall at the edge of a graveyard, breathing in desperate gasps. He lifted the sniper rifle.

There. At the far end of the cemetery. Ida's son was dropping to his knees in front of a headstone. He moved the scope to see Metcalf tightening a suppressor—raising the pistol.

Arnau Farre's rifle had jostled inside a duffle bag for three hours of rough road. Yesterday, it had vibrated all day on a train. The sights couldn't be trusted. He rested the stock on a flat rock, looked through the scope, and asked Ida to guide his bullet.

• • •

Ben heard a tight whistling sound, a thump, and then ... the distant blast of gunfire. He felt himself sinking against a weight that, he assumed, had something to do with his own dying. His face was falling into the headstone—he was aware of it and, in that millisecond, it seemed

210

strange to know such a thing. Ben's forehead slammed against Gerome Wallace's grave marker. Pain shot through him. But he wasn't dead. A body had crashed into him. Ben felt warm liquid flowing into his ear and down his cheek. A head was hanging next to his—over his right shoulder. He cried out and scrambled over the body of Briar Metcalf.

• • •

Arnau had held his breath through the 2.5lb. trigger pull. He watched, stunned, that the bullet had found its mark, sinking into his brother's skull. He kept his eye to the scope. After striking the headstone with his face, Benjamin Danvers was all arms and legs—pushing Metcalf off him. The kid was freaking out, covered in a slurry of blood and brain matter. He watched him jump to his feet and run back into the woods.

He leaned his rifle against the old rock wall. Exhausted, Arnau rolled over to let the stones take the weight of his back and head. He pressed his hands over the wound. Everything in him was trembling against his will. He was clammy. Arnau knew he was about to pass out—or die. There would be no chase back through the woods to find the kid and bring him somewhere safe. Benjamin Danvers was on his own. And would, likely, soon be dead. He prayed Ida would know how hard he'd tried. Maybe he'd see her soon. Apologize in person. Explain how he had failed her.

The pain deadened. His hand fell from his stomach and thumped into the frozen brown leaves. His eyes held a green pine branch swaying above him. It danced in the breeze. He stared at it until his eyes grew heavy and his vision blurred and the branch became a block of darkness against the gray sky. And then there was no color.

Arnau Farre felt himself drifting away—into sleep or into death. It didn't matter which.

50

Special Agent Emma Noble took the path from "America's Diner" into the woods. She was running in a hesitant jog, hoping the information was wrong. Praying it was a mistake. She'd bolted out of her early morning Hot Wash in the city and driven north at irresponsible speeds, hoping to catch Briar and Ben before they left. The call came in as she crossed the Connecticut line.

Emma stopped at the edge of the clearing and looked into the graveyard. A State Trooper stood in front of a body. She saw the splatter of red snow. She recognized the shoes. And the black overcoat. Emma knew it was Briar's body. There had been no mistake.

She couldn't look at him like this—not yet. Instead, she focused on small things: his black shoelaces, the half inch cuff of his pant leg, the white of his palm, the curl of his pointed index finger in the grains of snow.

"I'm sorry, Special Agent," said a trooper somewhere behind her.

She nodded because her voice would betray her.

Emma had the movie scene in her head; a loved one rushes to the body, hugs it, smooths back the hair and rocks it slowly until someone peels them away. Briar didn't have anyone in his life to hug his corpse. Right now, the closest thing to family he had was Emma. And she was having trouble screwing up the courage to look at him.

His face was a smear. Emma swallowed hard to keep herself from vomiting. She'd seen enough for now. She walked deeper into the cemetery, where no one could see the tears running down her face. She'd only known Briar Metcalf for a few days, but it had been enough. The man would never have won a congeniality award, but he didn't deserve to be lying dead in a frozen graveyard. He was a friend. Killed in the line of duty. A new face for the Wall of Honor. And he'd died alone.

Emma was seven rows deep. The ancient grave markers were weathered—their honorific words lost forever to the elements. She looked up the hill at the thousands of grave markers. This was the last thing Briar had seen. He shouldn't have been alone. She should have been here with him to meet Benjamin. Maybe things would have been different.

Benjamin Danvers.

Emma looked at the headstone in front of her, but she wasn't reading the name or the date. She was trying to understand how a simple breakfast meeting had exploded into *this*. What happened? Did gentle Ben kill Briar? She retraced her steps and knelt by the body of her partner. *Tell me, Briar.*

If not for his missing face, Briar could have been caught in a restless sleep: an open leg, a bent knee, an arm extended to the side—the other curled under him. She gently rolled him. His overcoat fell open. His Glock was holstered. Did that mean he hadn't sensed the threat? But what made him come into the graveyard?

Emma looked around at all the footprints in the snow. There was no telling if Briar had walked in alone or with someone else. That evidence had been trampled. She looked back over his body. In the snow, a few feet away, lay something she hadn't noticed when she'd arrived. A black, 9mm pistol with a suppressor. *Whose is this?*

"You guys didn't move anything, right?" Emma said to the troopers.

"Just as we found it."

Emma nodded. Her chirping phone interrupted. It was A.D. Monroe.

"Yes, sir. I'm here."

She listened to his rushed words of sympathy. Agents were en route. Reinforcements on the way.

"Sir, he was supposed to be meeting with Benjamin Danvers this morning. There's no sign of him."

"We'll look into it. Now, Noble, here's what's going to happen. You're going to go home. It's my understanding your SAC told you to do that very thing after your meeting this morning. I assume you misheard him. You were involved in a shooting yesterday. And now

213

this. You've been through more in 24 hours than most experience in a thirty-year career."

"Not yet, sir. I think I—"

"Or I can have someone take your badge, your gun, and your keys. Your choice. Have you heard me clearly? Go home and rest. Pass the baton."

Emma hung up and looked around the graveyard. She shook her head. No way. She wasn't going home—not with her partner dead and his killer on the loose. Not until she had some answers.

She studied the body and the 9mm below her. Briar was at the diner because of the meeting with Danvers. Emma reached into her brown coat and pulled out her phone. She dialed Benjamin's number. The ground began ringing—the sound coming from Briar's black over-coat. She rifled through his pockets and grabbed the phone, listening as Benjamin Danvers gave directions to leave a message.

Why do you have his phone, Briar?

Emma rubbed her hands over her face, trying to clear her mind. She bent next to the 9mm on the ground. She sniffed the barrel. It hadn't been fired. It wasn't the murder weapon. She exhaled and looked once again at the body. Briar's pant leg was pulled up, exposing his black socks. She lifted the cuff. There was an empty holster above the ankle.

That's your 9mm on the ground?

Emma looked into the tree line, reminding herself of her training—don't get wrapped around the axle before getting all the facts. Gather the evidence. See where it leads. Emma walked back down the path to America's Diner. Hopefully, the customers and staff saw something. A half-hour later, she learned the witnesses were sure of only two things:

— the person running out of the woods was covered in blood;

— he got into the nicest Land Rover you ever saw.

What they couldn't do was give any meaningful description of the person that ran away, other than he was in a panic. The man was of average height and weight. They disagreed on age, color of hair, and pretty much every other question Emma asked. The server remembered Briar because he was 'kind of pushy, you know?' She didn't notice the guy with him because, 'I'm not good at noticing the nice guys.'

Emma demanded a seventy-five-mile perimeter with a BOLO for a silver Land Rover suspected in an officer shooting. The law enforcement community would drop everything to assist. Off-duty officers wouldn't think twice about speeding back to work to find a cop-killer.

She looked around the parking lot.

"Who's the white van belong to?" Emma asked.

"Not sure," said a trooper.

"Run the plate, please."

Emma walked around the van. She looked into the window. Clothes were strewn around the seat. The ashtray was full of crushed butts. And there, out in the open, lying on the passenger seat, was a Beretta. Emma backed away from the van and looked at the snow by the edge of the lot. There were footprints and drops of blood. She pointed at two troopers standing by a vehicle.

"You guys mind? I need you."

They walked into the woods, following footprints and blood spatter. Emma could see where a person had slid down the hill and where they'd struggled to get up the other side. The farther they got into the woods, the more blood she saw. There was a red pool in the snow beside a rock wall at the edge of the graveyard. The brightness of a single, brass shell casing glinted in the blood.

Briar was shot from the rock wall.

"Whoever did this is in bad shape," said a trooper.

Emma looked up the hill, her eyes following the dragging track of bloody snow prints.

The witnesses at the restaurant had seen a guy covered in blood running to a Land Rover in the parking lot. Whoever they saw, it wasn't the murderer. The murderer's tracks were leading in the other direction. "Can you guys follow those? Maybe we'll get lucky and find him at the top lying face-first."

She sat on the rock wall, watching the troopers trudge up the hill. The conversation with the FBI's armory department was short. And it confused her. The armorer had ballistic information on every agent's service weapon. Emma had fired hers only a week earlier. The FBI didn't discourage secondary weapons, but in order to be government-insured, the armorer had to have fired the weapon and kept a record on file. Briar never registered his personal firearm with the Bureau.

She looked up the hill at the troopers whistling down to her. Their arms were up in the air. No dead body up there. Emma walked back through the woods toward the diner alone. There were a lot of unanswered questions, but two confused her the most.

Why pull the secondary, not your service weapon? Why a suppressor?

51

B en strangled the wheel, rocketing the silver Land Rover down the
interstate. He wasn't sure which highway he was speeding down
or even which direction he was heading. His focus was on speed. On
getting far away. Away from the graveyard. Away from "America's
Diner." He was hyperventilating into the windshield. His shoulders
were quaking and his neck was stiff. Ben brought his face into the
rearview mirror. It was a blood mask of burnt sienna and crimson—his
hair was matted with it.

For ten more miles he shot down the left lane, checking his mirrors
constantly until he realized no one was following him. Gradually, his
breathing returned to something approaching normal. He unburied his
foot from the gas pedal and used his blinker to move into the right lane.
He looked below the steering wheel. His corduroys were drenched in
urine. He tried to focus on what had just happened, what it meant, but
his mind was confetti. An FBI agent had just tried to murder him, but
he'd been shot dead before he could finish the job. Ben did an inventory
of what he knew, and what it meant:

Agent Briar Metcalf was dead. His body was lying in front
of a headstone in southern Connecticut. The FBI knew that
he was meeting Metcalf for breakfast. That probably meant
he was now the number one suspect in his murder.

217

Metcalf had hidden himself inside the FBI for decades. He was a Summerton orphan. They *were* everywhere. Ben couldn't trust anyone.

Alex Volkov and his people wanted him dead. Ben wasn't safe. And neither was Kate—he *had* to get her out of DC.

There was another thing on Ben's mind. He'd survived because someone had saved him. For all he knew, it was the hand of God. A miracle. The thing was, he hadn't even made an attempt to fight for his life. He'd walked placidly toward his own murder. If he couldn't save himself, how could he protect Kate? Ben sat in his own piss and made a promise. Never again would he surrender without a fight. Never.

He needed to get to Kate. Ben reached into the pocket where he kept his phone. It wasn't there. Metcalf had taken it back at the diner. He passed a blue highway sign advertising exit services: food, gas, lodging. He needed to buy a burner phone. He needed to regroup. And clean himself up. He took the exit and headed toward a huge Travel Center sign. Ben passed five columns of gas pumps for 4-wheeled vehicles. The back parking lot was six times the size—home to the big-rig crowd. Ben parked in unclaimed real estate by the air compressor and vacuum station.

He wiggled through the backseat of the Land Rover and grabbed his knapsack out of the rear. He found a bottle of Sprite, a third of it still left inside. He poured the flat fizz over a clean sock and scrubbed his face. With the help of the rearview mirror, he found the last bits of blood caked in his earlobe. Ben pulled off his red-stained white shirt and balled it on the passenger seat. He replaced it with a gray hoodie from his bag. He didn't have pants in the knapsack. There was no immediate solution for his soiled bottom half. He needed to clean himself up, call Kate, and get the hell out of there. If she didn't answer, he'd have to find her. It was a new ballgame. And he was *in* it. Not a spectator.

Ben walked toward the entrance, holding the knapsack in front of his crotch. He threw the bloody shirt into the trash and pulled open the glass doors. A coffee station took up the entire back wall. A miniature Taco Bell was to his left. This roadside oasis was a redneck country club, catering to professional, road-weary drivers. And, apparently, children of all ages. Ben walked down the aisles past American flag sweatshirts, Star Wars lightsabers, snack chips, candy, plastic medieval warrior helmets, anti-freeze, and Flintstone key rings before he found the case containing pre-paid phones. He chose a box that included a SIM card and 100 minutes. The selection of sweatpants was picked over. There was only one in his size—he grabbed it and headed for the cashier.

Ben walked down the hallway, ignoring the warning sign: "Professional Drivers Only." He passed the "cinema room" where a handful of drowsy guys watched a NASCAR rerun. He pushed open the door to the showers. It was a small room. Two shower stalls. He heard spray coming from one of them. Ben dropped his pants and threw them in the trash. He hung his gray hoodie on a silver hook and put his L.L.Bean boots under the bench.

He was naked and bent at the waist, stuffing his sock into the backpack, when the shower at the end turned off. The big trucker came out wiping a towel across his face, leaving nothing about his white, hairless body to the imagination.

He gave Ben a skeptical look. "You lost?"

"No." Ben said, stepping into the stall and shutting the door on the conversation.

"All right then."

Ben took a quick shower and pulled back the curtain. The trucker was waiting for him, standing in there in nothing but his white briefs.

"You're not a driver."

Ben didn't respond.

"You're the guy that was kidnapped, right? Your mom's the vice president."

"You've got the wrong guy."

• • •

Ben parked himself in a bright red booth in the Taco Bell. It took a minute to figure out how to work the new phone, but he got the SIM card inserted and activated. He would call Kate first. *Then what?* The FBI had been infiltrated. Everyone in DC was a stranger. So it could only be Kate. She'd help him figure it out.

I need you, Kate. It rang three times. Then clicked through on the fourth.

"Kate! Thank God. I've been—"

"Who's this?" asked a male voice.

Ben squinted at the phone. "Who's *this*?"

The voice replied, "Her boyfriend … Ben."

His heart raced. He sucked in his gasp and closed his eyes as the adrenaline whipped through him. *Calm. Stay calm.* "Can I speak to Kate, please? Is she there?"

She was. He could hear her in the background, her words getting louder as she walked toward the phone.

"*Who is it, babe?*"

"I don't know. Who is this?"

"It's, um—"

He heard Kate's voice growing more distant. "*I'm taking a shower. You coming, Benjamin?*"

"In a minute," he shouted. His voice quieted. "Sorry. She's unavailable. Call back later."

Click.

52

L ight and sound travel at different speeds. Eyes first. Then the ears. It's the same way with heartache and understanding. One takes a little longer. The heartache? Kate was showering with another man. Ben closed his eyes, swallowing back a tide of bile. It didn't take him long to understand what happened.

Kate would never cheat on him. It wasn't in her DNA.

"Who is it, babe?"

"You coming, Benjamin?"

She was talking to him. Or thought she was. In one horrible instant the truth became clear. Kate wasn't cheating—she thought she *was* with Ben. And the consequences of *that* realization were like a long line of dominoes knocking into each other.

Only one person could fool Kate into thinking she was with him. Someone identical. A twin who picked this moment to come back from the dead.

While Ben lived a life above suspicion—college, girlfriend, job— the Summerton cult waited for the resurrection of a boy burned alive in a boat explosion. After decades of brainwashing, his brother had become the perfect Trojan horse for whatever Alex Volkov had planned for the inauguration. Behold the prophesied Son.

Ben slammed his palm against the candy-apple table of the Taco Bell, startling a family out of their crunchy nachos. His heart was racing. And it was aching. If Kate believed that the man she was with was

221

Benjamin Danvers, so would everyone else. Tomorrow, his identical brother would be feet away from the president.

Ben wanted to believe that Kate would realize it wasn't him—that she'd immediately see that the man with her was not the one she'd been dating for the past two years. But Kate was sweet and trusting. The Summerton cult had likely trained his brother on enough aspects of his life to impersonate him for the few hours between now and the inauguration. *If* Kate noticed any weirdness, she'd simply chock it up to the shock of what he'd been through: the kidnapping, the death of Ida and Wendall, the reunion with his birth mother.

He ran his hands down his face—he should never have left her in DC.

Now his twin, the Son, would have access to the most important targets in the most secure place on the planet. He could do almost anything. And Kate would be beside him—in the crossfire. Or in the bomb radius. The virus was deep in the machine.

He had to get her out. On his own—without help. There was no one to trust.

Ben stared at a brown ketchup stain on the ceramic floor, mentally checking himself the way people do after a nasty fall, taking inventory of their limbs to see how much damage they'd sustained. Ben had been hollowed out. But he was alive. An hour ago, he'd been on his knees, waiting for a bullet. He was about to enter another room in hell, but by now he was familiar with the place—he'd been dragged through it all week like it was a goddamned open house.

Ben grabbed his knapsack and rushed to the exit door. He opened it halfway and froze. A State Trooper was standing in front of the hood of the Land Rover, talking into the radio on his shoulder. Another police car was pulling up to join him. There was a dead FBI agent. Ben was the prime suspect. His innocence would take days to prove, and by then, Kate might be dead. Hundreds or thousands of people might be dead.

Another arriving trooper jogged toward the building. In minutes they'd have the place sealed. Ben backed into the Travel Center. An idea crossed his mind. What if he made a scene and was arrested? That would neuter his twin, expose the deception. It would be easy. Everyone in the Travel Center had a phone. In minutes, they would broadcast the news that both brothers were still alive. That would spoil Volkov's plan.

And then? What would happen to Kate? She'd be in immediate danger. And would Alexander Volkov, a man who'd planned this for decades, not have a backup strategy? Of course he would. If Ben was going to protect Kate, he had to get out of the Travel Center without being seen.

He walked as fast as he could without attracting attention, past the lightsabers, the cinema, and the showers. He burst through the trucker's exit into the yard of eighteen wheelers parked between white lines—the rumbling harmony of forty big rigs. A score of bad ideas flew through his head: he could hide behind a rig, jump inside a cab, run down the road.

A red Kenworth with steel fangs attached to the grill rolled out and made a slow turn in Ben's direction. Teeth were unnecessary—eighteen wheelers were scary enough. He'd always believed that the drivers that attached fangs to the grill of their rigs had to be absolute assholes. But he needed this asshole. Ben moved into the Kenworth's path and waved his arms. The rig lurched and wheezed to a stop. He ran to the passenger side, pulled himself up by the grab bar and slapped at the window. The trucker was the same guy from the showers—he looked properly pissed at Ben's intrusion.

He leaned across and cranked the window down a few inches. "Get off my truck."

"We met back there. You're right, I'm not a trucker."

"I know. Get off my truck."

"I need a ride."

"No."

A State Trooper came around the corner of the building, looking around at the back lot.

"Please. I'm sorry if I was rude," Ben said.

"I don't know you. Get off my truck."

"But you do. You were right. I'm the guy."

"I don't think so. Get down."

The trooper had long strides and was walking toward the Kenworth. Ben pulled his wallet from the front pocket of his hoodie and flicked his driver's license through the top of the window. The driver squinted at it.

"It's me. Please. It's an emergency."

"What emergency?"

"My girlfriend. It's life and death."

"I don't know…."

The trooper was getting close.

"Please. You know who I am. People are going to die if I can't get back to DC. I'm begging. Unlock the door."

The trucker made a face and unlocked the passenger side. Ben ducked below the window as the trooper passed.

"You in trouble with the cops? I don't need that shit."

"It'll take them too long to realize I'm innocent. By the time they figure it out my girlfriend will be dead."

"You hurt anyone?"

"No. I swear."

The driver lowered the brim of his American flag hat and put the truck in gear.

"Get in the sleeper. Close the curtain."

There were four police vehicles surrounding the Land Rover and a fifth tearing into the Travel Center. Ben heard the trucker mumble something about regretting what he was about to do as he rolled out.

"Thank you," Ben said through the curtain.

"Homer."

"What?" Ben asked.

"My name."

"Thanks, Homer. How close can you get me to DC?"

"Going 95 South to Atlanta. I can put you down on top of it."

53

Emma Noble tucked her hair under her FBI baseball cap and adjusted her mirrored sunglasses. The shades were hiding a sunset of color from her broken nose that, in a few days, were sure to turn deep purple. Her hat came off when her partner, in a zippered black bag, was wheeled out of the woods and into an emergency vehicle. She said her goodbye quietly by the bumper.

She reached into her pocket when she heard the chirp of her phone. It was a text from Monroe.

FYI. Ben Danvers reported the Land Rover stolen last night. He's in DC. Took the train. Was never in CT. Not a suspect.

"You Agent Noble?" asked a State Trooper.

She nodded.

"I think we found the Land Rover," he said, passing her his phone.

She turned and walked behind the diner.

"This is Noble."

"Got a silver Land Rover matching your BOLO. I'm at a Travel Center off the highway, 'bout thirty clicks from you. Ran the plates. Get this, the vehicle belongs to a Kimberly Hancock. Any chance it's *the* Kimberly Hancock?"

"We don't need anyone jumping to that conclusion. Do me a favor—take the plates and put them in your trunk. Are you guys sealing up the Travel Center?"

"Doing it now."

"I'm on my way. Thank you."

There were more than a dozen law-enforcement vehicles surrounding the Travel Center, blocking the exits. Emma got a summary of what was happening from the first trooper on the scene. Police were already at work, getting statements and checking registrations from everyone on the property. The trooper delivered the bad news about the security cameras. A storm last summer fried the electronics. Management hadn't replaced the system. They could only rely on witnesses, and so far, they hadn't seen much.

Emma walked over to the Land Rover to see it for herself. She peeked through the window. In a minute, it would be towed to a lab. She sat on the concrete and leaned her back against an air compressor. Who drove the Land Rover here? Who was in the white van? Had there been two murderers intent on ambushing an FBI agent? She shook her head—no way she was going home yet.

Bags of evidence in clear plastic were piling up in front of the building. It was trash from every bin inside and outside the Travel Center. A team of experts would pick through it soon—analyzing receipts, checking fingerprints on coffee cups, whatever they could find. She didn't envy them. Emma raised her sunglasses. Through a clear plastic bag, she could see red. It was a bloody shirt. She snapped on blue rubber gloves and walked over. She pulled out the shirt and lifted it against the sun, looking for holes or cuts. There weren't any.

Emma thought about all the blood: Briar's in the cemetery, in the woods and by the rock wall, and now on this shirt. Three bloody people? *What the hell happened out there?*

She watched them drop another clear plastic bag of trash next to the others. There was a pair of balled-up tan corduroys inside. She opened the bag and inhaled a nose-full of urine. She pulled them out with gloved hands, shaking them straight. They belonged to an adult male. She shoved her hands in the back pockets. She checked the front left. Emma reached into the right and pulled out a white business card. She flipped it over.

Special Agent Emma Noble, Criminal Investigation Division
Federal Bureau of Investigation

She'd been in the field for five days, and in that time, she'd given out her business card to exactly one person. Benjamin Danvers. These were his piss-stained pants. And that was probably his bloody shirt.

But, Monroe's text said he was in DC. Ben was never here. So, someone had stolen his car and discarded his soiled pants at a Travel Center after assisting in the murder of an FBI agent? *If you're abandoning a vehicle, why throw out pants?*

It was a questionable career decision, but she needed to call A.D. Monroe once more. She exhaled and waited for his assistant to transfer the call into his office.

"Yes, sir. I understand. I'll be leaving in a minute. Can I ask…? Are we sure that Ben Danvers is in DC? The evidence doesn't suppor—"

"Noble, drop it."

"Please. Are you sure he's there?"

"I personally contacted the vice president's team. He's in DC with his girlfriend at the Grand FairPoint Hotel."

"I'd like to talk to him and—"

"Stop. Absolutely not. He's the son of our incoming vice president. He is not a suspect, and, if anyone is going to communicate with *that* family it will be me or the director himself. You're done now. Go home. I'm serious about this, Noble. You don't want to test me."

"Yes, sir."

Emma paced in front of the silver Land Rover. All the evidence pointed in the same direction—Ben Danvers had driven the Land Rover this morning. He'd been in the graveyard. And at this Travel Center. There was no way he was in DC.

And then—Emma had an odd thought. An improbable thought. Something that might explain how Benjamin Danvers could be at two places at the same time. Emma walked into the building and sat alone in the corner of the Taco Bell, thinking. *If* Benjamin Danvers had been at the Travel Center, he certainly wasn't here now. He could have hitched a ride. He could be anywhere. And he was probably scared. Scared enough to piss himself. Ben's phone was in her pocket—if he was out there somewhere, she couldn't contact him.

A teenager with a three-alarm pimple placed a diet soda in front of her. She sipped and watched the truckers on the other side of the Taco Bell. They had pushed three tables together. The men held hands and bowed their heads. A thin trucker with a ponytail and a black leather vest walked behind each man and laid his palm against their head and whispered something in their ear. It was highway church. The preacher prayed over a bearded man, taking his time with this one while the others kept their eyes closed and their heads bowed. The holy trucker lifted his hand out of the man's hair.

He looked up and found Emma staring at him. He straightened his arm outward, extending a prayer in her direction. She lowered her head and accepted the Taco Bell blessing—grateful for the moment of peace and the reminder of her faith. She raised her head and smiled. The guy nodded back.

Church was letting out. The truckers moved the tables back and shook hands and fist-bumped each other. Emma waited for the preacher.

"Thank you for the blessing. I needed that."

"We all do."

"My name's Emma. I'm with the FBI."

"They call me Vicar Joe."

"You mind if I ask a question? If you needed to get a message out to someone on the road—how would you do it?"

"Most likely, I'd call their cellphone."

Emma smiled. It made her face hurt.

"What if the person didn't have a phone, or you didn't have their number?"

"Depends on how important it is."

"Very important."

"I'd probably send out a 10-5."

"What's that?"

"It means 'pass it on.' CB radios have about a ten-mile range. So, passing it on requires a lot of rigs continually moving the message out. Most of the time, it doesn't get too far."

"Unless it's coming from someone they trust and respect, yes?"

The man nodded.

"A man like you."

"Are you asking me to do something for you?"

"Yes, Vicar Joe. I am."

54

Ben watched a blue minivan with five bicycles vibrating on its hitch whiz by. He closed his eyes. It was maddening. Kate's rescue mission was happening in slow motion. Homer's red Kenworth was content staying right where it was, mired in a line of trucks dripping down the slow lane of I-95. Ben pressed his fingers into his thighs every time a passenger vehicle zipped past. He had wrongly assumed that the kind of trucker who put steel fangs on his grill would drive a little fucking quicker. Homer drove without urgency—a decelerated Sunday morning drive.

It had been a long day already. He'd left his apartment early to get to the diner by 8 AM. Forty-five minutes later, he was flying out of the woods and into the Land Rover. An hour after that, he was hiding in the sleeper of Homer's Kenworth, pulling away from the Travel Center. They'd already been on the road for three hours, some of it stalled in tortuous New York traffic—bad enough that Ben almost jumped out of the cab to run past the two-mile queue of idling vehicles. He watched the minivan getting smaller in the distance. He reminded himself that the truck's slow pace was better than walking. For the first time, he didn't calculate how much sooner the passing car would reach DC before him.

He and Homer had done little talking. Mostly because of the white noise static coming out of the CB. It was deafening. Homer tried to explain that he didn't dial the squelch down because he was a professional, didn't mind the static, and could hear things from farther away with his radio set that way.

Ben minded the static. Very much. It was driving him crazy. And then, every fifteen minutes, it was interrupted with somebody a million miles away saying something inaudible to somebody else—and Homer would nod his head, like he'd heard it perfectly. Ben needed to get the hell out of this truck.

The radio farted a squawk of distant inaudible noise. Homer looked at Ben and raised his eyebrows.

"What?" Ben asked.

"You didn't catch that?"

Ben shook his head.

"It's going to come around again. Listen."

He was right. Two minutes later, the CB came in clear enough for him to hear.

"Got a 10-17 from our friend, Vicar Joe. Looking for a lost soul named Benjamin."

Ben tilted his head at the speaker.

"Call Noble. She trusts you."

He grabbed a chewed-up Bic pen out of the cupholder and wrote the contact info on the back of his hand.

"That was for you, wasn't it?"

Ben nodded.

"He said 10-17. That makes it urgent. You going to call?"

It was a good question. After this morning, trusting the FBI seemed like a terrible idea. But Agent Noble had been kind. If Briar Metcalf had an opposite, it was her. Nobel also wasn't in her fifties—she couldn't have been a Summerton orphan. Ben had a burner phone. He'd keep his location to himself. It was worth a shot.

• • •

Emma paced around her apartment. Tea had not calmed her, nor had the Downward Dog or any of the other yoga poses. Word had gotten out about Briar. Her classmates from Quantico were reaching out with sympathetic texts. Her partner was dead, but it hadn't sunk in yet. Her phone rang. She answered quickly. "This is Noble."

"You're looking for me?"

Emma inhaled and closed her eyes. She reminded herself to be careful. And gentle. "Benjamin? Are you okay?"

"No."

"Where are you?"

"I'm not going to tell you that."

"Okay. I understand. Are you safe right now?"

"Yes."

"I need to know what happened this morning."

"Your partner tried to kill me—that's what happened."

Emma closed her eyes.

"You still there, Agent Noble?"

"Yeah."

"Do you believe me?"

Emma pictured the scene—Briar's empty ankle holster and the unregistered, silenced pistol in the snow.

"Maybe. I don't know yet. Who killed Agent Metcalf?"

"My guardian angel. I don't know. I ran."

"So, to be clear, right now you're not in DC with your girlfriend? You're not at the Grand FairPoint Hotel? You didn't take the train this morning from Boston, and you didn't report the Land Rover stolen last night?"

Emma listened while Ben told her the story of Alexander Volkov, Summerton, and the Prophecy. And then about his twin brother, the Son. By the time he was finished, Emma had slid down the wall and was sitting with her butt on the floor, her head in her hands. For the first time all week, it was making sense. The *Tri Kolonoj*. The sudden reappearance of the long-lost, kidnapped son of Kimberly Hancock. She now understood why Volkov's people needed Benjamin Danvers dead. That he remained alive was a miracle.

"This Atamian woman thinks there's a hundred or more hidden in plain sight? Why?"

"They're planning something for tomorrow."

"At the inauguration. What are they going to do?"

"It involves my brother. They've gone to a lot of trouble. Probably an assassination. Maybe a terrorist strike—I'm not sure how many they're targeting. All I know is that Kate's in danger."

Emma exhaled. "Then ... we can't trust anyone."

"I'm not sure I even trust you, Agent Noble."

Emma nodded into the phone. "How are you going to get your girlfriend out?"

"I don't know."

"Keep your phone on. I'll call you back. We'll take your brother out of the equation. Kate's going to be fine."

"No. I need to get her out first. I don't want her in the middle of a takedown. When she and I are safe, you can go after my brother. Understand?"

"Keep your phone next to you."

Emma hung up with Ben and walked into the kitchen. She was shaking. *Briar Metcalf—a terrorist.* She thought about their long car rides. The conversations. Had she missed something? No. Of course not. There were no clues because she hadn't been looking. No one was. He was above suspicion—a decorated senior agent with the FBI. No one doubted him. Emma took a swipe at the coffee mug on the counter. *Fuck you, Briar!*

She stood over the pieces of shattered ceramic. That was the brilliance of Volkov's plan. You trust the people you know—the people you have history with. And if Briar Metcalf could be a terrorist, anyone could. Hell, Associate Director Monroe had a long chummy history with Briar. Was he part of this? How far up did it go? It was incalculable—the damage that could be inflicted by men and women in important positions trading on their history and friendships. Emma touched the hollow of her throat. She closed her eyes. *Who can you trust, Emma?*

She understood what she had to do. Her lip quivered and her eyes pooled. She swore she'd never play this card—the one she kept closest to her chest. He'd finally become the person her mother always knew he could be. And Emma was about to murder that one. And resurrect the other. But the stakes couldn't be higher.

She opened her phone and texted one word: BLOSSOM.

55

The good professor sat in a worn wooden chair by the window in his small apartment, looking down on Washington Avenue at the mix of pedestrians: businesspeople, bar-hoppers, and bums. He pulled a handkerchief out of his black pants and wiped small flakes of chipped lead paint off the windowsill. It was a studio apartment—one large room with high ceilings and brick walls. The refrigerator had milk, bread, and sandwich meat. And a carrot. The white stove might not have been working. Or maybe it worked fine. The good professor didn't use it.

A heavy wool blanket was tucked into his queen-sized bed, army-tight. The good professor slept alone.

Besides the wooden chair, the only other furniture was a side table with a bible and two framed pictures. One of a person he didn't see enough of. The other of a person he'd never see again. He prayed for both every morning and before turning out the light at the end of the day.

The good professor was an untenured academic at a St. Louis university. On meeting him for the first time, most young people couldn't help but stare at the two-inch scar that ran down the side of his serious face. The good professor had not always been a professor. And he'd not always been good.

He'd done his share of wielding Old Testament vengeance against the enemies of America—those who had hidden themselves behind iron curtains and desert bunkers. He'd been a messenger for a country that had denied his existence, and he'd delivered the news with the tip of a bullet or the blade of a knife. But that was in the past. He'd been reborn. And by the grace of God and his own dedication, he'd gotten out of the killing business—finally, in truce with his violent past.

He shook the flakes of paint from his handkerchief into the kitchen trash can. He poured himself a cold glass of milk, sat in his old wooden chair, and was taking his first sip when his cellphone lit up with a text he hoped he'd never receive.

BLOSSOM.

56

The black Audi with Maryland plates was parked at the rest stop outside DC, just where Agent Noble said it would be. Ben scanned the lot, wondering if anyone was waiting to kill him. Unless it happened to be the old guy walking his dachshund or the two kids screaming at their mother to get them something from the vending machine, he was safe. He climbed down off the red Kenworth.

While Homer waited, Ben checked the Audi's back left tire for the keys. They were right where she said they'd be. So far, Agent Noble had done everything she'd promised. Assuming the car didn't blow up five seconds after he started it, maybe he'd found someone he could trust.

Agent Noble said Kate was staying at the Grand FairPoint. Tonight, Kimberly Hancock was taking her family and senior staff to a pre-in-augural dinner at the Orchid Room in downtown DC. Noble had been a little cagey about where she was getting her information, but if it was accurate, he didn't care. Ben opened the Audi's driver side door. The phone was where she said it would be too. As requested, he threw his burner into the rest stop trash can.

He waved goodbye to Homer as the red Kenworth rumbled away. Agent Noble had made it very clear to the trucker that innocent lives were in his hands. People would be killed if he mentioned who his passenger was or anything he'd learned on the drive. Homer had agreed without hesitation. He was a Navy veteran. He understood what it meant to keep innocent Americans safe.

Ben pressed the start button on the Audi and waited five seconds.

Ten seconds. He hadn't exploded yet. He took that as a good sign. He shot back onto the highway and followed the directions already loaded in the navigation system. Fifteen minutes later, he pulled into an alley behind a row of commercial buildings. He parked in front of a yellow steel door. The alley was littered with broken glass and cans. Among the garbage piling up against the brick building was a small, broken ceramic mushroom. Ben picked it up and turned it over. A key was taped to the underside. He unbolted the door and walked in.

It was dark. It took him a minute to find the light switch. He was in a gallery of sorts—a museum filled with black and white erotic photography and sculptures of smooth brass penises. The art left nothing to the imagination. Men with women. Men with men. Something for everyone. In the middle of the room, an enormous onyx phallus stood proudly.

Black shades covered the windows at the front of the gallery. Ben unlocked the door but stayed inside. He peeked through the shade. Agent Noble said someone would be coming to him. A woman he could trust. A woman with a reputation for discretion. Ben had never met a hooker, but he'd seen them in the movies. He was watching for a woman in ankle-folding high heels, heavy lipstick, and a fuchsia leather skirt. He wasn't looking for a woman like Mika.

She looked both ways, then took the crosswalk like it was her personal runway, stepping fiercely in knee-high black leather boots. Mika moved like music—her long, airy brown hair bouncing in time with her hips. She wore her long jacket open so anyone looking might get a hint of what lay beneath her deep, V-neck blouse. Her lower half was wrapped in skintight riding pants, complete with patches inside the knees.

Two knocks. Ben opened the door and closed it quickly behind her.

"Mika," she said, extending her hand and giving him a curious smile.

"I'm Ben."

"Hoodie and sweatpants? I like my men casual." She looked him in the eyes. "Don't be nervous," she said, toying a finger near her glossy lips.

"I'm not."

She raised her eyebrows and leaned into him. "Baby, one look at you and I can see you're terrified."

Ben's face reddened against his will.

"This is my friend's place. He's out of the country," she said, shucking off her long jacket. Mika sat down and crossed her long legs. She stared at him awhile. "I hear you've had a tough week."

Ben nodded.

She reached for his hand and gently rubbed her soft fingers into him. "It's going to be fine. Mika's got you now."

"How do you know Agent Emma Noble?"

"I don't. I got a call from someone else—I can't say."

Ben decided it didn't matter who was paying her, as long as it worked. It was not a complicated plan. In fact, it was so simple it had a chance.

"So, you'll already be in the Orchid Room when they come in? And you'll call me when you have Kate alone?"

Mika nodded. "Just wait outside. I'll bring her out. I promise."

57

Emma lifted the ring under the lion's mouth and slapped it against the brass plate on the brownstone's thick front door. The sky was darkening. The temperature was dropping. Time was running out.

"Hey, Squirt. Come in."

"Where is he?"

Uncle Gunny pointed his thumb toward the back of the house. Emma made for the hallway, not noticing the impressionist artwork or the Chinese vases or the oriental rugs. She found her father in the kitchen, leaning against the marble.

"Emmaline."

It was magic, the way her father could say her name. When he said it that way, she felt a little taller—a little more sure-footed. He extended his long arms, and she hugged him back.

"I'm sorry. I didn't have—"

"You did the right thing. Exactly the right thing." The professor looked at his daughter's nose and winced.

"You should see the other guy," she smiled.

Gunny held up a bottle. "Thirty-year Scotch. I've been saving it for—"

"It's a coffee night," said Sam Noble.

The grinder pulverized the beans. Gunny packed the grounds into the portafilter and mated it with the stainless-steel espresso maker. It growled into service. When he'd made three, they got down to business.

Emma had given them the broad brushstrokes in a three-way call on her way to catch a plane out of LaGuardia. A car had appeared in front of Sam's door eight minutes later, courtesy of Uncle Gunny, speeding him to a private airfield. She put her small white cup on the marble.

"Okay, fill us in, Squirt."

It was time for Emma to give the sitrep. "Before I do, I have a question. Why does my Uncle have a high-priced hooker on speed dial?"

Gunny raised his eyebrows and looked at Sam Noble. "You gonna make me take the fall for this one?"

Emma's eyes widened.

"We've used her as an asset a couple times," her father said. "She's been helpful. That's all. Now, let's get to it. What do we know?"

Emma gave them a detailed account of everything she'd seen, and all that Benjamin Danvers had told her. They didn't interrupt, but she saw them exchanging looks. They'd worked together long enough to communicate with an eyebrow or a squint. Emma watched their reactions when she got to the part about the Father and Summerton and the virus in the machine. Now, they looked troubled.

Uncle Gunny recapped, "So, the Danvers kid was the squeaky-clean, normal twin that wouldn't raise any suspicion when he's discovered. He gets reunited with his mother a few days before the inauguration. A cult needs to kill him and replace him with the one they've been grooming so they can put him right next to—not just the new president—but the Joint Chiefs and the Supreme Court at the inauguration. We assume we're looking at some kind of mass-casualty event. And we have to assume that Volkov's got ears everywhere. We can't bring anyone else in. That about it?"

Emma nodded.

Sam Noble looked at his watch. "Eighteen hours. That's all we've got. Maybe less."

"The bad guys don't realize we know their dead twin is really alive," said Uncle Gunny. "That's something, at least."

Sam nodded, then looked at Emma. "Why hasn't the Danvers kid stepped into the spotlight and put an end to this?"

"He's worried about what they'll do to his girlfriend. He pleaded with me to stand down until Kate's away from the twin. I've seen them together. They're a sweet couple, Dad. He's right to be worried."

"Okay, then we let Mika do her thing. Our job is to get the twin. What do you think, Gunny?"

"It's going to be a tough pluck. He'll be surrounded by Kimberly Hancock's security detail. I'm sure Summerton will have someone on him too."

Sam shrugged. "He's the key to this thing. I want to find out what he knows, but if we can't take him with us—"

"We go extrajudicial," declared Emma.

Gunny turned. "We go what?

"Extrajudicial?"

"No," he said, shaking his head. "I've heard soldiers say a lot of weird shit before a raid. I promise you, going extrajudicial has never left anyone's mouth."

Emma assented. "Doesn't roll off the tongue. I get it."

"Are you two done?"

She nodded at her father as they got down to business. Emma was fascinated watching the men. They spoke in shorthand, feeding off each other—developing a plan that was risky, dangerous, and illegal. They were in their element. The operation required specific tools of the trade that Uncle Gunny had stockpiled for such an occasion. Emma didn't want to know what he'd amassed, but she was glad he was on her team. She hoped tonight's crimes would be limited to breaking and entering, burglary, and kidnapping. But whatever happened, the nation's security and the president were at risk—she could live with the consequences.

"It's pretty spooky though, right?" Gunny said. "Volkov brainwashed the Summerton kids with this prophecy back in the '70s—long before Kimberly Hancock had twins. How did he know—?"

"You're giving him too much credit," said Sam. "The story's not that original, is it?"

"What?"

"Half the world has been waiting over two thousand years for the coming of the Son. Volkov just put his own spin on a story that was already working. He said whatever it would take to groom a small army of kids into believers."

"Yeah, but how could he have known that Hancock would be the VP?"

"He didn't. But, remember, Kimberly Hancock has been a national figure since she first got elected to Congress. In her first term, the Boston papers predicted she would be the first female president of the United States. And why not? She came from a famous family. She was ambitious. Wealthy. No doubt, she got Volkov's attention. And he kept a close watch on her career." Sam Noble leaned against the counter. "You got to hand it to him. Volkov's a master at reading the tea leaves. And when Kimberly Hancock gave birth to identical twins? The script wrote itself."

"Jesus," said Gunny.

Emma tilted her head. "But if he's an anarchist, why wait so long? Why play such a long game?"

Sam nodded at his daughter. "That's the right question," he said, bringing his coffee cup to the sink. "The answer is that they needed time to soften the target."

"They?" she asked.

"I'd bet a paycheck that Volkov's not the one calling the shots. He's working for someone else."

Gunny's eyes widened. "You think he's state-sponsored?"

"Connect the dots with me: the malicious software intrusions worming into our secret government databases?"

Gunny nodded.

"How about the manipulation of our elections? Who's holding corporations hostage with ransomware? Fueling hate on social media? Our enemies are discreetly trying to take us down, attacking every seam and stitch that binds our country. They've been at it for decades, pulling at the fabric of our society—and it's working. America *is* coming apart." Sam lifted his chin. "If our enemies have been waiting for a soft target, they've got it. A mass casualty event at the inauguration tomorrow will cripple us."

58

The Orchid Room was once a rustic barn in the middle of a clover field surrounded by a wooden fence and grazing animals. A few years back, they lifted it off the ground, trucked it into DC and replanted it, transforming the old barn into a swanky cocktail bar for the wealthy. A large greenhouse was attached to it. Inside, intimate tables and white linens were framed by a jungle of bright summer flowers, plants, and vines. On this cold January night, it was the perfect tonic of warmth, humidity, and fragrance for a pre-inaugural meal for an incoming vice president and those closest to her—including her long-lost son and his girlfriend. The restaurant was closed for the event. Only a few VIPs were allowed access to the bar.

Mika was a VIP at every upscale bar in the DC area.

She sipped a Negroni and watched the trickling of suits and dresses entering through the barn and into the greenhouse. Many of these soon-to-be administration staffers were young. They walked with excitement, knowing they were only a few hours away from owning a cramped cubicle on Pennsylvania Avenue.

"Hey," said a guy a couple of barstools down.

Mika looked over. An obese porpoise in a blue suit was squeaking at her. She looked at his wrist. He wore a Patek Philippe watch conspicuously over his cuffed sleeve. She didn't hate the guy for it. Go with your strength. And if all you had in your corner was a wristwatch—work it.

She nodded and looked away. Maybe on another night she would have shown a little more interest. Men were teenagers in loose skin. A little less hair. A little more bravado. She had a tolerance for their odd shapes and sizes and kinks. As long as they weren't assholes. She had no patience for assholes. Mika caught the eye of the manager and winked at her. She always took good care of her network of referring partners—the well-placed maître d's and concierges in high-priced restaurants and hotels throughout DC. It was a symbiotic, discreet relationship that served the fetishes of the filthy rich.

This afternoon she'd asked Ben about his girlfriend's kinks. He blushed when she asked if Kate had any interest in women. He stumbled around the question. In the end, he said he didn't think so.

"You don't catch her looking?" she'd asked.

"Maybe their outfits, sometimes. Just innocent comments."

"Doesn't follow any of them into the restroom?"

"What? To have sex? No, of course not."

"No. Not sex. It's a benign little kink, more common than you think—following someone you're attracted to from a public place to a private one. You think she does that?"

Benjamin had looked confused. It wasn't odd that he wouldn't know. Most people didn't share what got them off. It was Mika's opinion that pretty much everyone should see a sex therapist—the entire population of adults in America were consumed by their fantasies. Few jumped into the deep end, but most everyone was staring at the pool.

"In town for the inauguration?" asked the porpoise.

Mika turned, "You?"

"They want me to attend the ball tomorrow night. Gratis. A 'thank you' from our new president. I pretty much turned Nevada for him myself," he said, trying to look down her blouse.

She opened her mouth wide and yawned in his face. It was Mika's foolproof conversation-ender. She employed it with regularity. She looked at her watch. They were running a little late. Mika considered another Negroni but decided against it. Sam Noble paid well. And he was one of the good guys. She didn't want to disappoint him.

Secret Service walked in first and then the small entourage. Mika buried her head in her Negroni ice water to keep from making eye contact with the guy walking behind Kimberly Hancock—the man who was *not* Benjamin Danvers. It was startling how identical they were. Now she understood how the woman by his side might confuse the two. The girlfriend wore a tight, yellow pencil dress. She was librarian-cute and carried herself with quiet confidence. Behind her walked a gigantic man with a head like a cantaloupe.

Mika watched the maître d' direct the girlfriend to sit under a vine of Carolina jessamine that matched the color of her dress. The restaurant manager returned and whispered into Mika's ear, inviting her to a small table with a direct sight line to Benjamin Danvers's girlfriend.

It was second nature for Mika to attract attention when she moved. All she had to do was stare at a random spot in the back of the room, keep her shoulders back, and sway almost imperceptibly. It was confidence. And Mika knew that confidence always attracted attention. She wondered if the girlfriend was watching. Mika made her presence known, bending at the waist to pick her napkin off the floor. Toyed with her shrimp cocktail. It didn't take long to realize that Kate wasn't interested. She was focused on her man, constantly reaching across the table to touch her boyfriend's fingertips. Her smile had a depth to it. She was in love. It was the wrong guy, but it took some women decades to see the imposter in the bodies of the men they'd once loved. It shouldn't be strange that the woman in the yellow dress hadn't noticed it in a few hours.

Mika wasn't sure how she would do it—she was okay with waiting, hoping an opportunity would present itself. If Kate didn't go to the restroom on her own, it would be tricky. But not impossible. *Confidence.*

Fifteen minutes later, Mika relaxed when Benjamin's girlfriend wiped her napkin across her lips and pushed her seat back. She tensed when Kimberly Hancock did the same. They were heading to the bathroom together—with a detail of secret service agents. Mika rose and followed the group toward the restroom. As expected, the secret service stiff-armed Mika to the side until Kimberly Hancock had completed freshening up—and had shared a little alone time with her son's girlfriend. Mika waited outside, hoping she'd remembered the details correctly.

They came out of the bathroom smiling at something said in the privacy of the toilets. The security detail surrounded them. It was now or never.

"Kate? Kate Malone?" said Mika.

"Yes?"

"Boston? St. Bart's, right?"

The woman in the yellow dress looked confused and hesitated while Kimberly Hancock continued past with her entourage.

"I'm sorry. Who are you?"

Mika had her opportunity and she needed to work quickly. This was the part she wasn't thrilled with—trying to convince a stranger that she was with a phony boyfriend— without getting slapped across the face.

"I have something for you. It's a note from someone. It's important you read it and then follow me back into the bathroom."

"I don't have time for this," Kate said. "Have a nice evening."

"Your life depends on it. I'm not exaggerating," Mika said, pulling a small paper out of her bra.

Kate made an impatient face and took the note. She read the small block handwriting. "What the hell is this?"

"He said you wouldn't believe it. But it's true. Follow me."

"This is ridiculous. He's right over there."

Mika shook her head. She took Kate's elbow and directed her into the restroom. Mika held up her phone so Kate could see the live-feed video of Ben lowering his hood.

"Thank god! Kate, it's me. Are you okay?"

"What the hell?"

"Kate, we're in trouble. The person at the table is my twin. Remember the agent that came to the apartment? She said he was dead. They were wrong. You're in danger. Get out of there."

"How do I kno—"

"You cried watching Guardians of the Galaxy. You thought about naming our puppy Sir Shits-a-lot. And, uh, last fall you spent the weekend trying to make turkeys out of popsicle sticks, cotton balls, and dead leaves."

Mika watched Kate staring at the phone.

"This is a joke, right?" Kate said, pushing her head out of the restroom door and peeking into the dining room. The man who was not Ben Danvers was staring off into space.

Mika could see that the girlfriend's world was beginning to unspool.

Kate looked down at the phone and held her palm over her mouth. "Where are you?"

"I'm outside, across the street—a block down."

Mika could see the panic in Kate's eyes. "You need to get out of here, sweetheart."

"How?"

Ben answered. "Make up an excuse. Just get out. Now!"

"Okay."

Mika took the phone back. "You okay?"

Kate shook her head. "No. I'm not."

Mika gave her a kiss on the cheek. "You'll be fine. Go find your man."

59

The lobby in the Grand FairPoint Hotel was jumping with noisy guests in town for the inauguration. The bar was overflowing with loud out-of-towners, spilling martinis and back-slapping. Emma Noble was glad for the distraction. She had pancaked her blackening eyes with concealer and covered them with tinted glasses. Emma kept her head in a book as she passed the front desk and made her way to the bank of elevators. She'd spent years studying crimes and criminals. Except for the overconfident or the terminally unlucky, most thieves didn't get caught in the act. If her father and Uncle Gunny were successful, no one would be reporting a crime tonight. All she had to do was not get nabbed going in or out of their suite.

Stepping into the lift, she spotted a group of drunks heading for her elevator. The doors began to close, but not fast enough. The drunks charged in before the elevator doors closed, filling the small space with boozy breath. She was mashed in the back, trying to ignore a guy staring at her. His nametag said he was David. From Joliet, IL.

"Heyyyy. Wherre yufromm?" he slurred at her.

Emma pretended she hadn't heard.

David stumbled in closer, breathing into her face. "I said, where you from?"

Emma turtled her head. "St. Louis."

David punched the arm of the guy next to him. "Cardinals suck! Cubs rule!" he said, pumping his fists above his head and jumping. The band of idiots followed suit and, for eight floors, the elevator rocked with the chant: "Cubs rule! Cubs rule!" Emma Noble exhaled. She was a diehard St. Louis Cardinals fan stuck in a cramped elevator with drunken Cub fans. The very definition of hell.

She exited on the 23rd floor. There was no one in the hallway. So far, so good. Earlier in the evening, she'd watched Uncle Gunny open a wall safe in his basement. He pulled out a leather binder and opened it on the couch with Emma sitting next to him. At first, she thought she was looking at pages of credit cards, each enclosed in plastic sleeves. But they were hotel keys—from all over the world. He flipped through until he found one from the Grand FairPoint Hotel.

Emma looked at him. "It's expired. How—"

"As they say in L.A.: it's all on the Strip."

"You're thinking of Vegas."

"You want to learn something about breaking into hotels or not?"

Twenty minutes later he handed her a plastic hotel key that he claimed would open any guest room in the Grand FairPoint.

Emma stood in front of suite 2315. She looked up and down the hallway, then pulled the blue key and held it over the electronic reader next to the door. It blinked with two red dots. She tried again. More red dots. The catch of the door clicked open from the suite next door. Emma turned her back on the person coming out. She laid the card on the scanner again. Red dots. *Come on.*

"Evening," said the woman, pulling a shawl over her shoulders.

Emma palmed the card over the reader again. More red dots. Uncle Gunny had convinced her that entry would be the easiest part of the job. She weighed her next move—all options seemed dangerous.

"Try rubbing it on your pant leg," said the woman.

Sure, lady. Emma wiped the blue card against her thigh. Green lights.

"Voila."

"Thanks," said Emma, keeping her face toward the door.

She locked the suite behind her. The bed was a mess of sheets. A pillow was on the floor. Other than that, the room looked fairly neat. She would search the place, and if she were lucky, she'd find the weapon they planned to use tomorrow. If it wasn't here, she'd settle for a computer or any kind of information. It was an enormous suite, but even so, commercial guest rooms didn't have many hiding places. There was nothing in the bathroom cabinets or in the toilet tank or under the lid. She grabbed the shaving kit and the clear cosmetic bag and shook them over the bed, inspecting the contents. Nothing interesting. She ignored the two ripped condom packages on the bedside table and opened every drawer. Except for a Gideon's bible, they were empty.

Emma got down on her hands and knees and looked under the bed and under the couch. She looked behind every painting and print on the wall. She turned over every cushion and examined every pillow. There was nothing to see. No weapons. No computers. She threw a hangered suit from the closet to the bed, then searched the two roller bags and the woman's weekender, running her fingers along the interior lining.

Nothing. The weapon was somewhere else.

Her Grand FairPoint burglary had likely been a waste of time, but she was bringing all of it back with her. Emma repacked the bags until they were bulging and heavy. She threw the weekender strap over her shoulder and strolled down the hallway with a suitcase handle in each hand.

Minutes later, she made her escape from the grounds of the Grand FairPoint Hotel, driving toward the mysterious address Gunny had given her. If all went as planned, they'd have the prophetic Son with them. Tonight, the men had the real challenge. And they needed to be perfect.

60

In another time, in another country, Sam Noble would have just shot the guy, not injected him with tranquilizer. He dumped the zip-tied limo driver into the boot and slammed the trunk down. He shared a look with Gunny, then grabbed the tactical rifle case and ran into the darkness. Yesterday, Sam Noble had lectured on the moral directive of conflict diplomacy.

Tonight, he would let his gun do the talking.

• • •

Ben Danvers hid in the shadows, leaning against the wall of a downtown jazz bar, the bass notes thumping through the brick, vibrating into the small bones of his back. From that dark place, he could see the sidewalk buzzing with couples in Burberry scarves strolling under ropes of Edison bulbs. The bars were hopping. A week ago, Ben and Kate were like those couples on the sidewalk, peering into bars, checking out the live music, walking arm and arm. A week ago, he'd been happy. Now, he was keeping to the shadows, his face hidden under a gray hoodie, trying to keep from being murdered while getting his girlfriend away from terrorists.

Ben's eyes were welded to the front entrance of the Orchid Room a block down the street. He watched Mika leave. A few minutes later, a gargantuan man came through the door. Ben recognized his bowling-ball head. It was Greer, the bodyguard who'd picked him up at the apartment in Boston. Now, the huge man was outside, holding the door for someone. *Come on, Kate.*

Ben exhaled. It was her. She was coming out the door in a yellow dress. He had a stupid urge to run to her. *Patience.* When she got closer, he'd walk out of the shadows, pull back his hood, and show her his face. Ben waited for Greer to walk back inside the restaurant. But he wasn't. He was still holding the door—waiting for another person to exit.

And there he was....

Ben stared at his identical twin brother in a fine suit walking out of the Orchid Room. He reached for Kate's hand. Ben's stomach clenched and he held his breath. Kate was looking down the block toward him, but his twin brother had her by the arm. Holding her back. She looked scared.

Greer scanned the line of vehicles parked across the road, then waved. A car down the street turned its headlights on and rolled forward. If Kate got in, Ben might never see her again. There was nothing he could do for her. He couldn't cover the distance. It was up to her. *She* had to do it. His brother took a step toward the curb, pulling her with him.

Get out of there, Kate.

Ben could only watch. Kate leaned into his brother's ear and said something. Whatever it was, he responded with a smile and then a chuckle. He released her arm and waved as she walked away. Kate took a few steps, glanced back over her shoulder, then quickened her pace toward Ben.

He stepped out of the shadows. She took one more cautious look back up the street, then sent Ben a tight nod from across the street.

Her eyes were wild. "What the hell is happening?"

Ben wrapped his arms around her. He didn't want to let her go.

"Ben, tell me what's goin—"

"You're out. Thank god. We gotta get out of here."

"I don't understand what's—"

"We need to move."

"Benjamin, tell me."

"We're not safe yet. They're trying to kill me—us."

"Kill you?"

"I have a car three blocks away."

"Where? Where are we going?"

"Please, Kate."

"Ben, I don't understand. What's *happening*?"

"I'll tell you on the way."

"On the way to where?" She looked above his eye and winced. "What happened to your head?"

Ben touched his index finger to the spot where he'd slammed into Gerome Wallace's headstone. That would be a story for later. "It's nothing."

They turned toward a commotion moving down the block. A group of rugby players were singing their way down the stairs of an Irish pub, joining a tide of people making their way up the street toward them.

"Ben, this is DC. You've been all over the news. We won't be able to walk to the next light, let alone three blocks to your car, without you getting recognized. Look at all those people."

She was right. By now, almost anyone with an internet connection would know his face.

"We can Uber," Kate said. "I'll call. You stay in the shadows until it gets here."

Ben nodded.

She dug through her black handbag, taking a second to search for her phone. She gave him a sad smile, then kissed him. "Get back there, babe."

Ben pulled his hoodie down and slipped back into the darkness. He leaned against the brick wall and sent an all-clear text to Agent Noble. Whatever plan the FBI agent had, it could commence now. Kate was safe. It was all going to be okay. Just a few more minutes. Just a few more miles. He silenced his phone and waited. Minutes later, Kate waved and Ben slipped unseen into the backseat of the car.

"Smooth jazz okay with you guys?" asked the driver.

Ben clicked into his seat belt and exhaled. For the first time in days, his stomach unclenched. He rested his ear on Kate's shoulder. She was safe now. It was all going to be okay.

61

Feston Greer watched the girlfriend in the yellow dress walk away. He didn't care if she came or went. It was the Son that mattered—all that mattered—and he would eat a bullet for him. Greer put his palm behind the Son's back and turned him toward the open door of the black Town Car across the street. He didn't have to do anything to make himself look tall or imposing—he was born with that. Still, he liked to bow-up in public, rounding out his shoulders and puffing his chest to accentuate his size. He clomped across the street, swiveling his head, knowing that when he did, people were thinking "there goes a man that you do not fuck with."

Greer was alert to the pedestrian traffic a few blocks down. It was early for this many drinkers to be spilling out of bars and onto the sidewalk. But they weren't threats. He opened the door and waited for the Son to settle in. He closed it carefully. Greer tapped his knuckle against the tinted driver's side window on his way around the hood. He got in the passenger seat and grunted to Neil behind the wheel, his head buried in a newspaper. The Town Car pulled forward, down the street and away from the bar scene. Greer pulled his seat belt around his colossal body and scrunched his neck down to wedge his massive skull under the moon roof. Cars were an uncomfortable, tight squeeze for the big man. It took a great deal of effort to get in and get out. And when he did finally get himself seated, he was pretty well stuck. Except for plane rides, cramming into a vehicle was the worst part of his job.

The driver, Neil, was finally acting professional—not chatting

253

everybody up. Greer had spoken to him about that. Maybe it had finally sunk in. The car's headlights swung across a sign for the park. But the park was in the wrong direction. Neil's compass was wired wrong again. This wasn't the way back to the Grand FairPoint.

Feston Greer whispered in a deep voice, "FairPoint. Straighten your shit."

It took effort for the big man to turn his thick neck toward the driver. Neil was looking to his left, fiddling with something by his feet. Greer noticed the ears sticking out from under the black cap. They weren't Neil's. They were bigger. Then a thick mist billowed through the car, clouding those strange ears from view.

• • •

Unlike the movies, in real life, it wasn't easy to incapacitate more than one person. Handkerchiefs dipped in chloroform were the most effective means of knocking out a single opponent, but difficult to administer simultaneously to multiple targets. The Russians thought they had found a solution. In 2002, they let the FSB test their sleep chemical against Chechen rebels after they took eight hundred Moscow theater-goers hostage. The FSB popped a lot of smoke that night, but their new chemical discovery wasn't ready yet—it killed 132 of the hostages.

Oddly, the most successful sleep solution didn't come from state-sponsored scientists, but from nine rural farmers in a Bolivian Mennonite colony. In 2004, they found that bull anesthesia, when sprayed through windows, could incapacitate an entire family, allowing the god-fearing farmers enough time to rape the women, the girls, and some of the men; they rigorously tested the chemical for four years on 151 of their brethren who, according to the local Mennonite bishop, didn't need post-traumatic counseling because they'd been asleep the entire time they were being raped.

Given the history of incapacitating chemicals, Gunny was already more than a little nervous about the efficacy of the smoke. Then he saw the guy who'd be sitting next to him—twice the size of a Mennonite.

Gunny popped the cannister, pushed the rubber mask over his face, jerked the wheel, and skidded to a stop. Thick mist fogged the vehicle. He had a split second to look in the rearview to see the twin's eyes roll back in his head. And then he felt a large fist crack him in the jaw.

Fortunately, the asshole was too big and the car too small for him to get much behind the punch—but it still hurt like hell. The drug wasn't affecting the guy. Gunny's left hand was trying to keep the mask on his face while his right tried to fend off the 350-lb bear. It wasn't going well. The bodyguard yanked the mask away and punched him once more in the jaw. Whether it was the punch or the bull anesthesia, the lights went out behind Gunny's eyes.

He never saw Feston Greer reach under his arm and pull the hand-gun. And he never heard the pffft-pffft of bullets rocketing through the windshield, punching into the big man's neck and chest. Uncle Gunny didn't see it, but he didn't need to. He trusted that Sam Noble was where he was supposed to be—crouched in a tree line with a good rifle and the best thermal scope money could buy.

62

Weaver's Storage was near a one-track road, a mile off a two-lane highway in rural Maryland. It had no paved parking lot, only a patch of brown winter grass. A chain-link fence surrounded the inside structures, three concrete buildings with four orange garage doors each. To the casual observer, it was a sad relic from the eighties—an unprosperous and useless business in the middle of nowhere.

Outside the chain-link was a slumping modular building with sun-faded plastic shutters. Emma Noble sat on a dirty sofa next to two roller bags and a weekender, waiting for her father and Uncle Gunny. It was a sparse office. The walls were white, the furniture cheap. The red second hand of an old clock clicked against the far wall. Emma watched the sweep of the hand, thinking about her father. She knew he was a skilled operator—she'd heard the stories, but those were after-action, highly redacted accounts from her father's friends while they sipped Budweiser. Back then, she would sit cross-legged on the carpet, watching the men laugh. It was hard to tell fact from fiction.

This was different. She was *in* it. She knew the stakes and the danger.

Headlights beamed through the windows. She jumped off the sofa and out the door, following the car across the brown grass and through the chain-link fence. The Town Car drove to building #3 and parked in front of the second orange garage door. Sam Noble rolled down the driver's side window.

"Your mom's birthday," he said.

Emma nodded and entered the date into the keypad. She heard the click and lifted the garage door. She stepped to the side, letting the car roll in. She hugged her father when he stepped out. Emma bent into the window to say hello to Uncle Gunny—instead she greeted a blood-soaked refrigerator of a man wedged into the passenger seat. She looked at her father. His face wasn't giving up any information. Sam Noble opened the back door and pulled the unconscious body of the Son from the car and laid him out on the concrete floor. His hands and legs were zip-tied. Emma quickly checked his pulse and his breathing—physically, he seemed fine.

"Dad where's—"

"Trunk."

"Oh, god."

Her father smirked and curled his finger for her to come see. Emma leaned in. Uncle Gunny was in the fetal position, his head resting on the naked chest of a bound and unconscious limo driver wearing nothing but his underwear.

"He's okay?"

"Yeah."

"Unlike the guy in the front.... What do we do with *him*?"

"Leave him where he is. How'd it go on your end?"

"Struck out. The bags are in the office."

Sam shrugged at his daughter. They both knew it was a long shot to have found anything in the suite of the Grand FairPoint. Emma looked around the small garage. There were a couple of boxes stacked in the back corner. Other than that, it was empty.

"What now?" she asked.

Sam lifted Gunny out of the vehicle and laid him gently against the wall of the garage. He looked at the bodies laid out on the gray concrete. His hands were on his hips. This was the posture her father used when he was getting to work on a project: cleaning the basement, planting the garden, washing the car, interrogating terrorists.

"He's our priority," he said, pointing to the twin.

"What about the driver?"

Sam slammed the trunk closed, and Emma had her answer.

"Emmaline, move those boxes. Your birthdate followed by your mother's."

She squinted at him and looked over at the corner. The boxes were filled with old sheets and clothes and some board games—none of it familiar. It was somebody's random shit. Emma moved the boxes away, and under an old rug was a silver hatch with a keypad.

Uncle Gunny's Bat Cave.

She looked over at her father. He was going through the twin's pockets. Emma entered the digits on the keypad and yanked up on the lid. Lights blinked from below, chasing each other up the black well and illuminating the ladder bolted to the side.

Sam turned to his daughter. "I need paracord. It's in the green trunk—under the grenades."

"Under *grenades*? I have to dig through grenades to find a rope? That's what they teach you at Marine safety camp?"

"Emmaline."

She gripped the ladder and descended. The walls were steel. This bunker hadn't been built by weekend warriors; it had been professionally constructed with defense funds, rounding errors peeled off of a $4.8 trillion budget. Thirty feet down, she hit solid floor.

The room was square—twenty across, twenty deep. It was an apartment of sorts: two bunk beds, a kitchenette, a couch with a bookcase, a small table with two chairs, a blue rug stretched across the concrete floor. Emma opened the cabinet over the microwave. Aluminum cans were stacked on top of each other: soups, dry noodles, sauces, meats, and vegetables. There wasn't a green trunk in this room. But there were three doors.

She walked through the first and found herself in a small communications room with rows of servers and blinking lights. The second was a smaller space with a composting toilet, bags of peat moss, and a rack of old *Sports Illustrated* magazines.

The third door opened into an arsenal. It was half the size of the living space and outfitted with handguns, assault rifles, shotguns, and sniper rifles. The weapons were organized across the wall, in cases, and in lockers. In the back was a steel, blast-proof door she had no desire to open. She found the green trunk next to a gun rack. She was careful removing the steel box of grenades on top.

Emma opened the trunk. Inside were an assortment of knives in a variety of shapes and sizes, two compasses, a garotte, and two pairs of black gloves, all arranged neatly in the wooden tray. She found the dense paracord underneath, looped and wrapped tight.

When she surfaced, Emma saw that Uncle Gunny had come back to life. He was leaning against the wall of the garage, rubbing his jaw.

"He lives!" she said.

"Your dad and I were having a little discussion about overwatch," he said.

"Stop your bitching, Gunny."

"The rhino punches me once—I get it. But twice? You've got a shitty sense of humor, Professor. You know that?"

"You used to be able to defend yourself. But now, I don't know—"

"Don't let your daughter see you being an asshole. Hey, Squirt."

"You guys are ridiculous," she said, throwing the rope to her father. Sam Noble handed Emma a cellphone.

"It's his," he said, pointing at the twin. "See if you can find anything interesting."

"What're you going to do with him?" Emma asked.

"We're going downstairs to have a conversation. We'll see where it goes from there."

Emma laid the twin's thumb over his phone and pressed. It opened to a black background with a purple moon in the corner. She leaned against the Town Car and looked through his messages first. She scrolled and found they all had one thing in common—they weren't in English. Esperanto maybe? Whatever language it was, it was going to take some time to decipher it. His email was a dead end—it required an encrypted password. She told her father that the phone didn't look promising.

"Maybe Gunny can take a crack at it."

Emma tapped on the photo app. She flipped through the first picture, then the second. She closed her eyes and tried to remember something from a few days ago. When she scrolled to the third, her heart flew into her throat. She expanded the photo, making sure she wasn't mistaken.

"Oh Shit!"

Uncle Gunny and her father looked over.

"What is it?" asked her father.

She showed him the picture and explained the problem. The conversation that followed was a short one. Minutes later, she was tearing down the dirt road, praying for a miracle. Uncle Gunny wasn't far behind.

63

The Uber driver rocked his head slowly to the beat of the smooth jazz breezing out of the speakers. But the mood in the backseat was anything but breezy. The weather had turned considerably more frigid. Ben looked at Kate. She was focused and intense—the muscles in her face flexing as she ground down on her teeth. He reached for her hand. She pulled it away, shifted in her seat, and looked out the window.

"Kate? You okay?"

"Peachy."

"I love you."

She nodded.

The realization hit him slower than it should have. What was wrong with him? Of course, she was upset. Kate had been tricked. Violated. This afternoon she hugged an imposter. Kissed him. Probably spent the afternoon making up with him in the suite of the Grand FairPoint Hotel. It had to be consuming her. A million things had to be going through her head—including guilt.

"It's okay," he said. "You couldn't have known. I don't blame you."

Kate hugged her black purse into her chest. "Not now."

"Okay." He leaned in and kissed her on the cheek. She let it land without turning.

"You sure you're okay?"

"I'd be better if you hadn't left me."

That was true. He abandoned her in DC with strangers. His leaving put her in danger. Kate had every right to be furious. He wanted to tell her everything that had happened: about Mrs. Atamian, the close call in the graveyard, how the FBI had found him. But this wasn't the moment. He needed to tend to her first.

"Can you pull in here, please?" Kate said to the driver. "Thank you."

Ben looked around. The car had turned off the main road. They were in an unlit parking lot. He hadn't really been paying attention to where they were. He wasn't sure if they were still in DC, Maryland, or Virginia. "Where are we?"

"Do you mind getting out?" Kate asked the driver. "We need to talk."

"Sure."

The driver turned off the car and opened the door. The vehicle bounced when he sat on the hood and lit a cigarette—the headlights faded to black. There was no light in the sky or in the vehicle. Only a red ember near the front bumper.

Ben stroked the back of her hand. "It's going to be all right, Kate. The worst part's over."

"It's not all right."

"Not now, but soon."

"You made me look ridiculous, running out on me like that."

"I know. I shouldn't have. I'm sorry."

"I didn't know where you were."

"I fucked up. I should have called sooner."

"My job is to know where you are, Benjamin."

"I know. And my job is to look after you too."

Kate shot him a look. "No, that's not your job. You don't look after me."

"I mean—we're in this together."

Ben felt the vehicle bounce again as the driver got off the hood and took another pull on his cigarette.

"It's over, Ben."

His stomach rolled. "What? What's over?"

"It's over," she said.

"I don't understand. Are you breaking up—"

"No. Not that."

He inhaled, "I thought you were putting an end to us."

"Not us, babe."

"No, of course not. I love y—"

261

"Benjamin. I'm not ending us." She leaned over and tapped the window. "Just you."

"Wha—"

"Sorry, babe."

Cold air rushed into the vehicle. Ben's door was opening. The driver had a handgun pointed at his face. He looked back at Kate. She was staring straight ahead, not watching as the guy yanked him out of the car by the scruff of his hoodie.

• • •

The first three photographs Emma saw on the twin's phone were of Ben and Kate, standing by a lakeside beach in front of blue waters with pine trees in the distance. She recognized them even though they were kids, no more than thirteen years old. And then she remembered what Kate had said a few nights ago in their apartment when she'd asked how they'd met: *introduced by a friend who works with Ben at Cambridge Hill. It'll be two years in April. Love at first sight.* That wasn't Ben in the picture, smiling with her in his wet swimming trunks. It was his identical twin. Kate Malone had grown up with Ben's brother. And the condom wrappers in the hotel told her they were more than just friends.

Emma sped down the road putting the pieces together. The cult specialized in having people on the inside. They needed to own the girlfriend—someone who'd make sure that, when the time came, Benjamin Danvers would answer the call and go to DC. Someone to smooth the transition from brother to brother. A person on the inside to help the Son with whatever they were planning at the inauguration.

Emma had helped Benjamin Danvers stumble into his own murder.

64

Sam Noble pulled out the kitchen chair in the bunker and studied
the young man in front of him. Like every interrogator who ever
walked into a room needing information, Sam Noble hoped it would
be easy—hoped the kid would understand the futility of his situation
and cooperate. One look at the twin's fuck-you face was enough to
dash that wish. Sam was going to have to work for it, and didn't have
time to make mistakes.

His career had spanned the evolution of interrogation—torture,
mind games, waterboarding, and everything in between. He'd seen
good men turn sadistic, employing methods that went beyond the pale.
Sometimes they got what they needed—often they didn't. But nothing ever worked when interrogators forgot that their goal was only to
extract information—not to mete out vigilante justice. All Sam wanted
was reliable information, and he was prepared to do anything to get it.

"Need anything?" he asked.

The Son said nothing, just stared at the bunk beds in the corner.
Sam watched his blink rate, getting a baseline. Lies and blinking.
Peanut butter and jelly.

"As you're probably aware, you won't be attending the inauguration. No one's coming to get you."

The twin didn't flinch. His chin was up, and he was scowling at
the wall across the room.

"You're probably wondering what happens now."

His eyes drifted toward Sam's.

263

"It's up to you. Not me. We're going to have a conversation. Or we won't."

Sam Noble stood and walked to the refrigerator. He pulled out a bottle of cold water. Gunny told him the gas had made him thirsty. He uncapped the bottle and set it in front of Ben's twin brother. "Go ahead. Have some."

The young man didn't move. Just stared.

"A sip of water doesn't make you a traitor."

He lowered his eyes to the water and considered the offer. After a minute of staring, he put the bottle to his lips.

"I'm glad we have a chance to talk."

"I'm not talking," said the Son.

"Fair enough. What should I call you?"

"I don't care," he said, staring back at the wall. "I want a lawyer."

"No."

"I get a lawyer."

"We're just two friends, talking. But if I *was* your lawyer, I'd tell you to cooperate. Want to know why?" Sam waited for the kid to look at him. "Because you didn't do anything. Yet. And you won't—because you're here with me. People will understand that you were mistreated. You can still have a good life—if you want it. Would you like that?"

The twin shifted in his seat. Sam Noble waited. It was the kid's turn. Sam would wait an hour if he had to.

"I am the Son that the Prophecy foretold. I have a destiny. This is merely a trial before my triumph."

Sam exhaled. They'd done a number on the kid, but at least he was talking.

"If you're meeting destiny, I think you're running a little late for your big sacrifice."

He looked at Sam. There was confusion in his eyes, probably realizing for the first time that he didn't know how long he'd been knocked out by the gas. His eyes scanned the room, pausing on the small alarm clock on the bookcase.

"You're no coward but," Sam made a wincing face, "it must suck—disappointing all those people who were relying on you. They were waiting their entire lives for you to do your thing. What's that feel like?"

The kid wasn't taking the bait.

Sam leaned forward. "You look bothered. Did you miss it? It's after 10 AM. You should be at the pre-inauguration church service with your mother right now—shouldn't you? Which means whatever weapon you were supposed to receive—you missed it. Right?"

The kid looked away.

"The Son didn't rise this morning. Does everyone just go home? Try again some other inauguration?"

"You wish," the twin said.

"So, there's someone else. They gave the weapon to some other asshole? Who? Who has it?"

The twin shrugged. "You think you're smart. You're a pig. You don't even know what you're looking for."

"I may not know what I'm looking for, but you're right, I sometimes impress myself. You were supposed to have a busy day today. So, if you were receiving something, it would have been in the lobby this morning, right? I'll check the cameras. Find out who has it. Or you could tell me and save me the work."

"It's a big lobby, but it doesn't matter. You can't stop it now."

"Tell me. Where is this weapon?"

"You'll never find it."

Sam frowned.

The twin raised his chin. "Must suck, disappointing all those people that were relying on you."

Sam looked at his watch and exhaled. "Whatever. So, you got, what? A two-hour head start? I can work with that."

"Four, dickhead." Another glance at the alarm clock. "How's it feel?"

He kept the answer to himself, but it felt pretty good. It was always fun when old tricks found new friends. Especially when they were low-tech. The kid was in the wrong time zone. Above ground, it was an hour before midnight.

Sam had the beginning of something he could work with. Sometime after 6 AM, somebody was handing over something to someone in the lobby of the Grand FairPoint Hotel. It wasn't a home run, but he could live with a few singles.

65

With every step the gunman took, the flashlight beam wobbled by Ben's feet. It illuminated only the worn, brown path before him—not the fields to the left or the canal to the right or the woods ahead. Ben walked stiffly. The only sound in that remote place was the crunching of his own footfalls and those of the killer's behind him. It was Ben's second forced march of the day. Tonight, there would be no guardian angel coming to his aid.

The treachery and manipulation washed over Ben—a stunning realization that everything in his life was stained with manufactured deceit. At first, he walked passively, resigned, ready to give up—to slip gentle into that good night. But the farther he trekked down the dark path the more his sadness and distress and impotence were replaced with anger and hate and madness.

The beam rose from the path by his feet and moved up over his shoulder. For a few seconds he saw the approaching woods and boulders brighten in front of him. The unsteady light returned to the path, and once again, his sight was limited to a few feet in front of his L.L.Bean boots. The killer was four paces behind. Every fifteen seconds, the beam rose again over Ben's shoulder, then lowered to the path.

When the gunman opened the car door, the weapon was in his right hand. Ben pictured him walking behind—flashlight in the left, gun in the right. Casually, Ben shortened his stride. The killer was three paces behind him now.

Ben had a moment to consider his life. If he had a crowning

achievement, it was in his victimhood. He was a world-class pussy. A first-ballot Hall of Famer, too naïve to see that the only woman he ever loved wanted him dead. The light bounced around the front of his boots. He shortened his stride a little more. Ben waited for the beam to come off the path once again. His rage was volcanic now. And he didn't care about consequences. There was nothing to lose.

The killer raised the flashlight. Ben saw it come up the side of his brown sweatpants, then hit the corner of his eye as it rose over his shoulder. The woods brightened, and for a moment, Ben was in darkness. He moved quickly, pivoting on his heels and swinging his arm at the flashlight. The gun blasted by his head—the deafening sound so close to his ear that it stunned him. Ben dodged off the path as the flashlight spun on the ground. When it stopped, it was pointing in the killer's direction—the beam shining against his calves. Ben snaked behind the silhouette. The killer swung his gun back and forth, trying to find his prey in the dark. Without the flashlight, Ben was invisible. The guy had only one choice. To bend down and get the light.

Ben charged, spearing his head into the man's spine. It was an illegal, head-first tackle that caught the guy by surprise, launching him off his feet. Ben heard the crack-thud of the guy's head slapping against the boulder. The gun flew out of his hand and clinked off a nearby rock. There was another sound. It was coming from Ben. An animal noise—grunts of rage that kept time with the staccato blows of his pummeling fists, attacking the man under him. The would-be murderer was not defending himself. His body was limp. Ben didn't notice—an adrenaline frenzy had overtaken him. With two hands he lifted the man's head, smashing his skull into the boulder. Over and over. Until, finally, Ben's agony became flaccid, devolving into heaving sobs. He was empty. Gutted. His ears pounding to the rhythm of his pulse.

The flashlight was on the ground. Ben retrieved it and pointed it at the man. His body was splayed unnaturally over a large, red-splattered rock. His eyes were open, but his face was pulp. Ben felt nothing about killing him. Gradually, his breathing slowed. He swung the light along the ground until he found the gun. His mind was hobbled. Ben stood in place. Rigid. Mechanical. Squeezing his eyes tight—waiting for his brain to reboot.

Ben rubbed the barrel of the gun against his forehead, feeling the friction of cold steel against his head. They'd loved each other. But like everything else in his life, Kate's love was nothing but a lie. She was only an actress. A pretender. A babysitter. Someone hired to pacify him until his murder. Ben stood there on the path, scratching the gun against his temple.

He had no plan, but his feet began to move. Ben walked slowly down the path, the beam wobbling in front of his feet, the gun gripped tightly in his right hand. The woods gave way to open fields—the canal on his left.

The parking lot was just up ahead.

• • •

The only light near Chain Bridge that evening came from the flashlight held by a man who could not hear his own footfalls. He walked a worn, frozen path through an open field. His ex-girlfriend sat in the backseat of the parked car, watching the beam rise and fall with the steps of the approaching man. She got out and stood in front of the bumper in her yellow dress, black purse by her side. She called out, asking how it had gone, but her question went unanswered. The woman asked again. The man was getting closer. Still, he did not answer. The flashlight beam moved from her yellow dress to her beautiful and familiar face—a waxwork of the sweet, first grade teacher he once loved. But now, the man had no feelings for her. He knew what she was. And he knew what she was going to do. And when he saw her reach into her purse and draw a handgun, it did not surprise him.

She fired five times. Wildly into the darkness.

The man raised his weapon. He fired; the way they'd taught him in Vermont when he'd earned a certificate for shooting at paper targets. Three shots to the chest. The woman in the yellow dress fell against the car. Dead before she hit the ground.

Ben shined the light across Kate's body. His mind was empty. But his gun was not.

He lifted the barrel.

And put it in his ear.

DAY 6

66

The tire bounced into a pothole, jarring Emma Noble in her seat, but she didn't slow down. She had Gunny in her ear, giving her the location of the cellphone they'd given Ben Danvers. Gunny was two minutes behind her, flying down the road in a red Mercedes, glancing back and forth from the road to his laptop.

Emma forced herself to stay optimistic, but it was a pretend kind of positivity. This afternoon, Briar Metcalf had tried to kill Ben Danvers and now, maybe his girlfriend had succeeded. The odds were high that he was already dead, but she wasn't giving up on him. And if that bitch had killed him, Emma vowed to find her and make her pay. Nobody deserved what they'd done to Ben Danvers.

Gunny said the phone was near Chain Bridge. It had moved a little but was now stationary. That didn't sound like good news.

"Squirt, wait for me. Understand?"

Emma didn't answer.

"I'm serious. Don't go in without—"

She ripped out the earpiece. Ben Danvers was in danger—wasting even a few minutes wasn't an option. She jerked the wheel, squealing into the Chain Bridge parking lot. Her headlights swung across a lone vehicle. She reached for her Glock and reversed the rental—the high beams lit up the vehicle in front of her.

Oh, God.

A body in a bloody, yellow dress was on the ground. Ben Danvers was standing above it with a gun to his head.

"Benjamin!" she yelled, jumping out of the vehicle.

Ben shielded his eyes against the brightness of the headlights, but the gun against his head, it didn't move.

"It's Emma. It's Agent Noble!" She reached into the car and turned off the blinding lights in favor of dimmers. "Hey, Ben," she said, gently. "It's going to be okay. Put the gun down."

He looked lost. And in shock.

"I'm coming to you now. It's gonna be okay. Put the gun down."

Emma had taken four cautious steps toward Ben when another vehicle came into the parking lot at high speed. The high beams of the Mercedes startled him. Ben turned the gun from his head and pointed it at Gunny's car.

"No!" screamed Emma, waving her hands. She was yelling at Gunny. He wasn't good with anyone pointing a gun at him. It always ended badly. Emma stepped in front of his high beams and looked into the windshield. She shook her head, hoping that he would read the situation and keep his gun in his lap. She turned back to Ben with her hands in the air.

"Ben, we need to talk. This is my friend. The one who helped you this afternoon. He's looking forward to meeting you." Emma continued walking toward him. "You can put the gun down now. It's over. I know what Kate tried to do. You're safe. I'm going to take care of you, okay? Put the gun down. Good. Just throw it over there. You don't need it anymore."

The gun landed by her feet. Ben looked at her with hollow, vacant eyes. Emma reached out her arms, touching his bicep and then his shoulder—pulling him into her. It was instinctive and unconditional. Motherly. His arms hung slack by his side and his face dropped into her shoulder. Emma put her hand in his hair, holding the back of his head while he wept into her, his body quaking with sobs.

"It's okay."

Emma looked down at the body of Kate Malone, wondering if a person could recover from what Ben had just been through.

"I killed her."

"I know," Emma whispered.

She sat with him on the hood and laid her hand over his wrist, lacing into his fingers and squeezing. There was a long silence. Uncle Gunny had the good sense to stay in the car. Neither spoke for a while.

"Thank you," he whispered.

"You were brave, Ben." She leaned her head to his shoulder and left it there while he recounted what had happened since reuniting with Kate outside the Orchid Room. She slid off the car and touched his arm. "Give me a minute to talk to my friend. Then we'll get out of here, okay?"

Emma walked to the driver's side window of the Mercedes.

"He took her out?" asked Gunny.

"Yeah, and there's another body in the woods. Can you take care of this so I can get him out of here?"

"The kid's a stud."

"He's a wreck. I'm taking him back to Weavers. I can look after him while you guys talk to his brother."

"No."

"No?"

"We need him. Sam says his twin is supposed to receive some kind of weapon or device in the lobby of the FairPoint this morning. Ben can get it for us."

"He can't. He's too fragile."

"We don't have any other options."

"He was about to put a round through his temple. There's no way."

"You'll figure it out. Nurse your baby bird. Get him ready."

"Jesus, you're not kidding."

"Put him in the suite of the Grand FairPoint. We'll meet you there later."

"He needs clothes."

"We'll bring his brother's. And, Squirt." He reached out the window and touched her forearm. "You did good."

Emma walked back to Ben. What he needed was sleep. And therapy. He needed to be in a safe place. What he *didn't* need was everything Emma was about to ask of him.

"You ready to get out of here?" she asked, squeezing his arm.

"Where are we going?"

"A suite at the Grand FairPoint."

"You're taking me to their room?"

"Yeah. You hate me?"

Ben shook his head.

"Let's have you catch your breath. Take a shower. We'll talk when you're rested."

Emma turned on the car. Her headlights illuminated the dead face of Kate Malone. She pulled away quickly, dropping the corpse back into darkness.

67

"Ben? How you doing?" Emma asked. She opened the bathroom door and dipped her head into the heavy steam. "Ready when you are."

He'd been in the shower a long time. Long enough that she felt she needed to make a welfare check. Emma didn't like leaving him alone, even for a few minutes. It had only been a few hours since he'd been suicidal, and it was far too early to think he'd completely given up on that solution.

She'd been watching Ben closely. He was having a rough go. For the first few hours, he simply sat at the end of the bed and stared at the wall. She tried engaging with him, but he didn't want to talk. All that Emma could do was sit with him and rub his shoulders.

At 4 AM, Emma decided she couldn't wait any longer. She whispered that she'd like his help and told him what they were planning. He gave her a one-word answer.

"Fine."

He was anything but fine. Given his current state, he probably wasn't legally competent to make a breakfast decision. It wasn't fair what she was asking him to do. But it was necessary. Her father and Gunny were in the lobby, watching—and they'd make sure he was safe. That was some consolation, but mentally, the plan would be an assault on Benjamin Danvers's sanity.

"Looking good," Emma said when he finally emerged from the bathroom in a blue suit.

He did look good. Except for the knot on his head, he carried none of the outward signs of his recent trauma.

She smoothed his tie in front of the full-length mirror. "How you feel?"

He didn't reply, but the look he returned was dog-pound sad. Emma wished he would talk. She couldn't gauge if he was even comprehending what was about to happen. He was in his own world.

"You'll be great," she said, patting him on the back.

Emma and the men had worked out a plan based on the information available—which was slim. The twin wasn't giving up much, but they were reasonably sure that a weapon or trigger was being delivered to the Son around 6 AM in the lobby. Other than that, they were in the dark.

The team expected Volkov to have eyes on the transfer, ensuring it passed without incident. If all went well, the delivery person and whoever else was in the lobby would leave quietly. There would be no takedown. Hopefully, the terrorists would leave thinking everything had gone to plan. But if there was a password or some verification that the terrorists expected, the plan was toast. In that case, they'd need to get aggressive. There was no way the terrorists were leaving the Grand FairPoint in possession of a weapon.

But the biggest concern was the thing that none of them said out loud—the most important covert operation in recent memory relied on a traumatized, unprepared, half-catatonic enterprise risk manager from Boston.

Emma raised her eyebrows and grinned like the tiny case she was opening was a birthday present. She gently lifted out an American flag lapel pin and fastened it to Ben's suit. "All right, 007. There's a tiny camera and a microphone in this pin. I'll be watching what you see. I'll be listening to what you hear. Okay?"

Ben nodded.

"Turn your head a little so I can get this in your ear. I can talk to you through this—I'll be your Jiminy Cricket this morning." She slid the small device deep in his ear, then walked to the other end of the suite and whispered into her microphone cord. "Ben, if you can hear me, raise your right arm."

He brought his hand up.

"You're all set." Emma looked at her watch. "5:30, right on time. I'm going to the lobby now. The others are already there. I'll tell you

275

to come down when I've settled in. Just be yourself. And listen to me: we'll figure this out together. And Ben," she looked up at him, "we'll all be there to make sure nothing happens to you. You're safe. We got you."

Emma smiled at him and gave him a hug. She prayed he wouldn't harm himself after she left. Or run. Or not come out of the room. There were problems with leaving Benjamin Danvers alone in the suite, but there was nothing to be done about it.

She exited the elevator. The lobby was already bustling on inauguration morning. Guests were lining up to check out of the hotel, others were huddled on couches in early meetings, some were milling around—drinking coffee, idling through the first hour of the day. Emma was sure that a few of those people were not here for meetings, or check out, or coffee—they were planted to make sure the Son received a package that would fulfill a prophecy.

Uncle Gunny was in a suit and tie, reading the *Wall Street Journal*. On the other side of the lobby, Sam Noble wore a cowboy hat low over his eyes, his legs extended: an early guest sleeping off a long night—his size and posture announcing, "Do Not Disturb."

Emma positioned herself in the deserted bar a few steps above the lobby. She put her head in a laptop, playing the eager junior employee getting an early start.

"Can you boys hear me?" she said.

Gunny shook out his paper. Her father lowered the brim of his cowboy hat.

"Okay, Ben. Come on down."

Emma watched her screen. He was in motion, thank God. His hand came up in front of his lapel camera. She watched him press the down button—saw his reflection in the polished silver of the elevator.

"Lookin' good, handsome."

Ben came out of the lift. As expected, people turned to see him. It was DC, after all. They read the papers and they knew who he was, but to their credit, they left him alone. He walked to a semi-private arrangement of comfortable chairs and low tables.

"You're a pro, Ben," Emma whispered, hoping she sounded convincing.

He stood like a cardboard cutout in front of a black sofa, his back to the lobby—staring at the wall.

"Ben?"

He wasn't sitting down. *Why isn't he sitting?* She looked up from her laptop and watched him. It looked like he might make a run for it. Ben took a few steps to the right, then retreated. The back of his knees knocked against the low table. He caught himself before falling over.

"Have a seat, Ben. Doing great."

She'd gotten him to sit, but he looked anything but casual. His hands were folded on his lap. He sat so straight in the cushion it looked like he was about to have high tea with the Queen.

Everyone was in position. It was 6 AM. Emma inhaled and waited.

6:05

6:12

6:25

Did they miss a signal? Was Ben supposed to have done something? Was he seated in the wrong section? There were so many ways this could fail.

At first, Emma took no notice of the woman puttering across the lobby, pushing her red walker across the white marble. She was smiling, her bent body and unsteady legs moving in a direct line to Benjamin Danvers.

Emma's heart raced. "Here we go," she murmured.

The woman sat next to Ben. "Good morning," she said.

He didn't respond. The lady looked up at him. Ben stared straight ahead, like she wasn't there.

Don't ignore her, Ben! Emma resisted the urge to yell into his ear. Whatever was going to happen, it was up to him.

"*Bonan matenon,*" the woman whispered.

"Shit," Emma blurted into her microphone. The woman was speaking in Esperanto. Was this the code? Now, Emma *knew* they weren't getting the package unless they took it. Her father and Uncle Gunny knew it too. The cowboy woke up; the businessman put down his paper. They had rehearsed this probability: Gunny would move on the delivery person, her father providing covering fire as necessary. Emma would jump in wherever help was needed. She had a hand on her weapon when she heard Ben speaking in her ear.

"*Bonan tagon ankaŭ al vi.*"

"Stand down," Emma whispered into her microphone.

The paper came up in front of the businessman's face and the cowboy went back to sleep. Emma was having trouble believing what she was seeing and hearing.

"*Dankon pro via ofero,*" the woman said.

Ben nodded.

She reached into the basket at the front of her rollator and pulled a small, blue thermos with an American flag out of a canvas bag. She put it into his hand, patted his knuckles, then pulled herself up and rolled back across the marble.

Emma didn't watch the woman leave. Her eyes were on Ben, sitting there on the couch in a fine hotel holding a blue thermos as if it was no big deal that he had, just now, saved the life of the president of the United States and who-knew-how-many others.

From where she sat, Emma thought she saw the smallest trace of a smile creep across Ben Danvers's lips.

68

Emma and Gunny followed Ben into the privacy of the elevator. She was stunned by what she'd just witnessed. And confused. "Ben, what just happened? What did you say to that woman?"

"I said 'good morning to you, too.'"

"That's it?"

He shrugged. "Then she thanked me for my sacrifice and handed me the thermos."

Emma stared at him, then looked over to a smirking Uncle Gunny.

"What now?" Ben asked, waiting for Emma to unlock the suite.

"You guys stay here," Emma said, grabbing car keys off the table. "I'm going back with Dad. Get some answers on what's in the thermos."

"You think I could get some food?" Ben said, looking at the former Marine.

"Son, after what you just did—yeah. Whatever the hell you want!"

• • •

"What do you think it is?" asked Emma, looking at the thermos.

Sam Noble shrugged. He wasn't going to share his theories with his daughter. There was only one thing to do: open it and see what happened. He brought his eyes up to meet hers and shook his head. "You can wipe that hero shit off your face, Emmaline. You're not getting anywhere near this thing. I'll open it in the bunker. If I'm not back in twenty minutes, leave. Do not go down—"

279

"Dad, I—"

Sam gave his daughter a one-arm hug and softened his tone. "Don't go down after me. Okay? Promise."

Emma nodded.

Alone, thirty-three feet below ground, in the bomb room of a steel bunker, Sam Noble held a magnifying glass over the blue thermos. There was nothing sinister about it. It was small enough to have fallen out of a kid's lunch box. Of course, it was anything but benign. To his experienced eye, there wasn't a trip wire or a secondary way of entry. He'd have to just unscrew it and see what was inside. If it was a dirty bomb, he was far enough underground to contain the explosion. But it could be anything. And whatever it was, Sam Noble understood that looking inside might be the last thing he ever did. He'd faced down death plenty of times. It held no great terror for him. He was at peace with his mortality but wasn't in any great rush for it.

He inhaled and twisted the lid. He had the cap in one hand and the blue thermos in the other—more than a little surprised to still be in one piece. Bubble wrap filled the interior of the plastic thermos. Sam gently pulled on the edge of the wrap with tweezers. Inside were two vials, each wrapped separately and secured with masking tape. He'd been holding his breath. Sam inhaled again through his nostrils and blew a steady gust out of his mouth. He was expecting a bomb. This was more clever and just as lethal.

It was chemical. A binary agent—each vial, independent of the other, a non-toxic powder. When combined, they would make a deadly cocktail. Russia had perfected something similar, a nerve agent known as Novichok. The poison was deadly and undetectable—an ideal weapon to smuggle into an inauguration.

Sam carefully separated the vials, putting each in its own secure container in opposite corners of the bomb room. It took no imagination to understand the damage this much chemical poison could do in the wrong hands. Benjamin Danvers had thwarted not just a presidential assassination, but an attack of epic proportions.

But it was a long way from over. There were questions. How many terrorists? Where were they? What else were they planning? They needed answers. The twin had been uncooperative the first go-around, and it was doubtful he'd fall for any more tricks. Sam was going to have to shake the tree—as violently as he had to. The twin *had* to talk.

69

Emma waited, staring at the orange garage door. So far, no smoke. No explosion. She looked at her watch. At the seventeen-minute mark, she exhaled. Like a curtain, the garage door lifted—revealing her father, center stage, and in one piece. He motioned her to join him.

"What'd you find? What is it?" Emma asked.

"Chemical toxin. Some really bad stuff. *Really* bad. I'm going to work the kid for intel: find out who's involved, see what else they're planning. I need you to go back to the hotel. I'll call when the little shit starts talking."

"James. His name is James."

"Fine."

She recognized the look in her father's eye—he wasn't going to be patient for information. Emma turned toward the office where the twin was tied with a black hood over his face. What would it take for Ben's brother to give up his secrets? What was the way in? Emma took a deep breath. The brothers had only one thing in common. And that might be enough.

"Dad, I'm gonna do it."

"What? Interrogate him? No. Absolutely not. I've sat across from him. Trust me, he won't talk to you."

"I can reach him."

He gripped her shoulder. "Emmaline, that's not going to happen. You've done great work. I'm proud of you, but let me take it from here. Go back to the hotel. I'll call you."

Emma pulled his hand off her shoulder. "I said I've got this."

"Let me remind you, you're a *rookie*. Not an operator. You've never even been *in* the room. This is real life. This is a national security crisis. You're not qualified. Don't make me tell you again. It's time for you to go, Emmaline."

"No."

"This isn't a game. Stop acting like a child. This is not up for debate."

She stared into her father's red face and lowered her voice to a whisper. "You're right. We're not debating. I know how to do it. And I will."

He narrowed his eyes. "How?"

"If I'm right, I may be the only person who can get to him."

Sam Noble blew an exasperated sigh. "Jesus—fine. Let's go, then."

She shook her head. "No. Just me."

"Emma—"

"You're going to have trust me. This is *my* case. It's *my* call. And you're *going* to let me do *my* job."

• • •

Fifteen minutes later, Emma was sitting in a wooden chair across the table from the scowling twin, his wrists zip-tied in front of him. His face was like his brother's, but different. Harder. There was no tenderness behind his eyes. This wasn't Ben. And he wasn't interested in being Emma's ally. She brushed perspiration from under her nose and tried to calm her breathing. She folded her hands on the table and said nothing. For five minutes, she didn't speak. Not until the twin looked at her.

"I'm Emma. Can I call you James?"

He shrugged and looked away, but she could tell he was paying attention.

"James, I have some things to tell you that will be hard for you to hear. Are you familiar with the term 'cognitive dissonance?' No? It's the feeling that happens when something you believe to be true is in direct conflict with fact. Failed prophecies cause cognitive dissonance."

The twin turned his head toward Emma.

"It's uncomfortable—it causes a lot of mental stress. And there are really only two ways to relieve it. The first, and easiest, is to make up a new bat-shit-crazy theory. The second is harder. A person needs to recognize that they've been duped and reconsider their belief structure. I'm hoping you'll choose the second."

"Your plan is to bore me to death?"

"No. I'm just warning you that what you're about to feel is cognitive dissonance. When the world fails to end at the appointed hour, when the alien spaceship doesn't show up on time, it leads to some confusing emotions. I'm just preparing you."

"Get to the point."

"The Father told you that you were destined to rise up and sacrifice yourself. America would fall and a more just society would take its place. Something like that, right?"

The twin didn't answer.

"But, James, you weren't going to do that alone, were you? There would be someone by your side. Someone you loved, with a destiny of her own. Wasn't there?"

He looked at her.

"I'm sorry. Truly. It gives me no pleasure to show you this."

Emma inhaled. This was the gamble. This was the moment. She placed four pictures on the table—pictures Gunny had taken of Kate Malone, dead on the ground in the Chain Bridge parking lot. She watched his reaction. His eyes widened. His breathing became more rapid. She watched his face melt into softness. He blinked at the photographs, then closed his eyes. She had seen the same look in Ben—the heartbreak.

Identical pain.

Emma gathered up the pictures and turned them over. She'd broken him open. Now it was time to show him the pieces. "The Father promised you'd enter paradise together, didn't he? It was important for you not to go alone. What you're experiencing right now? That's *not* cognitive dissonance—it's grief. And I'm sorry."

Emma waited, saying nothing for a few minutes.

"This morning, in the lobby of the Grand FairPoint Hotel, we received a blue thermos from a woman in a walker. It contains a chemical weapon. Do you believe me?"

"She would have died rather than give it to you."

"I imagine you're right. But she didn't give it to me. She handed it to your twin brother. Did you know he speaks Esperanto too?"

He was keeping a stiff upper lip, but Emma could see he was unspooling.

"There. Feel that? *That's* cognitive dissonance. You're realizing it was all bullshit. A lie. They kidnapped you—took away your life. They made you believe in a fiction. It's not your fault. The Father convinced a lot of people."

Emma let that sink in.

"Nothing's going to happen at the inauguration. America will not crumble. Soon, the rest of Volkov's followers will understand their mistake—just like you."

Emma exhaled. Her father would not approve of what she was about to do. But it was the only way. She reached into her pocket and pulled out a nail cutter. Two snips and the twin's wrists were free.

"The Father destroyed your life and your brother's. Kate is dead because of him. He's responsible. I'd like your help."

Emma Noble was patient. It took a half hour before the twin let loose the first drizzle of information: the followers still believed Ben Danvers had been killed in Boston the night before last. They thought he was dead. James hadn't had time to warn them before he was gassed.

In time, the drizzle became a torrent of intelligence. Emma had a clear picture of everything Alexander Volkov was planning.

It would have been a bloodbath.

• • •

Emma entered the hotel room. Ben Danvers was coming around. He was stretched across the bed, the suite's pillows propped behind his head. An empty plate on the edge of the couch was all that remained of his steak and eggs. His shirt collar was unbuttoned, his tie was off.

"You saved a lot of lives today, Ben."

He shrugged.

"Your brother's cooperating—to a point."

"What was it?" Ben asked, sitting up a little straighter.

"You intercepted a nerve agent. A lethal powder. Apparently, it works slowly, but it's lethal. Anyone who gets it on their skin dies within twenty-four hours. No antidote."

"How were they going to do it?"

"It was a suicide mission. Your brother and Kate were going to mix it with a gel. They would have applied it to the inside of their pants pockets. Every one of their handshakes today would have been deadly. It would have spread with every greeting and everyone they touched after it. It would have been a massacre."

"So, it wasn't targeted?"

Emma looked at him. He was definitely coming around.

"It *was* targeted. There were people waiting to make introductions to your brother and Kate. People who worked hard to get close to important people. They could be anyone— military, political, judicial. We don't know. The poison was going to be deployed at the Capitol lunch *and* at a defense reception before the inaugural ball. They planned to assassinate the president, the joint chiefs, the directors of the FBI, Homeland, CIA, NSA, and countless others."

"So, they could have taken out—"

"Everybody that mattered," Emma finished. "But, because of you, those people will go home to their families." Emma reached into her bag and pulled out his phone, the one she'd found in Briar Metcalf's pocket. "Take your phone. Get as far away from this place as you can."

Ben gave Emma a look she couldn't decipher. "Why?"

"You're a hero. A hero's job is to ride out into the sunset."

"It's not over. They're still out there."

"We'll mop up."

"Who? The three of you? You can't trust anyone. How will you do it?"

Emma stood up and leaned her back against the window. Her father had asked the same question. She didn't have a good answer for either of them. "What are you suggesting?"

"Let me do it."

"Ben, you can't. You've been through—"

"My brother was pretending to be me. They think Ben Danvers is dead. I'll attend the events. You'll see everything I see. If what my brother says is true, you'll know that the people introducing me are suspects. At least it gives you a place to start, right?"

The logic made sense, but Emma doubted whether he could handle more stress.

"I don't know, Ben...."

"If you were in my shoes, what would you do?"

Emma raised her eyebrows. Yeah, she'd do it. In a heartbeat.

"It's my turn to deliver a little payback," Ben told her. "Don't take this opportunity away from me."

She watched him look through the messages that had been left on his phone.

"A car is supposed to pick me up at 10:15 to take me to the church service. An aide's going to hand me my event passes. Face it, Agent Noble, I'm the best shot you've got."

70

The freezing rain pattered against the stiff fabric of Ben's black umbrella, making it almost impossible to hear Emma in his ear asking if he was "enjoying the weather." His vision was mostly blocked by umbrellas, but from what he could see, the inauguration looked like a soaking-wet funeral. And, so far, the new president's speech was turning out to be as lively as a eulogy.

For most of the morning, Ben Danvers had been herded by officials—directed into a church pew, escorted to a van, shown to his seat ten rows above the lectern. He'd had a brief exchange with Kimberly Hancock at St. John's Episcopal Church, where she'd turned in her seat, looking for him. From two rows ahead, she mouthed the words "Thank you," before the bishop called the congregation into prayer. Immediately after church, the Secret Service guided her into a limousine. That had been the extent of the mother and child reunion.

Freezing rain echoed in his umbrella and clinked against the metal grandstand around him. The inaugural prayers had been recited. The poems were read. Singers belted out their tunes. The new president had finally uttered the holy words, "So help me God."

Now, the man was in the middle of a mediocre speech about unifying the country. And his speech had already brought the audience closer together. There was clear bipartisan support for having him wrap it up and allow everyone to find their way to warmer, dryer conditions.

Somewhere in the procession of poets, and singers, and sheets of rain, his mother, Senator Kimberly Hancock, had become Vice President Kimberly Hancock.

The voice in his ear said, *"When the president finishes, you'll be brought to the lunch. This is your last chance to bail."*

Ben said nothing.

"Alright then. Good luck."

He had convinced himself he could do this. After all, his only job was to be himself for a couple of hours. Nothing hard about that. The new president finished his speech. Someone said a prayer. Then, it was all smiles and handshakes as the new administration made their way up the steps and into the warmth of the Capitol. Ben sheathed his black umbrella in the barrel by the door. He blew into his hands and followed the mass of people down the hallway, following signs to the Joint Congressional Luncheon in Statuary Hall. People recognized him, but everyone in the hallway was "somebody" and they had places they needed to be. A few said hello. Some patted his shoulder and said a kind word, but mostly, it was a cattle call for the cream of the crop to enjoy lunch at the invitation of Congress.

Ben handed his invitation to the woman outside the door and waited for his table number.

"It says reservation for two. Is Ms. Malone joining you?"

"She's a little under the weather. She's hoping to be here soon."

Statuary Hall smelled like flowers, and as Ben looked around, he understood why. There were vases on all fifty tables, on the long dais, in huge containers by the doors, and by the side of the giant statues of historic dignitaries that most in the room wouldn't have been able to name. Ben watched clumps of America's leadership filing into the room, making small talk and side-eyeing their table to determine how close they'd be to the dais. Emma had told him that there would be 250 seated for lunch, including the president and vice president. They would be the last to arrive and the first to leave.

Ben handed his overcoat to the checker, then looked for the nearest restroom.

"Stand there a minute. Let 'em see you."

Ben did as requested, then strolled to the restroom. Inside, he chose the last stall and sat down, looking up at the ceiling tiles and listening to men whistling into the urinals. When the restroom emptied, he whispered into his lapel pin:

"They're going to want to know where Kate is."

"You handled it fine. There's nothing we can do. Keep deflecting."

Ben returned to Statuary Hall and unbuttoned his suit coat. He slowly reached into the front pocket of his pants, and pulled out a white handkerchief and rubbed it over his hands. Ben recognized a few of the people in the room from the news, but most were strangers. It felt like fishing—who would be the first to show their traitorous face?

"Hey! Vice president's son. Am I right?"

Ben turned to face an eager couple in their mid-forties.

The guy stuck his hand out and shook Ben's. "Paul Majors— Chamber of Commerce. This is my wife, Nancy." He pointed his finger into Ben's chest, "Just wanted to say nice job. Man, you wake up one morning and, *boom*, you're the son of the next vice president. Outstanding. Hey, do me a solid and tell your mom that Paul from the Chamber says hi. Maybe she can return my call. You know? All right. I'll let you go. Keep up the good work."

Ben smiled at Emma singing in his head, *"Diiiiick."*

Mr. Majors and his wife weren't terrorists, but that stupid exchange would have left them dead by morning. Victims of an awful, poisonous end.

The attack began with a touch on the back of Ben's shoulder. "I thought your girlfriend would join you."

It was a woman's voice.

"Ben, I can't see her. Turn."

He faced a small woman in a pale pink suit.

"She'll be here soon," Ben lied.

"Maybe I can keep you company. Introduce you to some of my old friends." She smiled sweetly at him.

"You're doing great, Ben."

This was what Emma needed. An idea of where to start the investigation—focusing on the people that introduced him but didn't shake his hand. Anyone who touched his hand was obviously innocent—or suicidal. But just because someone made an introduction didn't make them guilty of being a terrorist. A first-year law student could mount a defense that would clear them of wrongdoing.

As the small woman in pale pink led him toward the group in the corner, Ben decided he would make it a little easier on Emma. He leaned into the woman's ear.

"*Ĉu vi estas amiko?* (You are a friend?)

The woman stopped and looked up at him.

"Ben? What are you doing?"

The woman whispered, "*Glorata estu la Filo.*" (Praise be to the Son)

"Holy shit."

The woman blinked her watering eyes and said, "Come with me, my dear boy."

They walked toward the corner, and the little lady became a swell of enthusiasm. She spread her arms wide, smiling at a litter of black robes. The introductions were swift. They smiled at Ben as he stuck his hand out, shaking each one. A simple greeting that would have taken out half the Supreme Court. The woman in pink returned Ben to the front of the room and left quickly, probably heading for a hazmat shower.

In fifteen minutes, two others tapped Ben on the back and introduced him to the people they'd spent decades getting close to while Emma recorded their faces and their voices speaking Esperanto. By the time lunch ended, Ben had shaken hands with the Speaker of the House, Majority Leader of the Senate, the Chief of Staff of the Army and Air Force, and seven senators. Plus the Supreme Court justices. And God only knew whose hands those people had touched.

Ben waved to his mother at the dais before she got up to leave. He looked around the table, aware of the places he'd put his hand—furniture, plates, cups, silverware. He thought of the busboys … the dishwashers. It numbed him to consider the devastation that the small blue thermos would have caused.

"Ben, get out of there. We have a problem."

71

Ben walked down the Capitol steps past the fencing and blue barricades. He pulled his coat collar up to his ears, as much to hide his identity as to protect his face from the sleet. He made a right on 2nd Street and jogged up the steps of St. Peter's Catholic Church. Mass was long over, but a prayerful few still kneeled in the pews. Emma was in the back row where she said she'd be. Ben dipped his finger into holy water, made the sign of the cross, and walked to a wall of red votive candles. He turned his head and saw Emma stand and leave the church.

"What's happening?" Ben whispered into his lapel.

"Shit's hitting the fan."

"What? How?"

"They know you're alive. Someone must have recognized you yesterday—there's a video of you walking out of the sex shop with Mika. TMZ uploaded it an hour ago. It's gone viral. Volkov knew your brother was at the hotel all day. The cult knows that was you, and you're alive—if you show up tonight without Kate, they'll kill you. Just to be safe."

"Who's 'they?'"

"The cell leader. Apparently, he's ruthless. We don't know what he's capable of, but he's got a reputation for paranoia. If everything isn't perfect, we think he'll go rogue."

Ben lit a candle, then folded a five-dollar bill and slipped it into the donation slot. "Do we know who this guy is?"

"Your mother's Chief of Staff. David Plimpton. You know him?"

291

"Yeah." Kimberly Hancock's old friend. The man she trusted more than any other.

"Ben, I can't put you in there."

"I'm not quitting."

"Did you hear me? If you show up without Kate, he'll kill you."

"I don't care. I'm seeing this through."

He heard Emma sigh.

"So, how're we going to do this?" Ben asked.

There was silence while the rookie FBI agent gathered herself.

"We need to kill you before *the reception."*

• • •

Emma was in the front seat of Uncle Gunny's black security van, her eyes on Ben making his exit out of St. Peter's Catholic Church. There was a lot about her plan that made her uncomfortable. This part was one of them. Emma had divided the van with a black curtain. One twin on one end. One on the other. She told Ben not to speak when he entered. Her father had given the same instructions to the twin who was already inside. The odds were pretty high that a two-minute conversation could lead to a brawl. Ben entered and closed the door behind him. They exchanged clothes. Ben's twin stepped out of the van with Gunny following two steps behind, making sure he didn't get lost.

• • •

Sam Noble focused his sniper scope on the parade-viewing stand. He was in the exact spot that Secret Service couldn't allow someone with a rifle, but Sam had unusual access to uniforms, badges, and clearance protocol. His scope had no one in it but the brother of Benjamin Danvers.

"Touch your nose, please."

Sam watched the young man raise his hand slowly. He itched it with his middle finger.

"Hilarious. Keep looking at the parade. Blink the wrong way and I'm sending a round through your buddy, David Plimpton, and then I'll put one in your ear. But I promise: if you do as you're told, I'll buy you an ice cream. The game's called Tiny Carrot/Really Big Stick."

Sam moved the scope over to David Plimpton. He was sitting six rows behind James. He wasn't watching the high school band from northern Idaho march past. The chief of staff for the vice president of the United States was staring at Kimberly Hancock's son, sans Kate Malone.

Sam looked at his watch. "We're a go."

He watched David Plimpton reach into the pocket of his jacket and pull out his phone. He held it against his ear while looking at the twin. Seconds later, he stood and walked down the metal stairs of the grandstand to find a little privacy.

• • •

"Who is this?" David Plimpton asked.

"It's Ben Danvers. I'm in trouble."

"I don't have time for this shit. How did you get this number?"

"You gotta listen to me. My twin is alive. He's impersonating me! Something horrible is happening. I can't find my girlfriend. She was with him!"

Emma made a wincing face—warning him about overacting.

"You expect me to believe that? I'm *looking* at Ben Danvers."

"I met you in Boston, at the airport."

"Not good enough," he said.

"We were in the car together—you said that you were in charge of the sails. My mother steers the ship."

Emma nodded at the improvement.

"Ben?"

"Someone's trying to kill me."

"Okay, I need to think this through. Where are you?"

"The Congressional Cemetery near, uh, a little chapel."

"All right. It's going to be okay. Stay right where you are."

"Okay."

"You did the right thing calling me. I'll send someone to you. Stay put. Ten minutes."

Ben hung up and looked at Emma. "How'd I do?"

Her eyes twinkled. "I wouldn't sell your shit and move to Hollywood just yet."

• • •

Nine minutes later, a white Porsche barreled through the entrance of the Congressional Cemetery. It slowed near the little brown chapel with the rust-red door. Ben moved out of the sheltering eave and made a hesitant wave at the car. He couldn't see the driver through the reflection of the gray sky on the windshield. It wasn't until he saw the black shoes, the thick pantyhose, and the wool skirt that he figured it out. David Plimpton had sent Riley McGraw to do his dirty work. Kimberly Hancock's public-perception expert climbed out of the car and gave Ben the same fake, stupid smile she'd given him when they'd first met on the Gulfstream. Talk about bad theater—she was rushing her part.

She'd barely rounded the hood of the car when she shoved her hand into her large, brown purse.

"Freeze! FBI," Emma yelled, sprinting from behind a headstone, rushing at the woman with a two-handed grip on her Glock.

Riley McGraw froze. She wasn't acting now—she was terrified.

"Hands where I can see them."

She lifted her hand out of the purse. Her fingers gripped a revolver.

"Drop it or I drop you!" Emma yelled.

Ben saw her doing the math in her head. It was a quick calculation, and before Emma could yell a second time, Riley McGraw took the easy way out, putting a slug through the roof of her mouth.

"Well, shit," Emma said.

The plan had been to promise leniency for her cooperation. All she had to do was to call David Plimpton and say, "It's done," then hang up.

Ben looked at Emma. "Send a text?"

"What? Just send a picture?"

"What else can we do?"

They put Riley McGraw's body into the trunk, but not before smearing her blood over Ben's face and shirt. He'd witnessed enough head shots in the past couple of days to know exactly where to apply the blood. Emma took pictures of Ben posing like a dead man in the back of Riley McGraw's car.

Between photographs, Ben Danvers couldn't help but smile. He was actually enjoying himself, bubbling with a carefree joy he'd never experienced before. It was likely a symptom of an impending break with sanity, but he had to admit, it was liberating—not caring if he lived or died.

72

Arnau Farre let the smoke from his cigarette drift lazily out of his nostrils and float in front of his fevered head and into his bloodshot eyes. He was infected from the knife wound—diseased and delirious, his guts boiling with the stuff of death. The cigarettes kept the nausea at bay—every few minutes, the last heartbeat of the old butt burned into the new. On and on. Over and over.

It was probably the fires of sepsis that were attacking him. And while talented doctors and great medicine might have successfully treated it, Arnau wasn't interested. He had resigned from life. There was only one thing that remained. The Prophecy. What was foretold when he was a child was finally coming to pass. It was coming tonight. He wanted to see it.

It had still been light when Arnau sat down on that hard, wet bench on the lawn of the Carnegie Library. He'd witnessed the fall of night and the drop of temperature. He sat in near darkness, the interior lights of the library casting a dull hue across the tuxedo he'd bought off the rack at Men's Wearhouse. The saleswoman offered to have it tailored while he waited. He refused. She'd been eyeing him, holding his stomach the way he was. He doubted she was buying the bullshit about suffering through a batch of bad clams. He paid cash and left. That was last night. The pain had worsened exponentially since then. But he could manage for a few more hours.

His mind, fevered as it was, did not assess the security presence across the street with a professional eye. It was merely activity: dogs, guns, fences, attitude—interesting things to watch while he smoked and tried not to think about the blistering fire spreading through his body.

Mt. Vernon Place Road bisected Arnau Farre's park bench and the Walter Washington Convention Center. The cops had closed it to regular traffic. The only vehicles getting through were those that had passed a checkpoint to drop off the volunteers and big-money donors with invitations to attend the inaugural ball.

Law enforcement visited Arnau's bench regularly. Every shift they came over, shined a flashlight into his eyes, and asked the same questions. With every visit he smiled through his pain and showed them his identification and invitation to the Ball. The K-9 units and the Secret Service made the confirming calls and kept learning the same thing. The tormented-looking chain smoker in the ill-fitting tuxedo was no threat.

And it was true. Tonight, Arnau Farre was no threat. The invitation to the Ball was a gift from the Father, secured by his man on the inside. The man who'd made everything happen. The smartest and most cunning of his brothers—and the most ruthless. All had done their part, but David Plimpton had been exalted by the Father. He held a special place in what was to come.

Arnau Farre's cigarette dangled off his lip. He watched the black limousine pull to the sidewalk in front of the steps of the Convention Center. Wincing pain greeted him as he leaned forward on the bench, narrowing his dilated eyes—confirming that it was the Son who was jogging up the steps to fulfill his destiny.

There was no doubt in Arnau's febrile mind that the unbearable, boiling infection consuming him was from Ida—a sign of her anger. He had broken his promise. Ben Danvers was dead, his body decomposing in a Porsche on the silty bottom of the Potomac River.

Arnau Farre pinched the life out of his cigarette and limped across the street. To follow the trail of the Son.

73

Ben's invitation was scanned twice—once outside the doors of the Convention Center and again at security. He emptied his pockets into a basket and stepped through the metal detector. He waited in a queue of tuxedoed men and sequined women for a wand to wave over him. The muffled, percussive thumps of live music drummed in the distance.

He was given two wristbands. One gave him VIP access to the presidential ball. The second, and more important, granted him entry into the National Defense Reception. He walked down the wide hallway, his black shoes clicking against the polished marble floor until they fell silent on a red, white, and blue rug in front of a wide door guarded by uniformed Marines.

Ben cleared his throat and took a deep, steadying breath. In the next hour, behind those doors, David Plimpton was going to make sure the president was dead. Either he believed Ben was the Son—believed that he'd be spreading nerve agent across the room—or, he'd take matters into his own hands.

A Marine opened the door. The Air Force Band played a light jazz tune from a platform between two large American flags. The logos of each military branch were displayed across the walls along with those of the CIA, NSA, Homeland, and FBI. Ben made a point of turning slowly around the room so Emma could see what he was seeing.

"The director's the short guy with red hair to your right. Monroe's next to him."

Emma didn't have to say it. Ben knew she was worried about how deeply the cult had infiltrated the Bureau. She was proud to be a Special Agent, but Briar Metcalf's treachery had spooked her. Until she knew who she could trust, every middle-aged man or woman in power was a suspect. Ben shared her fear.

More than half of the guests were in uniform. And most of those had polished silver stars across their shoulders. The rest, the spooks in suits, looked like insurance salesmen—pale, unhappy people with shifty eyes.

"Here we go. If you get a bad feeling about Plimpton, get out. And forget the Esperanto stuff, right?"

Ben scanned the room for Kimberly Hancock. She wasn't there yet. The only familiar face was David Plimpton's. He was smiling in a cluster of three-star generals. He took a sip of his drink and looked at Ben. Then he turned, no doubt, searching the room for Kate. When he didn't find her, his eyes settled back on Ben, carving him up with intense curiosity.

He felt the hand on the back of his shoulder and knew it for what it was.

"Uh, nice to see you again. Can I introduce you to some people?"

Ben turned his lapel pin toward an overweight gentleman in a dark suit. Sweat was beading under his nose. The guy was nervous and fidgety.

"Sure," Ben said.

The man guided him through the crowd toward Director O'Toole and Associate Director Monroe. In his ear, Ben could hear Emma's nervous inhale.

"Director, this is Benjamin Danvers, the vice president's son."

Ben shook the director's hand and Emma exhaled a *"Thank God"* in his ear.

But it wasn't Director O'Toole who concerned them most. It was Monroe. Briar had called him "Billy." He'd told Emma that they were old friends. It was A.D. Monroe who'd brought Briar Metcalf back into the case. There were a lot of reasons to suspect that "Billy" was working for the wrong team. Not only did William Monroe extend his hand to Ben, he held the grip—telling him about the death of a good man. Briar Metcalf. Yesterday, that good man had forced Ben to his knees in a graveyard. His face flushed with anger thinking about how he'd pissed himself waiting for a bullet to the brain.

"*I'm sorry to hear about the loss of your agent*," Emma said slowly into his ear.

"I'm sorry to hear about the loss of your agent," Ben repeated.

He let go of the hand and spotted David Plimpton staring at him again. He gave Ben a head nod toward the door. Plimpton and two of his men were waiting for him in the hallway.

"Walk with me."

"*It's going to be fine, Ben—stick with the plan.*"

Ben knew she was trying to calm herself as much as him. They turned down an empty hallway and walked farther into the bowels of the convention center. The men in dark suits kept pace behind. Plimpton was keeping his distance. At least some part of him believed Ben was carrying the deadly nerve agent. David Plimpton put his palm in the air and snuck a look back down the hallway. He stepped to Ben.

"What's going on?" he asked quietly.

Ben's voice cracked. "With what?"

"With what? Where's Kate?"

"She couldn't make it."

David Plimpton squinted. "What the hell does that mean? Couldn't make it?"

It was the question that Ben and Emma knew David Plimpton would ask—the one they had to get right. But there wasn't a good answer. The best they could do was offer up an excuse and hope that the pictures of "dead Ben" in the back of the Porsche were enough to convince him he was talking to the Son. That was all that mattered.

Emma spoke in his ear, reminding him what to say. "*I couldn't trust her. She let my brother escape. I zip-tied her to the bed.*"

Ben's heart was racing, but in that moment, looking at David Plimpton's stare, he realized it wouldn't work. The guy had spent his life in politics. He knew when he was being lied to. If he caught Ben lying, people were going to die.

"Well?"

"*She's tied up. I couldn't trust her,*" Emma said, more desperately.

"Something's not right." He shot a look at his two thugs, then stared back at Ben.

"*Get out, Ben.*"

299

His men moved closer.

"Either you can't tell me where she is or you won't. Last chance."

"Ben, please—get out."

"I killed her."

David Plimpton took a step back. His eyes narrowed.

"I killed her," Ben said again.

Plimpton raked his fingers through his hair. "You *killed* her?"

Ben closed the distance between them. "You think I'm lying?"

"Why would *you* kill her? She was your—"

"She wasn't who I thought she was."

Ben's hands were shaking, not from fear but raw emotion. He could almost feel the recoil of the gunshots—his mind replayed Kate falling off the hood in slow motion. He didn't fight the burning in his eyes. A tear fell down his cheek. He held his stare until David Plimpton nodded.

"You thought she was helping the kid. Keeping him alive."

Ben shrugged.

"Where is she?"

"Not here. That's all that matters."

David Plimpton was teetering between belief and skepticism. He needed a push in the right direction.

"If you don't believe me, why don't we shake hands and I'll head out the door. I'm already dead. You can't do anything to me."

Ben extended his hand and looked David Plimpton in the eye. The man with the perfect hair looked down at the invitation and stepped back. He grinned at Ben, then turned and walked down the hallway. He stopped and looked over his shoulder.

"You coming?"

74

The Air Force Band was playing some downright nasty jazz, the kind that used to waft out of 52nd Street smoky bar basements in New York. The drummer was laying down a beat that pounded only half as fast as Ben's heart. David Plimpton stood a few steps away, holding court with soldiers and suits. He looked casual and calm, and in the past two minutes, he'd glanced over at Ben twice and smiled.

David Plimpton wasn't going rogue tonight.

A blue-uniformed colonel marched to the platform and whispered into the bandleader's ear. Mid-measure, the swinging beat evaporated. Conversations ended. Silence hung in dead air. The band leader's white gloves snapped down, then flicked forward.

"Hail to the Chief" soared into the chandeliers.

Every man and woman and soldier came to attention, their eyes fixed on the double doors. The president entered like a man fighting against disbelief that the song was being played for him. The First Lady peacocked by his side without the burden of humility. Ben's eyes stayed on his mother. Kimberly Hancock was keeping a respectful distance behind them, walking with a confidence and bearing that the man in charge seemed to lack.

The president's short reception speech was a string of sound bites from his campaign. Even though the room had been hearing the words for a year, they were polite enough to nod their heads in kiss-ass earnestness.

ANDREW BRIDGEMAN

"And so, we must underscore our shared values and no longer pick the scabs of division. Let us not add new scars to old wounds."

Ben watched David Plimpton start the clapping that filled the room.

The president raised his hand, commanding them to silence. "I just want to say, it was Kimberly's idea to gather us all here this evening—together in one room. Like you, she's a fighter. When she speaks, understand: she has the full authority of my office. Her words are my words. Thank you, Kimberly."

The president allowed the applause to conclude his remarks. He accepted a red wine from a woman in a white jacket and the band jumped into a Brubeck tune.

David Plimpton leaned into Ben's ear. "Your mother is waiting."

Kimberly Hancock was surrounded by a circling army of dark suits and uniformed soldiers. David Plimpton broke through the line, nudging an admiral to the side so Ben could pass.

"Madam Vice President, I believe you wanted me to track down this gentleman for you," David Plimpton said cheerily.

"Benjamin. Finally," she said, waving the military brass away.

Ben felt her palm on the back of his shoulder.

She whispered into his ear, "I have someone I've been wanting you to meet. Come with me."

She kept her hand on his back, pressing him toward the president of the United States. Ben recognized the attack pattern. So did Emma.

"I'm sorry, Ben."

"Mr. President, I want to introduce you to my son, Benjamin."

Ben's head was swimming. He took the man's hand. The leader of the free world was saying something, but Ben wasn't listening. *She's one of them?* He tried to respond to the president, but his voice was stuck. He could only manage a weak nod. He glanced over and saw David Plimpton smirking at him. His mother's hand was still on his back, now guiding him away.

And then, the hand moved.

It slid down his shoulder, past his bicep, and over his elbow—it traveled down the sleeve of his black tuxedo. He felt her soft fingers running over his knuckles, clasping hers into his. She lifted his hand to her face and kissed the tips of his fingers.

Ben inhaled a fresh cleansing breath. He heard Emma whoop in his ear.

"Ben. It's over. You did it."

Kimberly Hancock smiled up at him. "Come with me. I want to show you off."

"Where?"

"With me."

"I need to do something first."

Ben dug a finger into his ear and walked to the director of the FBI. He held out his hand and O'Toole took it. "I've got someone that wants to speak with you," Ben said, pressing the earpiece into the director's palm.

• • •

Mother and son followed her security package down the wide marble hallway to the other side of the convention hall. A guy in headphones brought them through a narrow door and into the wings of a large stage. Ben was in darkness. He could hear the murmur of the crowd beyond the curtain. His mother was buried into his elbow, leaning on him.

"Did you find what you were looking for in Vermont?" she asked.

Ben nodded. "A little more than I was looking for."

"You'll tell me later?"

Their conversation was interrupted. The curtain divided, gliding open, drenching them in spotlight. Ben was center stage. Mother and son. Arm in arm. A week ago, Ben would have run from the light. But it had been a long week, and he'd come a long way—too far to walk back into shadow. His mother rested her head against his bicep. At the side of the stage, a woman in a long, shimmering black dress spoke into a microphone with a voice that sounded like salted caramel.

"Ladies and Gentlemen, the vice president of the United States, Kimberly Hancock. Accompanying her, in their first-ever dance, her son, Mr. Benjamin Danvers."

Applause thundered. Kimberly Hancock smiled and waved. Ben studied his mother next to him. For the first time, he recognized himself in her face: the thin lips and high cheekbones—the blue eyes. And for the first time, he had no misgivings about being her son. It was time. Time to become the person he was born to be.

Ben ignored his racing heart and walked away from Kimberly Hancock. He crossed the stage and stood next to the woman in the shimmering black dress. He held out his hand, waiting for her to give up the microphone. He squinted into the bright lights until the crowd went silent. A lone voice yelled something he didn't hear. The crowd laughed, then quieted again. Ben hesitated and looked down at his feet. He slowly raised his head and inhaled, staring out at the large audience.

"It's not Danvers. That's not who I am. My name is Benjamin Hancock." He turned and looked back across the stage.

His voice cracked. "Mom … I'm home."

Kimberly Hancock's shoulders quaked. She covered her mouth with her palm.

All that watched, in the convention center and those far beyond on TV screens, everyone felt it: joy—nonpartisan and pure. A mother's love for her child, decades of sorrow and pain giving way to relief, joy, and the hope of rediscovery. The evening choreography dictated that Kimberly Hancock leave her son and walk to the front of the stage to wave to the cheering crowd. The vice president took one step forward. And stopped. She didn't wave. The only thing Kimberly Hancock did on that grand stage, in front of the world, was to lay her palm on Ben's chest and weep into him.

The hall hushed in silence as mother and son embraced. The friends and colleagues, the volunteers and big-money donors stood, side by side, in their dresses and tuxedos—in quiet witness.

Most doubted that it was an accident; the shower of red and white and blue balloons—it wasn't meant for the vice president. Nor was the blast from the confetti machine. None of it was intended for the opening act. Still, the balloons fell as if on cue. Hundreds of them, raining down on Ben and Kimberly Hancock, bouncing off the stage and gathering around their feet. Ben looked up and smiled. His mother swatted a blue balloon as the crowd cheered from wet, happy faces. Red paper caught above Ben's eyebrow, and his mother joyfully picked it off his face.

The first notes of the song drifted from the speakers, and when the attendees recognized the tune, they reached for their napkins and tissues and each other. Ben took his mother's hand and they danced to John Lennon singing "Beautiful Boy."

75

Arnau Farre ignored the man across the table laughing at his own joke. He must have been somebody important to be seated this close to the stage, but to him, the guy was just a sheep, like everyone else. He lifted his fluted champagne glass and drained it in one swallow. The alcohol did nothing to cool Ida's burning punishment.

The stage was lit up with a million spotlights—the tables, the crowd, everyone else in darkness. No one could see what had become of Arnau Farre. He bit the inside of his lip, willing himself to remain conscious. In front of him, his back to the stage, was a Secret Service Agent. He looked like an asshole, scowling at everyone. They all looked like assholes—the agents hugging the stage every fifteen feet.

The curtains opened. The fancy people around him clapped. The new vice president, the bitch, was all smiles. Kimberly Hancock was about to serve the shortest term in history.

Things unfolded surprisingly. He did not expect the Son to make an announcement. It was unnecessary. And it was a curious thing to see the vice president sobbing into the chest of the man who had just poisoned her. The crowd was giving them a standing ovation. Arnau bit into his bottom lip, struggling against the scorching pain to rise with them. The giant was staring at him. Arnau clapped and forced himself to smile.

The mother and son moved toward the front of the stage. A blue balloon bounced off Arnau's shoulder. He brushed the confetti away from his face. He watched the woman on stage pick red paper from the Son's forehead.

Arnau's eyes widened and he blinked twice, trying to focus on the man on stage.

It couldn't be.

There was a knot above his left eye. In the same place where he'd watched Ben Danvers slam against a headstone in a Connecticut cemetery. Arnau Farre's mind was fevered, but it came to the right conclusion. This was not the Son. It was *Ida's* son.

It *was* Ben Danvers.

He was alive? Arnau looked around at the cheering crowd. How? And slowly, he came to understand that if *that* was Ben Danvers, then the prophecy had not come true. Which meant Ida had sacrificed herself for nothing. *Nothing.* All of it. The years away from each other. For nothing.

His mind was wheeling with fever, adrenaline, and insanity—his mental machinery wobbling off the rails. His hands shook with anger. He looked around at the clapping crowd—yelling and carrying on. Arnau balled his fist. It wasn't true. Ida had sacrificed herself for *something*—a cause greater than herself.

And so could he.

He couldn't bring down the government, but he could bring down Kimberly Hancock. And after that was done, Arnau would welcome the bullets that would speed him home—to the girl in the green dress.

"Mia juro, mia vivo," he whispered.

Arnau Farre found strength in adrenaline. He grabbed his fluted champagne glass and broke it over the table. He swung it across his body, smashing the jagged glass into the face of the giant in front of him. He reached his free hand into the grunting asshole's jacket, unholstered his gun, pointed it under the man's chin, and fired.

The pain was gone. Ida had lifted her punishment. Arnau Farre fired at the agent to his left, dropping him. Screams and overturned tables resounded through the hall as donors crashed into each other, trying to escape.

"Gun! Gun! Gun!"

The secret service detail rushed from the wings, desperate to save the vice president. But they were too slow. He fired twice.

• • •

Ben held his mother close as they swayed to the music. For the first time in a long while, Ben felt at peace. He ignored the audience, closed his eyes, and inhaled her perfume.

His eyes flew open at the sound of the first shot. He saw an agent fall. A man at the front was training a pistol on the stage—at his mother's back. Ben didn't think; he reacted. It was reflex, spinning himself into the path of the assassin's bullet.

He groaned at the pain searing into the middle of his back. And then another slug ripped into him. He was vaguely aware that he was crashing headfirst into the stage. His arms did not come up to break his fall. Through the tint of a red balloon, he saw secret service agents lifting his mother off the stage as she fought and kicked to reach him. He heard distant gunfire but did not see the assassin fall—an apology on his lips.

All the light that remained drained to black.

76

Nine hours later

Emma Noble pulled down on the neck of her bulletproof vest. She was staring out the window of the Black Hawk helicopter zipping over the tree line. Two choppers flew in formation beside it, each carrying a squad of fully loaded combat soldiers. She lifted her head to see the crew chief tap his wrist and stick five fingers in the air. In minutes, they'd be landing near a remote cabin in northern New York. Alexander Volkov was going down—dead or alive.

The FBI response had been swift. O'Toole was hesitant at first, but, in the end, he believed Emma. His conversation with Sam Noble had helped. They arrested David Plimpton and his two men before they could leave the Walter Washington Convention Center. Emma had uploaded the incriminating video she and Ben had recorded at the lunch and the reception. Teams of agents were already knocking down doors and taking away cult members involved in the plot.

There was enough happening to keep her mind occupied, but she couldn't get Ben Danvers out of her head. The best she could do for him was to get every one of these assholes behind bars or in body bags. Starting with Volkov.

She unclipped the harness after landing and waited for the soldiers to rush out. She wasn't going in with the teams. O'Toole had given her strict instructions to wait until the cabin was cleared. Emma watched as the soldiers spread out—weapons high—in synchronized movement, advancing on the cabin. She watched the windows break and heard the flash-bangs. A team barreled through the door.

Emma waited just beyond the sweep of the Black Hawk's rotors. Watching the cabin. Not blinking. For ten minutes she stared at the door, waiting for them to bring out a man or a body. Finally, the soldiers exited. One by one. Their weapons low. And Emma knew Volkov was already gone.

She walked slowly through the snow toward the rustic cabin, planting her feet in the footprints of the men that had gone before her. Emma hesitated, stopping in front of a green hemlock, its branches dappled with snow. Rows of neatly stacked firewood lined the outside walls of the cabin. She turned, taking in the surroundings: the ice-covered lake and the tall pines, imagining the children who swam and climbed and laughed here. She inhaled the cold air. No doubt, it was a magnificent place—to make kids into killers.

Emma entered. The old man had left in a hurry—a cigar stamped out well before its time, a bottle of expensive wine on the table next to it. A victory celebration snuffed out, just as it was beginning. Above the mantel was an old photograph of children standing in rows in front of the lake. Emma stepped closer and stared at the long-haired girl in front—in a green dress holding the hand of a disheveled boy.

She walked up the stairs, noting a silver garland weaving through wooden balusters. A door was open at the top of the landing. The pine-wood room was small—a child's room. There were only two pieces of furniture: a twin bed tucked below a half-moon window and a night-stand. Emma opened the single drawer and found a stack of envelopes secured by rubber bands. She sat on the bed and began to read.

77

One Week Later

Heavy snowflakes fell softly off the hood of the black hearse inching through the North End of Boston. The lights of two police cars cleared the path in front. Behind was a procession of bundled mourners making their way on foot. Papa Giordano waited for the long black vehicle to reach the restaurant before he shuffled out to greet it. His neighbors touched his shoulders, gave sorrowful nods, and cleared a path so he could walk first behind the coffin.

A crowd gathered silently on the sidewalks. It was a solemn North End funeral, and it didn't matter to them that this morning the nation was watching. This was *their* goodbye. It was personal. They watched and walked with respect and dignity.

The black hearse turned on Hanover Street and stopped in front of Saint Leonard's Catholic Church. The back door opened. The coffin slid out for the pallbearers. Papa Giordano's face bore the weight and the sadness of many such walks like this through the doors of Saint Leonard's.

. . .

Tasha Maidlow was watching the TV screen in her hotel room, looking at the close-up of the old man and his sad, weathered face. She took her best sweater, the mustard-colored cardigan that her grandmother had given her as a Christmas present, out of her suitcase. She glanced once more at the TV screen, still wondering who the funeral was for. Finally, the crawl at the bottom told her: *Funeral for Boston Domestic-Terror Victim Regina Puleo.*

Tasha turned off the tube and looked around her small room in the La Quinta Inn. She opened the curtain. In the distance, she could see the tip of the Washington Monument. This was as close to it as she'd ever been.

A receipt from last night's dinner at Cheddar's was on the dresser. She stuffed it into a manila envelope with the word "expenses" written in ballpoint pen. Barney was an overly officious ass and had been clear about the rules regarding expenses and the per diem, which was barely enough to buy a Denny's breakfast. But it was still exciting. Her only concern was leaving her cat with her brother for two days.

Tasha threw the spent coffee pouch into the trash and flipped the comforter toward the pillows. She checked the time. Then she checked her bag; her new legal pad was there, her favorite pen, her second-favorite pen next to it (in case of emergency), her black recorder, as well as her phone. She was ready.

Tasha looked into her bag three more times; once in the hotel lobby, once more in the Uber, and again outside the press briefing room at Walter Reed Hospital.

The room was too small for the number of reporters and television crews in attendance. Tripods and cameras blotted out the podium. All twelve rows were filled with reporters—the ones in the first pews had the best hair and teeth. The grooming got more disheveled and scraggily toward the back.

All the usual suspects were present: national news, world news, print journalism, cable outlets. Reporters jammed the aisles. A mash of press fought for space at the back of the room. Many, like Tasha, couldn't get in. The press briefing was supposed to start at 10 AM sharp. She'd gotten there fifteen minutes early. A rookie mistake.

Tasha ended up in the hallway outside the doors behind a lanky guy wearing a fedora. It was only when the man bent to speak to the reporter next to him that she got a glimpse of the podium. She never saw the team of doctors enter. She didn't see the hospital spokeswoman get behind the podium, but she sensed that something was about to happen from the body language of the reporters in front of her. Fedora lifted his recorder, blocking even more of Tasha's view.

She tapped him on the shoulder. "Could you at least take your hat off?"

"Who you with?" he asked.

"*Albany Inquirer.*"

"No," he said.

"Thanks, asshole."

Her favorite pen was at the ready, but she couldn't hear anything coming out of the speakers. She craned her head under the raised arm of Fedora, hoping to catch what the spokeswoman was saying about Benjamin Hancock's surgery. She couldn't hear. Or see. Tasha didn't catch the name of the next person to speak, but at least this doctor had a voice that carried.

"Benjamin Hancock is recuperating in the Presidential Medical Care Unit. We've just upgraded his condition. He's awake. And he's alert. Please. One at a time."

"Yes. It was a close call. Frankly, we don't know how he's alive. Obviously, someone upstairs was looking down on him."

"Yes, full recovery. The vice president is with him now. She's been at his side since the assassination attempt."

The room exploded with more questions.

"When will he speak to the press?" yelled a rumpled woman from the back.

The spokesperson returned to the podium and the room quieted enough for Tasha to hear her from the hallway.

"Mr. Hancock is making himself available to only one media outlet. Is the representative from—" the woman looked down at her notes and then back up at the expectant room of reporters. "Is Tasha Maidlow from the *Albany Inquirer* here?"

Tasha shouted and jumped from the hallway like she'd been called to the stage by Bob Barker. She raised her favorite pen so it could be seen above Fedora's hat. She pushed past the guy, then paused and looked up at him.

"*Albany Inquirer*, motherfucker."

The reporters were half off their seats, trying to see the woman coming forward. Tasha sidled through the mass of news professionals clotting the aisle. She smiled at the correspondents from Fox News and CNN and hopped up on stage. And that's when the former research assistant for Albany's fourth-favorite paper divided her fingers and gave the gawking reporters the Vulcan salute before being escorted to the elevator for her exclusive interview with Benjamin Hancock.

August

On the hottest day of summer, Benjamin Hancock worked shirt-less, rebuilding the once-rotted front steps of his Vermont home. As on most days that summer, he had labored all morning without stop, drenching himself in sweat that ran like a system of streams and tributaries—down his face, across his neck, and into the scars on his chest.

He jumped on the bottom step and bounced on the balls of his feet, testing his weight on the new treads. They were sturdy. He snuck a look down the grassy hill to the traffic on Route 7. These days, there weren't so many vehicles stopping in front of the house as before. And that was fine by him. He arched his back and rolled his neck from shoulder to shoulder, trying to get the kinks out; he was still suffering from pain and stiffness, but the summer heat was good lubrication for his injuries. The doctors couldn't tell him if the discomfort would ever go away. He suspected he'd have to get used to it.

The yellow two-story colonial had become the red colonial. The paint was Truckmeier's recommendation—mostly because he had gallons of it stacked in his shed, more than enough to cover half the house. Ben had built the scaffolding, chipped off the dull yellow paint and applied the red. It took weeks to do it, but after the white trim was brushed on, the colonial on the hill stood proud.

The work had healed him. He'd torn out the plaster walls, ripped out the old wiring, and hauled the mold and rot out of the house and into the green dumpster at the top of the drive. The interior of the old home was down to studs. The smell of its history was gone. The abuse and neglect and lack of care had been scooped out. All that remained of the once badly damaged home was the husk.

He grabbed for the gallon jug lying in the grass under the narrow shade of his sawhorse. He took a pull, letting the tepid water run into his dry throat. He ran his forearm down his face, mopping away pools of sweat. A distant car horn bleeped from down the hill. It was turning off Route 7 and making its way up the long drive. Ben squinted, then smiled when he saw it was a brown Solara with a U-Haul on the hitch. He pulled a Celtics tank top over his head and ran his fingers through his hair. He leaned against the split-rail fence until Tasha Maidlow got to the end of the driveway.

"Jesus. You have to be a fucking hick to live out here," she yelled before she was halfway out of the car. She gave him a quick hug before putting Mr. Spock's cat kennel in the shade by the garage. Ben's Aussie barked and plopped down next to it.

"I didn't know you were coming."

"You're a little difficult to reach. You even own a phone?"

Ben shook his head.

"Alrighty then. Where are we doing this?"

"Doing what?"

"The follow-up interview."

"We're not. That wasn't the deal."

Tasha made a face. "Come on. Give me a couple juicy bits for my new boss."

"The *Inquirer* was dumb enough to let you go?"

"*Boston Globe*, baby. Investigative Reporter. Start tomorrow. You gonna invite me in?" she asked, hopping up the porch steps and looking into the first-floor windows. "Jesus. There's nothing in there."

"Work in progress," he said, sitting on the top step.

Tasha sat next to him. He could feel her staring at him.

"What?"

"You don't know anything that's been going on, do you?"

Ben shrugged.

"You heard about Volkov?"

Ben turned quickly.

"Just fucking with you. They still haven't found him. He's probably in Russia or Belarus or someplace like that. Whaddaya think, Ben? Was Russia behind it?"

Tasha's hand was palming her phone—recording him. Ben made a sour face and shook his head.

"Come on, Ben! Please?"

"Don't. *The Globe* doesn't approve of whining."

317

"Fine," she huffed, putting down her phone. "Off the record."

Ben smiled.

She knocked her shoulder into his. "You doin' okay, buddy?"

"I'm okay."

"You ever meet your brother?"

"Twice. We're still feeling each other out. Lot of baggage to unpack there."

"Will your mother ask the big guy to pardon him? Get him out of jail before the trial?"

Ben shook his head. "She won't ask for favors."

Tasha nodded her approval. "You see her much?"

"Some. She's got a tough gig."

Tasha leaned forward, resting her elbows on her knees, looking around at the property. "I guess it doesn't *totally* suck up here." She looked over at Ben. "You heard Mrs. Atamian died, right? Two months after they found her husband's body. They buried her under the shade of the same maple tree. I wrote a nice piece on it. You should look it up online."

"I don't have a computer."

"Dude, you're a hermit."

"They say ignorance is bliss."

"You know that's bullshit, right?"

Ben shrugged.

"Will they make you testify at the Congressional hearings?"

"Hearings?"

"Now you're just being an asshole. You know how high this went? Five colonels and a general. Two federal judges. Slew of defense contractors. Tell me you know that."

"I know. But they haven't asked me. I'll testify if I have to but—you know."

Tasha bit her fingernail and looked down the hill toward the woods beyond the highway. She was quiet for a while before speaking. "Thank you."

"For what?"

"For everything, dummy. For the interview. For being a badass … and still managing to be sweet. I fucking love you, dude."

They talked and reminisced about their day at the Haystack and about her brother, Craig. It was a nice hour or two before she had to get back on the road. Tasha held the hug a while, then loaded Mr. Spock back into the car and got behind the wheel. Ben made a quick decision and put his palm out to stop her.

"What?"

"I've got something for you."

Ben ran into the house and came out with a stack of envelopes secured with rubber bands. Agent Emma Noble never put them into evidence—instead, she sent them to Ben. The love letters to Arnau Farre were all that remained of Ida's presence in Ben's life. He passed them through the window.

"What's this?"

"An interesting read. Do something good with it."

Tasha looked down at the envelopes and her mouth opened. "Ben, I—"

"Good luck at the *Globe*."

He watched her drive down the hill and waved at the distant bleep as her car made a left onto Route 7.

It was late afternoon when Ben's Aussie lifted its head off the shaded porch. Truckmeier was crossing the property line. The dog jumped and wiggled his nubby butt—the man was known to keep treats in his pocket. Ben saw the paper plate in his hands. Tilda had made cookies again. She was always finding reasons to send her husband over. She didn't complain when he didn't rush home. She knew the men needed each other—even if neither had much to say.

Ben put the cookies in the fridge and pulled out two beers. Truckmeier was already sitting on the metal rocker, rolling a cigarette, the dog's head nuzzling against his knee. Ben handed over a cold beer. He sat and looked down the hill, across Route 7, at the somewhat obstructed view of Harriton Reservoir. For hours the men shared each other's company, speaking intermittently of small things—the minimum conversation required on a summer night when the sky deserved the attention, its blue canvas splashed with streaks of orange and red that gradually deepened into purples.

The moon was full, and in the last light of day, the men sipped beer and watched bats jigging above the lawn and lightning bugs performing in the tall grass. Ben inhaled the fresh Vermont air as a cool evening breeze swept over the porch. But he was plenty warm. As warm and as free as he'd ever been. And with his back to the red colonial, he believed that he, too, could have a second story.

Better than the first.

THE END.

About the Author

Andrew Bridgeman has nearly as many twists in his own story as there are in his novel. A former rugby player, jazz singer, salesman, and entrepreneur, he finds inspiration in the characters he's crashed into along the way. Mr. Bridgeman studied creative writing at Dickinson College and earned his MBA from Washington University in Saint Louis. After decades in the St. Louis area, he now lives in New Hampshire with his wife, Kathy. He enjoys hiking in the mountains near his home, playing guitar, and exploring the US in an Airstream RV. This is Andrew Bridgeman's debut novel.

Acknowledgments

It's my first book, I'm going to need a minute.

My first thanks is to you. Thank you for being a reader. Thank you for being with me in the cramped unfinished room above the garage while I wrote this book. I knew you were there. I felt your presence—standing over my shoulder, demanding better. I guess, at this point, we've both done our parts. We good?

Nothing kills creativity like self-doubt, and I've had my fair share—spending years bleeding over three novels that ended up in the trash. Even after finishing *Fortunate Son*, there were doubts it would ever see the light of day. I owe a great thanks to the friends that kept me afloat. They did it with words of praise, small kindnesses, and sometimes just a well-timed wink and smile. Kerry Eielson and John Fanning, JOJ, Heather Larimer, Davia Larson, Jeremy Donnelly, Siobhan Wright, Emily Chenoweth, the writing group at Tuftonboro Free Library, my online classmates at the Dickinson College Alumni Writers Workshop, and my friends at La Muse Artist and Writers Retreat in Labastide-Esparbairenque, France. Your encouragement came at exactly the right times. Thank you.

Thank you to Robert Olmstead who many years ago taught me to listen to the sound writing makes when it's better than good. And to Susan Perabo at Dickinson College who critiqued an early draft of this book and pointed out things that needed work. Thank you, Bob and Susan, for being gentle with your writing students while demanding their best. There are thousands of us that are in your debt.

Thank you to my editor, Ed Stackler who helped me wrestle this very big story into submission—which is his job. And then he became my champion, which is not his job. He didn't have to be so damn generous. Thank you, Ed, for believing in this book and for your friendship. Thank you to agents Molly Friedrich and Hannah Brattesani for picking this novel out of the pile and introducing it to the literary world. Thanks to everyone at Mission Point Press—in particular, Doug, Chris, and Sarah. Thank you to Heather Shaw who ironed out a few wrinkles, then worked tirelessly to get this book over the finish line. And a heartfelt nod to the kindest, most competent publicist in the business, Kim Dower. Thank you for cheering this book into the world.

My brother, Steve, and my dad, Jim, read the earliest iteration of this book on the back porch—laughing and gasping in all the right places. Watching you fly through the pages was a gift and something I will never forget. Thank you.

Thank you to my son, Drew, for his encouragement, kindness, and unshakeable belief that this book was too good not to happen. And thank you to his amazing wife, Kara, who, although very sarcastic, is one of the most inspiring and deeply caring people I know. I love you both.

And a special thanks to my cigar buddy—my daughter, Jenny. You are the inspiration for the character, Emma Noble. You are tough, kind, funny, awkward, and beautiful. And a hero in your own right.

And most importantly, for my wife, I give my greatest thanks. Kath, you have enriched my life every day since walking into KC Legends Sports Bar in Peoria, IL, on May 10, 1990. Thank you for coaxing me out of the shadows to shine this dim light. I love you fiercely and forever.

COMING SOON

A Noble Sin

In a campground, a woman possessing an enigmatic link to Emma Noble's late mother is discovered dead, with traces of Sam Noble's skin beneath her fingernails. Emma searches for her missing father, but as she uncovers one dark secret after another, doubts about his innocence emerge.

Find out more about the series
and the author at
www.andrewbridgeman.com.

Excerpt from A Noble Sin

It had been a year since Emma was last in this room. She'd agonized for over an hour here, waiting to see if Director O'Toole would fire her for inadvertently helping a terrorist escape capture. He didn't. O'Toole let her off with a warning—it had something to do with her father. Some unspoken history between the director and Sam Noble.

Monroe walked past Emma to the unoccupied brown roller chair at the middle of the conference table and held the back of it, inviting her to sit.

"You know everyone, Agent Noble?"

She'd never seen any of them before, but based on age alone, she guessed it was a meeting of senior chiefs. "I don't believe so." She looked around the table. "I'm Special Agent Emma No—"

"They know who you are," said Monroe, walking away from the table to a chair in the back of the room. "Introduce yourselves, please."

The men and woman gave her nothing more than their name and section. They offered zero personal information and barely made eye contact. Emma had a better-than-average ability to read a room, and, looking around, she detected no warm fuzzies. Monroe raised his eyebrows and pursed his lips. He was smug as hell. Enjoying the moment.

"Can I ask what this meeting is—"

"The answer will unfold organically. Frank, can you *briefly* summarize the case?"

"Frank Byum, Chief Cyber Division," the bald man said as a reminder to Emma as he picked up the red folder in front of him and stood behind his chair.

Emma straightened, glancing around the table at the grim faces. Byum smoothed his tie and, before speaking, gave her the kind of apologetic face people save for wakes and funerals. It was brief, but long enough for Emma to get an uneasy feeling in her gut.

Frank Byum picked the remote off the end of the table and coughed into his fist before speaking. The men and women around the table weren't watching him. All eyes were on Emma Noble. They already knew what Byum was going to say. The dog-and-pony show was strictly for her benefit. They were watching to see how Emma would react.

"For the past fourteen months, Cyber and CID have been working in a joint operation—pursuing cryptocurrency theft with a special focus on ransomware payments. We've traced much of the activity to cartels and criminal organizations—seems it's an easy and profitable source of revenue these days. They are building out their infrastructure, recruiting hackers and others with exceptional computing skills. We think some have gone willingly. Most have not."

"Where are they operating from?" asked Emma, leaning forward.

"Wherever they want. They're difficult to track. We've developed a method to—"

Monroe grumbled, "Move it along, Frank."

Byum nodded. Emma suspected he had no more love for Monroe than she did.

"Six months ago, we caught a break, infiltrating a dark-web chat-room that appeared to be a loose confederation of crypto pirates, or 'Skimmers,' as they call themselves. We were monitoring the room."

Emma hoped her confusion wasn't apparent to the senior leaders staring at her. She didn't know anything about cryptocurrency or the dark web. Her specialty was criminal investigation. This case wasn't remotely in her wheelhouse.

"A month or two later, the chatter in the room changed. Something spooked them; we thought they might be on to us, but it was something else. They were being targeted. And they were scared."

The bald agent pointed the remote toward the screen at the front of the room. It brightened, displaying a photograph of a woman with a nose ring a few years older than Emma—early thirties.

"This is Maria Peterson. A software engineer. A few months ago, she was found dead in her Chula Vista apartment. Murdered." Agent Byum clicked the remote, showing a picture of the crime scene. "Shot three times. Twice in the chest. Once in the head." He clicked to a photograph of another woman with spikey red hair. "This is her room-mate, Lilith Hart, a respected coder that, we believe, had a side-hustle stealing crypto. She's missing. Evidence suggests the killer took her."

"Can you go back to the murder scene, please?" said Emma.

She focused on the picture of Maria Peterson slumped in her chair. The two entrance wounds in the chest were large—probably a high-caliber pistol. The proximity of the holes told her the killer hadn't fired wildly. She leaned forward, noticing the gunpowder stippling on the woman's nose and cheek. The last bullet, the headshot, was fired at close range. The murderer walked in on the victim and fired, making sure she was dead.

"Thank you."

Byum clicked ahead to a well-tanned, twenty-something blond man in a Speedo, standing on a catamaran—a beer and a cigar in his hand.

"A few days after Ms. Peterson's murder, this man showed up in the Boston office. He is Bryce Colliers. Calls himself 'Windjammer.' He came in scared, telling us he thought someone was coming after him. We had two agents bring him down for an interview, but in the short walk down the hall he got cold feet—changed his mind. Decided he didn't want to speak to the FBI after all. He was nervous. Evasive. He apologized and ran out. Our agents followed up with Mr. Colliers at his home. Apparently, he was right: someone *was* coming after him. The houseboat where he lived was ransacked. His dog was shot. There's been no sign of Collier since."

"What's the connection?"

"Like Ms. Hart, he was a coder. A little digging reveals they both attended the same hackers conference. Both won contests when they were there."

Monroe crossed his arms and cleared his throat.

"There have been others. I won't go into detail, but someone is taking Skimmers." He pointed the remote toward the screen. The polished image of an executive with salt and pepper hair flashed on the screen. "This is Ted Mortinson, a banker in northern Ohio. He's been on our radar. We suspected he might be setting up phony limited liability registrations—laundering crypto for someone. We didn't have enough on him to make anything stick. One of our investigators noticed his online footprint was similar to those of Ms. Hart and Mr.

Collier. We wanted to get a closer look. Yesterday, we got permission to execute a search warrant and bring him in for questioning. When our team arrived at his house this morning, an ambulance was in the drive. Mr. Mortinson was dead. Murdered in his study."

Byum clicked the remote, bringing up a photograph from the scene—the banker sprawled across his carpeted office with two gunshot wounds to the chest. One in the forehead.

"Thank you, Frank," Monroe said, getting out of his chair and walking to the front of the room and taking the remote out of Byum's hands. "I'll take it from here. Agent Noble, what do you see? First impression."

Emma shrugged. "Without a ballistics report to confirm, it's only a guess—but, by the look of it, the murderers were similar. Whoever did it is a pro." She looked at Monroe. "So, no witnesses to the killings or the kidnappings?"

"The murderer did a good job covering his tracks—until this morning. Had a little bad luck at Mortinson's home in Ohio. He literally ran into the cleaning woman on his way out the door. Fortunately for her, he kept running and didn't shoot her in the head."

"We get a description?"

"An excellent description. The woman's name is Margaret Banich. She's been very helpful, not only describing the man she saw, but recalling the out-of-state license plate on the killer's black truck."

"Let me guess, stolen vehicle?"

"Wrong. Not stolen. Banich's description is a match for the owner."

"Then we got him," said Emma, wondering why it was necessary for her to be in this meeting. "Who is he?"

Monroe lifted his chin, staring at Emma while he clicked his index finger down on the remote. The photograph that filled the screen was the driver's license of a man in his mid-fifties—strong, angular cheekbones and a dimpled chin. Emma blinked at the familiar face.

Monroe laid his palms on the conference table and pointed his finger at her.

"Where is your father? Where is Sam Noble?"

Made in United States
Orlando, FL
24 December 2024

56500536R00202